BRAIN DAMAGE

BY THE SAME AUTHOR

Writer-in-Residence
Strange Bedfellows
The Sensitives
The Snow Gods
The Sleeping Spy (coauthor)
The Death Freak (coauthor)
Mulligan's Seed
The Spanish Soldier
Spy: The History of Modern Espionage (coauthor)
Sister Bear

BRAIN DAMAGE

Herbert Burkholz

Atheneum
New York 1992

Maxwell Macmillan Canada
Toronto

Maxwell Macmillan International
New York Oxford Singapore Sydney

This is a work of fiction. Names, characters, places, and incidents either are the product of the author's imagination or are used fictitiously. Any resemblance to events or persons, living or dead, is entirely coincidental.

Atheneum
Macmillan Publishing Company
866 Third Avenue
New York, NY 10022

Maxwell Macmillan Canada, Inc.
1200 Eglinton Avenue East
Suite 200
Don Mills, Ontario M3C 3N1

Macmillan Publishing Company is part of the Maxwell Communication Group of Companies.

Library of Congress Cataloging-in-Publication Data

Burkholz, Herbert, 1932–
Brain damage / Herbert Burkholz.
p. cm.
ISBN 0-689-12009-5
I. Title.
PS3552.U725B73 1992 91-28547
813'.54—dc20 CIP

10 9 8 7 6 5 4 3 2 1

Printed in the United States of America

For

William and Elaine Sollfrey

1

David Ogden took a long time to die, and he did not die unnoticed. The course of his illness was followed in the nation's press and on the six o'clock news. David Ogden had tumors sprouting in his brain like mushrooms on a dewy morning. David Ogden was brain damaged, David Ogden was doomed. David Ogden, after four long months, was finally dead.

The attention called to Ogden's illness was less because of what he was than what he once had been. He was, at the time he was stricken, Deputy Director for Operations of the CIA, and as such he was accustomed to maintaining the lowest of profiles. He was also, however, one of the last of the original OSS boys, one of Wild Bill Donovan's daredevil band, which, with casual gallantry, had set occupied Europe ablaze during World War II; and as such he was fair game for exploitation. During his long illness, as he lay in a coma at Bethesda Naval Hospital outside Washington, his wartime exploits were chewed and rechewed in both the print and the electronic news media. Young David Ogden, who had made seventeen jumps into occupied France. Young David Ogden with Tito's guerrillas in the mountains of Yugoslavia. Young David Ogden, the terror of Trafalgar Square.

There was a life after the war, of course, a marriage and a family, and a steady rise through the ranks of the CIA, the successor to the OSS, but it was his wartime adventures that kept Ogden's name in the public eye while he lay in that darkened hospital room, mushrooms sprouting in his brain, for there was nothing about the activities of the Deputy Director for Operations that could have been printed. In truth, all of what David Ogden did during World War II was not one one-hundredth as fascinating, and as vital to the interests of his country, as what he accomplished in the last years of his life; but these latter-day actions were, by necessity, shrouded in silence. A few people knew, people who lived in that same silent world, and those were the ones who grieved during Ogden's illness. Grieved not for the death that was sure to come, for these people lived in a daily acceptance of mortality, but for the fine, incisive mind that was slowly being destroyed. It was a mind made for analysis, for meticulous attention to detail, and for the sudden impulse of a gambling thrust that could bring home a winner. It was the mind of an intelligence genius, and when Ogden finally died it was time for the grieving to end, not begin.

One of those who grieved for David Ogden was his successor, Alex Jessup. Ogden's protégé and second-in-command, Jessup lived through the four months of his mentor's illness in that grey arena where loyalty battles ambition. Jessup's war had been the Vietnam of the pacification programs run by the Agency, the Provincial Reconnaissance Units, the Strategic Hamlets, and the counterterror teams. During those Vietnam years he had worked under Ogden, and had come first to respect the man, then to admire him, and finally to enshrine him in something short of sainthood. He had risen with Ogden, tied to his star, and now he stood only a breath away from his ultimate ambition. The trouble was that the breath belonged to David Ogden. Jessup dreamed of being DDO the way other men dream of wealth and women, but at the same time he truly idolized the man he would replace, and if, during those months, he functioned as the *de facto* DDO, he did so with the daily hope that in some unfathomable fashion those mushrooms sprouting in Ogden's brain might be plucked out stem and spore. He was not a man for miracles; he knew that his hopes were fantasies, but while Ogden still lived he refused to relinquish them, and with that same sense of loyalty prompting him, he refused to assume the position and promotion that were properly his. He was DDO in everything but name, but while Ogden still breathed he could not get himself to take on the actual title, nor could he make the move into the suite of rooms on the executive floor that looked out through double layers of tinted glass onto the gentle Virginia countryside. He played the game by the only rules he knew, and then Ogden died, and with him died the restraints of loyalty. On the morning after the funeral, February bright and cold, Alex Jessup officially moved into the job and the office of the man he had admired most.

There was little ritual involved in the changing of the guard. The DCI, himself, along with the other deputy directors, stopped by that morning at eleven. Small glasses of good wine were lifted, and toasts were murmured, some wishing well for the future, others looking back at the past. That was all there was to it. There was no breaking of the papal seals, no salutes from plumed horsemen. Only one final task remained to make the assumption of office complete, and that was the emptying of David Ogden's private lockbox.

The office of each of the deputy directors contained such a box, a place to keep private, nonoperational papers. Official files were forbidden to the box, which was the ideal repository for the memorabilia of men who led such private lives. Something more than a safe, something less than a vault, it was a three-ply steel container the size of a small oven, set into the office wall and secured there by angle pins lodged in concrete. The box was virtually impregnable. It could be opened only by the voiceprint of the owner, and any attempt to force it would have reduced its contents to ashes. Under normal circumstances, when an office changed hands the occupant was on the spot to empty the box and leave it ready for the next user. David Ogden had not been on the spot. For the past four months he had been on his back and unable to communicate either in speech or in writing. During all that time the box had been untouched.

"It should have been opened before this," the DCI observed as he finished his wine and prepared to leave.

"Yes, I know," said Jessup, feeling the rebuke. The box should have been opened as soon as it had become apparent that Ogden was dying, but he had shied away from the act as being too final. "As you know, Director, it's for personal papers only."

"Still, you'd better get it open right away. Technical Services will do it for you. They're the only ones who can get the damn things open without blowing up the building." The DCI hesitated. "You'll send his things on to Amelia?"

"Of course."

"Go through everything carefully."

"Yes."

"Personally."

"Yes." The two men looked at each other in understanding. David Ogden, in a quiet way, had been a noted romancer of women. He had not been indiscriminate, but within his silent world his name had been linked in whispers: a senator's wife, a socialite, a television personality. His personal papers would have to be sifted before being sent to his wife.

"Amelia," said the DCI in a faraway voice. "Lovely woman."

"Indeed."

"I knew her as a girl, you know."

"No, I didn't know that."

"Oh, yes. Baltimore family, one of the Sutcliffe sisters. I never could understand why David felt the need for all that screwing around . . ." His voice trailed off, and then he said firmly, "I'll leave it in your hands."

It took the man from Technical Services, working from plans, almost an hour to bypass the voiceprint circuits on the lockbox, and another thirty minutes to cut the box open with a thermal lance. Inside the box was another container, this one unlocked. Jessup set it on what was now his desk.

The man from Technical Services looked unhappily at the mess he had made. "I'll call Maintenance. They'll clean it up."

"Later," said Jessup, ready to get at the box.

"Shouldn't take long."

"Later."

When the man was gone, Jessup opened the box. There were two compartments inside. He opened the right-hand compartment. In it were five large Manila envelopes, each with a woman's name written in pencil on the front. He felt a touch of queasiness in his stomach.

I don't want to do this, he thought. I really don't.

The name on the top envelope was *Sarah*. He opened the envelope, and emptied it onto the desk. The contents consisted of several Polaroid photographs, a packet of handwritten letters, and a sheaf of typewritten correspondence. Jessup grunted when he saw the photographs.

"Jesus," he muttered. "Sarah Brine."

There were three pictures of the movie actress, and in all of them she was nude and erotically posed. Jessup shook his head, and pushed the photos aside. The handwritten letters were bound by a thick rubber band. The paper on which they were written was cracked, and the ink had faded. Jessup went through them, skimming. As he expected, they were love letters from Sarah Brine to David Ogden. More than tender notes, they were explicit, descriptive, and highly complimentary. Jessup bound them up again, and turned to the sheaf of typewritten pages. They comprised a file of correspondence between Ogden and Gregory Lancer, head of Lancer Publications in Los Angeles. The dates on the letters were over ten years old. Again, Jessup skimmed. Ogden saying, *. . . spoken to several of my friends who are interested in investing in* Temptation. And, *. . . my check enclosed for my share of the* Temptation *project*. And, *. . . I can't think of anyone who could do a better job in* Temptation *than Sarah Brine*. And, *. . . must thank you for the consideration shown to Miss Brine. It won't be forgotten.*

Sarah Brine in *Temptation*, thought Jessup. Her first big break, the movie that made her a star, and David did it.

He turned to the next envelope marked *Jenny*. Again there were photographs of a nude and beautiful woman, but this time there was no instant recognition, and it took Jessup a moment to realize that the woman was Jenny Cookson, television anchorwoman and companion of the celebrated. As noted for her good looks as for her bulldog approach to journalism, Jenny Cookson had, over the past five years, made herself into the ultimate television interviewer, and in many ways had become almost as famous as the people who appeared on her program. Ogden, apparently, had been interviewed off camera. Again there was a packet of affectionate letters, and again a record of the payoff, copies of memorandum from Ogden arranging for Ms. Cookson to interview the Secretary of State, the First Lady, and a string of only slightly lesser notables.

Quid pro quo, thought Jessup. The queasy feeling was back in his stomach.

The third envelope was marked *Carla*, and Jessup was not surprised to find inside it a nude photograph of the wife of John MacAlester, the senior senator from Florida, for the long-standing relationship between David Ogden and Carla MacAlester had been grist for the Washington gossip mills for years. He examined the photo critically, and decided that it must have been taken years before when Carla had still been the vibrant young beauty from Tallahassee. There was the usual packet of letters, and along with them the record of the business side of the relationship: a series of notes to heavyweight senators of both parties deisgned to secure a seat on the powerful Foreign Relations Committee for the ambitious Senator MacAlester.

So neat and orderly for a record of sexual conquests, thought Jessup. First a photo of the woman like a trophy to be mounted, then the proof of her affection, and finally the record of the value received. For one, a starring rôle, for another an entrance into high places, for another a boost to her husband's career. What next?

Next was the socially impeccable Vivian Livingstone of Chevy Chase and Newport. No photographs of Mrs. Livingstone, too aware of her place in society, or perhaps too timid, but there was the packet of creased and dog-eared envelopes, still with a touch of scent to the paper, and at the bottom of the pile a copy of the notification that Mrs. Livingstone's son, Bradford, had been appointed to the United States Military Academy at West Point.

Jessup opened the last envelope and drew out a photograph of Maria-Teresa Bonfiglia, a star of the Metropolitan Opera; but this was no nude. The eight-by-ten glossy showed the veteran soprano in the costume of Puccini's Madame Butterfly, a rôle for which she had been critically acclaimed ever since her debut twenty years ago. There was no packet of letters this time, no scent of sachet, but the business end of the arrangement was there in the form of letters between Ogden and Otto Hartz, producer and impresario. Madame Bonfiglia was fast approaching the end of a distinguished career, and it was Mr. Ogden's warmest desire that she leave the musical stage in triumph. Therefore, he told Mr. Hartz, he was willing to underwrite personally the costs of a farewell tour by this magnificent soprano, if only Hartz would handle the details of production. Hartz would, indeed, and the last sheet of paper in the envelope gave the tour's itinerary: Denver, San Francisco,

Dallas, Chicago, Cleveland, Washington, and the final performance at New York's Carnegie Hall on the sixth of March.

An expensive tab to pick up, thought Jessup, for something that must have happened so many years ago. But then, David Ogden always paid his bills, no matter when they were presented.

The queasy feeling was back again. Jessup was in no way a prude, and Ogden's reputation as a sexual adventurer had been so well known that these confirmations of his adventures came as no surprise. What was surprising was the now apparent fact that over all those years Ogden had been trading favors for favors, using his influence as a way of wangling women into his bed.

And I thought he was doing it on charm. Well, I guess it wasn't pimping, but it was the next thing to it.

He stacked the envelopes, returned them to the right-hand section of the box, and sat staring at them. There would be nothing to send on to Amelia; this would all have to be destroyed. He shook his head sadly. Bedroom standards, he told himself. Don't ever measure people by bedroom standards. It was something that Ogden had taught him years ago.

He closed the compartment, and opened the other one. It contained only four thin Agency case folders. Jessup stiffened when he saw them. The covers of the folders were blank. No case numbers, no circulation slips, no registry stamps. There was only one proper place for a blank case folder, and that was in the Registry Office. Gingerly, reluctantly, he took out the topmost folder, and opened it. It contained a single sheet covered with a spidery handwriting that he recognized as Ogden's own. He opened the other three folders. Each contained a single, similar sheet of paper.

Jessup sat back to read. He read through the four folders carefully, then read through them again. When he was finished with them for the second time, he sat for a long while with his eyes on the place in the broken wall where the lockbox had been. He did not know it, but his face was grey and his eyes were heavy-lidded. He reached for the telephone.

2

I WAS drinking beer and eating Cajun shrimp with Manny Escobar and Bobby Montero when I heard about David Ogden. The shrimp joint was a shack off Route 90 outside of Houma, but there was a television set mounted on the wall and the word was on the eleven o'clock news. David Ogden, World War II hero, and number three man in the CIA, was dead. The news didn't move me much. The Agency owns me and my friends lock, stock, and barrel, but they don't own us body and soul. The relationship is love-hate, easy on the love. We do what they tell us to do, within reason, but that doesn't mean that we sleep in the same bed. Manny knew that, but he had to give me the needle.

"Bad news, Ben," he said. "Please accept my sincere condolences on the loss of your leader. I feel for you."

Bobby didn't know me that well, but he saw the way Manny was going, and he got into it. He laid a heavy hand on my shoulder. "Mister Slade, maybe you should go back to the motel and change into something black."

"Black, *tu culo,*" I told him.

"Oh, no, Mister Slade, not mine. Mine is pink; *como una rosa en el mes de mayo.* You gonna go to the funeral?"

"Not me. I might be tempted to piss on his grave."

Manny shook his head. "Bad luck to talk like that."

"Maybe you should just send flowers," said Bobby. He was big, and flabby, and his lips were greasy from the shrimp. "I heard about that guy, I heard he went crazy. I heard he had the brain cancer."

I nodded. "Tumors."

"*Menos mal.* In a job like that it helps to be a little crazy."

I didn't argue the point, it was too close to the truth. "You mean you don't have any crazies in your outfit? Is that what you mean?"

They looked at each other. They both were Cuban, and they worked for the DEA. They decided to laugh. Manny said, "You get crazies everywhere. Especially at the top."

"Shit floats," was Bobby's contribution. "Who gets this guy's job?"

"Man called Jessup."

"Is he crazy, too?"

"Give him time."

I pressed the icy beer bottle against my forehead. It was February, but the night was hot and moist, Louisiana muggy. The shrimp joint was five miles up the road from the 7-Eleven where the meet was supposed to go down at two in the morning. Tailgate party in the parking lot, fifty thousand in cash for a small barrel of China White. We had the money under the table in a carrying case that looked like the satchel your Aunt Edna left behind the last time she came to visit. Manny had it between his feet. He was slouched in his chair munching shrimp, relaxed and easy, but his feet were clamped on that case. He was out of the Drug Enforcement Agency in Washington, while Bobby was local. I was there on loan, which was common enough. The Agency farmed us out like mules to places like the FBI and the DEA. I had worked with Manny before, and he knew what I did for a living. It was different with Bobby. He knew that I had some sort of connection with the Agency, but he didn't know what it was and he didn't know why I was there. I was happy to leave it that way. He probably wouldn't have believed the truth, and if he had it would have made him edgy. Normal people get that way when people like me are around. Even with Manny, who was a friend, there was a wall between us. It was thin, but it was there. He knew that I could look into his head and see what he was thinking, and nobody normal likes that.

Bobby grabbed a handful of shrimp, and called over his shoulder for another beer. He stuffed shrimp into his mouth, chewed, and spat the shells onto the floor. He had the table manners of an alligator. He grinned at me, and said, "Yeah, I know. I'm a slob."

"As long as you know it," I told him.

"That's nothing," said Manny. He looked amused. "You should see him eat ribs. The bones fly."

"I'll pass."

The girl who was working the tables came with the beer, and Bobby watched her walk back to the bar, her haunches rolling. She was chubby, and she wasn't wearing much. She was fifteen at the most, and the chub was baby fat.

Bobby said speculatively, "You know what I'm thinking?"

I knew exactly what he was thinking. I was inside his head, tapping him. He was thinking in crude and graphic terms about taking the girl back to the motel with him. He didn't have much imagination.

"Come off it," said Manny. "She's just a kid."

"I know it, I know it." Bobby made a show of licking his lips. "Around here she's legal."

"Christ, you ought to be ashamed of yourself. You got a daughter that age."

"My daughter isn't bad for her age. You should try her sometimes."

"I already did. She's almost as good as your wife."

That was the level of the conversation. We sat at the table with the shrimp and the beer until after midnight, then we drove around until it was time to set up the meet. Bobby and Manny had been working on it for over a month, trying to make a buy from an organization that was flooding the lower parishes with quality coke. They were working without the local law, which Manny thought might be leaky. Bobby was working undercover, and it had taken him the month to set up the first buy. The buy was a teaser with no one due to get busted. If it went down smoothly then Bobby moved up the line to the next supplier, step-by-step, until they got to the people who were worth taking down. The meeting was one-on-one, only one of them with the merchandise and Bobby by himself with the satchel in the parking lot of the 7-Eleven at two in the morning. Manny would be there on a roof to back him up, and I would be there because Bobby couldn't wear a wire.

The trouble is television, too many drug agents wear wires. Well, the bad guys watch television, too, and now every time a major buy goes down the buyer gets a skin search. So it takes some balls to wear a wire these days, but there are times when it has to be done, mostly when recorded evidence is needed. That wasn't the case here. No one was getting busted, and the only need for a wire was to make sure that Bobby didn't get himself iced. He'd be sitting out in the open with a satchel full of cash, dealing with people he didn't know, and there had to be a way for him to call in the Marines. A wire back to Manny on the roof would have given him the protection, but they couldn't use a wire and so they had to use me. I do it without wires.

We split up at one o'clock. Manny and I left the car a half mile from the 7-Eleven, and Bobby went on alone, the satchel on the seat beside him. Manny and I went overland, down the embankment at the side of the road, and along a series of gullies, the sawtooth grass tearing at our ankles and knees. I was empty-handed, but Manny had his weapon in a gun bag over his shoulder. It was a sniper's rifle, a Dragunov with a telescopic sight. It wasn't heavy, but it was bulky, and it made the going difficult for him. The gullies were wet with runoff water, filled with slick rocks, and every time that Manny slipped he cursed softly.

We came out of the gully in back of the 7-Eleven, and climbed the emergency ladder up to the roof. The roof was flat and tarred, and with a waist-high façade at the front that gave plenty of cover. The parking lot below was dark and almost deserted. Only Bobby's car was there, parked directly in front of the store. I had picked the spot for him. My maximum range is one hundred and fifty feet, and the car was well within it. Manny set up the Dragunov on its tripod, zeroed it in on the driver's side of Bobby's car, and we settled in to wait.

I tuned into Bobby's head. Sitting down there in the car, staring out into the night, he was still thinking about that kid in the shrimp joint. He had her twisted into an impossible position. Or maybe it was possible, but not for anybody I knew. I told Manny, and he laughed.

"Bobby is okay," he said. "It's just that he's still growing up."

I figured Bobby for about forty. "How much further does he have to go?"

"Well, you know how it is. Some people never get there at all."

"He'd better be there tonight."

"Shit, you don't have to worry about Bobby that way. He's a good man on the job."

"It isn't a job for a middle-aged adolescent."

"Look, I've worked with him before. I'm telling you he's all right."

"If you say so."

"I say so." He was silent for a long moment. I didn't have to go into his head to sense his disapproval. "You don't like people much, do you?"

I didn't bother to answer.

"I guess it's that thing that you do, getting into people's heads, see what they're thinking. If I could do that, I guess I'd start playing God just like you."

"You know me better than that, Manny."

"I know you, and that's why I'm saying it. You see too much of the bad side of people, stuff that shouldn't be seen, except maybe by God. That's why you're down on people."

"You figure that God is down on people?"

"I've known it all my life."

"Then how come I'm not down on you? How come I think that you're a mature, stable personality without a blemish or a flaw?"

"Well, shit, that's me. Everybody knows I'm perfect." He grinned in the darkness. "But you're down on people, that's for sure. I guess you can't help it. Like what you said about Ogden, about pissing on his grave. You shouldn't have said that."

"The man was a prick."

"Maybe so. Bobby and me, we've got pricks in our outfit, too, but you'll never hear us say it in front of an outsider."

"You just said it."

"That was just to make a point. You'll never hear me say it again."

"I've got a different situation, Manny."

"How?"

I wanted to tell him how. I wanted to tell him how his outfit was engaged in a clear-cut battle that allowed for simple loyalties. I wanted to tell him how the chessmasters at Langley, men like Ogden and Jessup, moved their pieces around the board with an icy precision, casually sacrificing pawns for the good of the game. I wanted to tell him how many of those broken pawns I'd seen swept off the board in places like

Afghanistan and Nicaragua. I wanted to tell him all that, but just then a white El Dorado turned off the highway and into the parking lot.

Manny whispered, "Show time." He went into his crouch behind the Dragunov, his finger on the trigger and his eye fixed to the scope.

The El Dorado pulled up next to Bobby's car. There were two men in the front seat, which meant that they were breaking the agreement, but, then, so were we. The driver stayed behind the wheel. The dealer got out of the car and came over to Bobby's window. Bobby looked out, and grinned up at him.

"You got it?" asked the dealer.

"Sure, I got it," said Bobby. "You got yours?"

"I got it. Get out of the car and let's talk."

"I don't have to get out, I can talk from here." Bobby had the motor running, the gear engaged, and the clutch floored. He was ready to roll. "I don't see nothing. Where is it?"

"In the car. Come on, let's see your end."

"Hey, you crazy? You don't show me nothing, and you want to see my end?"

"Look, don't fuck with me."

"You're the one who's fucking around. Let's see the stuff."

"It's in the car."

"You said a barrel, so let's see the barrel."

"Get out of the car, I got to check you for wire."

"You check me once I see the merchandise."

"I check you, then I see the money."

"Bullshit, it don't work that way."

"You're jerking me off, you don't have any money."

"Hey, do things right. Show me the merchandise."

They were bellowing at each other. It sounded like the usual ranking, pushing for an edge, but by now I was into the dealer's head, and I knew it was a burn. I made a deep tap to be sure. There was merchandise in the El Dorado, but it wasn't for sale. It never had been. It had always been a burn, get the cash and run, and Bobby was due to go down. The dealer's weapon was in his belt, and he was ready to use it, but he wanted to see the money first. He was working himself up to it with all that shouting.

Manny whispered, "What is it?"

"A burn," I told him.

"You sure?"

I was sure. I was into the dealer's head, and I could see it clearly. "You don't have much time. You'd better drop him."

"Shit."

He didn't want to do it. Doing it would blow everything that they'd worked on for the past month, but he had no choice. He fired, and killed the dealer. The bullet went in through the top of the head. He didn't have to do it that way. He could have dropped the dealer without killing him, but his partner was under the gun, and he wasn't taking any chances.

The dealer went down, and when Bobby heard the shot he hit the accelerator. The car raced across the lot to the far end, skidded into a one-eighty, and came roaring back directly at the El Dorado. The driver of the El Dorado had a weapon out the window, firing. Bobby kept on coming. Manny put three shots into the roof of the El Dorado, and the driver popped out with his hands up. Bobby braked just short of hitting him, then he was out of the car and had the driver spread out on the hood. He was quick, and he was sure, and he wasn't thinking about teenage poon.

Bobby had the driver cuffed and his face in the gravel by the time that Manny and I got down to the lot. Manny knelt over the body of the dealer. The dealer's hands were empty; his pistol was tucked in his belt. Manny eased it out with a pencil, and dropped it into the dealer's right hand. He closed the hand around the butt, then let it go. The pistol dropped to the ground.

I must have made a noise, because Manny looked up at me, and asked, "You feel like playing God again?"

"No," I said, "but how do you know he was right-handed?"

"I don't. I'm just going with the odds."

Bobby came over and looked at the body. "The bastards," he said. He had a hard time getting the words out. He was breathing hard. He knew how close it had been.

It was time to bring in the local law, and Bobby was elected to drive into Houma to get them. Before he left, Manny took the satchel from the car. "The way they pay the cops around here," he explained, "they don't eat too regular."

When Bobby was gone, we checked to see that the driver was secure, and then we sat on the hood of the El Dorado to wait. The frogs started up in the stillness, masses of them croaking in the wetlands behind us. Manny said, "You ever go for frogs when you were a kid?"

"No."

"Didn't think so. Don't find many frogs in the big city."

"Wrong. Little town in north Texas, but no frogs worth going for."

"You don't talk like Texas."

"Not any more, it's been a while." I could have told him that he didn't talk like Cuba any more, but he knew better than that.

"We used to go for frogs when I was little. Not here, in Cuba. Big bastards, meat like a chicken leg. Catch enough and the whole family had frogs for dinner."

"Do you go for them here?"

"Not worth it. Too much work for what you get. I guess it's something for kids to do." And then, without a pause, "What do you think of Bobby now?"

"He did the job," I admitted.

"You see him come straight at that sumbitch?" He jerked his chin at the driver on the ground.

"I saw it."

"He didn't have to do that. He could have let me finish it, but that's the way he is. He gets the blood up and you can't stop him."

So Bobby was a slob and a cretin, but he could do the job. That didn't change my opinion of him, but it was the wrong time to say something like that. All I said was, "You were right. I had him wrong."

Manny nodded, satisfied. "What he doesn't know is that you saved his ass."

"Part of my job."

"Yeah, I know, but it's one hell of a job. I don't know how you do it, but there's nobody like you. You're one in a million, kid."

He was wrong, and he was right. There were many others like me all over the world, and we were, in fact, one in a million. That was the statistic most commonly used. It wasn't exact, but it was close enough: one sensitive for every million of population. I had heard it all my life. I was one in a million.

It was a long night with the police, and with a fussy type from the office of the prosecuting attorney of the parish. They weren't happy about having us in the neighborhood without notice, but they never are and it's something they live with. All they could do was look disapproving. I was carrying DEA credentials for the job, and so there wasn't any heat on me, but the paperwork was staggering and it was midday before we got back to the motel. That was just the local formalities. We slept through the afternoon and the night, and the next day we went up to New Orleans to take care of the federal end of it. I faded into the background there. I couldn't show my DEA papers to the Feds, and there was no justifiable reason for an employee of the Federal Center for the Study of Childhood Diseases to have been involved in a drug operation. So Manny carried the ball at the Federal Court House on Camp Street, and by the late afternoon it was all over.

We went back to the hotel to shower and change, and Manny and Bobby were ready to party. They had been on the job for a month, and they had some steam to blow. "You got to come along," said Bobby. His lips were loose and wet. "There's this place in the Quarter, they got bucking bulls and the girls with no clothes on."

Manny added, "They make great ribs, too."

I flashed a vision of Bobby drinking boilermakers in a cowboy bar and playing Henry the Eighth with a side of pork. I tried to look regretful. "Count me out, I'm beat. I really am. I need an early night."

"You can sleep tomorrow," said Manny. "Come on, you'll have a good time."

"Right now my idea of a good time is a broiled lobster and a bottle of wine, but I want them served in my room with the bed so close that I can fall into it."

"Chickenshit."

"That's me."

"We'll miss you." He gave me a tight smile. "Aside from playing God, you're also a bit of a snob, aren't you?"

"Just a bit, Manny, just a bit. I try not to let it show."

But I didn't get the lobster, I didn't get the wine, and I didn't get to sleep that night. An hour later Sammy Warsaw called from the Center and told me to get my ass up there. Sammy is like a brother to me, but he runs the Center now, and he tends to be peremptory. "No excuses," he said. "I want you here by noon tomorrow."

"Sammy, in case it slipped your mind, I just came off a job and my bones are breaking. Tomorrow I'll probably slide down to the coast, lie in the sun, and maybe try for some snapper."

"You'll be here tomorrow."

I figured the days. "Maybe Friday."

"There's a flight out of New Orleans in an hour. Be on it."

"Forget it."

"Do you want me to make it an order?"

I laughed. We don't give each other orders. "Now I know you're joking."

"No joke, I'm calling in the troops."

"All of them?" I couldn't imagine him recalling every one of the two hundred-odd aces that we have spread out all over the world.

"The senior aces," he said patiently. "You and Vince, Martha and Snake."

"And you." He was the boss now, but he still was one of us.

"And me," he agreed. "I want you all in my office at twelve sharp."

"What is it, World War III, or did somebody lose the key to the Men's Room?"

"All I know is that I got a call about an hour ago. I'm supposed to have the five of us on tap at noon tomorrow. There'll be some visitors from the Agency arriving about then."

"Delaney?" Roger Delaney was the Deputy Director for Science and Technology, and as such he controlled our finances, our security, and our assignments. He was the one person from the Agency who had access to the Center.

"Delaney and a few others." Sammy sounded unhappy.

"That's against the rules."

"I'm afraid that we're bending the rules this time."

"Then it has to be something hot."

"And you have to be here."

"You're a hard man, Sammy."

"Do you want this fucking job? You can have it, you know."

I hung up, and an hour later I was on my way home.

I have an apartment in Manhattan in a cold and sterile building, but that isn't what I call home. I have a cottage on the Jersey shore, but that isn't home, either. There's that Texas town where I was born, but it never was home to me, and never will be. Home is a state of mind, and mine is in the state of Virginia. To get to my home you leave Washington on Interstate 95 going south into the Virginia countryside for almost an hour. You pass the Marine base at Quantico, and leave the Interstate at Fredericksburg, following the state road southeast with the Rappahannock River on your left and the Nathan Bedford Forrest Military Reservation on your right. You skirt the perimeter of the reservation edging southward, and after three miles you turn onto a dirt road that is marked by a faded sign that reads: FEDERAL CENTER FOR THE STUDY OF CHILDHOOD DISEASES—AUTHORIZED PERSONNEL ONLY. From the turnoff you can see the first of the manned gates and the tops of the buildings beyond the fence. When I reach that turnoff, I know that I'm home. When you reach that turnoff, you've gone as far as you can go.

I left my rented car at the manned gate, and passed into the Center on foot. Inside me was a rolling excitement, a childish glee. It was birthday time and Christmas rolled into one, for this had been my home from the age of twelve, and coming back was like no other feeling in the world. Only Center personnel could clear the gate; Agency people stayed on the other side of the wire. On their side were the barracks, the motor pool, and the security headquarters; all squat and functional buildings. On our side was the fieldstone and ivy-covered structures of the Center: the separate living quarters for the aces and the students, the double-winged administration building, the mess hall and lounge, the long, low block of the hospital and research complex, the athletic fields and the swimming pools.

Sammy met me at the gate. He ran the place now, but he was guided by a courtesy long out of fashion. His greeting, however, was anything but courteous. The guard at the gate could have heard him, and so he spoke to me head-to-head.

Late, as usual, he said. *What is it with you, can't you ever be on time? The others are up in the office.*

Don't blame me, blame Delta. Are the visitors here yet?

Not yet. They're as bad as you are. Worse.

Any idea what it's all about?

He shook his head. *I don't know any more than I knew last night. We'll find out soon enough.*

What are the rules? No tapping? One of the many agreements that we had with the Agency people was that we did not go into their heads. It was a rule that we observed at our convenience.

Sammy shrugged. *Use your own judgment.* He was sore about them bringing in unauthorized personnel, and he wasn't trying to hide it.

We walked together up the tree-lined road that led to the administration building. It was a quiet day, and the only noises that came to us were those of the birds, and the shouts of a faraway group of kids on the soccer field. The place looked more like a small-town college than anything else, and with good reason. No matter what the signs said, our side of the wire had only one function, the study and training of sensitives. The Federal Center for the Study of Childhood Diseases was a fiction to discourage the curious, and the actual workings of the Center was classified information. Aside from our own people, only a selected few in high places knew of the existence of the Center. It was the same with all the other countries that used sensitives: the research center was always affiliated with the intelligence branch of the government. It had to be that way. In our case the budget of the Center ran into more money than any institution in the private sector could handle. Only the government could afford to pick up the tab, and that meant the CIA. The Agency and the Center were joined hip and thigh in a relationship that was often strained, but never had been broken.

The layout of the Center showed the nature of that relationship. We were on the inside of the fence, and they were on the outside. They were very much in control. In exchange for all the money, in exchange for the Center, in exchange for our very existence, we worked for them. They owned us, every single one of us.

"The kid," said Martha, "is a monster. I'm sorry to have to put it that way, but that's what he is. A monster."

"The kid," said Vince, "is a kid. And all kids are monsters."

"Not like this one. He's truly nasty."

"He'll grow out of it," said Snake.

"He refuses to study."

I said, "Motivate him."

"He disrupts the class."

"Apply peer pressure."

"And," Martha made her final point, "he's a terror with the girls."

"There you are," said Vince. "I knew he couldn't be all bad."

Sammy smiled, but did not look up from his work. We sat in his office waiting for our visitors from the Agency, Sammy at his desk, and the rest of us spread over couches and chairs. Sammy's work was a stack of requisition forms, and he checked each one carefully before putting his initials on it. He never had wanted to run the Center, never had wanted to have anything to do with administration, but now he had the job and he was doing his best with it. He had been happiest in the field when the five of us had worked as a team. We were all the same age, had come to the Center in the same year as children, and had grown up together with ties far tighter than actual kinship could have produced. Not that we were in any way alike. Sammy Warsaw, with his frizzy hair and his batwing ears, his sharp wit and keen intellect, was the first among equals. Vince Bonepart, big and black, had the profile of an Assyrian god and the body of an NFL linebacker. Martha Marino was everybody's Earth Mother, gentle to the bone, while Claudia, called Snake, was as slim as a boy and as daring as a wildcat. And then were was me, Ben Slade.

We rarely operated as a team anymore, and Sammy had called us in from independent assignments: me from Louisiana, Vince from his translation post at the U.N., and Snake from an interrogation in Seattle. Martha had not had to travel at all; she was on temporary assignment at the Center, teaching. We all took a turn at that once every year, working with the kids whose powers were the same as ours, but who still had to learn how to handle them. The Center had a staff of teachers for the normal curriculum, but it took a sensitive to teach another one how to live with the responsibility that went with the talent. I had always found it to be a rewarding experience, but Martha had caught a rough one with Little, and he was driving her up the wall.

"He's anything but little," she said to Vince. "He's only sixteen and he's almost as big as you are. And nobody calls him Amos anymore. Chicken Little, that's his name now."

"I like it, but why Chicken?"

"That's his favorite game. You know, going head-to-head with cars, first one to turn away is chicken. Well, Amos never turns. Never."

"Here in the Center? Where do they get the cars?"

Snake laughed. "Where did we get them when we were here?" She had a right to laugh. When we were kids, nobody was quicker or better than Snake at lifting a jeep from the motor pool.

"The other day he talked another kid into doing it with forklift trucks. Can you imagine two forklifts going head-to-head? It was like a pair of saber-toothed tigers."

More laughter.

"You can laugh," said Martha, her voice troubled, "but I'm really worried about the boy. I'm beginning to think he's not right in the head."

The laughter reached a new level. "Did I hear you right?" I asked. "Not right in the head? Do you remember what you were like when you came here? Do you remember what we all were like?"

The laughter stopped in sympathy for Martha. There was nothing she could say in answer to those questions, although she knew the answers well enough. Before coming to the Center, we all had been quite mad.

The Center had found Martha in a home for retarded children in Omaha. She had been there for a year. She heard voices in her head that no one else could hear. When she heard the voices she went wild. She screamed for hours, she clawed her body, she soiled herself. When the Center found her she was under constant restraint and sedation. She was twelve years old.

The Center had found Vince tucked away in the corner of a drug-abuse program in Boston. Vince also heard the voices. His parents had abandoned him when he was seven, and after that he had lived in the streets. He had learned from his elders how to boost drunks and how to shoot smack. The smack kept the voices quiet. He was kicking when the Center found him, and the voices were back, filling his head with their howls. He was twelve years old.

The Center found Claudia in a religious commune in Idaho. The members of the group worshipped snakes. They also worshipped Claudia. When Claudia heard the voices she went into a trance and made hissing noises. That, to members of the commune, made her part of the godhead, a higher form of snake. They kept her in a cage and fed her what the snakes ate. When the Center found her she had not spoken a word for months, and she moved by slithering across the floor on her belly. She was twelve years old.

The Center found Sammy in an expensive sanitarium north of New York City. His parents had placed him there. He was catatonic, incapable of voluntary movement. He could not speak, and his limbs remained fixed in whatever position they were placed. His eyes stared straight ahead, unblinking. He had been that way since he first heard the voices. He was twelve years old.

The Center found me locked in the back bedroom of a shack in Freeman, Texas, just south of the Oklahoma line. The room had a bed, a chair, and a slop bucket. I was chained to the bed, and I was naked. My body was covered with old scars and fresh welts. The man I called my daddy said that the voices I heard were the tongues of the devil. He was a shade-tree mechanic and a part-time preacher, and he knew about devils. At the end of each day he whipped the devil out of me with a razor strop, and then prayed for my deliverance. When the Center found me I could not stand or sit, and my body was a festering wound. I was twelve years old.

That's what we had been, my generation at the Center, and other generations, before us and after, had come from the same sort of background: the abused, the imprisoned, the seemingly mad. At the Center we were cleansed, we were nourished, we were treated, we were loved, and we were taught how to live with the voices in our heads. They were the voices of the world around us. The lust of the satyr, the sloth of the slob, the greed of the avaricious, the jealousy of the discontented, the righteousness of the fanatic, the despair of the helpless, the flaring orange delight of the arsonist, and the screaming crimson of the psychopath—those were the voices that had howled around within our heads like winds in a cavern, and had blown us away into another world. It took time to learn how to live with those voices, and by the time we were sixteen most of us had managed it. Amos Little was one of the exceptions.

"I hate to say this," said Martha, and we all knew what was coming.

"Go ahead, spit it out," said Vince.

"He may be a deuce."

Nobody laughed at that. There was nothing funny about one of the kids turning out to be a deuce, a failed ace. It didn't happen very often, but it happened. A kid would come into the program with all the potential ability of a true sensitive, but the ability would never develop. A kid like that was left in limbo, neither a normal nor a sensitive, capable of limited communication, but useless in the field. There was nothing to do with a kid like that; he was in the system, and couldn't get out, but he could never truly be a part of it. He was a deuce, and around the Center the deuces were the hewers of wood and the haulers of water. I had known a few happy deuces, but I hadn't known many.

Snake asked, "What makes you think so?"

Martha shrugged. "The usual. He has a great deal of difficulty communicating head to head. He can do it, but not easily, and not all of the time."

"Any pain?"

"He says that it hurts his head when he tries to do it."

It was the classic sign of the failed ace, and it brought more silence. Sammy looked up from what he was doing, and said, "That doesn't have to mean that he's a deuce. I've known kids with the same problem, and they've broken through."

"So have I," said Martha, "but . . ." She waved the thought away. "I hope you're right."

The telephone rang. Sammy picked it up, said a few words, put it down, and announced, "Our visitors are here."

3

THE Prisoner dreamed every night, and every night the dream was the same. He dreamed of a young girl, ten or eleven years old, whose face was smooth and oval, whose eyes were dark and deep, and whose hair was a wave of chestnut that a loving mother had drawn into braids. That was what The Prisoner saw at the start of each dream, but at the end of it the oval face was shattered, the eyes were sightless, and the little girl's hair was matted with blood and bits of brain.

In his dream, The Prisoner knew that it would not have happened if the child had not screamed. It would not have happened if the mother had been able to control her. In an airplane operation the silence and obedience of the hostages are essential to the success of the mission. It has to be that way, but the little girl had screamed, had gone on screaming, and so Amir had hit her on top of the head with his pistol. Even then, she had not stopped, and Amir had had to hit her several times before she was silent. That was the way that The Prisoner remembered it, although sometimes his memory played tricks on him, and in recollection it seemed that it had been Murad, not Amir, who had beaten the child. Amir or Murad, one or the other. Both of them were dead now, hunted down by the Zionist murder squads. Of the four on the mission, only Zahra and The Prisoner were still alive, she undercover in Paris, and he in the camp that he thought of as a prison.

He wondered if Zahra ever dreamed of the child, and he doubted it. It was eight years now since the airplane job, eight years since the four of them had snatched Pan Am 307 out of the sky, but it was only during the last six months that the face of the child had begun to come to him in the night. He wondered at that, because down through those years there had been much more blood and many other faces, but the face of that child was the only one that was able to unsettle his sleep.

The Prisoner always woke at the end of the dream, but he did not wake in horror or in sweat. Nor did he cry out. The dream was a companion now, and he had learned to live with it. At the end of the dream he would open his eyes, and repeat to himself the words of Muhammad Taqi Partovi Sabzevari.

"It is Allah who puts the gun in our hand," he would whisper to himself, "but we cannot expect Him to pull the trigger as well, just because we are fainthearted."

Then he would sit up in his cot and look around in the darkness at the other men sleeping in the long, rectangular tent that was open at both ends to the breezes of the desert. Each night when he woke from his dream he would check to see that they all were well. There were twenty-two others who slept in the tent, and as their leader The Prisoner could have slept in a tent of his own, but he preferred to be with his brothers. The only time that he used a private tent, and they all did then, was during the monthly visits when the women were sent in from the outside. But other than that single day each month, they lived communally, sleeping, eating, and training together. The number of them varied. There were twenty-two now, but The Prisoner could remember a time when there had been as few as six. They came and they went, some never to return, and whenever that happened The Prisoner would remind his men that, unlike other religions, which consider death to be the end of a man, in the vision of the Qur'an death is not the end of life but its continuation in another form. He told them that man's evolutionary movement toward infinity continues after death. He told them that death is no more than a hyphen between the two parts of man's existence. He told them that sincerely, for he believed it all, most of the time.

And then, having checked to see that his men were well, he would lower himself to his pillow again, and compose himself to return to sleep. A lesser man at a time like that might chase the dream of the little girl by conjuring up a soothing vision: a golden day, a verdant field, a ring of children playing gaily. But that was not the way of The Prisoner. Instead, he would turn his mind to the broken bodies of all the Arab children he had seen in his life, the children of Gaza, of the camps in Beirut, of the villages of the Bekaa. Some of the children had been the victims of poverty and malnutrition, others had been slain by the Nazarenes, and still others by the Zionist warplanes. There were many that he could count, hundreds, perhaps thousands, and as he lay on his cot The Prisoner would stack them into piles in his mind, one pathetic corpse on top of the other, until the pyramids of their bodies managed to mask one broken, oval face, and then he would sleep undisturbed until dawn.

4

SAMMY was sore. He was hopping mad, and the only reason that he wasn't actually hopping up and down was that he didn't want to give our Agency visitors the satisfaction of seeing how upset he was. There were five visitors, and only two were acceptable on the premises. One was Roger Delaney, the Deputy Director for Science and Technology. Bluff, hearty, and not too bright, he was our liaison, and the only Agency official with unrestricted access to the Center. With him was Alex Jessup, the new DDO, who was there with Sammy's reluctant permission. Jessup had asked for it, and Sammy had granted it. It isn't easy to say no to the number three man in the outfit that owns you. So Delaney and Jessup were welcome in the Center, but the other three definitely were not. They stood against the wall of Sammy's office, and stared at us with cold eyes. They were young, and they were cold. Everything about them was cold, and everything about them screamed security. They had good tailors, their clothes did not bulge, but they had the look that goes with being armed. They had no business on our side of the wire, and Sammy so told Delaney.

"Can't be helped," Delaney replied. "Necessary evil, I'm afraid."

"Bullshit, you can't march into my office with a bunch of thugs and . . ."

"Sammy, we're carrying something rather sensitive, you see."

"That?" Sammy pointed to a large metal box that Jessup had set on a table.

"Exactly. Now, if you'll just give me a chance to . . ."

"Is that what the guards are for? You think we're going to pinch it?"

"No, of course not."

"Then get them out of here. They make me nervous."

"Afraid I can't do that." He turned to Jessup for help. "Alex, perhaps if you explained."

Jessup cleared his throat. "As Roger said, the material we have here is highly sensitive. It would have been impossible for us to bring it from Langley without some form of security."

Sammy said, "Then you should have held this meeting at your office, not mine."

"Your presence at Langley would have been noticed. For reasons of security, I wanted to avoid that."

"So you brought along your storm troopers. What kind of security is that with them standing here listening? What kind of clearance do they have?"

"Their clearance is my business, not yours." Jessup turned angrily to Delaney. "What kind of a ship are you running here? I thought these people were under your control."

Delaney smiled nervously. "Control isn't quite the word to use. The Center is an independent organization."

"We own it, don't we? We run it, don't we?"

"We own it, Alex. We don't run it."

"Then maybe it's time that we did. Who the hell do these people think they are?"

I said to Sammy, head-to-head, *This jackass is beginning to irritate me. Do you mind if I tap him?*

Be my guest, Sammy said disgustedly. *He doesn't deserve any courtesy. We might as well all go in.*

The five of us went into Jessup's head, and rummaged around. He had a disorderly mind, but at the very front of it was the name of David Ogden. Something about the lockbox on the table. And some files. And some code names: Gemstone . . . Sextant . . . Madrigal . . .

Domino. And binding it all together was a solid block of ice-cold fear.

We came out of Jessup's head, and Vince said, *This is one unhappy dude. He's so scared he's shitting peach pits.*

Martha, who looked for good in everyone, asked, *Do you think that's why he's acting this way? Because he's frightened?*

Don't give him any points, said Snake. *He's acting this way because he's a prick.*

Delaney was trying to calm Jessup down. "You have to understand that you can't deal with these people the way you can with Agency personnel. They are very highly strung, emotional, artistic . . ."

"Artistic." Jessup spat the word.

". . . sensitive people. That's what they're called, and that's what they are. They're sensitives. Because of what they can do."

"I've heard about what they can do, and I don't believe half of it. God damn witch doctors. Remember, this was your idea, not mine."

Delaney shrugged. "If you can think of a better way to handle the situation . . ." He let the sentence hang.

"No, I can't. You know damn well I can't. That's why I'm sitting here dealing with these . . . these . . ."

He never got the word out. Snake stretched lazily, and said, "You're not dealing with me, chum. Sammy, if those goons against the wall are staying, I'm leaving. I want to get in some racquetball, anyway. How about it, Vince?"

"Sounds good," Vince told her. "You ready to get your ass whipped?"

"In your dreams," she said.

Martha stood up. "I have a ton of papers to grade."

I yawned widely. "And I've got some sleep to catch up on."

Jessup looked around wildly. "What is this? What's going on?"

"What's going on is this," said Sammy in his mildest voice. "You're apparently afraid of something. In fact, you're filled with fear."

Jessup stared at him.

"Now fear is a reasonable excuse for bad manners, but if you want to talk to us about the files that David Ogden left behind, you'll have to get rid of your security people. If not, then this meeting is over."

Jessup looked as if he had been slapped in the face. He stared at Sammy helplessly. He had heard about sensitives, but he had never actually seen one in action. More than that, he had never fully believed that we existed. When he had thought about us at all, he had thought of us as carnival tricksters. Now he was face-to-face with the reality. Either there had been a massive breach of security, or he was sitting in a room with five people who could pick his brains at their leisure. I almost felt sorry for him.

He recovered nicely. It took him a moment to regain control, a moment of slow breathing and concentration, and then he went back in the saddle. He turned to the cold young men, and said, "Out. Wait for us at the gate."

"On the other side of the gate," Sammy added. Once they had filed out of the room he put on that meek and mild voice of his again, the one he used around appropriations time each year. That was why he was running the show. He could do things like that. "Mr. Jessup, we started off on the wrong foot here, and I don't want the situation to get any worse. With all respect, you have something to tell us, and we're ready to listen. Please go ahead."

Jessup nodded. He recognized the oil. It was a commodity he dealt in every day. "How much do you know already?"

"Only what you've been thinking about during the past few minutes. No details."

Jessup frowned as another thought struck him. "What's happening now? What sort of privacy do I have?"

"Total privacy," Sammy assured him, lying casually. "What I did before, I did as a demonstration, and to save us all some time. No one is working on you now."

"You can count on that," Delaney rushed to say. "These people have their own code of conduct, and they stick to it." He realized how lame that sounded. "Most of the time."

Most of the time, echoed Vince, and we laughed silently.

"So," said Sammy, prodding. "Tell us about David Ogden."

He told us. He started slowly, but picked up speed as he went along. He told us much that we already knew: about Ogden's illness, the inoperable tumors in his brain, the weeks in the hospital when he lay in a coma, and the final release. Then he told us about the lockbox that had just been opened.

"Frankly, a mistake in judgment was made," he said, staring at his hands. "The box should have been opened earlier, but we assumed that it contained only personal papers. There seemed to be no need for an indecent haste. As I said, that was a mistake, and we're paying for it now. In addition to several highly personal items, the box contained four file folders that . . ." He broke off for a moment. "You say that I'm frightened, and I admit that I am. The contents of those folders could seriously compromise the credibility of the Agency. They might even threaten the composition of the Agency as we know it today."

He looked around to see if we were properly impressed. I wasn't. It sounded like a case of the keys to the Men's Room, an internal Agency flap. Someone, probably Ogden, had dropped the ball somewhere, and the Agency image would suffer if the story got out. I felt like yawning again, and not only because I had missed a night's sleep.

"These files," said Sammy. "What do they contain?"

"Four blank case folders. In each one is an assignment to an agent who is identified only by a code name. The assignments apparently were made just before Ogden entered the hospital. The assignments are . . . bizarre, to say the least."

"Do you intend showing them to us?"

"I do, yes, but before we get to that I'd like to explain my position here. Ever since this situation came to light, after the lockbox was opened, an executive committee has sat in almost continuous session to consider what action should be taken. Several plans were developed, and all of them were discarded for reasons that will become apparent. It was Roger Delaney here, who suggested that we bring you people in on the problem, and, frankly, I must tell you that I was against the idea. I don't really understand what it is that you people do, or how you do it, and I have to admit that you make me uncomfortable. But as Roger has pointed out, we've run out of options. You'll understand that better after you've seen the files. For the moment, you're the best bet we have."

We all nodded understandingly, but that doesn't mean that we were giving Jessup our undivided attention. While he was making his statement, Vince and Snake were silently arguing the relative merits of racquetball and squash, Martha was considering the possibility that

Jessup's ill temper was the result of a high-fat diet, Sammy was wondering if he might be able to maneuver a budget extension in return for the favor that was about to be asked of us, and I was thinking about security. Like everyone else in his line of work, Jessup was obsessed with the concept, yet he had mentioned an executive committee, which meant that between seven and ten people already knew about the Ogden files. Then there were the three heavyweights that he had brought with him, and now he was about to entrust the deep dark secret to five of the most irresponsible people I knew. Between fifteen and twenty, by my count. I once had to deal with Carlo Marcello, the Cosa Nostra boss in New Orleans. Carlo had a sign on the wall of his office, that read: THREE PEOPLE CAN KEEP A SECRET IF TWO OF THEM ARE DEAD. Old Carlo knew what he was talking about, and he was only two-thirds right.

Jessup opened the lockbox. There were two compartments in it. He opened the left compartment, and took out four thin folders. He looked at the folders, and read off the names. "Domino, Madrigal, Sextant, and Gemstone. To begin with, we have no records of these names, no idea who these agents are. From the contents of the files, it appears that these are people with whom Ogden worked in the past, people he could trust, and who owed him a high degree of loyalty." He hesitated. "It is not unknown for someone in Ogden's position to maintain such outside connections. It is contrary to accepted procedure, but it is not unknown."

Which meant that he had a few of his own.

"But we know nothing more than that, not even if these are males or females. I'm going to ask you to read the files now. Pass them among you and read all four of them. To save time, please note that each assignment sheet contains the same opening paragraphs, an introduction of sorts. The individual assignments follow the opening."

He passed out the folders, and we read. On each assignment sheet, the opening paragraphs were:

> Dear old friend, I have a task for you, one which I am sure you will approach with the same unquestioning devotion and fierce dedication that you have displayed to me so often in the past. I must tell you, however, that this is likely to be the last assignment

you will ever receive from me. Tomorrow I enter Bethesda Naval Hospital for an exploratory operation. The good doctors will open up my head and peer at my brain, and although I know not what they will find, I have my strong suspicions. There have been signs: blackouts, severe headaches, hallucinations, flashes of vivid color, and the odor of freshly sharpened pencils in my nostrils. Yes, I have a good idea what they will find. They will look inside my skull, shake their heads sadly, and close me up again with nothing to be done. Perhaps not. Perhaps my pessimism is misplaced, but I rather think that I am right, and so I have a task for you.

You know me as an arrogant man, and I do not deny it. More than that, I revel in it, for I have accomplished much in my life, and my arrogance is well earned. Even my enemies grant me that. I have lived my life at a level far above that of the ordinary man. I have shaken nations. I have changed the lives of hundreds of thousands. I have dammed up the rivers of history, and have set them on new courses. And having done all that, I find myself reluctant to leave this world in the way of the ordinary mortal . . . facing the unknown alone. There was a time, long ago, when a man such as I am went into the darkness accompanied by a slaughter of jesters and slaves, with the body of his faithful dog at his feet, with a sacrifice of virgins all around, and with a ceremonial fire that roared on the altar. In my well-earned arrogance I see myself as the direct descendent of such men, entitled to the same ceremonials, and the same companions on my voyage. I am willing to make concessions in numbers, but I insist on the symbols. I must have my sacrifices, my jester and my virgin, my bulldog and my sacred blaze. I wish them, I demand them, and I am calling on you, who have served me so well in the past, to make one of them possible.

Those were the opening paragraphs on each sheet. Then, individually, these followed.

Gemstone, your job is the fire, and even as I write these words I am visited by nostalgia, by the odor of rose bushes burning. Do you remember the aroma? Gasoline and roses in the villa in Quon Trac, the garden burning in the night. Do you remember how the odor blocked the smell of roasting flesh? You were good at it, Gemstone, as good as they come. I remember how you loved it all. I remember the look in your eye and the smile on your lips when you smelled the rose bushes burning, and now I have another blaze for you to set.

I want you to burn down a house. Not much of a job for your talents, I know, but it is the ceremony I have chosen and it will serve as a symbol for my pyre. The Southern Manor is a rather tacky little rooming house in the town of Glen Grove, Florida. It is a typical haven for the retired and the elderly, and I want it destroyed. I want it burned to the ground and made uninhabitable sometime between the dates of 28 February and 4 March. This is the blaze that I want for my altar, and I ask it of you. Should the opportunity present itself, you may throw a rose on the embers.

Your usual fee has been deposited in the Zurich account. Gibraltar Rules apply.

Sextant, your job is the virgin. Yes, I know that in the age in which we live the term is likely to be figurative, but this is the one I have chosen. Her name is Lila Simms, and she is a sixteen-year-old high school junior who lives in the small town of Rockhill, New York, in the Hudson Valley. There is nothing distinctive about the girl; she is a normal, decent teenager. Her interests are prosaic: dancing, rock music, tennis in the summer, skiing in the winter. Her school grades are average, and although she dates frequently, she has no steady boyfriend. This is the sacrifice I require, and I want it performed within the time frame of 28 February to 4 March. These are your instructions.

I want her raped, Sextant. Not just raped, but gang-raped by many men. I do not want her life, in fact I forbid you to take it, but I want her brutalized and I want it done in a fashion that will insure the maximum public attention and notoriety. My aim is her humiliation and her degradation; that will be sacrifice enough. Do this, Sextant, to speed me on my way.

Your usual fee has been deposited in the Geneva account. Gibraltar Rules apply.

Domino, I want you to slay me a bulldog to lie at my feet, but here I must confess to a weakness. I have ordered the deaths of many men, and have borne silent witness to the deaths of many others, but I have never killed an innocent animal, not deliberately, and I cannot order you to do so. The action is beyond me. Strange, but there it is, a weakness I have had all my life, and so this killing must be symbolic.

If you search among the small colleges of the northeast part of our country, you will find that Polk College, in New Hampshire, and Van Buren College in upper New York State, are traditional rivals in the sport of basketball. Each year they play against each other in the final game of the season, and the winner of that game will goes on to play in the Easter Holiday Tournament of Champions at Madison Square Garden. Having said that, I must point out that Van Buren is given little chance of getting into the tournament this year. Polk is too strong for them, even though Van Buren may well have its first winning season since its glory days of twenty years ago. Even now, well in advance of the game, Polk is heavily favored by the bookmakers.

And so, your assignment. The Van Buren team is called the Cavaliers. The Polk team is known as the Bulldogs, and therein lies my symbol. Van Buren must win. Polk must lose. The Bulldog must die. It's as simple as that, and I don't care how you do it. Bribery suggests itself, but I leave the details in your hands. Those hands that have served me so well, and now this final task, faint echo of past triumphs. But do it for me, as you always have. Slay me my bulldog on the first of March.

Your usual fee has been deposited in the Bern account. Gibraltar Rules apply.

Madrigal, I would have a jester to ride by my side on this darkest and longest of journeys. How wise the old ones were to take along a fool who could whistle in graveyards and mock eternal night. A jester, mind you, not a source of true wit or humor. I credit myself with a sufficiency of satire, and a sense of the ironic; I need no help in those departments. What I must have is a clown, a low-down thigh-slapper, a baggy-pants comedian, a mouther of banalities. In short, a buffoon, and I have found just the man.

His name is Calvin Weiss, and he is the entertainment director of the cruise ship S.S. *Carnival Queen*, one of those pathetic vessels that call at ports throughout the Caribbean. Visualize him, Madrigal, alive with a feverish energy, his eyes popping and his face sweating as he strives every night to amuse still another boatload of the brainless. Imagine what the mind of such a man must be like, stuffed full of punch lines and stale gags, blackout skits and rimshot whammos. What a delight he will be on the journey, what a shield against the gloom. Slay him for me, Madrigal. I need him. March first is the date that I give you. Have him for me then.

Your usual fee has been deposited in the Zurich account. Gibraltar Rules apply.

Sammy collected the folders, and returned them to Jessup. There was silence in the room. Jessup said, "First, let me point out the obvious. These people must be stopped. Today is the sixteenth of February, and these assignments are due to go into effect on the last day of the month. So, a certain amount of urgency is involved. And having said that, I'd now like to hear your opinion of the mental condition of the man who wrote these files."

Sammy looked at me, and said, "Ben, around the circle."

Which meant that I was to speak first. We all had been born in the same year, but I was the youngest by a month, and it was a tradition with us that the youngest spoke first. So it was me, then Martha, then Vince, then Snake, and then Sammy, who was our eldest by a matter of weeks.

"I have to assume that the man was deranged," I said. "These assignments were made just before he went into the hospital, and the tumors had already taken root in his brain. I don't think that I need to comment on the nature of the assignments, since they were obviously written by a madman. He has ordered, in the name of the Agency, a murder, a rape, an act of arson, and a possible fraud. At the risk of sounding overly technical, David Ogden was a nut case."

Martha said, "Agreed. Totally bonkers."

Vince said, "No question about it."

Snake said, "Crazy weirdo."

Sammy said, "Make it unanimous. The man was brain damaged."

Jessup nodded his satisfaction. "I'm glad to hear that. Those of us who knew David Ogden well, and that includes everyone on the executive committee, knew him to be a decent and honorable man. The David Ogden we knew could never have made those assignments. A different man made them, a man with a damaged brain. And having said that, I will now ask if there are any questions."

"I have one," said Vince. He looked unhappy. "You say that Ogden was an honorable man, and in his right mind he never would have made those assignments. Are you also saying that the DDO, or anyone like him, never sanctioned a killing, or an arson, or a rape, in the name of military or political expediency?"

Jessup stared at him icily. "Do you expect me to consider that a serious question?"

Vince shrugged. "No, I guess not. We both know the answer. It's happened many times, too many to count, but this time it's a friend of yours who did it, a megalomaniac who was gratifying some pretty dark impulses. You may see a difference in terms of morality, but I don't."

"Vince, lay off," said Sammy. It was his turn to look unhappy, for Vince had said the m-word. You don't use a word like morality around people like Jessup and Delaney. For diversion, Sammy rushed into the breach. "Mr. Jessup, what intrigues me most about these assignments is the apparently random nature in which they were made—an unknown girl, an obscure comedian, a tiny college, a run-down rooming house. Do you have any idea how Ogden chose these targets?"

"Not at the moment. We're working on that."

"Any connection between them?"

"Apparently not, but we're working on that, too. Yes?"

Martha had several questions. "What we have here are a set of handwritten notes. Are they copies? Are they memory aids? Were they ever processed? Were the instructions issued orally? Do you know if they were ever actually issued at all?"

"Good questions, all of them, but I can only answer one of them with certainty. These assignments were never processed through any Agency machine, or by Agency personnel. As for the rest of it, we simply do not know, but when it comes to assumptions, we have no choice. We have to assume that the assignments were made, one way or the other. We have to assume that these projects are already in motion."

"What about the time frame?" asked Snake. "Everything goes down between the last day of February and the fourth day of March. Is there any reason for that?"

"Not that we know of." Jessup hesitated. "However, I have a theory of my own. I think that David miscalculated how long he was going to live. Conceding that he was out of his mind, still every madness contains its own interior logic. I think that David wanted his symbols, his sacrifices, waiting for him when he arrived to begin what he called his long, dark journey. He wanted everything to be in place by a certain time."

"But they weren't waiting. There are still two weeks to go."

"As I said, he miscalculated. At least, that's the way I see it. Any other questions?"

"Yeah, one," said Vince. "What's in the right-hand compartment of that box? All we've seen is the left side."

"Nothing important. Some of Ogden's private papers."

"Could you be more explicit?"

"I'm afraid not. As I said, they're private, and they don't concern us here."

"By private, do you mean intimate?"

"Well . . . yes."

Vince sighed. "Sammy, do you want to do this, or should I?"

"Go ahead," said Sammy. "Just try to do it without insulting anybody."

"Not so easy." Vince stood up. He towered. "Mr. Jessup, I don't know yet why you're here, but it's pretty clear that you're going to ask us to do something for you. Which means that sometime soon my ass is going to be on the line because of you. Now I'm not about to risk it without knowing what I'm walking into. You can't feed me half a loaf of information. I have to know everything. And if I haven't made myself clear enough, if you refuse to tell me what's in that compartment I can get the information out of your head in thirty seconds flat."

Vince sat down. Sammy muttered, "Smooth, real smooth. Very diplomatic."

"Yeah, I got the touch."

Jessup's face was set into hard lines. "Very well, since you put it that way. The compartment contains five large envelopes, and each envelope contains . . . mementoes . . . of David's relationship with a particular woman. Five women in all." He went on to detail the contents of the envelopes, and he gave us the names of the women: Sarah Brine, Jenny Cookson, Carla MacAlester, Vivian Livingstone, and Maria-Teresa Bonfiglia. He was clearly uncomfortable. When he was finished, he said stiffly, "Does that satisfy your curiosity?"

"For the moment," said Vince. "One more point. Gibraltar Rules. What does that mean?"

Jessup looked surprised. "No contact, no recall, of course."

Delaney, who knew how little attention we paid to formal procedures, said, "Alex, perhaps you'd best explain."

Jessup said patiently, "Under Gibraltar Rules, there is no contact between Control and Field once the assignment is made, and there is no possibility of recall. None at all."

"Are you saying that even if you knew the names of these agents, you couldn't call them off the job?"

"Exactly. Under Gibraltar Rules, the Field is required to ignore any and all orders for recall. Once the project is rolling, it cannot be stopped."

"For how long?"

"For the period of the time frame. Once the time frame expires, the assignment expires as well."

"A five-day frame," Delaney pointed out. "Starting less than two weeks from now."

"Jesus."

I don't know who said it. Maybe we all did. There was silence in the room as the facts sank in. Somewhere out there were four unknown field agents, highly trained and supplied with funds, loyal to the memory of a madman, committed to a series of crimes in his name . . . and beyond recall.

I could see it coming, and so could the others. Not for the first time, we were going to be asked to pull some Agency chestnuts out of the fire, and what irritated me most was that there was no real need for us to be involved at all. There was a simple course of action for Jessup to follow. Take Lila Simms and Calvin Weiss out of circulation for the period of the time frame by stashing them each in a safe house. Warn the coaches of both college teams, and kill any chance of a fix on the game. As for the rooming house in Florida, request a round-the-clock watch on the property by the local fire department. It was as simple as that. It was, after all, for a period of only five days. The assignments would expire when the time frame expired, and everything would return to normal.

The trouble was, it was too simple. If he played it that way, Jessup would have to tell both Weiss and Simms why they were being protected. He would have to tell both of the coaches, and he would have to tell the people in Florida. Equally distasteful, he would have to bring in squads of Agency people, each of whom would have to know at least a piece of the picture. Cover stories could be concocted, good stories prepared by master deceivers, but the Agency lived in a goldfish bowl these days, and there was always the risk that the cover would fail.

It was a risk that Jessup was unwilling to take, and just the thought of it had frozen his guts with fear. When he and Delaney spoke to us about averting a tragedy, they weren't talking about murder, or arson, or rape. They were talking about public relations and image building. To them, the real tragedy would be if the word got out that the DDO, before he died, had ordered up a series of horrors on a mad caprice. In their worst-case scenario they could see it all laid out on the eleven o'clock news. That, to them, meant true tragedy.

So they were handing it over to us, and that in itself showed how little they knew about sensitives. Either, like Jessup, they thought of us as tricksters, or they jumped to the other extreme by investing us with powers that existed only in their imaginations. If you were to listen to some of the stories that they told around the water coolers up at Langley they'd have you believing that an ace could read minds in the Kremlin from a thousand miles away, lift a two-ton truck by sheer willpower, and think himself from Kansas City to San Diego in the blink of an eye. It was all nonsense, born out of ignorance. A sensitive, because of his neurological imbalance, is highly receptive to the thoughts and emotions of others. He can hear those thoughts as if they were spoken. That is all he can do, and he can do it at a range of two hundred feet at the most. All the rest of the talk is wishful thinking. Delaney knew that, but Jessup didn't. Jessup had started out thinking of us as tricksters, and now, in his desperation, he had decided that we were demigods, and the answer to his prayers. It would have done us no good at all to tell him that we were neither.

"Mr. Jessup," said Sammy, "it looks to me like you've got yourself one hell of a problem."

"Yes, I do," said Jessup. "And now you have it, too."

5

THE place that The Prisoner thought of as his prison was, in fact, an armed encampment in the Libyan Fezzan. Beyond the camp, to the north, were seas of dusty gravel and long drifts of sand that rose up into the volcanic massif of the Jebel Soda. To the south, past the oasis palms, were dunes that ran in graceful arcs of beige, and gold, and bisque down to the arid slice of the Wadi Tengesir that cut across the plain. Despite the palms, and the kaleidoscope of shifting sands, it was an altogether desolate place.

The encampment was circled by three tiers of barbed-wire fencing and a field of mines. Surface-to-air missiles poked their snouts at the skies, and a regiment of tanks was based nearby. The perimeter of the camp was guarded by a crack unit of the Libyan Army, and supplies were trucked in from Sokna to the north. All of this effort was exerted for the safety and convenience of the twenty-three men who actually occupied the camp, but the effort was wholly external. There was no staff within the camp to service the men. The occupants cooked their own food, policed their own grounds and latrines, conducted their own training, and held their own formations. Only their spiritual leadership came from the outside in the person of an imam who visited the camp once each week. Their temporal well-being was the responsibility of

The Prisoner, and even he was subject to the orders of a committee that sat far away in Beirut.

The Prisoner thought of himself as such because he was forbidden to leave the camp without the permission of the committee, and that permission had been denied for the past eleven months. He had been operational for seven years before that, involved in the hijacking of three aircraft, the bombing of a railroad station in Rome, the abduction of two members of the royal family in Saudi Arabia, and a string of other ventures which, although successful, had, in the end, cost him his anonymity. His face and his name now were known to the world. True, it was not the face and the name with which he had been born; plastic surgeons and export forgers had taken care of that, but enough about him was now known to convince the committee that, if not forever, at least for the foreseeable future he should be taken off field operations. He was too valuable to put at risk in the outside world, and so for the past eleven months the camp in the Fezzan had been his home and his prison. From there he had sent men out on missions that should have been his. Some of the missions had succeeded, some had failed, but none had borne his personal stamp. For eleven months he had stormed and fretted in his prison although, in fact, there was nothing to prevent him from leaving save the unenforceable directive from the faraway committee. He could, at any time during those months, have ordered up a vehicle and driven through the gates of the camp into the outside world. That he had not done so, had never even thought of doing so, was a tribute both to his sense of discipline and to his reluctant agreement that the decision of the committee had been proper.

Still, he stormed and fretted in his self-made prison, his life made bearable by his faith, his love of music, and the weekly visits from the imam. He prayed at dawn, at noon, at midafternoon, at dusk, and after dark; and those prayers were bright beads on the strings of his day. The rest of his time was a routine grind: calisthenics, small arms drill, obstacle course, endurance runs, political orientation; all of this punctuated by indifferent meals. In the late afternoon the men played soccer on a section of packed-down plain, and after that there was a private hour that each man held for his own. The other men spent that hour on their cots in the sleeping tent, but The Prisoner spent his in a smaller tent that served the camp both as a squad room and as a *tekiyeh*, a place of religious gathering. The Prisoner did not go there for religious purposes. On the contrary, it was during that hour that he displayed what his men considered to be his only weakness, a love of western music, grand opera in particular. There was a phonograph in the squad room and a stack of old records that belonged to The Prisoner, and each day at that hour he lay there on a pallet, his eyes closed and his being as one with the music of Verdi and Puccini, Wagner and Strauss that rolled out over the sands.

The Prisoner looked forward to the weekly visit by the imam as much for the single letter that he never failed to bring as for the religious guidance that he provided. The Prisoner was the only man in the camp to receive mail, for these were Holy Warriors cut off from the world. A grudging exception was made for The Prisoner. His reputation and his seniority allowed him to demand the privilege, and it was, after all, only a single envelope that was carefully examined and its contents read before being forwarded on. Always from the same source, and written in the same hand, the letter came to The Prisoner by a circuitous route, being mailed first to a blind address in Paris, forwarded from there to the Libyan embassy on the Via Nomantana in Rome, and sent from there by diplomatic bag to Tripoli. On those days when the imam brought the letter, The Prisoner would retire with it to the squad room, read it once, then again, and spend the rest of his private hour in apparent meditation. On those days he did not play music.

The imam who visited the camp was a man of true holiness, but he was also a practical man who knew when to close an eye. He was aware of the women who were brought to the camp every month, but he chose to ignore them, just as he chose to ignore the western music that The Prisoner played on his phonograph. The main concern of the imam was to keep his Holy Warriors finely tuned, and much of his time was spent in trying to convince The Prisoner that his enforced idleness was a form of positive action.

On one particular day, alone with The Prisoner, the imam compared his situation to that of a *hegira*, and asked if The Prisoner could not see it in that light. The Prisoner considered the idea. He understood *hegira* in the historical sense as the flight of the Prophet from the hostile people of Mecca, and he also knew that in another sense the word meant a going away, an emigration, a withdrawal. But he could not see how it applied to him.

"I have not accomplished *hegira*," he said softly. "In the past year I have accomplished nothing at all."

"Foolish words," said the imam. "Listen to the words of Gholam-Reza Fada'i-Araqi." In a sing-song voice, he recited, "In its Islamic meaning, *hegira* signifies the withdrawal from a society in which true believers can no longer live in accordance with their faith. In such a society, conditions of life are so hard that the true believer must either die, or renounce his faith. It is then that the third choice is suggested: that of cutting onself off, even to the point of going into exile. That is what you have done, and it is a true *hegira*."

"I was offered no choice," The Prisoner protested. "I was ordered to stay here. I was ordered into this exile."

"And you accepted the order willingly. Remember this. The way of the *hegira* may be chosen only with the understanding that the period of withdrawal will not be too long, and that it will be used for the purpose of gathering forces in order to return and destroy the enemy. That is what you are doing."

"How long is too long? What you call *hegira* seems like nothing more than cowardice to me."

The imam raised a warning finger. "No excuse will be accepted from those who submit to the rules of a Satanic society and who do not accomplish *hegira*. Those who can withdraw but refuse to do so for whatever reason, will be held responsible. As they lie dying, they will see angels, who will ask, 'Was not Allah's land vast enough to offer you a corner of peace?' How will you answer them?"

"I will tell them that I have had enough of peace. I am a man of war."

"You are not thinking clearly. Remember that most of the hundred and twenty-four thousand prophets sent to mankind by the Almighty have been forced at one time or another to perform *hegira*, either to go into exile or to go into the desert. Abraham, Moses, Jesus, and our own Prophet all were forced into exile."

"I do not belong in such company."

"Do you not?" The imam leaned forward intently. "The *hegira* is a means of struggle for those who have no links with this world, those who cannot be enslaved by earthly possessions and interest. Does that not describe you?"

The Prisoner thought: Does that describe me? Have I nothing left?

"It is you," said the imam.

The Prisoner bowed his head. He thought of the girl with the broken face. "Yes, it is I."

6

SAMMY made the assignments, and he gave the Polk College job to Vince. Vince frowned when he heard it, and shook his head.

"You got a problem with this?" asked Sammy.

"Definitely."

"I don't see it." Sammy was genuinely surprised. "You go up to New Hampshire, you get close to the team, and you tap their heads. You find out which of the players are in on the fix, and you take it from there. What's the problem?"

"We don't even know if there *is* a fix. This Domino could have some other angle."

"You've got to be kidding. Domino's instructions are simple, the Polk Bulldogs have to lose, and there's only one way to guarantee that. There has to be a fix."

"Maybe, but I still don't want it. Let me switch with somebody else."

"No switching, not unless you have a damn good reason."

"How about this one. It's racist. Just because it's basketball, you figure that you have to put a black man on the case. That sucks, Sammy."

Sammy said calmly, "I'll let that one go by. You call it racist, and I call it common sense. They've got a twelve-man squad at Polk, and seven of those kids are black. The coach is white, but the assistant coach is black, and so is the team manager. You think I'll get the same results if I give the job to a white man?"

"How about a white woman? Martha would love it, all those young studs running around in their underwear."

"Martha has her job, and you have yours. You'll have to give me a better reason than that."

"Basketball is the stupidest game in the world. Did you know that eighty-seven percent of all college games are decided in the last two minutes?"

"So what?"

"So why don't they play just the last two minutes? The hell with the rest of the game."

"Get serious, will you? That's no reason."

"Then how about this one? I can't take the cold. Look at the others. All right, Martha gets the rape job, and that's no day at the beach, but Snake goes to Florida on the arson job, Ben gets to go on a Caribbean cruise while he bodyguards that comic, and good old Vince gets to visit that iceberg in New Hampshire."

Sammy shrugged. "Dress warm."

"I'm not going to any New Hampshire."

"You are."

"Old Hampshire is more like it. Clotted cream, fishing in the Avon, strolls along the chalk downs. Send me there, Sammy, that's my style."

Sammy stared at him for a moment. "There's something else, isn't there? Something you aren't saying."

Vince hesitated, then shook his head.

"Come on, open up. What's bugging you?"

"Forget it."

"Meet you head-to-head?"

Vince nodded. He and Sammy opened up, dropping the mental blocks that were part of their everyday equipment, and doing it that way, head-to-head, Vince was able to show what he had not been able to voice.

You're asking me to put the finger on a brother.

Doesn't have to be a brother doing the fix.

The odds say yes. How the hell can I tag some ghetto kid who's looking to make a dollar the only way he can?

Not the only way. It's crooked, Vince.

Crooked? Just about everything in this country is twisted out of shape, there's no reality any more, and you're worried about a lousy basketball game.

Don't preach to me. I'm worried about the job. The game is just a part of it.

Not my part, not if it means handing some black kid over to the law.

Who said anything about the law?

How else?

That's up to you. All I care is that the game gets played on the level. You work it out whichever way you want.

No law?

Not if that's the way you want it. Just get the job done.

This straight?

When did I ever?

Never, Vince admitted.

You know, you remind me of my grandmother.

You got a black grandmother?

I've got a Jewish grandmother, and she goes into instant mourning whenever she reads in the paper about some Jew who's screwed up. Makes no difference what he did—a holdup, a swindle, an axe murder—if the guy has a Jewish name it's like the disgrace is on her own family. She shrivels up and walks around all day shaking her head and muttering to herself. She takes it personally, not just the shame, but the burden of responsibility. Which is stupid, because nobody can carry that much weight, not even my grandmother, and she's one tough old lady. You can't carry it, either.

Easy to say. You know what you've got, Sammy?

Besides a Jewish grandmother?

You've got leadership qualities, that's what you've got.

Listen, any time you want this fucking job . . .

Less than twenty-four hours later, Vince struggled along a plowed path on the Polk College campus that led from the Administration Building to the athletic fieldhouse. His head was lowered against a cutting wind. He was dressed in boots and parka, ski pants and long johns, watch cap and fur-lined gloves, but he was cold to the bones. His fingers, toes, and nose were numb, and the rest of him wasn't far behind. The campus was covered by three feet of snow. Bare trees were sheathed in black and ugly ice, the same ice hung from eaves and windows, and the sky was the color of lead. It was a dismal scene, relieved only by the splashes of color on the bedsheet banners that were posted on every wall. Painted in Day-Glo orange, and red, and green, they all shouted the same message. BEAT VAN BUREN.

Got nothing against that, thought Vince, but why can't they beat them in tennis, or baseball, or something else that you play in the sun?

He picked up his pace, and the PR guy beside him had to jog to keep up. The PR guy was young and enthusiastic, and his head came no higher than Vince's shoulder. His name was Willard, and the weather didn't bother him. He pointed to one of the signs, and said, "As you can see, the whole school is up for the game."

"Lots of rah-rah," Vince agreed.

"School spirit."

"Can't run a school without spirit."

"It's our big game of the year. It may not be Army-Navy or Yale-Harvard, but it's traditional."

"Can't beat tradition. The battle of Waterloo was won on the playing fields of Eton."

"Hey, I didn't know that."

"Believe it."

"I didn't even know they played basketball at Eton. I guess you guys know all those things."

"Believe that, too. If we don't know it, it didn't happen."

In Vince's pocket were papers that named him as a reporter for *Hoops* magazine, the national review of college basketball. Willard lit a candle in front of a copy of *Hoops* every night before he went to bed. A call to the offices of *Hoops* in Kansas City would have confirmed that Mister Bonepart was, indeed, on assignment for the magazine, but no confirmation had been necessary. The athletic director's office had accepted his credentials without question, and had assigned Willard as his gofer, apologizing for the fact that Head Coach Haggerty was out of town on a scouting trip.

"Don't worry about Haggerty," said Willard as they worked their way toward the field house. "The Chief will take good care of you."

"What chief?"

"Chief Thunder. The assistant coach, Boyd Preston."

"An Indian?"

"No, that's just what they call him."

"How come?"

Willard grinned. "You'll see."

Coming out of the cold and into the fieldhouse was like coming home for Christmas. The place was warm, brightly lit, and noisy. The stands were empty, but the team was on the court, working out under the eye of a short and wiry man with a clipboard and a whistle. Vince paused to let the heat sink in, and along with it the smells of sweat and liniment, the squeak of shoes on the hardwood floor, the grunts of the panting players, the slap of the ball, the pounding sound of a solitary runner circling the metal track high above the court, and over it all the booming voice of the man with the whistle.

"I wanna see some quick," he was shouting, "I wanna hear some thunder. Hey, Willy, move it, make him commit. That's it, hands up. Willy, *move*. You tired, son? You weary, Willy? You have a big time last night, you so weary? Let's see some feet, Willy, let's hear some thunder . . ."

The team was working a half-court drill, red shirts defending against the white shirts, and Vince tried to match numbers with the names on the sheet of paper that Willard had given him. *Devereaux, Clancy, Holmes, Chambers, Jefferson.* A white-shirted player cut to the basket, faked once, went up with a defender all over him, and passed off blind to another white shirt, who scored. Vince nodded in admiration. He thought little of basketball as a sporting event—there had to be something wrong with a game that depended on deliberate fouling as an essential tactic—but he was able to admire the balletic grace that the best of the players so casually displayed. As an exhibition of style, it was magnificent, but he couldn't take it seriously as a sport.

The man with the whistle tipped back his head, and roared up at the ceiling, "Melton!"

The lonely runner who had been circling the overhead track had stopped, and was leaning over the rail, staring down at the court. "Yeah, chief."

"I don't hear any thunder."

"Just taking a break."

"Thunder, Melton, thunder. Or maybe you're weary, like Willy over here. You weary, Melton?"

"No, chief, I'm okay."

"Then let me hear it."

Melton pushed himself away from the rail, and started up again, his feet pounding the track.

The chief smiled, and said, "Not bad, but I gotta have more thunder." He pointed a finger at a white-shirted player. Vince made him as Willy Holmes, a guard. "Willy, get up there and give me some thunder."

Holmes pulled a face. "Hey, chief . . ."

"Yeah, I know, you're weary. Twenty laps'll fix you fine. Let's hear some thunder, son."

Holmes shook his head, but he trotted over to the stairs that led up to the track, and soon the sound of the pounding overhead doubled. The chief smiled again. "That's the way I like it, lots of thunder. Now, let me see some feet."

He started the two squads through the drills again. Vince said to Willard, "Chief Thunder, huh?"

Willard grinned. "Now you know."

"When can I see him?"

"After the drills. Won't be long."

It took about ten minutes. Vince stood with Willard and watched the two squads work against each other, unhappily aware of what was coming. First this Chief, then the players; tap them all and find out how many of the kids were in on the fix. Because he knew now that Sammy had to be right. There had to be a fix. It was the only practical way for Domino to carry out his instructions, and besides, fixing basketball games was as American as—he searched for a simile, and let it go. It wasn't important. What was important was how many—and which ones. And, please, if there was any grace left in the world, not all of them would be black.

The Chief dismissed the squads with a blast of his whistle, and sent them to the showers. He strode over to Vince, and put out his hand.

"I'm Boyd Preston," he said.

Willard said quickly, "This is Mister Bonepart . . ."

"I know who he is," Preston interrupted. "The AD's office called. *Hoops* magazine, we're honored. I didn't think you people bothered with the teams down here in Division Two."

Vince said, "It's all basketball, coach."

"Call me Chief, everybody does. There's only one coach around here, and that's Haggerty. How come you're here?"

"You've got a big game coming up."

"We play Van Buren every year, but you never came around before."

"Then it's about time. How does the game look to you?"

"I'm not the one to ask, I just keep the troops marching. Coach Haggerty gives all the interviews, and he's out of town."

"So I heard. Well, what would he say if he were here?"

Preston smiled. "That's easy. If the coach was here, he'd say that Van Buren is a tough team that can't be underrated. He'd say that this is a traditional game coming up, and in traditional games the stats don't mean much. He'd say that on any given day any team can beat any other team, and that we can't afford to be overconfident. That's what the Coach would say."

Vince grinned his appreciation of the conventional wisdom that every coach in every sport spouts before a big game.

Preston went on. "But if you're asking me, which you're not, I'd say that we're going to wipe up the floor with Van Buren. They can't touch us. We're bigger, we're faster, we're smarter, and we play the Big D."

"Offense is skill," Vince quoted piously, "but defense is soul."

"Exactly, and our kids have the soul. We'll cream Van Buren, but you can't quote me on that. For the record, all I can say is that we can't afford to be overconfident."

Vince grinned again, warming to the man, and decided that it was time to tap him. He went into Preston's head. He was in and out in a twinkle, but while he was there he found a neat and orderly mind. He found a fierce pride. He found a deep well of dedication. He found many other things, but he found no larceny. If the fix was on, Preston had nothing to do with it.

Satisfied, Vince said, "I'd like to speak to the players, if that's all right with you."

Preston frowned. "Let's go someplace where we can talk."

Preston's office was a cubbyhole next to the head coach's office. Both rooms opened onto the locker area, the training center, and the showers. The locker room was hot and damp, and those players who had finished with their showers looked up curiously as Vince and Preston passed through. Preston closed his office door, and motioned Vince to a chair. He was still frowning.

"There's something you have to understand," he said. "You're probably used to schools like Indiana, and UCLA, and DePaul—you know, the basketball factories where the teams are half pro already. Maybe you don't know what it's like down here in Division Two. These kids of mine, that's all they are, just kids. They're good athletes, and they know how to play the game, but, let's face it, they're never going to play pro ball. Not in the NBA, not in the Continental, not even for some European team. They're just not good enough. When they leave here they go straight into the real world, nothing glitzy like the pros, and . . . my point is, I don't want them getting any kind of a swelled head because the man from *Hoops* is here. You understand?"

Vince nodded. "I'll go easy on them."

"Another thing. We both know how it works at some of those factories—athletes who never graduate, play four years and they're out on their ass with nothing to show for it. That doesn't happen here. Overall, Polk graduates ninety-two percent of its athletes. On this team, the average is even higher."

"Impressive."

"Let me give you a couple of examples. Take our starting five. As guards we have Willy Holmes and Jack Clancy. Holmes is the point guard, and he'll be in med school next year. Clancy's the shooting guard, and he's a Marketing major with a three-point-seven average. Center is Dion Devereaux, an English major, and the editor of the yearbook. He writes poetry and nobody makes jokes about it. The power forward is Jerry Jefferson who's doing Engineering, and the small forward is Ted Melton, and all I can say about Melton is that he's doing a double major in French and Economics with honors. Those are the starters, and the other seven men aren't all that different. No Phys Ed majors, no courses in Leisure Alternatives, you know? I'm not saying that we've got a bunch of geniuses here, 'cause we don't, but they're not just a bunch of jocks, either. I'd like you to remember that when you write about them."

Vince, who had no intention of writing anything at all, said solemnly, "I promise you that."

"Fair enough."

They went out to the locker area. Preston banged on a table for attention, and twelve heads turned their way, curious eyes appraising the stranger.

"Listen up," said Preston. "This gentleman is Mister Vincent Bonepart from *Hoops* magazine . . ."

Low murmurs. Someone whistled softly.

". . . and he's here to do a story on the team. Why *Hoops* would want to bother with us is a mystery to me, but the man is here and I want you to give him your respectful attention. Answer his questions, and try not to sound too stupid." He turned to Vince. "They're all yours."

Vince spent the next hour chatting with twelve young men in varying stages of dress, making notes that he would never use. He spoke to some of them individually, and some in small groups. He kept the conversation light and easy, and after a while he found that he was enjoying himself. He spoke French with Ted Melton, and talked about T.S. Eliot with Dion Devereaux. Willy Holmes was interested in orthopedic medicine, but agreed that it was too early to think about specialties. Jerry Jefferson wanted to build bridges, and Jack Clancy already had his first million figured out. Those were the starting five, and it went on that way with the other members of the team. As a group, they were bright, sober, interesting people, and definitely not a bunch of jocks. At the end of the hour he was glowing with good will.

Then he tapped them, and the glow disappeared. It didn't take long, he was in and out. He was looking for larceny, for a driving greed, for a hidden shame, and he found all of that. He found it twice. Willy Holmes, who was headed for med school, and Dion Devereaux, the poet. Twenty-five thousand dollars each to throw the game with Van Buren; half paid in advance, and half on delivery.

Preston, beside him, said, "Something wrong?"

It must have shown on his face, the anger boiling within him. He throttled it down, and composed his features. "Just my stomach. I can never get used to that airline food. Look, you've got a great bunch of kids here."

Preston beamed. "Thank you for saying so. Is there anything else I can do for you?"

"No, you've done fine," said Vince, a sour taste in his mouth. The boiling anger had been replaced by a feeling of disgust and betrayal. "Thanks for your help. I have to get going now."

"Well, you come back anytime. You'll be welcome."

Vince got out of Polk as quickly as he could, and the sour taste remained in his mouth during the flight to New York. He called the Center from LaGuardia airport, and told Sammy what he had found.

"What are you going to do?" Sammy asked.

"I know what I'd like to do, I'd like to strangle the bastards. Two kids with every advantage, and they're screwing it up."

"You sound involved."

"I feel like your grandmother."

"Don't let it mess up your head. What are you doing in New York?"

"Got some people I want to see."

Sammy knew better than to ask. "It's your deal, you play it whichever way you want."

"We're still agreed? No law?"

"That's understood." Sammy hung up.

Vince went through two bourbon Manhattans and half a bowl of peanuts while he worked on his approach, and then he made another call. Ida Whitney answered, and he said his name.

"Good Lord," she said. "Out of the blue."

"Yeah. I'm sorry to have to do it this way, but I have to see Lewis."

"What kind of a hello is that? We don't hear from you for years, and that's all you have to say?"

"I said I was sorry. Is he home?"

"You mean you want to see him now? Right now?"

"Why not?"

"Because he's dressing, and we're about to go out, that's why not."

"I'm at LaGuardia. I can be at your place in less than an hour."

"Impossible, we're due at the borough president's reception."

"Screw the borough president. This is important, Ida."

"To whom?"

"To me. Maybe to Lewis, maybe to you."

"More important than the BP?"

"More important than one more political cocktail party. Don't go out. Wait for me."

"Just a minute, let me ask Lewis."

"Don't bother, I'm on my way."

Going against the traffic flow, it took twenty minutes from the airport to Sutton Place South. Lewis and Ida Whitney lived in an apartment building that looked, felt, and smelled like old money. Not that the Whitney money was old; it was so new it squeaked, and Vince could remember when there had been no Whitney money at all. That had been back in the days of the South Harlem Rescue Committee when Ida and Lewis had lived on crackers and cheese for weeks on end. The SHRC, a storefront legal advocacy group, aimed at aiding young black kids caught up in the criminal justice system of an uncaring city, with Lewis fresh out of law school and Ida the unpaid legal aide. It had been a time of hope, of promise, of unstained idealism, and it also had been a time of hectic eighteen-hour days, with crackers and cheese to keep them going.

Not any more, thought Vince as he rode up in the elevator. Maybe stone-ground wafers and Brie, but no more rat cheese and saltines with a jug of Kool-Aid to wash it down. No more penniless, idealistic lawyer, either. Hotshot attorney with corporation clients plugged into the political power structure. Plugged into more than that, they say. We'll see how much more.

"It's an interesting story," said Lewis Whitney, "but I don't see what it has to do with me."

"I'm coming to that," said Vince. "Just give me a few minutes more."

Lewis looked at his watch, and complained, "We're late as it is."

"Let him finish," said Ida. "You won't lose any points with the BP, and those receptions are a bore, anyway."

She smiled at Vince, and he nodded his appreciation. The Whitneys had not changed much over the years. Ida still was slim and lovely, Lewis still a commanding figure, although a thicker one; and sitting in their carefully understated living room, they looked not too different from the cheese and cracker days of the SHRC. Just richer.

Lewis sighed, and said, "All right, let me see if I've got this straight. You say that a couple of kids on the Polk College basketball team are fixing to throw a game, and you want to stop it."

"Right."

"You want to keep those kids out of trouble."

"Right."

"So you can't blow the whistle on them, can't go to their coach, or the cops, or the State's Attorney, or whatever they call it in New Hampshire."

"Right."

"But the one thing you haven't told me is how you know about this."

That was the tricky one. To Lewis and Ida, Vince was nothing more than his cover job, a translator at the United Nations. They knew nothing about sensitives, nothing about the Center, and that was the way it had to stay.

"I want you to take that part of it on faith," Vince said carefully. "It's going to happen, believe me. Will you take my word on that?"

"But you can't ask me . . ."

Ida put her hand on her husband's arm. "He's entitled to that much, Lewis. He's an old friend."

Whitney nodded reluctantly. He looked at his watch again. "Go ahead."

"Let me state a hypothetical situation. Let's say that I'm a gambler, a real high roller, and I want to put the fix on a game. How do I go about it?"

"I haven't the faintest idea."

"Do I stroll up to the nearest basketball player, and say, hey sonny, you want to make some easy money? Obviously not. All that gets me is a boot in the ass, and maybe the cops. If I want to cut a deal like that, I go to a professional. Somebody who's been there before. Somebody who knows the angles. Somebody who is highly organized, if you know what I mean. I want to know who that somebody might be."

"You're asking me?"

"I'm asking you. I need a place to start, someone to steer me in the right direction. I need a name, Lewis."

"I don't like the way this conversation is going." Whitney's face was set in hard lines. "How the hell would I know something like that? I'm a reputable attorney."

"Time to cut the horseshit, Lewis. Sure, you're reputable. You sit down to dinner with the mayor, but you break some bread at some other tables, don't you? You're plugged into power, you're plugged into money, and you're plugged into the mob."

"You just ran out of time."

Vince stood up. "Two black kids, the kind you used to fight to save. I'm trying to save these two."

Lewis started up out of his chair. "Get out of here."

"Remember Floyd Washington?"

Puzzled, Lewis slumped back. He frowned, and shook his head. Ida said, "Vince, let's not get into that."

Lewis turned to her. "You know what he's talking about?"

"A long time ago." There was a touch of weariness in her voice. "The Washington boy. Hooked on horse, and he held up a liquor store. You handled the case."

"You did more than handle the case," said Vince. "You saved that kid. You kept him out of jail, you got him off drugs, you gave him some hope and a life to lead."

The lines softened in Whitney's face. "Washington. Yes, of course I remember."

"And now you represent the people who sell the drugs to kids like Floyd Washington."

This time Lewis came all the way out of his chair, and his arm was back. "You son of a bitch, nobody says that to me."

Ida jumped up, and grabbed her husband's arm. To Vince, she said, "That isn't so."

"It isn't? Okay, maybe it isn't, literally. Maybe he doesn't represent pushers and dealers, but he's connected with the people who do. He's part of the structure, and he could get me a name if he wanted to."

Ida turned to her husband. "Could you?"

Lewis did not answer. He was staring coldly at Vince.

"Lewis?"

He did not look at her.

"Lewis, if you can do that, then you have to."

Whitney looked at her for the first time. He nodded slowly. He disengaged his arm from her hand. He marched from the room, closing a door behind him. Ida sank into a chair. Vince stayed on his feet. After a while they heard the muted sound of Whitney's voice through the door, but they could not make out the words.

"He used to have a lot of heart," said Vince.

Ida sat looking at her hands. "He still does, he's a good man. It's just that . . . it's a different world now."

Vince let that one go by. They waited. Ida said into the silence, "I used to be in love with you."

"I know."

"But you didn't . . . you weren't . . ."

"I was, but not enough. You're right, you got a good man."

She shrugged helplessly. "It's just . . . different."

Lewis came back into the room. His face was still cold. He said, "I'm not going to write any of this down, and neither are you. The name is Carmine Giardelli, and you can find him at the Royal Buccaneer in Atlantic City. He keeps a suite there. You can tell him I sent you. Do you have that?"

"I've got it, and thanks."

"You stayed away for years. If you really want to thank me, stay away a few more."

"If that's the way you want it." Vince glanced at Ida, but she would not look at him. He left.

7

VIOLET Simms read her mail at the breakfast table. She did not receive many letters, but she enjoyed the ritual of slitting open the envelopes before starting in on her grapefruit and coffee. It was a civilized way to start the day. On this particular morning, she set aside the junk mail and the flyer from the supermarket, and was left with three envelopes. One of them was addressed to her granddaughter.

"This one's for you," she said, and handed it across the table.

"For me?"

"Has your name on it."

Lila Simms, at sixteen, was rarely alert at that time of the morning, particularly on school days. She stared dully at the envelope, and continued to spoon up her cereal. She couldn't imagine who would be writing to her. She let the envelope lie on the table as she finished her breakfast.

Violet asked, "Aren't you going to open it?"

"Must be an ad." Lila stifled a yawn. "Somebody's trying to sell me something."

"Don't have to buy, you know. Go ahead and open it. It won't bite."

Lila tore open the envelope. She read, her eyes still glazed and dull. She turned the paper over, read the other side, and then went back to the beginning and read the whole thing through again. By the time she had read it for the second time, her eyes were no longer dull.

"I don't believe this," she said, excitement in her voice. "I simply don't believe."

Violent asked indulgently, "What don't you believe? What are they selling?"

"Look at this. Just look at it."

Lila passed the sheet of paper across to her grandmother.

National Association for Recreational Skiing
Hammond, Va. 23671

CONGRATULATIONS

The National Association for Recreational Skiing is pleased to advise you

LILA SIMMS

that through a computer-operated lottery of high school students throughout the country, you have been chosen as one of five winners of the prize listed below.

A *one-week, all-expense-paid skiing holiday at Hightower Mountain in the Adirondacks.*

No purchase necessary. This is a final and unconditional prize.
See other side for details.

"It's one of those lottery things, that's all," said Violet. "There ought to be a law."

"I don't think so, gran. I think it's for real."

"No, honey, it's one of those things where you have to buy something to win."

"It says no purchase necessary." Lila came around the table to stand in back of her grandmother. "Look, right there."

"Oh. Well, you know how they work these things. They put your name in with a zillion others, and they have a drawing maybe a yaer from now."

"No, look. 'This is a final and unconditional prize.' " Lila turned the page over, and pointed. "The week starts on Saturday."

"*This* Saturday? That's only three days . . ." Violet peered at the print on the back of the page. "Supervised by a trained ski instructor provided by the NARS—transportation by bus—accommodations at the Holiday Inn at Hightower." She searched for flaws, but could find none. Still, she protested, "There has to be a catch. Nobody ever wins these things."

"Somebody has to, otherwise it wouldn't be legal, would it?"

Violet said doubtfully, "I suppose. But why would they pick you?"

"It says random selection. A computer did it."

There it was, the magic word for this generation. If a computer did it, then it had to be real. "But what's this National Association . . . or whatever? I never heard of it."

"Oh, I have," said Lila, who never had heard of it, either. "It's very big, the biggest. I can go, Gran, can't I? It's Hightower. It's supposed to be fantastic skiing there."

"I can't let you go off with people I don't know."

"It says trained supervision, and there are four other kids. Please, Gran. Please?"

Violet shook her head, not so much in disapproval as in resignation. Raising a grandchild all on her own had been both a joy and a cross to bear, and the next few years would bring the worst of it. She tried to remember what her own daughter, Lila's mother, had been like at sixteen, what she had wanted and needed, but all she could recall was a time of total confusion. She spoiled Lila somewhat, she knew she did, but this—to send her off with strangers? Still, a week, all expenses paid, and she did love skiing so much.

"Gran, please?"

Violet shook herself briskly. "We'll see, we'll talk about it later. I have to think about it."

"But we don't have much time."

"Time enough to think. We'll talk this afternoon, after school." She glanced at the clock. "And you'd better scoot, or you'll be late."

Lila gathered her coat and her books. She kissed her grandmother's cheek, and hugged her shoulders. "Please think about it," she pleaded. "Please think real hard."

"I will, I promise." Violet looked up, and smiled. "We'll see."

Lila nodded happily. She knew her grandmother, she knew that smile, and she knew that she was going to Hightower Mountain.

About an hour after Lila raced off to school, Martha marched into Sammy's office at the Center. She was just back from two whirlwind days in Rockhill, New York, on the Simms assignment. She threw her report on Sammy's desk, and waited while he read it.

Sammy:

Here's what I have so far on the Sextant operation.

Rockhill is a small town in the Hudson Valley, the east bank just north of Rhinebeck. It's a pleasant place, quiet, with shady streets, and a high school straight out of a 1930's movie. Mickey Rooney and Judy Garland, you know? The sidewalks are clean, there's no graffiti, and aside from a bowling alley and a roadhouse out on the edge of town, the lights go out at eleven. I wouldn't mind living in Rockhill someday.

I spent my first day there using my cover as a field agent for the New York State Department of Social Services, researching crimes of violence in the area. I hit the chief of police, the high school principal, a couple of pastors, and came away with the impression that Rockhill is virtually free of serious crime. Sure, once in a while a teenage party gets out of hand, once in a while the buckos out at Jimmy's Grill, the local roadhouse, take on a load and start bopping each other, once in a while a kid gets himself busted for smoking pot on the village green—but that's about it. Again, I wouldn't mind living there.

I spent the next morning at the hall of records. Lila Simms was born 11 June 1976. Mother listed as Julia Simms, died in childbirth. Father listed as "unknown." Lila's residence, 29A Linden Avenue, Rockhill, is listed as being owned by Mrs. Violet Simms, who turns out to be the kid's maternal grandmother. Tax valuation $57,500. Real estate and water taxes paid up to date. No mortgage, no outstanding liens. Lila has lived with her grandmother all her life.

Late in the afternoon I got close enough to Lila to do an Alpha tap. Couldn't get her to stay still long enough for a Delta, but we're not interested in anything deep. Turns out to be a perfectly normal sixteen-year-old, into rock music, tennis, and skiing. Likes boys, dates around, but nothing steady. Deep attached to her grandmother, and no memories of her parents, which isn't surprising since she never knew them. Worried about her school grades, but not to the point of panic. Somewhat bored with her life, somewhat restless, somewhat curious about the big wide world out there, but that's nothing unusual. She is also, believe it or not, exactly what Ogden was looking for, a certified virgin.

So there's your background, and here's the problem. My brief is to keep this child from being raped within the time frame, but my brief also specifies that she cannot know what is going on. Nor can anyone else connected with her. This, my dear Sammy, is a virtual impossibility. Given the limitations of our mandate, I see no way in which we can protect Lila Simms unless—and this is my point—we remove her from her present environment.

Thus:

(1) Sextant will come after her in Rockhill.

(2) Given our limits, there is no way that we can protect her in Rockhill.

(3) We have to remove her from Rockhill, and place her in an environment that we can control.

(4) How do we do that, and at the same time preserve the limitations of our mandate?

(5) Turn page for the answer.

Sammy turned the page and found himself looking at a duplicate of the notification to Lila Sims, advising her that she had won a week's vacation at Hightower Mountain. He read it carefully, then looked up, and smiled.

"Not bad. Fast work."

"The Workshop did it. We were up all night. I haven't been to sleep yet."

"When will Lila get it?"

"She got it this morning." When Sammy raised an eyebrow, she added, "Jerry Becker in Postal took care of it. He owes us."

"You're close to a breach of security there."

"Sometimes you have to bend the mandate. I had to get it to her today. Sextant's time frame begins in four days, and I want her out of there in three. Of course, I'll be leading the party."

"You'll need transport."

"The Workshop is organizing a minivan."

"Rooms at the inn?"

"All the logistics will be locked up by this afternoon. There's just one other point that I have to clear with you."

"Yeah, I see it coming." Sammy sat back, and his smile was gone. "You need four teenage kids to fill out the group."

"Four kids who can ski. Four seniors I can trust all the way down the line. I want George Shackley, Pam Costis, Linda Bryce, and Terry Krazewski."

"They're not operational."

"Okay, you had to say that, but who else can I use? I know they're not operational, but they're all seventeen, less than a year away from assignment. They're not aces yet, but they're damn close. They can do the job, and I need them. Now, are we going to sit here and argue all morning, or can we cut to the bottom line?"

"Who's arguing? You can have them."

"I can?" Martha's surprise showed on her face. "I thought I was going to have to wrestle you."

"No, they're the obvious choices, and, as you said, sometimes you have to bend the mandate. But you can only have three, you can't have Krazewski."

"Why not?"

"He's in the infirmary with the flu. Not a chance."

"Sammy, I have to have four."

"So take four. Take Little."

"Chicken?" Martha stared at him. "You're kidding."

Sammy shrugged. "It's up to you, but he's the only other senior."

"But he's a disaster."

"I know."

"He's a menace."

"I know."

"He's a monster."

"I know."

Very slowly, and carefully, Martha said, "Sammy, we both know that he may be a deuce. It's taking a hell of a chance."

"I know that, too. Do you have a choice?"

She shook her head. "I guess not."

On the night of that same day, Sextant prepared to go out on the town. He had been working hard, and it was time to play. He had been in Rockhill for a week, doing the painstaking research that was the hallmark of his work, establishing a clear pattern of his target's routine. After a week in Rockhill he knew what time Lila Simms went to school, where she ate lunch, who she met at the Dairy Queen, what time she came home, and where she went in the evenings. He knew the food she ate, the clothes she wore, and the pace of her walk. He could pick her out in any crowd. After a week in Rockhill he knew as much as he needed to know, and now, with the time frame of his assignment only four days away, he was ready to make his move. But first it was time to play.

Sextant was fifty-three years old, but he looked to be less than forty. His body was slim and hipless, his face unlined, and his hair a rich chestnut that needed only an occasional touching. Preparing for the evening, he inspected his wardrobe in the closet of his motel room. The leather and chains wouldn't draw flies here in Rockhill, much less what he was after. The bell-bottoms and bolero jacket? Not very subtle; might as well wear a skirt. Cowboy boots and stone-washed jump suit? Too campy by far. What was needed was a touch of swish, just a touch. He decided on pencil-thin Italian slacks, a ruffled shirt, and a blazer that nipped at the waist. He laid the clothing out on the bed, showered and shaved, and, standing in front of the bathroom mirror, he went to work on his face. He used a Revlon misty rose for a base, a soft beige Max Factor cream puff, and a Maybelline liner for his eyes; a touch of shadow, and then ever so lightly with the velvet black mascara. He worked slowly, and when he was finished, he inspected himself in the mirror.

"Just enough," he murmured, and dabbed a drop of Persian Mist behind each ear. "Wouldn't do to cause riots."

Jimmy's Grill was ten minutes out of town on Route 9. Outside it was fake bluestone and neon strips. Inside it was Naugahyde and pickled pine booths, a moosehead on the wall, and a flashing BUD sign behind the bar. The food was burgers, fries, and chili dogs; and the music on the box was country. The place was as dim as a cave full of bats, and it smelled of stale beer and Lysol.

Sextant made a calculated entrance, moving with just enough of a sway to draw eyes as he walked to the bar. He put his back against it, leaned there languidly, and surveyed the scene. The customers were mostly men, and they looked like men who worked with their hands, men who wore Levis and steel-capped boots, flannel shirts and gimme caps. They sat around in groups of three, and four, and five, and most of them were drinking beer. Some of them were hard-working men relaxing at the end of the day. Those were the older ones, and Sextant ignored them. He was looking for animals.

"What'll it be?" said a voice in his ear.

Sextant turned. The bartender was a young man with a full beard. He wore a red T-shirt with a Maltese cross and the legend: R.V.F.D. ENGINE CO. NO. 2.

"A glass of white wine, please."

The bartender poured, and Sextant sipped. The wine was disgusting. He gave a counterfeit sigh of pleasure, and said, "Lovely." He tipped his head toward the juke box, and asked, "Rockin' Chair Money?"

"That's it."

"Junior or senior?"

"Senior. I don't believe Hank Williams Junior ever cut that song."

"I'm sure you're right. My name is Ralph, what's yours?"

"Uh . . . Patsy."

"Are you really a fireman, Patsy?"

"What? Oh, the shirt. No, I just picked it up somewhere."

"*Quel dommage*! I absolutely adore firemen, don't you?"

"How's that?"

"Just think of what they do. Dashing into burning buildings, throwing their arms around people and rescuing them. It's all so sweaty and manly."

The bartender looked uncomfortable. "Yeah, they do good work, I guess."

"Good? Only good?" Sextant leaned closer. "Let me tell you, my dear, from personal experience, that firemen can be absolutely fantastic."

The bartender took a good look at the ruffled shirt, the languid manner, and the made-up eyes. He swallowed hard, and moved down to the other end of the bar. Sextant smiled, and forced himself to take another sip of wine as he looked around the room. He was as out of place as a rose in an onion patch, and he knew that there were eyes on him. His own eyes settled on three men sitting at a table near the far end of the bar. They were young, early twenties at the most, and they sprawled lazily in their seats. Two were tall, lanky, and lantern-jawed, and they looked enough alike to be brothers. The third had a beer-gut that hung over his belt, and small eyes set in a fleshy face. He got up, and came over to the bar. He whispered something to the bartender. The bartender nodded. Beer-gut laughed, and went back to his table.

Perhaps, thought Sextant. Perhaps.

He finished his wine in one convulsive gulp, held up his glass, and called out archly, "Bartender, another wee drop of ambrosia, please?"

That brought more eyes to him. The bartender came back, looking unhappy. Sextant pushed his empty glass across the bar, but the bartender did not take it. He said, "Look, mister, you don't really want another drink."

"Oh, but I do. It's delicious."

"No, you don't." His voice was firm. "What you want is to pay me for the one, and find yourself another place."

Sextant registered surprise. "Are you refusing to serve me?"

"I didn't say that. I was making a suggestion."

"Not a very friendly one, I must say. You make it sound as if I'm not welcome here."

The bartender held up his hands. "I didn't say that, either. The law says I gotta serve you so long as you're not drunk, and you're not. I'm just trying to give you some good advice."

"But why? I thought we were getting along so nicely."

"Now look . . ."

"I thought we had established the beginnings of a true rapport."

Patsy said indignantly, "We didn't establish anything. You gonna take my advice?"

"Certainly not, I have no intention of leaving. I like this place, and I'm enjoying myself." Sextant manufactured a shiver. "It's so . . . gritty."

"Suit yourself," the bartender muttered. He poured wine, slopping some on the bar, and went back to the far end. Beer-gut came over to confer with him, and, again, there was laughter.

Sextant turned his back on the scene. Wait for it, he told himself. He counted silently to ten. When nothing happened, he counted to twenty. He was up to eighteen when he heard the sound of someone sliding onto the barstool next to him. He turned around.

"Hi there," said Beer-gut. "I hear you like firemen."

Sextant pouted. "Oh, he *told* you."

"Nothing wrong with that, Patsy's okay, he's just trying to be friendly." Beer-gut grinned, showing teeth the color of tobacco juice. "He said you liked firemen, and that's me."

"You're a fireman?"

"Rockhill Volunteers, best damn company in the Hudson Valley."

Sextant said doubtfully, "You don't look like a fireman to me."

"Hell, what's a fireman supposed to look like?"

"Sort of . . . athletic. I mean, how do you get up and down those ladders?"

"You mean this?" Beer-gut patted his belly. "That don't stop me from doing what I want to. Never has, and never will." He winked. "You know what I mean?"

"I haven't the faintest idea what you mean." Sextant flashed a glance at Beer-gut's table. The two men who looked like brothers were grinning broadly. Patsy stood at the end of the bar with a worried look on his face. "I don't believe you're a fireman at all."

"You're a hard man to convince."

"Prove it then. If you're a fireman, where's your tool?"

"Say what?"

"Your tool. That long iron bar that the firemen carry. They call it a halligan."

"Oh, that tool. Well, hell, you don't expect me to carry it around with me, do you? It's out in my van."

"I don't believe you."

"Wanna bet? I'll bet you fifty bucks it is."

Sextant looked at him with cool contempt. "You're bluffing. Go ahead and get it."

"Bring it in here?" Beer-gut shook his head. "No way, might cause a panic, people think there's a fire. You want to see it, come on out to the parking lot, and I'll show it to you."

Sextant looked away. "How boring."

Beer-gut shrugged. "Suit yourself, pal, but that's the only way you get to see my tool."

Sextant looked back. "Let me see if I understand this. We go out to the parking lot, and look in your van?"

"Right."

"And if you can show me your tool, you win and I give you fifty dollars?"

"That's it."

Sextant glanced at the table again. The other two men were gone. He slid off his stool. "Let's go."

They left the bar, Beer-gut leading. The parking lot was dark beyond the pool of light by the door. Their shoes crunched on gravel. They turned a corner past a dumpster, and past the exhaust fan from the kitchen. Sextant caught a blast of foul air, and tightened his lips.

"Where's your van?" he asked.

Beer-gut's voice came floating out of the darkness. "Right back here."

"I don't see anything."

"Don't wet your pants, it's just a little ways."

Beer-gut stopped beside a Chevy van that once had been white. Now it was grey, and matted with rust. He slid open the side door, bent over, and reached inside. He said, "Should be around here someplace." He straightened up. He had a softball bat in his hand.

Sextant said quietly, "That's not the tool I was looking for."

"I know that, sweetheart." Beer-gut tapped the bat against his leg. "But this is what you're gonna get."

Sextant stood very still. He heard the scrape of shoes on gravel behind him, and he knew that the other two were there. He said, "What is this?"

"It's time to teach you a lesson, faggot." The bat went tap, tap, tap. "You don't belong here. You got told that, didn't you?"

"Now, look . . ."

"You got told to get out, but you wouldn't. You think you can come into a decent place like this and go prancing around . . ."

"Look, let's just say that you won the bet. I'll give you the fifty."

"Fuck your money, and fuck you, faggot. This isn't for money, this is for what's right and what's wrong." A torrent of filth poured out of his mouth as he worked himself into a rage.

Sextant said calmly, "Now I'm sure you're not a fireman. A fireman would never use such language. A fireman is a noble creature."

Beer-gut raised the bat. "God damn you . . ."

Behind Sextant, somebody said, "Hey, stop talking so much and pop him one."

Beer-gut swung. Sextant moved inside the arc of the swing, and put his left fist into Beer-gut's belly. He turned his shoulder, and put his weight behind it. Beer-gut's eyes widened, and he doubled over. He dropped the bat. Sextant chopped down at his neck with the edge of his right hand. Beer-gut went flat on his face.

Sextant whirled to face the other two. They came charging at him awkwardly. He laughed. He waited until they were close enough, and then moved with the grace of a dancer. He kicked the first one in the pit of the stomach. He took out the second one with the same chop he had used on Beer-gut. They both went down. The second one lay without moving. The first one twitched and groaned. Sextant put two fingers to the side of his neck, pressed, and the groaning stopped. He straightened up, and looked around. He saw nothing but darkness, and heard nothing but the faint sound of the music from the tavern. He nodded in satisfaction.

He loaded the three men into the van, climbed in, and slid the door shut. He found the interior light, and flipped it on. There was a coil of greasy rope on the floor, but he preferred the fishing line he had in his pocket. He bound the three men hands and feet, and looked around for rags. There were none, but there was an old newspaper. He made wads out of the paper, and used the wads for gags. He checked the eyes of the three men; they were still out. He settled back to wait.

While he waited, he scrubbed at his face with a handkerchief, trying to remove the makeup he had used. Now that it had served its purpose he wanted it off as quickly as possible for, despite the masquerade he had just performed, he was not gay. Nor was he straight. He was a man without sexual interest, and had always been so. It was a drive that he lacked, but the lack did not bother him. He felt in no way incomplete, for he had his own compensations.

After a while he realized that the scrubbing was getting him nowhere, and he put the handkerchief away. He would need some cream and a proper wash. He sat back and waited. Beer-gut was the first to open his eyes. He looked around wildly, and strained to get free. He managed to raise his feet a few inches, and bang them on the floor. He did it twice.

Sextant said, "Stop that or I'll hurt you."

Beer-gut stopped, but his eyes were still wild. The other two came around slowly. They also strained, and then slumped back.

"Let me have your attention," said Sextant. He spoke in a low, calm voice. "We have something to discuss, and I'm going to take those gags out of your mouths, but you're going to keep your voices low, and you're not going to make any noise. Is that understood. Nod if it is."

They glared at him without moving. He sighed, and murmured, "I thought not."

He put his hand on Beer-gut's upper arm. He did something quickly with his fingers. Sweat popped out on Beer-gut's face, and he made a strangled noise behind the gag. Sextant did the same to the other two, and got the same result.

"I can give you that sort of pain any time I want to," he said. "And I should also mention that I enjoy doing it. Now, are you going to play nicely?"

Three heads nodded. Sextant flipped the wads of paper out of their mouths. They were breathing heavily. Beer-gut was the first to speak.

"Who the hell are you?"

"Just a guy who likes firemen."

"Shit, you ain't no faggot. Ain't a faggot alive can hit like that."

"Don't be too sure of that."

"Well, are you?"

"You'll never know."

"What is this?" asked one of the others. "What you want with us?"

"Actually," Sextant said brightly. "I want to offer you a job. All three of you."

It took a moment for that to sink in. Beer-gut spluttered, "A job? You did this just to . . . you said a job?"

Sextant nodded.

"Mister, this is one hell of a way to run an employment agency."

Sextant did not smile. "I had to be sure of what I was getting. I need three animals, three thoroughly loathsome creatures without a scrap of moral sensibility. I think you'll do nicely."

"That's just calling names," said Beer-gut. "You let me loose, and we'll see who calls names."

"You were loose when I took you out. Do you want to try it again?"

After a moment, Beer-gut shook his head. "You can hit, that's for sure. What's this job you're talking about?"

Sextant told them. He told them in detail. By the time he was finished, all three were grinning broadly.

"Are you sure you won't have some coffee?" asked Violet Simms. "I have it hot in the kitchen."

"Thanks, but I really have to be going," said Martha. "We have a long drive ahead of us."

"What time will you get to Hightower?"

"Late this afternoon."

"With the roads all icy, yes. You'll have to drive slowly."

They sat in the Simms living room, an orderly place that had been dusted and polished to perfection. Lila was out in the van with the other kids. The four from the Center had been drilled for two days, learning their cover stories pat. Martha had been pleased and impressed by the way they had taken the news of their assignment. There had been no explosions of juvenile excitement, nor, as far as she could tell, had there been any signs of anxiety. They had been told in detail the nature of the mission (there had been some debate with Sammy over that), and they knew that their job was to provide a ring of warning and security around Lila. They had reacted with an air of cool professionalism that was partly assumed, but also the result of their training. Even Chicken had kept himself under control, although he had been visibly disappointed when he learned that they would not be carrying weapons. Now they were out in the van with Lila, with instructions to make her feel welcome, while Martha chatted with her grandmother.

"We'll be driving slowly," Martha assured her, "and the radio says that the weather looks good further north. There's nothing to worry about, really."

"I know that, Martha." They had known each other only fifteen minutes, but they were using first names. Martha had that way with people. Violet reached out to touch the younger woman's arm gently. "I can see that you're a responsible person. It's just that this all came up so quickly. I'm still not used to the idea."

"We can thank the post office for that," Martha said briskly. She had no wish to dwell on the subject. "Lila should have received her notice weeks ago, along with the others."

"Well, it all worked out," Violet conceded, "and she's thrilled to be going. I'm sorry to be such a worrier, but it hasn't been easy for me, raising my daughter's child."

"From what I can see, you've done a wonderful job." Martha stood up. "I really must go now, and please don't worry. She's in good hands."

Violet watched from the doorway, as Martha went out to the van. The roof-rack was loaded with skis, and the rear area was filled with luggage, boots, and poles. Lila sat up front, Pam and Linda behind her, and George and Chicken in back.

"Okay, let's roll it," said Martha, as she got into the van and started up. "Call out for pit stops, but let's try and keep it to a minimum, okay?"

There was a murmur of assent. Head-to-head, Martha said, *Let's have your reports. Pam?*

Nothing unusual. She seems like a nice kid. I don't think we'll have any trouble with her.

If we have any trouble, it won't come from Lila. Linda, anything?

Same as Pam.

George?

She's sort of . . . innocent. We'd better watch our language with her.

Good point. Chicken? There was no answer. *Chicken?*

Martha sighed to herself. As usual, Chicken wasn't tuned in. *Will one of you please poke him?*

George, who was sitting next to Chicken, did it. He did not do it gently. Chicken jumped, and was about to poke back when George nodded at Martha.

Chicken, do you read me?

Uh . . . yeah, I got you.

I know it hurts, but you have to stay tuned to me. Will you do that, Chicken?

I'm sorry, I'll try. What do you want?

I was asking the others about Lila. What do you think of her?

I think she's cute.

Great.

Well, she is.

Go back to sleep. The rest of you, keep alert.

All this in the time that it took to start the car, and pull away from the curb. Martha drove down Linden Avenue, and made a left at the corner. She had already made her turn when another van, which once had been white and now was matted with rust, pulled out to follow.

8

SNAKE parked the rental Trans-Am at the curb in front of the Southern Manor, and sat there with the motor and the air-conditioning running, reluctant to leave the sanctuary of the car. The Florida sun was heavy, unkind, and her destination did not beckon. The Southern Manor was a two-story house of faded stucco with a sagging wooden porch, a sign that said ROOMS embedded in a gravelled yard, and a rusted flagpole without a flag. The other houses on the street were much the same. This was hardscrabble Florida, tracts of land that were virtually treeless, flat and sandy, dull and discouraging.

She looked again at the Southern Manor. David Ogden wanted it burned, and at the moment that didn't seem like such a bad idea.

I am, she told herself, about to become a house-sitter. I am supposed to sit around on my butt and make sure that somebody doesn't torch this monstrosity, which is just plain stupid. I love Sammy, he's my brother and I know that he's got the brains in the outfit, but he sure screwed up on this assignment. He gives the college gig to Vince, and I can't argue with that because I don't know the first thing about basketball, and I don't want to. He gives Ben the cruise ship, and that makes sense. But he gives Martha the Simms girl, and he makes me the house-sitter, which is all wrong. Martha is soft, and I'm steel. Martha is sweet, and I'm sharp. Martha says please, and I say gimme. The Simms kid needs a hard-nosed, hard-assed bitch. That's me. This job needs an earth mother who can make friends and talk to people. That's Martha. So why, Sammy?

She stared at the house with distaste, and the house stared back. The only way to guard the place effectively was from the inside, which meant renting a room. She dredged up memories of cheap rooming houses: lumpy mattresses, stiff grey sheets, ancient air-conditioning, one bathroom to a floor, and a sign in every room that said NO COOKING.

Someday, Sammy. Someday.

She went into the house to rent a room, and ten minutes later she was still trying. Bertha Costigan, the owner of the Southern Manor, was a cheerful woman of middle years who was perfectly happy to sit her down, give her a cold Coke, chat with her, and complain about the weather. What Bertha Costigan could not do was rent her a room.

"I wish I could, but I simply can't," she explained. "I have six rooms, and they're all occupied. I wish I had six more, a dozen more. I'd rent them all this time of year."

"What about doubling up?" Snake asked. "Maybe I could share a room."

"Afraid not. I don't have any other young women staying with me right now, and even if I did, most people don't like to share."

"Anybody leaving soon?"

"Not likely. You see, I don't have what you call transients here. Most of my people have been with me for quite a while. Now, Mrs. Moskowitz, she's been here close to five years, Mr. Pasco the same, and the Roveres maybe four. Poor Mr. Teague has been here the longest." She lowered her voice. "He's an invalid, can't move around." Her voice shifted up. "Then there's Mr. Krill, about a year, and Mr. Ramirez, six months or so." She lowered her voice again. "Mr. Ramirez, he's Cuban, but he's one of the good ones." She showed the palms of her hands. "So you see, there's nothing I can do for you."

"If it's a question of money—something extra?"

"I'm sorry." A firm shake of the head. "You'll have to try somewhere else."

"I was counting on this place."

"There are plenty of others. There's nothing special about the Southern Manor."

You got *that* right, thought Snake. What do I do now, pitch a tent in the street? The time frame starts tomorrow.

The front doorbell rang, and the landlady went to answer it. Snake caught a glimpse of a heavy-set woman standing on the porch. Mrs. Costigan said, "Morning, Ellen, right on time."

"You know me, like clockwork," said the woman. "How about this weather?"

"Pressure cooker."

"And it's gonna get worse." The woman came in, and disappeared down a hallway.

"Ellen Coombs, county nurse," Mrs. Costigan explained to Snake. "Comes by every day to see to Mr. Teague."

"What's wrong with him?"

"Nothing wrong with the man except he's got the disposition of a junkyard dog. Believe me, I know, I was a nurse once, myself. And not any country nurse, either. I was an R.N. in a hospital, Buffalo General up north. Trained at St. Mary's."

Snake tried to look admiring. "If there's nothing wrong with him, why does he need a nurse?"

"It's just that he can't move around anymore, bedbound they call it. Stays in his room all day and all night. Ellen comes by to make sure he's clean and cared for. I could do it myself, but my nursing days are over."

"Sounds like he belongs in a nursing home."

"That's what they say, but he won't have it. Stubborn old goat, he says this is his home, and this is where he stays." She added proudly. "That's what I mean about my people. Real loyal."

"Bertha?" The nurse poked her head out of the hallway. "I have to shift his bed today. Can you get someone to give me a hand?"

"Hold on for a minute." The nurse's head vanished, and Mrs. Costigan said with quiet contempt, "County people. That woman doesn't know what real nursing is. Can't even move a bed by herself."

"Can I help?" asked Snake.

"Bless you, no. I'll get Barney." She went to the foot of the stairs, and called up, "Barney? Barney, you up there? Ellen needs some help."

There was the sound of a door opening, and a voice called, "Be right there."

A young man came scampering down the stairs. He wore only shorts and sandals. His torso was a muscular V, and his skin glistened. He looked as if he worked out daily. When he saw Snake, he flashed a smile at her. To Mrs. Costigan, he said, "What's up, Mom?"

"Ellen needs a hand with Mr. Teague. Would you mind?"

"Sure thing." He looked at Snake with interest. "Hi, you just visiting, or are you moving in?"

"I wanted to move in, but there's no room."

"I told her," said Mrs. Costigan. "I'd be pleased to have her, but there you are."

"Too bad." Krill was still showing teeth. "You'd be an adornment around here."

Mrs. Cotigan said, "Barney?"

"Right." He winked at Snake. "This place would fall apart without me." He went down the hall.

"Always willing to help," said Mrs. Costigan. "Not like some these days."

"Your son?"

"Lord, no, that's Barney Krill, one of the roomers. He just calls me Mom, that's his way. Well, if there's nothing else I can do for you . . ." Her voice trailed off, waiting.

Snake nodded, and said goodby. She went out on the porch and stood there, trying to figure her next move. The door opened behind her, and Barney came out. He stood next to her. He was cat-quick in the way that he moved.

"That didn't take long," said Snake.

"Just a bed to shift. I wanted to catch you before you left."

"Why?"

"Why not? Pretty girl like you."

Snake stared at him.

"Well, you know . . . I thought I could give you a hand, help you find a place. I know most of the cheap places, and if you came here you must be looking for cheap."

He looked down at her confidently, the smile still fixed on his face. The flesh along his pectorals jumped.

Snake said, "You flex them like that, you might break one."

"No problem, I've got spares. Listen, why don't we go get a drink, or something, and then we can find you that room."

"A drink at ten in the morning?"

"Okay, coffee."

Snake looked at him, considering the idea. He was obnoxious. His smile was insincere, and his flattery was clumsy, but there was the off chance that he might turn out to be useful. She was still debating with herself, when he said, "A penny for your thoughts."

"No, thanks." She reached into a pocket, and came up with some coins. She found a penny, and handed it to him. "That's my line. A penny for yours."

"Huh?"

She jumped into his head. She rummaged around, working her way past the blatant sexuality and self-esteem. She didn't know what she was looking for, but she knew it at once when she found it. She almost laughed, and when she came out of his head, she was smiling. She didn't smile often, but when she did she could light up a room.

Krill thought the smile was for him, and his own smile rose to his eyes. "Let's go," he said. "There's a place down the street for coffee."

Snake shook her head. She was still smiling. "No thanks. I don't think I'll have any trouble finding a room."

"Might not be so easy."

"I'll manage."

The smile disappeared. "Suit yourself."

"I always do."

She went down the steps to her car, leaving him to stare at her back. She drove around until she found a telephone. She called Sammy at the Center, and told him what she needed.

"He calls himself Barney Krill, but his real name is Barry Kagen," she said. "He's wanted in Akron, two counts of grand theft auto."

Sammy said, "So what?"

"So I want you to pull a wire in Akron, get the police there to call the county people down here. I want this guy picked up by tomorrow morning, the latest."

"You sound sore. What the hell did he do to you?"

"Not a damn thing. I just want his room."

Late the next night, installed as the newest roomer at the Southern Manor, Snake sat by herself on the sagging porch in a rickety glider, rocking back and forth as she went over the events of the day just past. It was a dark night, the street was unlit, and the only light on the porch came from a single yellow bulb. The air was light now, almost pleasant. The inside of the house was quiet with the silence of sleep, and the only outside noises came from insects, from a yapping dog, and from the faint rumble of trucks along the interstate, half a mile away. It was a time for reflection, and, under different circumstances, it would have been time for a daily report. But there wouldn't be any daily reports on a job like this, only a final summary at the end of the time frame. Still, she formed the report in her mind as she rocked back and forth.

Sammy:

Thanks for pulling the wire in Akron. The state police picked up Kagan, aka Barney Krill, about ten this morning. I was parked across the street, and saw them take him. I waited a decent interval, then went into the house and found Mrs. Costigan collapsed in a blubbering heap. Just couldn't believe that sweet, friendly Barney was a car thief. I told her that the world is filled with evil, and asked if I could have his room. She brightened up when she realized that she wasn't going to lose even one day's rent. She practically fell all over me. I made sure she changed the sheets.

Once I was inside, my first job was to check the physical layout for fire risk. What I found was part good, and part bad. First, the bad.

The building is stucco, which doesn't burn easily, but there is enough of a frame construction involved to make the place flammable. Just about anything will burn if you crank the temperature high enough, and the way that the professional torches are using accelerants these days, the house could go up in a flash. Am I assuming that Gemstone is a torch? I think I have to. Ogden picked him (her) specifically for this job, and I can't get it out of my mind that his instructions to him (her) referred to a burning villa in Nam, and the smile on his (her) lips when he (she) smelled the burning rose bushes. So I have to figure Gemstone for a pro who will know how to use an accelerant, maybe gasoline and maybe something more sophisticated, and probably placed at the bottom of the stairwell to create the maximum draft. So that's my key area of observation, but I can't defend it twenty-four hours a day, and that's the bad part.

Here's the good. Almost nobody parks on the streets here. Cars are kept in driveways or carports, and, in the case of the Southern Manor, in a small area around at the side of the house. This means that I have a clear field of observation for any strange vehicles entering the street or parking there.

Also good. The house is filled with smoke alarms, well placed, and all functioning if those little red lights mean what they say.

Even better. About fifteen years ago a local ordinance was passed here that requires all hotels, nursing homes, and rooming houses to install a direct-wire alarm to the nearest fire station. The alarm here is in the parlor, a red button behind a glass panel. Break the glass, push the button, and the alarm is transmitted over the wire. A number pops up on the dispatcher's board, and he knows where to send the equipment. No delay in dialing 911, or anything else like that. If I need the troops, I can have them here in minutes.

So that's the physical situation. I figure to keep an all-night watch during the time frame, and grab whatever sleep I can during the day. When the job is over, you and I will take about a week off.

After I checked the physical layout, I spent the rest of the day tapping the residents of the Southern Manor. I realize how unlikely it is that Gemstone is one of them, but it had to be done, and how I wish I could have skipped it. Sammy, you and I both know how much like a sewer the human mind can be, which is why every ace I know avoids tapping heads unless it's for business. Or, or course, for love. Okay, sex. But not casually, not for the fun of seeing what someone is thinking, because it isn't worth it. Too much like diving for pearls in a cesspool. But today it was business, and it had to be done. First I checked out the two hired girls who help around the house, nothing there, and then

I went to work on the residents. Sammy, you've got to see this collection yourself to believe it. So far I've got myself one pussycat, a piano-playing psychopath, an elderly grifter, a pair of thieves, and a woman who iced her husband. I tell you, Barney Krill is an angel compared to some of these people. I haven't gotten to Mr. Ramirez yet. He's the Cuban, he's off somewhere in the *barrio* today, and considering what I've found so far, I can hardly wait to meet him.

Mike Teague is the pussycat, and no matter what Mrs. Costigan says, he really is bedridden. He lies there all day, and his head is filled with memories of punching bags and boxing gloves, the smell of liniment and sweat, and the thud of flesh hitting flesh. Mike was an athletic trainer all his active life, first with teams, then with fighters, and the walls of his room are covered with photos of the people he calls "my boys." Ballplayers of every sort, coaches, managers, but mostly boxers. Mike is one of those people who never met an athlete he didn't like, he's incapable of malice, or envy, or greed. He spends his time writing postcards to his boys, a dozen a day, and he gets that many in return. He never forgets a name or a face, and he can tell you in graphic detail what Willy Pep did to one of his boys that night in Cleveland back in Forty-seven. Sure, he's short-tempered and grouchy, who wouldn't be, tied to a bed that way, but he isn't any junkyard dog. He's a pussycat, and he certainly isn't Gemstone.

I tapped Jeremy Pasco next. He's a slim little guy, about twenty-five, with dark hair that he slicks back, and a mustache that's hardly worth mentioning. Pasco comes from Dallas, but he hasn't been back there in years. He makes a living playing cocktail piano six nights a week at the Flamingo Lounge on Third Street, and he spends most of his days at the track. He's a loser in more ways than one. The ponies don't love him, and the way he sees it, the rest of the world is down on him, too. You know the type. Nobody appreciates him, nobody recognizes his talent, nobody ever gives him a break, and every time he stubs his toe it's because some son of a bitch put a rock in the road. He once had ambitions as a concert pianist, but that's only a dream now. He's past it, he hasn't practiced seriously in years, and he's going to spend the rest of his life playing "Misty" and "Stardust" to the same old bunch of drunks. But there was a time when it could have happened, until somebody put that stone in the road. The guy with the stone was his younger brother, David.

Jeremy and David Pasco were born two years apart, the only children of two musicians. Papa Pasco was a violinist with the Dallas Symphony, Mama taught piano at home, and their boys were raised in a world of music. Both kids were introduced to the piano at an early age, and both took to it with a natural ease. They were good, everyone said so, and by the time that both were in their teens, people were predicting brilliant futures for them. If it had been a horse race, Jeremy would have been the favorite. At that stage in their development, his playing was the more considered, the more sensitive, and his technique was more advanced than his brother's. He was on the way up, and the first rung on the ladder was the All-Texas Youth Competition. Winning the All-Texas would open the right doors, and for two years Jeremy worked with the competition as his goal. He was nineteen when his parents thought he was ready. They entered him and, almost as an afterthought, they entered David, too. They expected little from the younger brother, but they thought that the experience would be valuable for him. Jeremy was the rising star.

It didn't work that way. At nineteen, Jeremy had progressed as far as he ever would, while David had matured into an accomplished artist. Both brothers made it into the final round, but David was the winner, and Jeremy finished out of the money. When the decision was announced, Jeremy threw his arms around his brother and hugged him exuberantly, grinning broadly as if he, himself, had won. It was a family triumph, he told his parents, and hugged his brother again.

The Pasco family went to bed late that night after a champagne supper. Jeremy sat up in his room and waited until he was sure that the others were asleep. He knew exactly what he was going to do. At two in the morning he packed a small bag, looked around his room, and said goodby to his childhood. Then he went down to the parlor, found his mother's sewing box, and took her pinking shears. He went up to his brother's room. David lay on his back, his mouth open, snoring. Jeremy put his pinking shears around his brother's right index finger, and paused. David did not move. Jeremy squeezed. He was surprised at how easily the shears cut through flesh and bone. He cut off David's finger at the second joint, severing it completely. He grabbed his bag, and ran. He went out of the house and down the street with the screaming in his ears. He did not look back. Not then, not ever.

He's been pounding the piano at places like the Flamingo Lounge ever since, and he still feels that he got a bad break. That's Jeremy Pasco. He isn't much, but he isn't Gemstone, either.

Clara Moskowitz is an eighty-five-year-old flim-flam artist who scores off susceptible elderly widowers, a first cousin to the octagenarian lady sharks who cruise Collins Avenue in Miami Beach. Clara prefers to work the provinces, and she does well at it. Nothing spectacular, not a fortune, but every so often she'll meet some poor sap who was married to one woman for fifty years, and who, now that she's gone, does not know how to make it on his own. Clara shows him how. Nothing physical, not at her age or his, just a little hand-holding, lots of sympathy, a commanding presence, and before el sappo knows it, Clara has taken over his life, his checkbook, and his CMA account at Merrill Lynch. Unlike her Miami cousins, she never marries the mark. She's already buried three husbands, and she can't take the strain of those funerals anymore. She just turns the sap upside down, and when there's nothing left to shake loose she sends him back to South Dakota, or Wisconsin, or wherever to live off the reluctant generosity of his children. The way Clara sees it, she gives value for the money, and there must be something to it, because no one has ever filed a complaint. She's a neat little piece of work, our Clara, but she isn't Gemstone.

Then there's Mr. and Mrs. Rovere. Paul and Patsy are in their late fifties, and the story they give out is that Paul took an early retirement from his job back in Kingston, New York. Dicey heart, a small pension, but they manage with it. Breakfast at The Clock, lunch at Denny's, the early-bird special at the Fisherman's Net, sit on the porch in the evenings and rock away the hours. It isn't a bad story, and they actually do come from Kingston, but their name wasn't Rovere then. It was something quite different back home where they were pillars of the Dutch Reformed Church, and Paul was the chairman of the building fund. Yeah, you got it. His retirement began the day he cleaned out the fund, and they headed south. He got away with something just short of 200K, and it seemed like a good idea at the time, but it isn't working out. They had just enough brains to steal the money, but not enough to know what to do with it. Instead of putting it to work, they've been nibbling away at it for the past four years, and it's almost gone. They don't sleep well. They lie in bed with the covers over their heads, wondering which will come first, the law, or the day when there won't be enough left for the early-bird special at the Fisherman's Net. They're pathetic people, but neither of them is Gemstone.

The last one I tapped was Bertha Costigan, and I peeled that woman's mind like an onion. On the surface I found a placid, kindly widow whose life revolved around her rooming house and the people who live there. On the next layer down I found that she's had a lifelong love affair with the state of Florida, not the drab place where she lives, but the fantasy Florida of the travel brochures and the television commercials, the white beaches and the emerald water, the orange groves and Disney World. Under that I found a deep pride in her former profession; years ago in Buffalo, New York, she was a well-respected nurse. Buffalo, that was the next layer down, and when I reached it, it almost froze me stiff. Buffalo, with its snow, and ice, and freezing winds; and on that level of Bertha's mind I found a reservoir of hate. She hates Buffalo, she hates the cold weather, and she hates the years that she spent there. That time includes the years of her marraige, and she hates her husband, too. Late husband. She hated him when he was still alive, and even though he's been dead for twenty years, she hates him still. In her mind he comes across as an inconsiderate, domineering son of a bitch, but for Bertha the worst of his sins is that he never moved her to Florida. Harry was an actuary with the Metropolitan Life, and when they first were married she told him how much she despised the cold, and sleet, and snow that battered Buffalo every winter. She begged him to get her out of there, and he promised that he would. He promised her the Florida of her dreams, and that was the part she could never forgive, for he never delivered. The years went by, and every year there was another reason why they couldn't move south. There was Harry's job, there was his ailing mother, there was the cost of moving. Each year he came up with something else—once he actually announced that he was allergic to oranges—and after a while it was clear to Bertha that Harry wasn't going anywhere. She knew now that he had never intended to fulfill her dream, and that for as long as he lived she would be stuck in Buffalo.

So she killed him, and moved south with the insurance money.

Sammy, I'm not kidding, she really did. She doesn't know that she did it, or rather, she knows, but she's buried it so deep that it's gone from her conscious mind. I swear, I had to go down *eleven* layers before I found it, but there it was, tinkling like a lonesome bell.

. . . *Treviton every three hours* . . . *Treviton every three hours* . . . *Treviton every three hours* . . .

Do you see it? Husband Harry has a massive heart attack, and once he's off the critical list they send him home from the hospital because, what the hell, his wife is a registered nurse, and she can take care of him. Bed rest, TLC, no excitement, and Treviton every three hours. She's administered Treviton to more cardiac patients than she can remember, there's nothing difficult about it for her, and for the first four days she keeps to the routine. Never occurs to her not to. But this is Buffalo in February, and on the fifth night the wind comes sweeping up the lake, and the Grey Goose Express unloads three feet of snow on the city. That does it. The next time that Harry is due for his dosage, she goes into his room and looks out the window. The streets are blanketed, the snow is coming down in curtains, and she can almost feel the freezing winds that are blowing outside. She looks down at the Treviton on the tray beside the bed, she looks down at Harry asleep there, she looks outside at the snow again, and without allowing herself to think about what she is doing she picks up the tray and walks out of the room without administering the medication. It's as simple as that. She sits up all night in the kitchen drinking coffee and listening to the whistle of the winds outside. The hours go by, three, and six, and nine, but she never leaves the kitchen. She never goes back to the bedroom. It's a long night, just long enough, and Harry checks out just before dawn.

That was twenty years ago, and, as I said, she doesn't remember it that way. Talk about suppression, she's got it buried so deep that it would take a shrink with a degree in civil engineering to blast it loose. When she thinks about it at all, she remembers that she nursed poor old Harry round the clock, never left his side, but his heart just gave out. Snap of the fingers, quick like that. She did her best, but it wasn't enough. It was God's will, and who could blame her if she chose to move away from the scene of such sorrow? That's the way she recalls it, and she really believes it.

Are you ready for the cream of the jest? Harry the actuary, Harry the Met Life guy, Harry the conservative one, had only about half the life insurance coverage that she thought he had. Through all the years of their marriage he had denied her the Florida of her dreams, and he did it again from the grave. There wasn't nearly enough for the white beaches and the emerald waters; there was hardly enough for the hard-scrabble sands of Glen Grove, and a rooming house to give her an income as she grew older. Isn't it enough to make you weep for the old gal? Yeah, me too. But whatever you think of Bertha Costigan, she isn't Gemstone.

That leaves Julio Ramirez, the only one I haven't met. From what I can gather, he's a slim, dark, well-mannered guy in his thirties who scrapes together a living as some sort of an entertainer in the Cuban community here. Of course, the *barrio* here isn't anywhere as big as what you find further south, but . . .

Snake stiffened, and braced herself to stop the rocking of the glider as a car turned the corner and came into the street. She got to her feet, and moved quickly out of the light and into the shadows at the end of the porch. The car slowed as it neared the house, and she tensed, ready to move again. It was a jump to the front door, and three quick steps to the alarm. The car turned into the parking area near the house. The headlights went out, the motor went off, and a door slammed. She heard footsteps on the gravel, on the stairs, and a man walked onto the porch. He was also in shadow. He stopped, looked around, and said cautiously, "Is there someone here?"

"I'm sorry," said Snake. "I didn't mean to startle you."

"Where are you?"

"At the end of the porch." She stayed in the shadows.

"What are you doing here?"

"Who wants to know?"

The man laughed softly. "Take it easy, I didn't mean it that way."

"I'm new here. I moved in this morning."

"I see. I live here, too. I'm Julio Ramirez. And you?"

"Claudia." She tried to make out his face, but the shadows covered him.

"Welcome to the Southern Manor, Claudia. Will you be staying here long?"

"Maybe. Who knows?"

"You probably won't. Nothing happens here, nothing exciting."

"Did I say that I was looking for excitement?"

He laughed again. "No, you didn't. Goodnight." He turned to go inside.

"Goodnight."

His back was to her. He was the last one, and she decided to tap him on the spot. One quick sweep of his head was all that she needed. She tapped, but nothing happened. She frowned, and tapped again. Still nothing. She tapped a third time, but it was like banging against a wall. She couldn't get in. He had a block up, a mental barricade that no normal person could have erected. Only an ace could have done it.

He wheeled around to face her. Head-to-head, he said, *Who the hell are you?*

You felt it?

Of course I felt it. You hit me like a sledgehammer.

And you brushed it off like a feather. You're good.

I used to be.

Do we talk?

If you wish.

Walk into the light.

They both moved at the same time, and stood facing each other under the porch light. They stared at each other. Snake saw a lean, dark-haired man with smooth olive skin and a thin mustache. Her eyes widened. So did his.

Snake.

Rafael.

The moment hung on tip-toes, and then they had their arms around each other. They kissed. He cupped her face in his hands, and kissed her again. They both grinned broadly. They both were close to tears. Snake stepped back.

"I don't believe this," she said. "What are you doing here?"

He looked dazed. "How did you find me?"

"I didn't. I mean, I wasn't looking for you."

"Then why . . . ?"

She shook her head. "You look older."

"How kind of you to say so. You don't."

"Who's Julio Ramirez?" She had known him as Rafael Cañero.

He shrugged. "Just a name."

"What do I call you?"

"Make it Julio, I'm used to it. When you said Claudia—I always thought of you as Snake."

She put her hands on his shoulders, and stood back. "Let me look at you."

She looked long and hard at the man who once, for a brief time, had been her lover. In those days, Rafael Cañero had been an ace in the employ of the *Dirección General de Inteligencia*, the Cuban version of the CIA—how long ago? Six years back, she figured, at the United Nations when he had been attached to the Cuban mission, and she to the American. His cover job had been as the commercial attaché, and hers had been as a translator, but both had done what all sensitives do. They were snoops.

They had been lovers for three months, and it had been a time of desperate loving, for by the rules of the topsy-turvy world in which they lived they were forbidden to know one another. They were on opposite sides of the political fence, security risks if they exchanged so much as a word, but they had managed. As sensitives, they had their own ways, and it had started during one of those slam-bang cocktail hours in the North Delegates' Lounge where drinks were still a dollar apiece and the place was packed every night with all ranks and all nations. Doing it the way aces did it, head-to-head from opposite ends of the bar with the crowd in between unaware of what was going on.

Hey, you down there in the blue dress and the pretty eyes—yeah, you, the Yankee ace—you read me?

It isn't blue, it's aqua, and which one are you?

The good-looking guy in the grey pinstripe suit.

From here I can see four grey suits, and none of the guys inside them look all that great.

You got to be kidding. Look, I'm raising my glass now.

Oh sure, the Cuban.

You know me?

I've seen you around. What's on your mind?

I could get arrested for what's on my mind.

Save it for your dreams.

No, I mean really arrested, because what I got on my mind is to come down to your end of the bar, say hello, maybe buy you a drink, but if I do that we're both in trouble. A Cuban and a Yankee, both aces, not so good.

My people wouldn't be happy.

Neither would mine. Bright lights and lots of questions, you know?

I know.

So I was thinking . . . you got a keeper?

No, we don't work it that way.

You're lucky. I've got a keeper, but he doesn't have the brains that God gives to goats. I can lose him easy if I want to.

Now why would you want to do that?

Come on, what do you say?

It's risky.

What isn't?

Plenty of things. Watching television. Washing my hair. Things like that.

Sure, if you play by the rules then nothing's risky. You always play by the rules?

That did it. Where and when?

You know Woody's on Third Avenue?

Sure.

Half an hour?

I'll be there.

That was the way it began, and from there it had escalated into three months of frantic loving, months of meeting on the sly, drinking in bars that no one knew, using motels in Jersey and Queens. Three months of looking over their shoulders before diving into bed, and then one day it was over. He was ordered back to Havana, and that was the end of it. There was time for a quick farewell, one last night of laughter, and then he was gone. Until now. Now he was here with his arms around her, and the years had dropped away.

She rested her head against his shoulder, and said, "We have some things to talk about."

"We can talk in my room."

"I don't think so. We'd better talk here."

"Oh?" He took his arms away. "Sorry, didn't mean to push."

"It isn't that."

"Then what?"

"I think we have to talk business."

He laughed. "What a Yankee you can be, always business first. You're not exactly overwhelmed by this reunion, are you?"

"More than you think, but we still have to talk. You can start by telling me what a Cuban ace is doing here in Glen Grove."

"Wait here, I'll be right back."

He went into the darkened house, and returned in a moment with two cold bottles of San Miguel beer. He gave one to Snake.

"Mrs. Costigan keeps a few bottles in the refrigerator for me," he explained. "She thinks it helps to remind me of home. Actually, it's made in Tampa and it tastes like Bud, but I drink it. It makes the old lady happy."

Snake took a sip. "You haven't answered my question."

"I don't see that I'm obliged to."

"You're not, but I'm hoping that you will."

"For old times sake? You're here on a job, aren't you?"

"Of course, and I assume that you are, too."

"As a matter of fact, I'm not."

"Oh sure, you just decided to take your vacation in Florida this year."

"It's simpler than that. I don't work for anyone anymore. Not the DGI, not anyone. I'm retired."

Snake said flatly, "You wouldn't kid an old lover, would you? No ace ever retires. My people don't allow it, and neither do yours. No agency allows it."

"Who said I asked permission?"

"You mean you came over?" She knew that could not be. If he had defected to the Agency, she would have known about it.

"You're not listening to me. I said I was out of the business."

"Do you mind if I tell you that you're a lousy liar?"

"I don't mind at all," he said cheerfully, "but it's true. Do you want me to prove it?"

"How?"

"I'll open up long enough for you to take a look. Just long enough. You can see for yourself. Do you want that?"

She was suddenly unsure. "If you do."

"Go ahead. I have nothing to hide anymore."

He opened up. She went in and saw that he was telling the truth. She came out quickly. He slammed the gates.

"You saw?" he asked.

"Yes. It's still hard to believe, but I saw. I'm sorry, it didn't seem possible. When did you . . . ?"

"About five years ago."

"What happened?"

"It's a long story."

"I'm not in any hurry. Is there any more beer?"

"Enough."

"Then go ahead." She moved to the glider, and sat with her legs tucked under her. "Tell me all about it."

He leaned against the porch railing, and grinned so broadly that his teeth gleamed in the night. "All right, you asked for it."

9

MADRIGAL'S job was to kill Calvin Weiss. My job was to stop Madrigal, and the job was impossible. Weiss was the entertainment director on the S.S. *Carnival Queen*, a cruise ship that sailed out of Florida's Port St. James, on a regular eight-day run to Nassau, San Juan, St. Thomas, and St. Maarten. The *Queen* had seven bars, four lounges, and a casino. She had a swimming pool, a gymnasium, and two saunas. She had a cavernous dining room, three card rooms, two cafes, a sports area, a skeet range, and the facilities of a small city. She carried one thousand and twelve passengers, and a staff of over four hundred, any one of whom could have been Madrigal. And I had to keep Weiss alive.

"Impossible," I told Sammy.

"Difficult," he agreed, "but you'll manage."

"How? If there were twenty of me, I couldn't keep Weiss covered every minute."

"Right, so you don't try to cover him. The job is to find Madrigal before he can do anything."

"Look, I don't know if Madrigal is a man, a woman, or a cocker spaniel. How do you expect me to find him, tap fourteen hundred heads?"

"Just keep your mind open, tune in to anything you can. With your luck, you'll pick up something."

"Is that the best advice you can give me?"

"With your luck, that's all you need."

My luck. He has a thing about that word. He likes to say that I have more luck than brains, and to prove it he points to the way that I win at cards. He ignores the fact that what I do at the card table has nothing to do with luck. I win because I know what everybody else at the table is holding. I go into their heads, and peek at their cards. To put it baldly, I cheat. Yes, I agree that the way I play doesn't fall within the code of the gentleman gambler, but, you see, I don't believe in gambling. Life is uncertain enough.

With those instructions in mind, on the night that the *Carnival Queen* sailed from Port St. James, I was not shadowing Weiss all over the ship, nor was I desperately trying to tap any of over a thousand heads at the seven complimentary cocktail parties and imitation luaus going on. I was, according to instructions, trusting to my luck, which meant that I was sitting in the card room on the Promenade Deck trying to decide which way to go on a two-way finesse for the queen of hearts. My partner's name was Betty Ireland, our opponents were Jim and Ellen Kreiske, from Cleveland, and the stakes were respectable enough to keep me awake. The contract was six spades, doubled, I looked to be a trick short, and there was no squeeze or endplay in sight. I needed the finesse, and there was no clue from the bidding as to where the queen lay. It was an even shot either way, and anyone else would have flipped a mental coin, but that would have been gambling, and I don't believe in gambling. Instead, I went into their heads. I tried Ellen Kreiske on my left, but she didn't have it. I tried her husband, and there it was, the queen of hearts along with two small ones. I crossed to the dummy, led the ten of hearts, and when Jim didn't cover, I let it run. I cashed the ace and the king, collecting the queen, and claimed the contract.

"Six spades doubled," I announced. "Nine hundred and ten."

"Way to go, partner," said Betty. "Well played."

"Luck," said Kreiske. He was a grumbler. "Could have gone either way."

"Sheer luck," his wife agreed.

But, as you can see, luck had nothing to do with it. Still, I have to admit that Sammy has a point about my luck, for there have been times when I've done something thoughtless, or careless, or downright stupid, and the luck has pulled me through. That's the way it was earlier that day, before we sailed, when I staked out Weiss's home in Port St. James. He lived on a shady, well-kept street lined with cookie-cutter houses, the sort of street where you express your individuality by the color of your garage door and the size of the flamingo on your lawn. Weiss's door was lime green, and his flamingo wouldn't have broken any records. For no good reason, I was disappointed. I had expected more of a statement from a man who made his living making other people laugh.

I got there early in the morning, parked down the street, and waited for him to show. The *Queen* sailed at five in the afternoon, and so I had plenty of time, but, despite what Sammy had said about covering him, I wanted to see him on his home grounds and familiarize myself with the way he moved. I settled down to wait with the motor running, the air on high, and that was the first stupid thing I did that day. I wasn't there twenty minutes when the cruiser pulled up, and parked behind me. Two cops got out, and came over. They both wore dark glasses, and one of them was chewing a toothpick.

I lowered the window, and said what everybody says. "What's the problem, officer?"

Toothpick said, "Would you step out of the car, please?"

"I'm just sitting here."

"Out, please. Now." I stepped out into the heat, and he said, "License and registration, please."

I gave him the papers. He looked them over, and gave them back. "Mr. Slade, do you have any business around here?"

"No, just passing through."

"Parked at the curb?"

"Is it a no-parking zone?"

He didn't like that. "Do you know anyone in this neighborhood?"

"Not a soul."

"Then I'm going to ask you to keep on moving."

"You running me?"

"That's it."

"I don't get it. What did I do?"

"It isn't what you did, it's what you're going to do." He shifted the toothpick to the other side of his mouth. "You are going to drive straight down Mason Street to the first light, hang a left onto Cordell, and go four more lights to the entrance to the Interstate. You will not stop for a cup of coffee, you will not stop to rest your weary head, you will barely even stop for the lights along the way. You will get onto the Interstate, north or south, makes no difference, and you will leave the confines of Port St. James at once. That's what you will do. Have I made myself clear?"

"Clear enough, but I'm not sure that you can do this."

"Mr. Slade, I assure you I can. I can do it hard, or I can do it easy. Which is it going to be?"

I couldn't figure it. Sometimes a cop will run a stranger in a small town, but not when the small town is in south Florida where strangers are the bread and the butter. Still, I should have done it. I should have tugged my forelock, and gone quietly, but that would have left Weiss uncovered, and so I made my second stupid move of the day. I reached for my wallet, and both cops stiffened. I smiled. I showed them the silver shield and the green plastic card that identified me as Commander Benjamin Slade, Office of Naval Intelligence, Criminal Investigation Division. Toothpick wasn't impressed.

"Around here that doesn't mean shit," he said. "I know a place in Miami where you can buy one of those things for ten bucks."

"Not one like this."

Toothpick asked his partner, "What do you think, Eddie?"

"The lieutenant said to run him."

"He didn't say anything about the U.S. Navy."

"I don't work for the Navy, I work for the lieutenant."

"Yeah, there's that." Toothpick asked me, "You gonna move?"

"Sorry, but I can't oblige you."

"Have it your way."

He was quick, and he was good. He hit me once in the belly, doubled me over, and clipped my head with his knee as I went down. The pain burst in my cheek, and went to my neck. I tried to get up, and he gave me the knee again. This time I lay on the ground without moving.

"Get up," said Toothpick."

"Not me," I told him. "I like it down here."

They threw me into the cruiser and took me to the substation, one of them driving my car. They turned me over to a lieutenant named Ford. He was short and tubby, and he looked as if his shoes hurt. When he saw my face, he glared at the cops.

"I told you to run him," he said. "I didn't tell you to make hamburger out of him."

The two cops shifted uncomfortably. Toothpick put my ID on the desk. Ford stared at it, and said, "What the hell is this? The navy?"

Eddie said, "You said to run him, boss, but he wouldn't run."

"The fucking U.S. Navy?"

"He wouldn't run," Eddie repeated stubbornly.

Ford's mouth opened and closed a couple of times. He looked like an unhappy fish. He suddenly shouted, "Get out of here. Get the hell out of here."

The cops went out. Ford peered at my face. "That hurt much?"

"I can live with it."

"Sit down, sit down." He got a bottle of Wild Turkey out of a desk drawer, poured into paper cups, and handed me one. "That should take the edge off it. What the hell have we got here?"

"Your people tried to run me. I got sore, and I showed them the tin. Then the fun started."

"You working?"

"If I were, would I tell you?"

"No, I guess not. You should have let them run you. I mean, what the hell?"

"I know. Like I said, I got sore."

"Not so good in your line of work. If it is your line of work." He tapped my ID with a fingernail. "Take me an hour to check this out. If it's a phony, you could tell me now and save us some time."

"It's real, all right. Look, I'll show you. Port is left, starboard is right. That's sailor talk. Can I go now?"

"Jesus, one of those." He sighed, and pushed himself out of his chair. "Sit there like a good little sailor, and don't move."

He went out, and came back in a few minutes. "Like I said, about an hour."

"What do I do for an hour, just sit here?"

"You want to pass the time, you can tell me why you were staking out the Weiss house."

That didn't figure. I'd been parked up the street. "You've got me. What's a Weiss house?"

He sighed again. "Suit yourself."

He went to work on some papers, and ignored me after that. I sat back, stared at a wall, and wondered how I was going to explain this one to Sammy. He had to find out. The computer check would go to the ONI, but then it would be shunted to the Center. The check would come back confirmed, but Sammy would see the paperwork. Lie, I decided.

The check took less than an hour. After a while, a woman came in and handed Ford a printout. He read it, grunted, and gave it back to her. He pushed my shield and card across the desk to me. He leaned forward, and said quietly, "Okay, so you check out, but that doesn't mean that I can let you hassle Mr. Weiss. He pays his taxes just like everybody else around here."

I shook my head. "I'm not trying to hassle anybody, and I don't know any Weiss."

"Look, you think you're the first one who tried to get at him? You're the fourth, sailor, four that I can remember. One guy actually popped him as he was coming out the door, damn near broke his jaw. We stopped the other two, and now you come along."

"Is that why you tried to run me?"

"We keep an eye on that street, but that wasn't it. His wife called it in. She saw you from a window. So it doesn't make any difference what kind of a badge you're carrying. I want you out of town."

"I guess you know what you're talking about, but I'm still in the dark."

He sat back, and shrugged. "If that's the way you want to play it, but let me give you a piece of advice. If you can't control your wife, get rid of her, but don't try to settle it here on my turf."

"Is that what this is all about? Wives?"

"And husbands. Three of them, and now you."

"This Weiss sounds like quite a guy."

"From what I hear, he's the greatest cocksman since Errol Flynn, but what happens on board the *Carnival Queen* is none of my business." He gave me a steely cop look. "What happens here in town is very much my business, and I've got enough business to worry about without a bunch of angry husbands buzzing around that house. You understand? You've been warned."

"I understand, but you've got it wrong. I'm not even married." I stood up. "Am I free to go?"

"Sure, I've got nothing to hold you on. You want another piece of advice?"

"I already heard it. Get out of town."

"That definitely, but something else. There are two ways out of this station. You turn to the right, and you go out the front. You turn to the left, and you go out the back. I'd go out the back if I were you."

"Any particular reason?"

"Mrs. Weiss is waiting out front. She says she wants to see you. You don't want to see her, do you?"

"I don't even know the lady."

"Now you're talking." His eyes turned shifty. "What my boys did . . . can we keep that off the record?"

"I've been drinking your whisky, haven't I?"

He grinned. "Off you go, sailor."

I went out of his office, stood in the corridor, and looked at my watch. It was only eleven-thirty. Left or right, stupid or lucky? I wasn't sure which, but I had the feeling that I had exhausted my capacity for stupidity, at least for one day. I turned right.

She was waiting for me in the reception area, sitting on one of those wooden benches that they make for the cop shops, the hardest, saddest benches in the world. In an age of premolded plastics, they still make those seats of misery, or maybe the old ones never wear out.

She stood up when she saw me, and I knew that my luck had kicked in. She was a beauty, a tall and slender blonde. She was ten years past the best of it, and those years showed in her eyes, but she was still a beauty.

She stood in front of me, and said, "Mr. Slade, I'm June Weiss." Her voice was throaty, with a catch in it. "I've been waiting to see you."

"The lieutenant told me."

She stared at me with a concentration that was disconcerting. "I'm sorry, this must seem strange to you, but you're the first one I've ever seen. I never saw any of the others. I had to see what you looked like."

"Why?"

"It was important to me. Would you mind if we went someplace, and talked?"

"About what?"

She looked at the busy station. There were at least a dozen people in the room. She put a hand on my arm. "Not, here, I can't talk in a place like this. Please?"

She knew how to do it. Come close, touch you lightly, let you breathe her, and use that throaty voice to say please. It worked just fine on me. I felt a soft plum in the back of my throat, and I had to swallow hard.

We walked out into the sunlit street, and I managed to say, "Where do you want to go?"

"My car is right here. Will you follow me?"

To the ends of the earth, I thought, but all I said was, "Yes."

I followed her car to an X-brand motel near the Interstate. It was a cheap-looking joint with a faded façade, and the parking lot was a checkerboard of weeds. The bar in the rear was called the Tropic Moon, and it stank of antiseptic. It didn't seem like her sort of place, but I told myself that I didn't know anything about her. We were the only customers in the room. She wanted a gin and tonic, I ordered a beer, and we sat at a table silently. She stared at her glass without drinking, and I wondered what she wanted. I could have gone into her head to find out, but I was reluctant to pry. Instead, I put it into words.

"What did you want to talk about?"

"Do you have a picture of her?"

"Who?"

"Your wife. Do you carry a photo?"

I finessed that one. "No, I never got into the habit. Why?"

"I wanted to see what she looked like." Her eyes shifted away from me. "I'm told . . . I hear that Calvin's women tend to look like me. I was curious."

"Why don't you ask him?"

She smiled faintly. "It's not something we talk about."

"Maybe you should."

"What good would it do?" There was a tired note in her voice. "I don't know why I should tell you this, maybe because we're in the same boat together, but during the season Calvin goes to sea for eight days, and then he's home for two. Eight days of chasing every woman in sight, and two days of resting up for his next adventure. That's his routine, and it doesn't leave much time for small talk."

"Children?"

"Are you serious? Do you think I'd still be here if there weren't children? Two boys, fourteen and ten. You?"

"No, no children."

"Does she look like me? Your wife, I mean."

Another finesse. "Not really."

"Are you still in love with her?"

And another. "That's not something I talk about."

"I'm sorry, you're right, it's none of my business."

She took a tiny sip of her drink, and fell silent. Again it was time to go into her head, and again I did not want to. It would have been like marching through a rose bed in jackboots.

I asked, "Is that all you wanted to talk about?"

She shook her head. "No, there's something else. It's about Calvin. I want you to leave him alone. You're not the first one to come after him, or did you know that?"

"The cop at the station told me."

"Ben . . . may I call you that?" I nodded. "Please leave him alone."

"It sounds as if you still care about him."

"He's a miserable son of a bitch, but I don't want him dead," she said calmly. "Marrying Calvin was the biggest mistake of my life, but my children need a father. He's betrayed me, he's humiliated me, he's tortured me with those women of his. But it's my mistake, I'm stuck with it, and he's still the father of my children." She reached across the table, and put her hand on top of mine. "Let it go, Ben. He's gone by now, he's on board the *Queen*, and he'll be gone for eight days. I'm asking you, please, don't be here when he gets back. I know what you must be feeling, God knows I feel the same way, but I want you to leave him alone."

"You sound as if you thought I was going to kill him."

"I don't know. I don't know what the others wanted, either. Maybe they just wanted to hit out in anger, and maybe they wanted to do more than that. But whatever it is, I'm asking you not to do it." She looked away, and in a voice so soft that I could barely hear it, she said, "There are other ways of taking revenge."

Her words hung between us. For the third time, I knew that I should go into her head, and for the third time, I backed away. I said, "Maybe you'd better spell that out."

"Do I have to?" Her chin came up. "What would you say if I suggested that we get ourselves a room here, and spend the afternoon making love?"

I tried not to smile. That explained the cheap motel, a place where she would not be known. "What would I say? I'd say that you're hurt, that you're angry, and that you don't really mean it."

She stood up. "Wait here."

She walked out of the bar. She had a good walk. She was back by the time I had finished my beer. She tossed a room key on the table.

"Well?" she asked.

Well, indeed. Part of me wanted her, the sticky plum was still in my throat, and another part of me knew that there was everything wrong with it. Forget that I was on the job; I had dallied on the job before. Forget that my case was her husband; he had nothing to do with the moment. Forget the time factor; I had plenty of time before the *Queen* sailed at five. Easy enough to forget all that, but what I could not forget was that this was a bird with a broken wing who was trying to fly in the face of a gale. I was a long way past bagging wounded birds, at least I thought I was, but the plum in my throat made me wonder.

I stood up, and said, "Let's go."

The room was right on line for a sleaze motel: a waterbed, a VCR with a stack of cassettes, a mended rip in the carpet, a stain the size of a watermelon on the wallpaper, and the same pervading odor of antiseptic. She walked around the room touching things. She ran a finger over a surface, and stared at it.

Without looking at me, she said, "It's pretty bad, isn't it?"

"I've seen worse. Do you want to leave?"

"No, it doesn't make any difference. Or does it?"

"Not to me, but are you sure you want to do this?"

"Of course I do. Just give me a minute.

She went into the bathroom. She wasn't gone long, and when she came back she was naked except for a towel she had wrapped around her. The towel didn't hide much. She gave me a bright smile, and said, "You still have your clothes on."

"I'm slow that way."

"That's all right, I want another drink, anyway. How about you?"

"I'll pass."

"Please, let's have another drink. Could you order up something from the bar?"

"Not in a place like this. I'd have to go get it."

"Would you mind terribly?" She peered at the bruise on my face. "Did the police do that?"

"Yeah."

"Because of me."

"No, because cops do things like that. Some cops."

She leaned against me, and brushed the bruise with her lips. "Poor you."

I put my arms around her, and the towel dropped away. She smelled of violets. It was like holding a warm, soft statue, but it was still a statue. She put her hands at the back of my neck, and I kissed her. She held the kiss for a moment, then twisted away. She slipped out of my arms, and covered herself again with the towel. She sat on the edge of the bed, and looked down at her folded hands. I could not see her face.

"I'm sorry," she said in a tiny voice. "I wasn't—I wasn't ready."

I took her arm, and pulled her to her feet. "Come on, get dressed. We're leaving."

"No, wait." She pulled against me. "Where are we going?"

"Anyplace. Out of here."

She planted her feet. She wouldn't move. Her face was close to mine, and her eyes were wide. "You don't want me. Is that it?"

"That's stupid, you know what you look like. I'm flattered that you thought you wanted me, but you don't, and we're leaving."

"But I do. I mean . . . want you." She took a breath. "I came here to make love. That's what I want." She was suddenly in my arms again. She said quickly, "I know I'm doing this all wrong, but I'll be all right, really I will. I just need something to relax me. Please, get us a drink, and I'll be ready when you come back. I promise."

I didn't think much of her promise, and I didn't get us a drink. Another drink wasn't going to change anything. Instead, I did what I should have done earlier. I trampled the rose bed, I went into her head, and it was sad in there.

I saw a time, long ago, when all of her life had been love, and warmth, and friendship, and I saw how much that had changed. I saw a time of decision back then, saw the decision made, and saw how much she later regretted it. I saw a young love lost, and never regained, saw her daydreams of what might have been. I saw her as a girl who once had been adored, and I saw her as a woman who had forgotten her beauty. I saw the man of long ago, the man she turned away.

I saw her need, and I saw that I could not supply it.

She needed absolution for mistakes of the past, she needed to set back the clock. She needed me to tell her that birds with broken wings can fly, that everyone gets a second chance, and that it all works out in the end. She needed to dream of a different decision, and she needed me to help her with the dream. She needed me for a lot of things, but she didn't need me for a lover.

"Go home," I told her. The plum in my throat was still there, and I had to work to keep my voice steady. "Get dressed, and go home. There's nothing I can do for you."

I turned, and walked away from her. At the door, I looked back. She was staring at me, still clutching that towel. I left her standing there, and went to catch the *Carnival Queen*.

Nine hours later, I squared the deck for the last time that night, and collected two hundred and twenty dollars from the Kreiskes. I took the money into the Cockatoo Lounge, and spent some of it at the bar. While I was there, I followed Sammy's advice and kept my mind open, taking in the flow from the crowded room. Not completely open, I would have been swamped, but open enough to pick up streams of thought. It was, as usual, a sad business. Unless you do what I do, you have no idea what garbage runs through most people's minds.

. . . off-white with a skin like that makes her look like an oyster . . .

. . . Mary had a little lamb . . .

. . . right in the middle, I'm ready to come, and she asks me if I made the car payment . . .

. . . wedgies, already, she still thinks it's the fifties . . .

. . . Jesus, what an ass . . .

. . . to school one day it was against the . . .

. . . could have sold at 44, but he had to be greedy . . .

. . . can't help it if it hurts, can I help it if it hurts? . . .

. . . could bury my head in that all night . . .

. . . rules. Mary had a little . . .

. . . must have been the lobster at dinner . . .

. . . three seventy-five a gross less ten percent . . .

Satisfied, Sammy?

I lowered the volume. The second purser was at the bar, natty in uniform, drinking slowly. That was part of his job: to stand at the bar, show the uniform, answer questions, and drink slowly. I waited until he was ready, and bought him one.

"Cheers," he said, lifting his glass. "Saw you in the card room earlier. Any luck?"

That word again. "Can't complain."

"Absolutely amazing, you card players. Spend all this money on an eight-day cruise, and never leave the card room."

"I'm not as bad as that," I assured him. "I have other interests."

"Should hope so. Lots of things to see and do. You traveling alone?" I nodded. He looked at me owlishly. "Lots of things."

"Female things?"

"That's the word I was searching for."

"I thought you had mostly couples on board."

"Mostly, yes. We get about three-quarters couples and one-quarter singles. That still leaves several hundred bodies groping around in the dark."

"And the married ones?"

"More so than the singles, some of them. I don't know why it is, but you get people out beyond the three-mile limit and all the rules disappear. Especially with the regulars."

"Who are they?"

"The repeaters. On any given trip, at least one-third of the passenger list has been with us before. Some of them come back two or three times a year. There are people on board who know their way around this bucket of bolts better than I do."

I heard the word then. I was still tuned in, and I heard the word that snapped me back to full attention. *Calvin.*

And then another. *Hey, there's Calvin.*

And then a flood of it. *Calvin's here . . . look, there's Calvin.*

"Of course, Calvin has a lot to do with it," said the second purser, looking toward the door. "Some of the regulars come back just to see Calvin."

A strident voice called, "Hey, you people, loosen up. Whadda you think this is, a morgue?"

I turned to see Calvin Weiss come into the room. He was short and sandy-haired, with peaked eyebrows and a button nose. He threw up his arms in a greeting to the crowd. "Never saw so many stiffs in my life," he yelled. "Not that I got anything against something stiff, but there's a time and a place for everything."

"That's our Calvin," murmured the second purser, and explained, "the entertainment director. On the first night out he hits all the lounges and loosens up the people."

"Funnyman?"

"He thinks so. Amazingly, so do a lot of other people."

Weiss called over to a fat man at a far table. "Hey, Kaplan, you back again? I hope you brought your wife this time."

The fat man protested, "Come on, I always bring my wife."

"If that's your wife, then I just changed my position on the abortion issue." He paused. "And in her case, I'll make it retroactive."

He got his laugh, and began to go from table to table, saying hello to the people he knew, introducing himself to the others. Watching him work the room was like watching a politician at the state fair. He greeted men with a firm handshake, gripping the elbow with his free hand. He greeted the women with the burlesque of a bow. He never stopped talking, and he never stopped moving, working one table with his eyes already on the next. He bowed over a seated woman, stared down the front of her dress, and said something that made her laugh.

"I'll never understand it," said the second purser. "He's rude, he's crude, and he's obvious, but they adore him. Of course, most of them would also like to kill him."

That sat me up straight. "Do what?"

"Kill him." The second purser said it cheerfully. "Actually, I wouldn't mind killing him, myself."

I heard it then in the ear of my mind. I had missed it at first, but now it was like a mental murmur coming from every part of the room, building in volume as Weiss went from table to table. People were thinking: *Kill Calvin, kill Calvin, kill Calvin.* Not just one, but dozens of them. They were all thinking the same thing. I couldn't believe it. My eyes went around the room, staring at all the innocent faces that were covering murderous minds. *Kill Calvin, kill Calvin, oh God, how I'd love to kill Calvin.* Their thoughts roared in my mind.

"Actually," said the second purser, "as much as I'd like to kill Calvin, I can't. I'm ineligible. Only a passenger is allowed to kill Calvin."

I held on to the bar for support, and said, "I think you'd better explain."

10

AFTER a while, The Prisoner stopped going to the women who were brought by truck to the camp each month. The women were the scourings of the brothels of Benghazi. They were unwashed and shapeless, long past the freshness of youth, and in any other circumstance the men of the camp would have rejected them scornfully. But these were men who now loved without women, who were enjoined by a fierce discipline from seeking the traditional substitute, and so the day before the monthly visit was marked by a keen anticipation, heroic posturings, and a ribald good humor. On the day of the visit there was an animal roar when the truck came through the gates, a rush to claim the dubious prizes, and later on, after the women had left, the inevitable braggings of who had done what, and how many times.

In the beginning, The Prisoner was no different than the men he led. He made the jokes, coupled with the whores, and if, in the evening, he did not join the crowing of the cocks, he nodded and smiled at each gasconade. But after the first few months, that changed, and he no longer went to the women. He was at the gates each month when the truck arrived, making sure that order was maintained, but once the men had made their choices, he would absent himself from the scene. He offered no explanations for his conduct, he simply stopped, and it was an indication of the esteem in which he was held by his men that his abstinence did not lessen him in their eyes. In a world in which masculinity was judged by the simplest of standards, they did not judge him as they would have judged themselves. He was, to them, beyond such measurements.

On that day each month when the other men went with the women, it was the custom of The Prisoner to retreat to the privacy of the squad-room tent, and while the rest of the camp was busily rutting, he would play his music on the phonograph. No Verdi or Puccini at those times, no opera at all, but music from a small collection of tapes that he kept at the bottom of the pile. "Rhinestone Cowboy" and "Laughter in the Rain," Elton John singing "Philadelphia Freedom," "San Antonio Stroll" with Tanya Tucker. Yeah, and "Dust and Ice." Songs of a certain part of his life, a certain year, and that one day each month was the only time when he allowed himself the luxury of thinking about it. Linda Rondstadt singing "You're No Good," and with the volume turned down low he could close his eyes and let himself drift away back to those days when the four of them would lie around for hours in the Poodle's rooms playing the music and drinking herbal tea.

In the beginning there were only three of them. Later, after the Poodle came along they were four, but at first there were only the three college seniors, and they were inseparable. Mutt, Jeff, and the Pom-Pom Queen, but those were names that they used only among themselves, private names for their private world. Mutt and Jeff because one of the guys was short and the other one tall, and the Pom-Pom Queen because she was a blooming beauty on the cheerleading squad, shaking those puffs of blue and gold at all the games. Mutt and Jeff, and the collective girl of their dreams, they went everywhere together, and they were tight. It was an odd situation, but they were tight, and they told themselves that they would always be, no matter what happened. And something was going to happen that senior year, they all knew that. With two best friends in love with the same girl, something had to happen, and they swore that when it did they would still be tight, all three of them. One of the guys was going to win her, one of the guys was going to lose her, but that wasn't going to break up the team. They were young enough and innocent enough to believe that, and during the senior year they went everywhere together, Mutt and Jeff paying court while the Pom-Pom Queen made up her mind. It was a neat little triangle until the Poodle came along.

Came along? She came tagging after them like a playful puppy, yipping at their heels, begging to belong. She was a pest, she was a pain, she was everybody's kid sister. Worst of all she was only a junior, but after a while it was easier to let her tag along than to try to chase her, and then there were four of them. She wasn't part of the team, but she was there, and she turned the triangle into a square. She balanced things out. She was as dark as the Pom-Pom Queen was fair, as eager as the Pom-Pom Queen was cool, as concerned with the woes of the world as the Pom-Pom Queen was indifferent. She was the Poodle, and in the spring of seventy-five it was in her rooms that they gathered to lie around, drink her herbal tea, and listen to the music.

Seems like maybe half my life
Been driving down some bumpy road
Eating the dust that I make for myself,
Hauling some other man's load.

The Prisoner hummed along, thinking back to those bittersweet days. Sweet because the Pom-Pom Queen had been the first of his loves. He had loved others since, perhaps more fervently, but the Pom-Pom Queen had been the first, and hers was the love with the place in his memory. Sweet, too, because of Jeff. Now he was bound by knife and blood to twenty-two brothers whose destinies were entwined with his in a fashion far removed from a simple college friendship; but when he thought about those days, and how it had been with Mutt and Jeff traveling down the road together, the memories had to be sweet. Sweet, as well, because of the Poodle, who had started out as the little sister, and who had turned into something quite different.

Sweet, but bitter, as well. Bitter because someone had to win, someone had to lose, and he had been the loser. Bitter because, after the loss, he had realized for the first time that the cards had been stacked against him. Bitter because, despite all the promises, the team was never the same after that. And bitter because of what happened to the Poodle.

Other half of my life it seems
I'm driving up some icy hill
Sliding back more than I'm making up,
Cursing the cold and the chill.

Humming along, The Prisoner would rest, allowing himself the luxury of those bittersweet memories, and after a while he would sleep. It was always a peaceful sleep, with none of the horrors that visited him in the night. He was aware of this difference, and it was one of the reasons that he allowed himself the monthly luxury. He was a man of dedication, and he knew that such memories defined a weakness within him, but he was willing to trade the weakness for the sake of sleep.

11

IT took Vince over a week to get to Carmine Giardelli, and during that time he cooled his heels at the Royal Buccaneer Hotel in Atlantic City. The gambling czar was unavailable. He was in Vegas for the weekend. He was in Miami on urgent business. He had to go to San Juan for a day. And so on. Mr. Giardelli would be back in Atlantic City shortly, Vince was told, just be patient.

Patience was too much to expect, but Vince had played the game, he had waited, and now Giardelli was back. Vince paced the length of the living room as he waited for the summons to see the big man, his shoes sinking into ankle-deep carpet, his fingers curled around a pony of brandy that was almost as old as he was. His suite at the Royal Buccaneer was middle-America's vision of what Atlantic City was all about. It had a sunken marble bath, a sunken marble living room, and sunken marble windows that opened onto a sunken marble sea. It had a candy-cane couch, a heart-shaped waterbed, and a spiral staircase that went nowhere. It had black and red flocked-velvet wallpaper, crimson drapes, and a walk-in closet big enough to hide a hippo. It had a *faux* Monet in the bathroom, a *faux* Van Gogh in the bedroom, and a lithograph of Elvis over the chrome and onyx bar. It had the style and warmth of a scream in the night, and it was all on the house.

Everything was on the house; Vince was comped. The suite, his food and drink, the services of a butler should he wish them, all came to him with the compliments of the management. Only the highest of rollers were comped that way, high credit, low risk players who could be counted on to drop a bundle at the tables two times out of three. For the Royal Buck, as for any other casino hotel, it was simply good business to comp the heavy hitters, and it was good business to comp a distinguished visitor, as well. Vince was distinguished. He had been sent by Lewis Whitney, he was there to see Carmine Giardelli, and that was enough to get him the same sort of treatment that would have been lavished on an Oklahoma oil man who bet with both hands.

Giardelli's man arrived promptly at nine. His name was Anthony, and he was young and round-faced. His suit was made of shantung silk, his shoes had been made on the bench, and his cologne was a breath of fresh mint. He smiled easily.

"Are you comfortable here?" he asked. "Everything to your satisfaction?"

"Everything's fine," Vince assured him.

"Mister Gee wants you to be comfortable. Anything you want, just ask for it."

"I'll do that. When do I see him?"

"In a minute, I have to go over you first. Nothing personal, just part of the routine."

Vince moved his feet apart, and held out his arms. Anthony's fingers probed quickly and expertly for weapons or wires. Close up, his minty cologne had an overtone of freshly cut grass. "You're hard as a rock," he said. "You work out?"

"When I can."

"I never seem to find the time,"

"What's the cologne?"

Anthony looked surprised and pleased. "Kentucky Spring. You like it?"

"It's you. It is definitely you."

Carmine Giardelli was the lay-off man for every major sports book between Washington and Toronto. Anything that the local book couldn't handle, anything too big or too complex, went to Giardelli, and "laying it off with Carmine" was a stock expression in the business. He didn't handle horses, but in football, basketball, baseball, and hockey Giardelli was to the local bookmaker what Lloyds of London was to the insurance underwriter. He was the specialist, he handled the overflow, he made the books balance.

Giardelli kept a penthouse apartment at the Royal Buck. It was soberly decorated, with none of the glitz of the luxury suites downstairs. Anthony led the way to a room that was bare except for a Ping-Pong table. Giardelli and a woman were playing, both standing back from the table and slamming power shots mixed with cute little slices. They grunted when they hit the ball, their faces ran with sweat, and their Reeboks squeaked on the floor. Giardelli wore only shorts. He was a tall man in his sixties with a lined face and lively eyes. The woman wore shorts and a halter top. Her lithe body said that she was about twenty, but her face swore that her body was lying. They both saw Vince come into the room, but they didn't stop playing. They were good, reminding Vince of the films he had seen of the Chinese masters of the game. The rally went on until Giardelli's backhand clipped the edge of the table, and fell away for the point.

"Seventeen–sixteen," he announced. He glanced at Vince. "Be right with you. I'm on a roll here."

"Roll, my ass," said the woman. Her voice was hard and edgy.

"Take your time," said Vince.

The action surged back and forth, and the score went to twenty–nineteen, Giardelli up. He said to Vince, "Just another minute while I put her away."

"Put your money where your mouth is," said the woman. "Fifty says you don't make it."

"We already got fifty on the game."

"Another fifty on the point."

"Sucker bet. You got it."

Giardelli stepped back to serve. The woman reached behind her back, and untied her halter top. She pulled it over her head, and let it drop to the floor. She moved up and down on her toes, ready to receive, and her breasts bounced with the motion. Anthony, beside Vince, made a sound deep in his throat. Vince glanced at him. His lips were tight with disapproval.

Giardelli grinned, and said, "Forget it, Shelley, it's not gonna work."
Shelley snapped, "Shut up and serve."
"They're cute, but I've seen 'em before."
"Serve."
"Take more than that to . . ."
"Serve, God damn it."
Giardelli served. The ball broke sharply away from Shelley's forehand for an ace. She waved at it futilely, then slammed her paddle on the table in disgust.
"Bingo," said Giardelli. "Pay me."
Shelley threw her paddle at him. It hit him in the forehead, and bounced to the floor. She marched out of the room.
Giardelli called after her, "Hey, you owe me a cee," but she was gone.
"You're bleeding," said Anthony.
There was a cut over Giardelli's left eyebrow, oozing blood. Anthony grabbed a towel from a hook on the wall, and dabbed at the cut. Giardelli pushed him away roughly.
"It's nothing," he said.
"There's blood all over your face." Anthony tried to dab again.
"Leave it alone," Giardelli ordered. He took the towel, and pressed it to his forehead. "That is one hell of a woman, but she sure is a lousy loser."
"Better let me put something on that cut."
"I'll take care of it. You think I never saw my own blood before?"
Anthony said in a prissy voice, "You should wash it out, and then get some iodine."
"Christ, you sound like an Italian grandmother."
"It could get infected."
"Anthony, she cut me with a Ping-Pong paddle, not a rusty knife." Giardelli held out his hand to Vince. "Sorry you came in on the middle of this."
"Happens in the best of families," said Vince.
"Give me a minute to clean myself up, and I'll be right with you."
"Take your time, and take care of that cut."
"Another Italian grandmother. You got some Italian blood in you?"
"You never know, do you?"

"Anthony, take Mister Bonepart into the living room and give him a drink." Giardelli took the towel away from his forehead, and looked at the red stain. "Christ, she got me good."

Vince followed Anthony into the living room, and found a comfortable chair. Anthony asked him what he wanted to drink.

"There was some dynamite cognac in my room."

Anthony nodded his approval. "Napier, thirty years old. You've got the palate."

Anthony went to the bar, and Vince said to his back, "Do they always play for blood?"

"The boss is a good player. Shelley just thinks she is."

"She's quite a girl."

"Girl? Did you see that face? That's wrinkle city."

"That's also a great body."

"From the neck up, she's gotta be forty. She is also a dumb cunt with no class."

"You always talk that way about your boss's women?"

Anthony brought the cognac. "I've been with Mister Gee for eight years. The women, they come and they go. This one, she'll be gone before the robins come home."

"You comfortable?" asked Giardelli from the door. He had put on a terry cloth robe, and there was a strip of plaster over one eye. He took a glass of mineral water from Anthony, and settled into a deep sofa. After a thirsty sip, he said, "So tell me about my old friend, Lewis Whitney."

"He's fine. He sends his best."

"I never see him anymore. He used to come down here for the weekend with that lovely wife of his, but now I never see him."

"He's a busy man."

"That's no excuse, we're all busy. You gotta make time to enjoy, you tell him I said that."

"I will, and I'll try not to take up too much of your time."

"Hey, for a friend of Lewis, I got all the time in the world. He said I should listen to you, so I'm listening. Something about a fix on a basketball game?"

"That's right, next Saturday night."

Giardelli shrugged. "So what else is new?"

"You don't seem surprised."

"Listen, my friend, you know how many college games get shaved every week? Team is favored to win by seven, but they only win by three. The team still wins, but a couple of players make a payday, and some wiseguy wins a bundle. Happens all the time, it's as American as pepperoni pizza."

"I didn't say anything about a shave. It's a dump."

Giardelli leaned forward. "An actual dump? You mean the favorite is gonna lose?"

"That's it."

"I don't get it, why bother? A shave is just as good, and the team doesn't take the loss."

"That's the way it's going down."

"Crazy, that's crazy." Giardelli took a cigar from the humidor on the table beside him. He offered one to Vince, who shook his head. Giardelli lit the cigar carefully, and blew smoke. "I don't understand people any more. Maybe it's me, but I don't understand. What teams?"

"Polk and Van Buren."

"Never heard of 'em."

"Division Two."

"That's why I never heard of 'em. Anthony, call Caruso and check it out."

Anthony went to the telephone, and spoke briefly. He hung up, and said, "Polk over Van Buren by five and a half."

"Any heavy action?"

"Not so far. Caruso wants to know, should he put a flag on it."

"Not yet. We'll see."

Shelley came into the room, and the conversation stopped. She had changed into tapered slacks and a frilly blouse. Both men watched as she went to the bar. Anthony did not move to help her. She poured gin and tonic into a glass, and stirred with a finger. She licked the finger, and walked over to Giardelli. She threw two fifties in his lap.

"Does your head hurt?" she asked.

"No." Giardelli put the money in the pocket of his robe.

"Next time I'll use something heavier."

"You do it again, and I'll show you what really hurts."

"You ever do that, and I'm out the door."

"I don't have to do it. Anthony'll do it for me."

"Him?" She stared at Anthony, who was leaning against the wall. "I don't think so, Carmine, I really don't. If he ever touched me, he'd never sleep easy again."

"I'd sleep," said Anthony. His voice was cold. "I never have trouble sleeping."

"Hey, loosen up, the two of you," said Giardelli. He looked uncomfortable. "We got a guest here. Shelley, this is Mister Bonepart."

Shelley looked at Vince with interest. "You play table tennis?"

"I used to. We called it Ping-Pong."

"Table tennis," she insisted. "You want a game? Dollar a point."

Giardelli said admiringly, "What a hustler. She's gotta make her money back."

Vince smiled, and shook his head.

"I'll spot you three points," said Shelley.

Vince shook his head again.

"And I'll keep my clothes on."

"Some other time."

"Shelley, we're talking business here," said Giardelli.

"Pardon me for breathing. You want me to go?"

"No, it's nothing you can't hear."

"Can I order something up?" Her voice lost its hard edge, and turned little-girl sweet. "I'm hungry. Losing always makes me hungry."

"So does winning. Order whatever you want."

"I think maybe lobster."

"This time of night? You looking for indigestion?"

"I can eat lobster anytime."

Giardelli nodded to Anthony, who moved to the telephone. "Order a lobster, and steak for the rest of us."

"Not for me," said Vince.

"Order for four, maybe he'll change his mind." Giardelli turned his attention to Vince. "So, go ahead, what's this fix got to do with me?"

"The people that I represent . . ." Vince paused, and Giardelli nodded an agreement that the people did not need to be named. "These people would be very happy if the scam doesn't go down."

"Very noble, very civic-minded. All they got to do is blow the whistle."

"Vince shook his head. "My people don't want publicity. They are very anxious to see that the game gets played, but that it gets played straight."

"How do you expect to do that?"

"I want to get to whoever put the fix in. I want it called off."

"And you think I can do that?"

"I was hoping that you could point me in the right direction."

Giardelli spent time with his cigar. He inspected the length of the ash, he drew, he inspected it again. He sighed. "After a while you get a kind of a reputation in this business. People say 'lay if off with Carmine.' They say 'Carmine, he knows everything.' They say a quarterback in some jerkwater school in Oklahoma gets a sore elbow, and Carmine knows about it. They say the goalie in Calgary has a fight with his wife, and Carmine hears about it. They say all kinds of crazy things, but to tell you the truth, most of that is bullshit. Sure, I hear things, everybody hears things, but I don't pay much attention to that kind of talk. I can't afford to. I got enough to do just running my business, and this thing that you're talking about, it's not my business."

"You've heard nothing?"

"Nothing."

"And there's no way you could find out?"

Giardelli said patiently, "Let me explain something. If the fix is really in on this game . . ."

"There's no question about that."

"Okay, you come to me from Lewis, so I know that you're not some kind of a kook. So it's real, but if it's real there's only two ways it could happen. Either the guys who are pulling it are connected, or they're free-lance. If they're connected, I would know about it, and if they're not then there is no fucking way I would know who they are. So there it is. I got nothing for you."

Shelley went to a console against the wall, and flipped a switch. Loud music filled the room. She snapped her fingers, and swayed to the music.

Giardelli said, "Turn that off, we're talking."

Shelley ignored him. She did a little dance step, and twirled around.

Anthony went to the console, and turned off the music. Shelley glared at him, and kept on dancing.

Vince asked, "And there's no one you could send me to?"

"No one who would know more than I do. Look, Vince . . . okay to call you Vince?"

"Sure."

"Vince, even if I could do something like this, which I can't, once a deal gets started it has a momentum, you know? People put in the money, and you can't reverse something like that. Not once the money is in."

"My people understand that. They know that the bottom line is always money, and so they've authorized me to make you an offer."

Giardelli threw up his hands. "I just finished telling you . . ."

"Please, hear me out. They'd like you to act as broker on this deal. They're willing to guarantee a lump-sum payment to cover everybody's losses if the fix doesn't happen. The money would be paid directly to you, and you would see that it reached the proper parties, no questions asked. Your fee would be included. The only stipulation is that the game is played on the level."

Giardelli did his cigar routine again. When he was satisfied with the ash, he asked, "How much of a sum?"

"Half a mil."

"That's an impressive figure. Your people must be anxious."

"They're very . . . concerned."

"I can see that." Giardelli stared at the ceiling. "It's tempting, very tempting."

Vince waited.

"And I'd like to oblige Lewis."

"He would be grateful, and he'd show his gratitude."

"But I have to say no. I wouldn't know where to start. There's nothing I can do for you, Vince, nothing at all."

"That's final?"

"Final. No hard feelings?"

"Certainly not."

"Then that's it."

Not quite, thought Vince. It's time to tap.

He went into Giardelli's head. The old man was playing it straight. He knew nothing about the fix.

He went into Shelley's head. She was Domino.

He stood up, and said, "I want to thank you for taking the time to see me."

"You going? Those steaks'll be up in a minute."

"Sorry, but I have things to do."

"Whatever you say. I wish I could have helped you."

Shelley came dancing over, still without the music. "You going?"

Vince nodded.

"Come back any time," said Giardelli. "You'll be welcome."

"Table tennis next time," said Shelley. "I promise to take it easy on you."

"It's a deal,"said Vince, "but we'll have to play by my rules."

"You got special rules?"

"That's right. Gibraltar rules."

Her eyes narrowed, and she frowned. "I play American rules. That's good enough for me."

"We'll see," said Vince. "Maybe you'll like mine better."

He went back to his room. He stripped the top sheet from his bed, put it in the bathtub, and let the cold water run. When the sheet was soaked through, he wrung it out, and brought it back to the bedroom. He went to the bar, made himself a drink, and settled down to wait. He figured to wait at least an hour, but the knock on his door came after only twenty minutes. She stood in the doorway dressed for the street, a cape thrown over her shoulders. The cape hid her hands.

"We have to talk," she said. "Do I come in?"

"Of course."

He stood back to let her pass. As she came by him, he chopped at the base of her neck with the edge of his palm. She went down noiselessly, and the pistol in her hand slid out from under the cape. He picked it up, kicked the door shut, and carried her into the bedroom. He put her on the bed, and checked her eyes and pulse. She was still out, but not for long. He stripped her clothes off, and found another pistol tucked in the back of her waistband, and a thin blade taped to her thigh. He wrapped her in the wet sheet, rolling her over and over.

He left her head free, but the rest of her was trussed as tight as a Christmas turkey.

He waited again, watching her, and again he was struck by the apparent disparity between a youthful body and a middle-aged face. After a while, he decided that it wasn't just age. It was the face of a woman who had seen too much, and who had been marked by what she had seen.

Her eyelids flickered. Her eyes opened. Her eyeballs rolled wildly. She tried to move, and found that she could not. She strained silently against the wet sheet once, again, and then stopped trying. She breathed in deeply, and breathed out slowly to relax herself. She looked up at Vince, and her eyes were calm. It was an impressive performance. She had gone from unconsciousness to full awareness, and an acceptance of her situation, in a matter of seconds. It was more than impressive, it was wholly professional.

"Who are you?" she asked in an even voice.

"Just a messenger."

"You said something upstairs."

"Gibraltar rules. That was just to get your attention. Your mission is aborted. Your instructions are to discontinue the operation at once, roll it back. The fix is off, that game has to be played on the level."

"What are the chances of getting out of this straitjacket?"

"After a while. Right now I want you immobile. You came in here carrying."

"What did you expect?"

"Exactly that. Do you understand the message?"

"You're starting in the middle. I don't even know who you are. How about some ID?"

"You know better than that. I could show you all the ID in the world, and it wouldn't mean anything. Your code name is Domino, your mission is to kill the bulldog, and your orders came from David Ogden. That's all the ID I need."

She accepted that. "You said abort?"

"More than that. I don't know how you set up the fix, but you're going to have to unfix it, make it like it never happened."

She managed to shake her head. "You said something about Gibraltar rules. If you know the words, you know what they mean. The mission can't be aborted. We're in the time frame."

"The man who gave you the mission is dead."

The lines in her face deepened. "I read the papers."

"Other people are running the show now, and the decision is to abort."

"That's their decision, not mine."

"You're not in a position to refuse."

"I have no choice. Gibraltar rules."

"Screw the rules, your job is dead." Vince felt his anger flaring, and he throttled it down. "Look, I can roll this thing back without you, but it would be a lot easier if you worked with me. How did you set up the fix?"

She said nothing.

"Come on, we're talking about a lousy basketball game, not nuclear weapons."

Again nothing.

"This doesn't make any sense. No matter what the rules are, this is crazy."

"It doesn't have to make sense. David Ogden wanted it, and that's all that matters."

"David Ogden had tumors eating at his brain when he gave you those orders. He wasn't responsible."

"David Ogden with half a brain was more responsible than any man I ever knew. This is what he wanted, and this is what he gets."

"You're going to have to tell me, Shelley, one way or another."

She smiled. It was a hell of a time to smile, but there it was. She said, "What do you know about the *Mukhabarat?*"

"The Iraqi Security Service."

"Number Ten Flowering Square?"

"Their interrogation center in Baghdad."

"I was in there for eleven days. Do you know what it's like in there? There's nothing refined about the Iraqi technique, nothing sophisticated. I was beaten every day, over and over. I was raped every night, over and over. I took it for eleven days, and I didn't talk."

"Everybody talks."

"I didn't. On the twelfth day, David Ogden got me out."

"Nobody gets out of there."

"I did. An exchange, the kind you don't read about in the newspapers. David Ogden brought me back from hell. So if David Ogden wants something . . . wanted . . . he's going to get it. No matter what."

"You're still going to have to tell me."

She shook her head and he saw the look in her eyes. He had seen that look before in the eyes of the righteous and convinced. He had seen it in the eyes of a backwoods preacher shouting down sin. He had seen it in the eyes of a twelve-story leaper at the moment when she knew that she was really going to jump. He had seen it in the eyes of an Afghani guerrilla about to charge a Soviet tank with a hunting rifle in his hands. He had seen it, and he knew what it meant.

She was still smiling. "Do you think you can beat it out of me? You're welcome to try."

"No, I'm not going to do anything like that. I don't have to."

He prepared himself for a Delta tap, a deep probe on all levels for as far as he could go. He went into her head, entirely focused on what he was doing. He never heard a footstep behind him, or any other sound. Later, all he could remember from the moment were the odors of fresh mint and newly cut grass, just before the world fell in on him.

He came up out of it with a bitter taste in his mouth, and his head throbbing like an angry pulse. He opened his eyes, and tried to focus. He was lying on the bed, and there was someone lying next to him. The someone felt like a sack full of sand that was pressing against his back.

"He's coming around, lieutenant."

There were two uniforms standing over him, and two more in suits. He tried to put a hand to his aching head, but his hands wouldn't move. They were cuffed behind his back.

"Keep still," said one of the uniforms. "Don't go moving around."

The other uniform was talking into a mouthpiece, and someone on the other end squawked back at him. He clicked a button, and announced, "Wagon's on its way."

Vince tried to shift his weight away from the sack of sand. The first uniform bent over, and slapped him across the face. "I told you to keep still."

"Lay off," said one of the suits. He squatted next to the bed. "Can you stand up?"

Vince mumbled, "What's happening?"

"Can you stand?"

"Why should I?"

"I'm gonna read you your rights, and I want you standing when I do it."

"What did I do?"

"Come on, get up. Big guy like you can stand on his feet."

The suit put a hand under Vince's elbow, and pulled him up. He stood next to the bed, swaying. The other suit was down on the floor. There was a pistol lying on the carpet, and he was trying to poke it with a pencil into a transparent bag. The first suit read Vince his rights, and said, "Did you understand that?"

"I heard it, but I don't remember it. What's happening here?"

"Turn around and take a look."

Vince stood without moving. He did not want to turn around. He knew now that there was a body on the bed, and he did not want to see it. He thought about the *Mukhabarat* and Number Ten Flowering Square. He had known her for only a few hours, but he still did not want to see it.

The suit grinned at him. "What's the matter, got the jumps? Big guy like you got the jumps?"

Vince took a deep breath, and turned around. The body on the bed was what was left of Carmine Giardelli. He let out his breath, and said, "When do I get to make my phone call?"

12

MARTHA and her five kids rode the double chairlift that serviced the north face of Hightower Mountain, rising up over meadows of spun-sugar snow and slopes that were dotted with skiers carving tracks. Martha rode with Lila Simms, George and Chicken had the chairs up ahead, while Pam and Linda rode behind. Below them the countryside stretched out in a checkerboard pattern of blacks and whites, its geometry broken by a snaking river and the coil of the highway that bent around the base of the hill. It was their first trip of the day up the mountain, and it was the sort of day that skiers cherish: fresh powder, clear skies, and an edge to the cold that sets the blood singing. A plume of snow from a neighboring peak was a feather in the cap of the day.

Lila, sitting next to Martha on the lift, pointed to the slope below where a pair of skiers were carving patterns. "Look at that," she said excitedly. "Fresh powder there. I want some of that."

"You'll get it," Martha assured her. "It isn't going anywhere."

"You get enough skiers on it and they'll pack it down to nothing." The girl was dressed all in blue: ski pants, parka, and knitted cap. Even her skis and boots were the same shade of blue. She waved her arm in an exuberant circle to take in the mountain, the sky, and the snow. "Fresh powder, I love it. Powder up to the hips, that's heaven."

"If you want really deep powder, you have to go west. Ever skied out there?"

Lila's face lit up. "No, but I'd love to. Do you ever take groups there?"

"Uh . . ." Martha had to recall her rôle as a guide. "Sure, once in a while."

"Do you think I could come along sometimes?" Lila flashed a bouncy grin. "I'd love to ski Aspen, or Vail, or one of those places."

The girl's good humor was infectious, and Martha smiled back. "Hey, we just got here. Let's do this mountain first."

"I'm sorry, I didn't mean to sound greedy. I know how lucky I was to get this trip, and everyone's been so friendly. Pam, and Linda, and George . . . and Chicken."

Martha picked up the hesitation. "Any problems with Chicken?"

"No, not at all. It's just that he's different."

That's for sure, thought Martha. "How do you mean?"

"Well, he's cute, but he's sort of crazy, too."

Cute? Chicken? What does this kid use for brains?

"He keeps looking at me all the time."

Great. I'm supposed to be keeping this virgin *intacto*, and one of my team has the hots for her. "Let me know if he bothers you. I'll keep him in line."

"He doesn't bother me." The sunny smile was back. "I sort of like him. He reminds me of someone I once knew."

And if he puts one finger on you I'll turn him into a soprano.

Lila giggled. "Not a person, actually. It was a puppy I once had. He was a cute little fella, but sort of crazy. Always peeing on the carpet or barking in the middle of the night. Crazy, but cute."

"And Chicken reminds you of . . . ?"

"He has the same sort of look on his face sometimes."

"Some puppy," Martha said, laughing. "Look, I don't want to sound pompous, but we tend to discourage personal relationships on these trips. You know?"

Lila nodded solemnly, but Martha knew that the message had not gotten through. It was a disquieting thought, for a romance was the last thing that she needed right now. Getting Lila out of Rockhill had been the obvious opening move in a defense against Sextant, but Martha knew that the girl's vulnerability had only been lessened, not eliminated. She knew that she was up against an accomplished professional, and that any defense she might mount against Sextant would be no more effective than the tools she had to work with: four teenage kids without field experience. She damned the Agency for giving them a job with such unattractive odds, but she comforted herself with the manner in which most of the kids were conducting themselves. Pam and Linda had quickly formed a female bond with Lila, and George had assumed the rôle of the considerate, if disinterested, older brother.

The weak link was Chicken, who was so out of tune with the others. On the basis of his record at the Center, he had no business being on the job. His grades were poor, his attitudê indifferent, and, most important, he was losing his ability to work head-to-head. Along with the other members of his class, he had arrived at the Center at the age of eleven with all the latent abilities of a sensitive, but during the past year, when those abilities should have been peaking, they had started to ebb. Often he could not hear what the others were saying when they went head-to-head, often he couldn't get through when he tried to speak to them that way, and always the effort was accompanied by a severe pain at the base of his skull. Chicken was on his way to becoming a deuce, a failed ace.

The physicians at the Center had language to explain the erosion of Chicken's skills. They spoke about the neurological imbalance that lay at the core of a sensitive's ability, and how, in some few cases, the neurological network slowly returned to a balanced, or normal, state. The condition was rare, but not unknown, and once the balance was complete the skills were gone. It happened perhaps once in every five hundred cases that an ace turned into a deuce, and there were always one or two of them around the Center. There was no way in which they could be sent back into the normal world, for they knew too much, and so they stayed bound to a life that had abandoned them. They became the hewers of wood and the fetchers of water, auxiliaries to those who once had been their peers. To be a deuce among aces was a sensitive's nightmare, and Chicken was facing just such a life.

Poor bastard, Martha thought. Poor, pathetic bastard.

She pushed the thought aside; it was time to check the troops. To the lift in back of her, she flashed, *Pam? Linda?*

Pam here.

Linda here. Any instructions?

Just keep your heads open. Report anything that looks even slightly suspicious. George? Chicken?

George here.

Chicken? No answer. *Chicken, do you copy?* Still no answer. *Damn it, Chicken . . .* Martha caught herself. *George, tell him to keep his eyes open and stay alert.*

You try telling him. He's off in another world. I think he's in love.

Just what we needed. You mean Lila?

Who else?

That isn't love, it's teenage lust.

I know that, and you know that, but Chicken doesn't. Maybe if you fixed him up with her . . .

That's enough of that. Nobody's getting fixed up on this trip.

Hey, who made that rule? asked Pam from behind, and Linda chimed in, *You mean we're supposed to live like nuns?*

I said enough, Martha told them. *George, tell Chicken what I said, and the rest of you keep alert.*

George poked Chicken, and said, "Martha says to keep your eyes open."

Chicken nodded absently. Open for what? Villains? Guys in black hats? His mind was on Lila, but not on the job. The girl attracted him, he wanted her to notice him, but he didn't know how to get her attention. He had little experience with "normal" girls, even the females at the Center seemed always to defeat him, and he was painfully aware of his limitations. His appearance was against him. He was overgrown and clumsy for his age, with a moon face, squinty eyes, and features that were not yet fully formed. He had no social graces, words did not come easily to him, and when he talked with girls he tended to mutter the first idiocy that came into his mind. So he did crazy things. He stole trucks at the Center, raced them and crashed them. He stunted, he bragged, he lied outrageously. He did everything he could to get the world to pay attention, but all that the world ever did was to frown.

So far, Lila hadn't frowned, but she hadn't paid much attention to him, either. Still, he had the feeling that she liked him, and there had to be a way to make her notice him, a way to light up her eyes. But, as always, he couldn't think of what to do, or to say. Angry at his helplessness, he gripped the safety bar in front of him, and squeezed. He squeezed as hard as he could, as if squeezing could give him an answer. He looked down at his hands. Fastened to the safety bar was a metal plaque that bore a warning. DO NOT BOUNCE ON THE CHAIRS.

Yeah, he thought. Yeah.

He shifted his weight in the seat, and gave a little bounce. The chair shivered, and the tremor passed up through the supporting bar to the cable. The chair rocked back and forth. He did it again, just a little bounce, and the same thing happened. One solid bounce, he figured, would send the chairs rocking all along the cable. He was about to try it when he felt George's hand close over his wrist in a tight grip. George twisted and squeezed, and pain shot up Chicken's arm.

"Hey, cut it out," he said.

"Don't do it again."

"Do what?"

"Bounce."

"I wasn't."

"You were, and you were about to do it again. That's kid stuff, Chicken, and it's dangerous. Get her attention some other way."

"You're hurting my wrist."

"If you try it again," George said sweetly, "I will break your fucking hand."

"Look, I really wasn't . . ."

"You were. You were about to pull one of your stupid stunts."

"How did you . . . ?" Chicken knew the answer before he finished the question. George had been in his head, and he hadn't been aware of it. He had felt nothing. The knowledge hurt more than the pain in his wrist, and he muttered, "You can let go now. I won't do anything."

George took his hand away. He stared straight ahead as if nothing had happened. They rode together silently, until Chicken, rubbing his wrist, said, "We used to be friends."

They had been more than friends. George and Chicken, Pam and

Linda, Terry Krazewski back at the Center in the infirmary—as members of the same class they had been taught to think of themselves as brothers and sisters. George sighed. "Look, I'm still your friend, still your brother, but shit, Chicken, this last year . . . there sure are times when you burn my ass. And it isn't just me."

"I know." Chicken looked away. "The others, too."

"You really can't blame them, some of the things you do. You act so crazy sometimes."

"That's me, the crazy Chicken. You ever stop to wonder why?"

George shifted uncomfortably in his seat. It was a subject they avoided. "You mean because you're losing it?"

"It's getting worse."

"I know. I was in and out of your head just now, and you didn't even know it."

Chicken said quietly, "It scares me, George."

"It would scare me, too."

"I get scared and I do crazy things. It's like I can't help myself."

"I understand."

"I don't want to be a deuce, George. I think I'd rather die than be a deuce."

"Don't talk that way."

"Why not? You'd talk that way, too, if it happened to you."

"Is it totally gone?"

"No, sometimes it's there. They've been giving me medication. They say it may help. It's a zinc oxide combination. It's supposed to slow things down, maintain the imbalance."

"Does it work?"

"Sometimes." Chicken shrugged. "Most of the time it doesn't do a damn thing for me."

"So what happens next?"

"We wait and see. That's all they can say. Wait and see."

With unconscious cruelty, George said, "That isn't much."

"It's all I've got."

George searched for words, and found none. He finally said, "Hang in there."

"Yeah."

Two chairs back, Pam and Linda fretted over Martha's ban on social activity. They were accustomed to the easygoing sexual standards of the Center where, once you were old enough, the only taboo was making it with a member of your own class. They had assumed that the same standards would apply in the field, and now this.

"It's going to be a cold couple of days," said Linda.

"Cold all over," Pam agreed. "Cold on the hill, and cold in bed."

"You know that big fireplace back at the lodge?"

"Big enough to roast a rhino."

"I was sort of looking forward to sitting there tonight with some mulled wine, soft music, and a slab of muscle."

"Anybody in mind? We just got here."

"How long does it take?"

"Not long," Pam admitted, "but you'd better forget it. You heard what she said."

"She can't watch us all the time."

"She's got eyes all over."

"It isn't fair, she's treating us like kids."

"We are kids," Pam pointed out. "And we're on a job."

"Come on, you've heard the way the aces talk. Being on the job doesn't mean that you can't have some fun. The trouble with Martha is that she's old, she's forgotten what it's like. She's got to be thirty, at least."

Thirty-four next November. It was Martha, jumping into their heads. *An old crone. An absolute hag.*

"Damn," Linda whispered.

Let me have your attention, I have some points to make.

Yes, Martha.

Yes, Martha.

Point number one. When you're in the field, you never know who might be listening in. This time it was me, next time it could be somebody nasty. So keep it buttoned up.

Right, Martha.

Okay, Martha.

Point number two. Since your thoughts seem to be concentrated somewhere below the waist, let me drop one little word into your shell-pink ears. The word is rape. It's a short, ugly, nasty word, and we're here to make sure that it doesn't happen to the kid who's sitting next to me. It is something that should not happen to any woman, and it is something that must not happen to this one. I didn't think that I'd have to explain that to two females, but apparently I do. You are here for one reason. You are not here to have fun, and you are not here to meet boys. You are here to protect Lila Simms, and you will do exactly that, even if it means, as one of you so quaintly put it, that you have to live like nuns for a couple of days. Is that clear?

Yes, Martha.

Yes, Martha.

Okay, carry on.

Both girls giggled.

All right, I mean don't carry on. I mean . . . Martha allowed herself to laugh. *You know what I mean.*

The chairlift ended just above the three-thousand-foot level at the top of the Cascade Trail, a steep slope, studded with moguls, that dropped into a series of ess-turns before it broadened into a well-kept *piste.* The temperature at the top was minus four, and a strong wind swirled the snow. Martha led the kids to the lip of the trail, and spoke to her own gang head-to-head.

Pay attention. If I thought I could get away with it, I'd keep us all together in a pack, but I don't want Lila wondering why. After all, this isn't a ski school and there's no reason to stay together, so we'll have to split up. I'll stay as close to her as I can, and the rest of you try to keep in sight. Remember, no booming off by yourselves. If you get separated, try to join up, and if you can't we'll all meet for lunch at the cafeteria. Understood?

There were three affirmatives.

Chicken?

Nothing.

Chicken?

But all that Chicken heard was a faint buzzing as she tried to get through. He strained to catch her words, but they just weren't there. The ability, which once had been so natural to him, now was a sometime thing that came and went, racking his head with pain. He felt the familiar anger building inside of him, and the pressure. The hell with it, he thought, and while the others were checking their bindings and using the lip balm, he turned to Lila, and said in a low voice, "What do you say we bomb the liftline?"

She looked at him curiously. "Do what?"

"Straight down the hill under the chairlift. Shake up the mountain."

"Is that the way you ski?"

"Sometimes. Come on, it's fun."

"It's also pretty hotdog."

"Nothing wrong with a little hotdog once in a while."

"I don't know. You mean, just us?"

"Sure, why not?"

She hesitated, and he knew that she was going to say yes, but just then Martha called out, "Okay, troops, let's hit it."

Martha did a graceful *rouade* to turn onto the track, and started down the slope. Pam, George, and Linda followed close behind. Lila looked at Chicken, shrugged helplessly, and followed the others. They skied the slope easily, not pressing, just working back and forth across the hill.

Chicken watched them go, and he did not move. She would have said yes, he knew it. He felt the pressure building in his head, felt it behind his eyes. He knew that he was close to the edge, ready to blow, and just for the moment a finger of sanity reached out and tried to pull him back. He brushed the finger aside. He jabbed his poles in the snow, and slid over the edge and onto the slope. He headed straight down the fall line, dropping into a racing tuck. Below him, Martha and the others were doing the hill in leisurely traverses.

Kid stuff, he thought. *Bomb the mountain.*

That's kid suff, too, if you keep your eyes open, he told himself. *How about trying it with your eyes shut?*

Come on.

Why not?

Can't ski with your eyes closed.

Who says?

You mean . . . all the way?

For as long as you can keep them closed. New way to play chicken.

Wow . . . first one to open his eyes . . . ?

You got it.

But there's only me.

Even better. If you have the balls for it.

You calling me chicken?

It's your move.

I like it.

Then do it.

Chicken closed his eyes. He was transported at once into a world of wind, speed, and darkness. He panicked, and opened his eyes. He jammed them shut again.

Open your eyes.

No,

Open them.

No.

He dropped down the hill like an elevator with its cable cut. He was totally out of control. Even if his eyes had been open, he would have been out of control. He kept them firmly shut. It was flight, it was fear, it was wild, it was . . .

Fun? Open your eyes.

No. *All the way this time. No matter what happens, I go all the way.*

All the way? Sinatra on skis?

He didn't go all the way. He didn't go very far at all. Skiing like that, he had to hit someone or something, and he did. He hit Martha. George and Linda were off to the side, out of the way. Lila and Pam saw him coming. They both called *track*, and scooted to safety. Martha, traversing the hill, had most of her back to him. Someone else called *track*, and she started to turn, but by then it was too late. Racing down the mountain with his eyes screwed shut, Chicken hit her squarely, knocked her over, and broke her leg.

Sextant saw the accident from where he stood in the lee of a slatted snow fence at the top of the Cascade Trail. He saw Chicken bomb the hill, saw him hit Martha, saw them both go down. He saw Chicken shake himself and get to his feet, but Martha did not move. He waited and watched. He watched as a small crowd gathered on the slope, watched as two red-jacketed ski patrolmen appeared, watched as they called for a stretcher-sled. Martha still had not moved, and he wondered if she might be dead. No such luck, he decided, not from a fall like that, and then he heard words drifting up the hill from the crowd.

". . . broken leg . . ."

". . . damn fool hotdog . . ."

"Where the hell is that sled?"

He watched as the sled appeared accompanied by two more patrolmen, watched as they loaded Martha onto it, watched as they started her down the hill with the kids following. He watched until the sled was out of sight. He nodded with deep satisfaction. He did not know who Martha was, did not know her name or her connection with his target. He knew only that his job had just been made easier.

He shifted his weight on the snow. His rented boots pinched at his toes, his rented skis were a touch too long, and his hastily bought ski pants were tight at the crotch. But despite these discomforts, he was fully at ease. He had been at ease on skis since childhood. Skiers cavorted on the slopes below, and he watched them with a mild contempt. He had been born and raised in the Julian Alps of Yugoslavia where children had skied as soon as they could walk. Skiing in that world had been a means of transportation, a necessity, and it amused him to see people ski for sport. Most of them look graceful enough, but he wondered how long they would have lasted in the mountains of his youth.

He lit a cigarette and breathed in deeply, savoring the combination of tobacco and frigid mountain air. From where he stood he could see, far below, the curve of the highway that wound around the base of the mountain. Further down that road, and out of sight, was the Northern Inn where his target and her friends were staying, and further still was the rented house where he had parked his three animals. He had left them with a case of beer and strict instructions to stay put, for his purpose this morning was only to reconnoiter. He needed an adjustment to the new terrain. He had expected to do his job back in Rockhill, he had not anticipated the sudden removal to a ski resort, but Sextant was nothing if not flexible. There or here, the job would be done.

The job, yes. He wondered at the nature of the job he had been given, although his wonder did not extend to questioning his orders.

To question an order from David Ogden was unthinkable to him, even an order that came from the grave. Still, he wondered. He had killed for David Ogden in the past. He had lied and stolen, he had inflicted tortures, and all for David Ogden. But rape? How strange that Ogden should ask this of him. Memory intruded on his thoughts, and he shivered. He knew that his forehead and his palms were damp. It was a familiar chill, one that came to him often, and it had nothing to do with the frigid air or the snow on which he stood. The chill was part of the memory. It had always been that way.

Why me, he wondered. Of all the people you could have chosen, David, why did you have to pick me? Did you want to see how icy I can be? Is that what this is, one final test to prove that I'm still the man you made me? Did you think that the memories would get in my way? No, David, I'm ice, all right. I don't have to prove that anymore, and if this is what you want, you'll get it. You always did. I'll do the job, David, don't worry about that, and fuck the memories.

The memories dated from 1943. He was six years old then, his name was Vlado Priol, and his father was part of a partisan band that operated against the occupying Germans in northern Slovenia. There were many such bands in Yugoslavia then, and this one was based two thousand meters high on the side of Mount Krn in the Julian Alps. The country there was wide and desolate, and in the wintertime the partisan camp was virtually impossible to reach for someone who was not a native of the region. Even if you were born in the shadow of Mount Krn, it still was a job of work. To make the trek you started from the bottom of the mountain in the morning, skiing first over miles of trackless terrain, through stands of snow-laden trees, and then along a ridge that was overhung with needles of ice. It snowed every morning in the wintertime, and you moved through it blindly. When the terrain tipped up you climbed for as long as you could on your skis, then took them off, strapped them onto your back, and kept climbing on foot. You climbed through the morning, around noon the snow would stop, and once the air was clear you could look back to see what you had left behind: a white world far below, with the town of Ravne and the railroad etched in. Then you started to climb again, laboring through most of the day until just before sunset when you came to an indentation in the mountainside about a mile across. It was a depression shaped like a punchbowl with steep and icy slopes, and on the far side of the bowl the north face rose up to form the dark peak that gave the mountain its name. At the base of that peak was a ridge that was dotted with caves, and it was in those caves that the partisans made their camp. They felt themselves to be safe there, protected by the mountain from their enemies.

The partisan band was led by a man named Cankar, but that was not his real name. Like many in the partisan movement he had adopted a *nom de guerre*, in his case the name of an early Slovenian playwright and patriot. This modern-day Cankar was a lean and leathery old man with broad mustaches that curled at the ends, and he commanded a band of three dozen men, and a handful of women. Four of those women had children with them, and one of those children was Vlado Priol.

The Germans in the area were part of the 156th Regiment of the *Alpinkorps*, and Cankar's band raised all kinds of hell with them by severing lines of communication, blowing up ammo dumps, and derailing trains. They would sweep down from their mountaintop camp on skis, strike quickly, and then scamper up like goats to the safety of the heights. In the warm weather they stole horses and raided into Italy, and up along the Austrian border. They lived on what they stole. They were lightly armed, they had two mountain-wise mules for transport, and they had a radio, which was their only link to the outside world. They also had a young American officer who had parachuted in, and who provided their liaison with the Allied forces in Italy. He belonged to an organization called the OSS, and his name was David Ogden.

Sextant started down the mountain just as the sled bearing Martha made the first of the ess-turns below the moguls, and disappeared from sight. He skied effortlessly, running the fall line and skimming the moguls. He had no style, he just skied.

Speeding down the mountain, he thought, Yes, I remember you David, the way you were then. Just the way I remember being hungry most of the time, and so cold in the winter. I remember my mother warming me, and feeding me, and singing songs in the night. I remember our cave, and searching for wood for the fire, and the flickering shadows on the walls. I remember when the men went raiding, and the women and the children were left alone, and when the men came back I would look to see if my father was there, and then I would look for you. I remember a lot, David, but I often wonder if these memories of mine are made up of things that I actually saw, and heard, and felt, or if they are only a recollection of the stories that you told me later on. Even now, at my age, a childhood memory still can be sharp and clear, but it also can be overgrown with layers of legends, and that is what I suspect has happened. Much of what I remember now I first heard from your lips, and I have the feeling that the stories improved each time that you told them. Still, the memories are there, no matter what the provenance, and they stick in my mind like burrs on a sheep. I remember you the way a child remembers, for to a boy of six the world is peopled by the tall and the wise. You weren't the wisest to me, that was my father, but you were certainly the tallest, and wise enough. Later on I worked it out that you couldn't have been more than twenty that year, maybe nineteen, and compared to people like Old Cankar and my father, you were a baby when it came to mountain fighting. But you learned, oh yes, you learned.

At the bottom of the mountain, he found the first-aid station and waited outside. He did not have to wait long. They brought Martha out on a stretcher, and loaded her into an ambulance. The legend on the ambulance read BENSON CITY HOSPITAL. He went to his car. He had just enough time to pick up his three animals, and get to Benson City, twenty miles away.

The kids followed the ambulance in the van, and once they got to the hospital, four of them went inside with Martha. Chicken did not go in, he stayed in the van. No one told him to stay there. No one needed to. He knew that he was not wanted inside. Only Lila had spoken to him during the drive from the mountain. His peers from the Center, his brother and sisters, had ignored him. They had not even bothered to ask how he felt. Clearly, he had come out of the collision unhurt, and Martha's leg was broken. The words were unspoken in the van as they drove, but the words were there, just the same. Chicken had done it again, and if anyone rated a broken bone it was the master screw-up himself.

Now he sat alone in the van, cold and shaken. He could have turned the motor on, and the heater, but he didn't. He punished himself with the cold. This was, he knew, the ultimate failure. His adventures of the past had always been met with a shake of the head and a sigh of exasperation. He knew those sighs well. He had heard them often enough during the past year from both his peers and his mentors. But there would be no sighs this time. He had jeopardized the mission, and he had put the most popular ace in the Center out of action. They were finished with him, he knew it, and he knew what would be waiting for him back at the Center. With his abilities fading, and now this—they'd make him a deuce, for sure. Alone, cold, and miserable, he bent over until his face was close to his knees, shaking his head.

Why? he asked himself. Why do I do it?

The question was rhetorical. He knew the answer, and the answer wasn't good enough. He shook himself against the chill, and went inside.

The other kids were sprawled on chairs around the hospital waiting room while Martha was in the emergency section. The waiting room had been designed with cheer in mind. There were cheerful colors, cheerful chairs, and cheerful drawings by children on the walls. There was a tank full of cheerful fish who bubbled and stared, magazines filled with cheerful stories, and cheerful giant snowflakes glued to every window. It was the most depressing place that Lila had ever seen.

She had more than one reason to feel depressed. She was worried about Martha, and her dream trip had begun to turn sour, but what bothered her just as much was the way that the other kids were treating Chicken. Sure, he had done something stupid. It was irresponsible and inexcusable to bomb the hill that way, but that was no reason to treat him like a leper. She had sensed the atmosphere in the van on the way to the hospital, and she had seen the look on Chicken's face. It was the same, sad, puppy-dog look that first had drawn her to him, and just as she had with that dog long ago, she had wanted to put her arms around him, hug him, and tell him that he was forgiven. If she had been alone with him, she might have done just that. That dog, she remembered unhappily, had never learned not to pee on the rug.

She looked up when Chicken came into the room. The others saw him, but they turned their heads away. Chicken's eyes moved across the room, and he chose a seat away from them. He slumped in the chair, and stared at his knees. That face, thought Lila. All he needs is a button nose and a pair of floppy ears. She stood up, walked across the room, and sat down next to him. She put her hand over his. He turned to her, confusion on his face.

"You look like you need a friend," she said.

He nodded.

"Well, you've got one."

He nodded again, and they sat silently that way, his hand under hers.

Do you see what's going on there? Pam spoke head-to-head with the others. *Our favorite screwball just got himself adopted.*

How could she? asked Linda. *After what he did.*

She doesn't know that he had his eyes closed.

For that matter, how do we know? Just because George says so?

He did, said George. *I'm sure of it.*

How could you tell? His goggles were down.

I tapped him just before he hit Martha. I was in his head, damn it, and his eyes were closed.

The head talk stopped when the doctor came into the room. He was a short, dark man in greens, and he needed a shave. George jumped to his feet. "How is she?"

"It was a clean break and a good set," said the doctor. "No problems."

"Are you sure?"

The doctor yawned. "Do you have any idea how many legs I do every winter? Stop worrying, your friend is okay. She's resting now, I have her sedated."

"How long will she have to stay here?"

"I want her here overnight. If things look good in the morning, I'll put the cast on, and she can go."

"Can we see her now?"

"Just for a few minutes. She's drowsy, and I want her to rest."

George turned to the others. "Come on."

They all stood up except Lila. She shook her head, and said, "I'll wait here. Hospital rooms give me the yips."

Pam frowned, and said quickly, "You really should come with us."

"It's only polite," Linda added.

Lila was firm. "Tell Martha I'm sorry, but I can't do it. I'd probably throw up all over the place. Even sitting right here is hard enough."

"Are you sure?" asked George. "We really should all stay together."

"Why?"

"Uh . . . well, you know . . ."

"I'll stay here. I know what would happen."

No good, said Pam. *We can't leave her alone.*

Linda asked, *Why not? It's just for a few minutes.*

The orders say that she has to be covered at all times.

George cut in. *Pam's right, someone has to stay with her. Chicken, do you read me?*

Yeah, I've got you. A little fuzzy, but I've got you.

Congratulations. It was not said kindly.

It still happens sometimes.

I want you to stay here with Lila, keep an eye on her.

Why me?

Because the rest of us have to talk to Martha. We have to know what to do next.

And I don't?

Not as much as we do. Not after what happened.

I wanted to tell her I was sorry.

That's a little bit late, and it can wait. Right now you stay here.

You running things now?

That's right. Until Martha can take over again.

Hold on, said Pam. *Who elected you God?*

We'll work that out later. In the meantime, Chicken stays here.

Chicken shrugged, and sat down. Lila said, "What's the matter?

"I'm going to wait here with you." He gave her a jaunty grin. He had come a long way on a few minutes worth of hand-holding. "I don't much like hospital rooms, either."

Lila covered his hand with hers again. "That's nice, we have something in common."

"Yeah." He gave her hand a tentative squeeze. "I wonder what else. What's your favorite food?"

"Chocolate chocolate-chip."

"Cookies?"

"Ice cream."

"Hey, how about that? Me too."

Yecch, said Pam. *Now it's my turn to throw up.*

Chicken, listen up, said George. *This job I just gave you, it's important.*

I know that, said Chicken without breaking his conversation with Lila.

You're in the deep shit now, you know that, don't you?

Yeah.

Don't make it any worse. This is no time to pull one of your stupid stunts, you understand?

I understand.

Just sit here and keep an eye on her. We'll be right inside.

I heard you the first time, George. "Baconburgers or cheeseburgers?"

"Cheese," said Lila.

"Me too. Home fries or french fries?"

"French."

"Play nicely, kiddies," said George. "We'll be back as soon as we can."

As soon as the others were out of the waiting room, Lila jumped up, and grabbed Chicken's hand. "Let's go."

"Go where?"

"Outside. I told you, I can't take hospitals. Even the waiting room makes me feel funny."

"It's cold out there," he said, but when she tugged his hand he followed along.

It was cold, it was snowing heavily, and the afternoon light was fading fast. They walked around the building to keep warm, and then through the parking lot, walking hand-in-hand, which now seemed the natural thing to do. They walked with their heads down against the driving snow, their eyes on the ground, and walking that way they did not see the four men looming out of the whiteness all around them, closing in.

13

YOU want to know why I am here, said Julio Ramirez, aka Rafael Cañero. He said it to Claudia Wing, aka Snake, and also known as his onetime lover as they sat in the dark on the porch of the Southern Manor.

I am here because I am a man of passion, that's why. You know me, Snake. Passion rules me, I am passion's little plaything. Passion pulls my strings like a master puppeteer, and when passion pulls I caper and leap. I am a slave to passion, I admit it.

You smile. Why? Do you think that I use the word in its limited, sexual sense? Well, we were lovers once, and so you know that I am a passionate man in that area, but I am also much more than that. Mine is a passion for all of life, an overwhelming need to chew life like an apple and spit out the core. My passion is to risk, to dare, to fence with fate, and that is why I am here.

It began when I was ordered back to Havana from the U.N., after we said goodbye to each other. On my first day home I reported to my team leader for my next assignment, and I was told to see Patrício Chavez over at the *Dirección General de Inteligencia*, which didn't please me at all. This Chavez is what your outfit calls the DDO, he runs all the operations, and he is not one of my favorite people. He's a mean, narrow-minded son of a bitch, and he is also one of the trickiest bastards that you'll ever meet on the face of the earth. I tell you, he's slick as oil, everything he says has three or four meanings, and you never really know what he's getting at. He was trained by the Jesuits before the revolution, the same school in Santiago where Fidel was trained, and maybe that's where he gets it from. There was one stunt that he pulled in Angola that cost us some very good people just because he outsmarted himself, and ever since then he hasn't rated very high with our aces. Not that there's anything we can do about it. We're in the same boat as you are. The CIA runs your Center, the DGI runs ours, and that's the way the world spins. So I wasn't very happy when I was told to report to Chavez; first because I loathe the little prick, and second because why would the DDO himself be giving me my next assignment? I always got my orders from my team leader, not from some normal, but, what the hell, there was nothing I could do about it. I went in to see him, and there he was sitting behind a desk as big as a tank in a tailor-made uniform that must have cost him a month's pay, no faded fatigues for this guy, and he told me that I was going straight back to the States.

"Don't bother unpacking," he said, "you're going to Miami. I'm putting you in with Mendoza and Fitch."

Now this came as no big surprise. This was duty that I was due for in the normal rotation of things. But I'd better tell you first about Mendoza and Fitch, and I don't give a damn if I'm talking out of turn. I meant it when I said that I'm out of it, out of it for good. So if you want to give this to your people at Langley, go right ahead. I don't care. It's not that I'm switching sides, it's just that I'm out of it.

Mendoza and Fitch is a stock brokerage house in Miami, a covert operation of the DGI. The DGI owns it, runs it, and staffs it with their agents. They've been in business for years, and most of their clients are Cuban expatriates. Cute, huh? The DGI making money off the exiles, but there's more to it than that, a lot more. The name of the game for Mendoza and Fitch is hard currency, something that Cuba is dying for. They can't trade with the United States, the peso is worthless off the island, and so they don't see much of anything hard. They're constantly strapped for convertible currency, so Patrício Chavez with that Jesuit mind of his comes up with the idea of planting legitimate businesses in the States as a way of funneling cash back to Cuba. This was years ago. I don't know how many covert ops he established, maybe a dozen, and all of them in south Florida where the DGI agents could blend in with the exile population. There was a trucking company, an outfit that made aluminum siding, a cigar factory, and some others that I never got close to. Some of them made good, some of them didn't, but they all had one main purpose, and that was to send dollars back to Cuba. Mendoza and Fitch is by far the most successful. As a stock broker and a financial consultant, Mendy services the cream of the expatriate community in south Florida, the families of all those fat cats who grabbed their cash and ran when Fidel came in. Mendy is good. Mendy makes money for its clients, it makes money for the house, and it makes money for Cuba. Chavez is very proud of the Mendy operation, not only for the money but because of the other function it performs. You see, there is always at least one sensitive working out of the Mendy office in Miami, dealing with the customers, and look who those customers are. The financiers, the bankers, the politicians, the high rollers in the exile community all use Mendoza and Fitch, and there's always a sensitive in the office to tap their heads. There's always a sensitive to sit in on the board meetings, the planning sessions, the late-night get-togethers when the movers and shakers make the decisions. You know what that means? It means that nothing goes on in the Cuban exile community that Mendoza and Fitch doesn't know about, and if Mendy knows, then Chavez knows, and if Chavez knows, then Fidel knows. He thinks of the exiles as his deadliest enemies, and he wants to know what they're thinking and planning. And he does, every minute of the day, thanks to Mendoza and Fitch.

So, Mendoza and Fitch is an intelligence gold mine . . . right? Wrong. In theory, that's the way it should be, but in practice it's virtually worthless. Why? Because, as the old proverb goes, you can't make chicken salad out of chickenshit, and you can't gather intelligence when there's no intelligence to gather. You think those high-powered expatriates, those captains of industry sit around all day plotting how they're going to overthrow Fidel and take back Cuba? You think they're busy hiring assassination teams to hit the Maximum Leader, slip him an explosive cigar? You think they're dreaming about another Bay of Pigs, only better? Forget it, that was yesterday. You know what they think about now? First they think about money, how to get it and how to keep it. Then they think about power, how to get it and how to use it. After that, the men think about women, the women think about men, and they both think about their kids, their education, the future, the marriage. They think about clothes, about food, about the weather, about the Dolphins, and all the way down at the bottom of the list they think about Cuba. *Algún día,* they think. One of these days we'll be able to go back to Cuba. You see what I'm getting at? I'm not saying that these people aren't sincere, it's just that they have other things to think about. American things, because they're Americans now. So, *algún día*, but that's tomorrow, and this is today.

So, for a sensitive, tapping the elite of the exile community is about as valuable, in an intelligence sense, as tapping a Rotary luncheon or a meeting of the Elks. But Fidel wants it, and Fidel gets it. I know, I did the job for almost a year. I sat in on those board meetings as Mendy's rep, I went to all the cocktail parties, I sat in the luxury boxes at the Dolphins games, I mingled with the *crema de la crema*, and I passed along every juicy little item I uncovered. But, believe me, it wasn't worth chickenshit.

But I wasn't thinking about that when Patrício Chavez told me that I was going right back to the states. A tour of duty in Miami sounded like heaven to me, because like any other Cuban you'll ever meet I start to shiver when the temperature drops below seventy-five, but I still didn't understand why it was Chavez, himself, who was giving me my orders. He was all genialtiy. He sat me down, offered me a cup of coffee with the usual five sugars in it just to let me know that I was back in Cuba for the moment, and asked me what I knew about the chain of command at Mendoza and Fitch.

"Only what I've been told," I said.

"Let me hear it."

The way I understood it, the entire operation was under the control of Jaime Figueroa, a DGI agent who functioned as managing director, and who supervised the herd of brokers who serviced the customers' accounts. Like many other houses, Mendy also traded on its own account, but that's where the comparison with a normal brokerage operation stopped. There were four house accounts, and they were designated as Alpha, Beta, Gamma, and Delta.

The Alpha account belonged to the Communist Party of Cuba, it was run by a representative of the PPC, and its take was thirty-five percent of Mendy's net profit.

The Beta account was the Army's plum, run by a top colonel, and its take was also thirty-five percent.

The Gamma account, with fifteen percent, was somewhat different from the others in that it was under the direction of a senior official from the Ministry of Sugar, and was used to help influence prices on the world sugar market.

The Delta account, with fifteen percent, was the property of the DGI, and was always run by a sensitive. That was my next assignment. I stopped talking, and looked at Chavez expectantly.

"What about the bank accounts?" he asked.

"Each division has its own numbered bank account in Switzerland, and all monies are channeled there first for transfer to Cuba.

I must have been smiling, for he said, "You find this amusing?"

"Somewhat. Don't you?"

"Not at all."

"The Communist Party of Cuba is trading on the New York Stock Exchange, and you don't find that at least . . . ironic?"

The geniality vanished, and he turned cold: cold eyes, cold thin lips, cold fingers that formed a steeple in front of his face. "If Jesus Christ were alive today, he'd be a member of the Communist Party. Jesus said, 'Give up your property, and follow me.' Fidel says, 'Give your property to the revolution, and then follow *me*.' Now, that's irony. What you're talking about is economic reality. Do you understand the difference?"

"Yes, *compañero*." It was that Jesuit training of his. "We haven't discussed the Tau account yet."

His eyes narrowed. "What do you know about the Tau?"

"The way I understand it, nine percent of the DGI money in the Delta account is rolled over into a separate and a distinct account, the Tau, for use in special operations overseas. Do you have any instructions for me on that?"

"The Tau account is no concern of yours."

That confused me. "If I'm handling Delta, don't I have to know about Tau?"

"Someone in Geneva handles Tau. Forget about it."

"That's contrary to procedure," I protested. "If I'm going to have the responsibility, I have to have control."

He shook his head.

I didn't like it. My ass was on the line if something happened to that money. I said stiffly, "I must ask why."

"Why? You ask a lot of questions."

"I've only asked one."

"Sometimes one is one too many."

"I still have to ask it."

He looked amused. "Are you familiar with the teachings of Saint Augustine?"

"No."

"I thought not. Let me tell you a little story about him. It seems that a group of theologians once approached that holy man, who was then the bishop of Hippo, and asked him a question that had been bothering them. What, they asked, had God been thinking about just before he created the heavens and the earth. The good bishop reflected, and do you know what he said?"

"No, *compañero*."

"Saint Augustine said that God was thinking about making a hell for people who ask such questions." He smiled faintly. "Now, is there anything else that you'd like to ask?"

I shook my head. If any man could make a hell for me, it was Patrício Chavez.

"Good. Now, you may have wondered why I wanted to give you this assignment personally." I nodded. "Have you also wondered why the head of the Delta division is always a sensitive?"

The question confused me. "I assumed that it was for intelligence-gathering purposes. Our particular . . . talents."

Chavez frowned. "Please, between ourselves, we can dispense with that fiction. We both know how little true intelligence is gathered in Miami." I kept a straight face. He was as much as saying that we did it just to keep the boss happy. He could say it, but I couldn't. "Don't misunderstand," he went on, "I want you to keep on doing your little tricks over there. Exercise your particular talent, as you put it, and send me all the juicy gossip you dig up, but remember to keep your priorities straight. Your main job is to keep an eye on Jaime Figueroa. The son of a bitch has been stealing us blind."

"Figueroa? The managing director?" I didn't know what to say. "But he's one of ours. He's DGI."

"That doesn't make him an angel, does it?" Chavez was back in his genial mode, treating me as a confidant. "By now you should have learned that in this business you trust nobody. Figueroa is a thief, I'm convinced of it. He's skimming money off the top of the operation."

"A serious charge."

"The man is a master at making money disappear. That's why I always have a sensitive there, to get into his head and see what he's doing."

"Have you caught him in anything?"

Chavez shook his head angrily. "Not yet. He's a clever devil. Even with a tap on his head, he's getting away with it. I would have gotten rid of him long ago, but the man has friends, important friends. I need proof, and the day I get that proof Jaime Figueroa goes to the wall." He pointed a finger at me. "Get me that proof and you can name your next assignment. I can be generous to those who work with me."

"This man is stealing from the state," I said, and my voice must have shown how shocked I was.

Chavez nodded his approval of my indignation. "That is exactly what he is doing, and I want you to help me to prove it."

I sat there, stunned. This may sound naive to you, Snake, but the idea sickened me. Figueroa was stealing money from Cuba. You knew me back then, I was never much of a flag waver, but at that point in my life I was a lot less cynical than I am now. I was still in love with my country then, because . . . Let me tell you something about Cuba.

You want to tell me that Cuba is a police-state dictatorship? You're right. You want to tell me that life in Cuba is oppressive, with no free press and no dissent? You're right. You want to tell me that my own outfit, the DGI, was controlled from Moscow by the KGB? Right again.

But if you want to tell me that the average Cuban isn't better off today than he was before the revolution, then you're wrong. Dead wrong. I'm talking about medical services, I'm talking about education, I'm talking about job security. Much better off, and I know what I'm talking about. After all, I'm what they used to call a true son of the revolution, because I was born on the first of January, 1959. The date doesn't mean anything to you? Okay, Yankee, a little history lesson. On January 1, 1959, Fidel Castro toppled the government of the dictator Batista, and rolled into Havana at the head of a rag-tag army at the precise moment when, some fifty miles to the east in the province of Matanzas, my mother grunted, groaned, and gave me birth.

The precise moment? Maybe not, but close enough so that from my earliest days I was called a true son of the revolution. Everyone who was born on that day was called a true son or daughter of the revolution, and you want to hear something else? I was born in a log cabin. How about that for proletarian roots? If I had been born in America that would have insured my future as a politician, but to tell you the truth, where I came from every raggedy-assed kid was born in a *bohio*, the Cuban version of a log cabin. Trees for the framework, strips of palm for the sides, fronds to thatch the roof, two rooms inside and the kitchen out back. That was your standard working-model *bohio*: no running water, no electricity, beans and rice at noontime, rice and beans at night. That's how this son of the revolution was raised, along with three brothers and two sisters, by a mother who slaved for us and a father who cut cane in the fields. I tried to live up to my name. I joined the UJC, and later the Young Pioneers. I listened carefully when my teachers explained the revolution to us, listened to the leaders from the CDR, listened to the torrents of words that poured out of the radio whenever Fidel decided to stage one of those mind-numbing four-hour extravaganzas. I marched in all the demonstrations and parades, I banged on the drum, I waved the banner, and I shouted "*Venceremos*" until my throat went sore. And while I was doing that, my father cut cane in the fields.

A bad business, cutting cane. The old man was up with the sun to wait for the workers' bus that took the cutters to a different field every day, and those fields were hot and smoky, burned over the night before so that the earth was steamy underneath your feet and your body turned black from the soot. Heavy work with the machete in the heat and smoke. One slash to cut down the stalk, slash, slash to take off the leaves, and three quick chops to cut the cane into even pieces, each about a meter long. By the end of the day the old man was covered with soot, exhausted, and when he got home he had just enough energy left to clean himself, eat his meal, and smoke a cigarette before going to sleep. Sometimes he smoked that cigarette, or two, or three, sitting outside in front of the *bohio* with his children gathered around him, and often he would talk to us about sugar. He was a simple man, unschooled, and sugar was all that he knew.

"After the revolution," he would tell us, "Fidel said that it was the sugar that kept our people poor, and that we would have to raise other crops. Well, they tried them, many of them, but always they had to come back to the sugar. Because of the money it can bring, you see? It's a bad thing to be so dependent on a single crop, but that's the way it is. Sugar is Cuba's blessing, and Cuba's curse, but let me tell you something, children. It's a hard life cutting cane, but as hard as it is, it was worse before the revolution. We don't have much now, but back then a man like me had nothing."

More than anything else, my father hoped that his sons would not have to work in the fields, that the revolution would bring us something else to do, but it didn't happen that way. One by one, my three older brothers went to cut cane, and for a very short time so did I. Only when they discovered that I was a sensitive was I saved from a life in the fields, although I like to think that I would have found something better than field work in any event. But who knows about those things?

So I was eleven years old when I worked in the fields along with my father and brothers, and that was the year that Fidel decreed a ten-million-ton *zafra*. That was 1970, and in the years before that the sugar crop had never come close to that figure. Five million, six million tons was the absolute top, but in 1969 Fidel announced that the goal for 1970 would be ten, and if you weren't livng in Cuba at that time you have no idea how that plan turned the country inside out. More land was cleared, more cane was planted, and people from all over the island were drafted to help in the effort. The goal became a national obsession, I mean there were billboards all over that said, 'What Are You Doing for the Ten Million?' Once the harvest started there was a steady parade of the big shots who came out to the fields to lend a hand, with the TV and the newspaper cameras following them around. I remember Marshal Grechko, the Soviet Minister of Defense, cutting cane, and there were groups from North Vietnam and East Germany. Fidel came, of course, slashing away with his machete for the cameras, but let me tell you this: after the cameras were finished he stayed and cut cane for the rest of the day. It was a magnificent effort, but in the end it failed. There was no ten-million-ton *zafra* that year, not even nine. Eight and a half was the final figure, and the failure wrecked the country for years to come. But I wasn't around to see the end of it. All I saw was the beginning.

Like I said, it was a national obsession, and I had to be a part of it. I was only eleven, but in Cuba that's close to being a man, and I had been swinging a machete for years. I worked every day in the steamy, sooty fields alongside my father and my brothers, and I was proud to be a part of it. Then, one day in the fields I began to hear the voices, and after that I was crazy for a while.

You know how it is, it's the same with all of us, the voices in your head when you're about eleven, and then the craziness. I stopped being crazy when they took me to the Center in Havana and explained the facts of life to me. The facts of a sensitive's life. They told me what I was, and what I could be, and after that I didn't have to worry about cutting cane. But I never forgot what the fields were like, and I never forgot the stories that my father told us about how it had been before the revolution. The revolution didn't make him rich, but it brought him more than he had ever had before. And now, according to Chavez, someone was stealing it from him. The way I saw it, if Jaime Figueroa was stealing from the state, then he was stealing from my father, and that made me sick.

It also made me boiling mad. It made my face flush and my ears burn; it made me sweat. My passion, you see, my inability to do things by halves. For just that moment I was out of my head with indignation, and if Jaime Figueroa had been standing there before me I would have cut his throat without a quiver.

But it was Patrício Chavez who stood before me, not the other, and again he nodded his approval of my indignation. "Get me the proof," he said again, "and I'll put that thief up against the wall."

"You can count on it," I told him, my voice trembling with emotion, for I was blinded by this passion of mine.

Yes, blinded. So blinded that I forgot for the moment what a devious bastard this Chavez was. So blinded that I did not stop to question what he said. So blinded that I did not bother to tap him.

Yes, we have the same rules that you have. It is forbidden to tap an officer of the DGI without written authorization, but you know how often that rule is broken. We all do it, regularly and without qualms, but this time I didn't. Blinded by my passion, I accepted what he said, and went to prepare for my new assignment.

I should have tapped. If I had, I would have saved myself time and trouble. There was only one thief involved in the operation, and the thief was Patrício Chavez. So I should have tapped, but on the other hand, even if I had tapped him I never would have dreamed that by the end of the year I would have stolen more money from Mendoza and Fitch than Chavez ever had dreamed of.

Crickets chirped as Rafael Cañero, aka Julio Ramirez, fell silent. Far away, trucks rumbled over the Interstate, and a faint breeze rattled palm fronds.

Snake said softly, "You bastard."

From the darkness, a surprised Julio asked, "Me?"

"How long were you in Cuba?"

"When?"

"You know when. Then."

"A week, maybe ten days. Just long enough to learn my new cover and get fitted out with new ID."

"And then you went to Miami as Julio Ramirez."

"No, my new name was Jorge Guardado. Julio Ramirez came later."

Snake brushed that aside as unimportant. "But ten days after we played that farewell scene in New York you were back in the States."

"Yes."

"And you never once got in touch with me. Not a note, not a telephone call. Nothing."

"Snake, be reasonable. It's the way that we live. How could I?"

Snake thought about it, and decided to be reasonable. "You couldn't," she admitted. And then, after a moment, "Did you want to?"

"You know the answer to that."

She decided not to press it. "So you turned into a thief."

"In a sense."

"And now you're on the run."

"In a sense. It was a little more complicated than that."

I started work at Mendoza and Fitch in December of 1986, and I was there until October of the following year, which, if you're quick with dates, tells you why I eventually left. I started there just before the new year, and I learned a few things quickly.

I learned, as I had expected, that the intelligence to be gathered from Miami's exile community was minimal. It was gossip, nothing more; juicy gossip that I faithfully forwarded to Havana every month. If Fidel enjoyed the reports, they at least had entertainment value.

I learned, contrary to what I had expected, that the people who dealt with Mendoza and Fitch were not only the fat cats and the power brokers of the exile community. They were, for the most part, middle-class Cubans with modest accounts who were trying to inch their way up the American ladder.

I learned that there was nothing to pin on Jaime Figueroa. I tapped the man every day for a week, and found nothing. After the first couple of taps I spoke to Pablo Obregón about it. Pablo was the ace I was replacing, and he had stayed on for a two-week transition period, filling me in on office routine, and introducing me to the heavy players on the Delta account. When I asked him about Figueroa, he made a face of disgust.

"A waste of time," he said. "I've been into his head for a year now, and I haven't found a thing. If he's a thief, then I'm the bishop of Santiago."

"But Chavez said . . ."

"Look, I got the same pep talk before I came here." He spoke in Chavez's icy voice. "Get me the proof and I'll put that thief up against the wall." His voice returned to normal. "It just isn't there, believe me. If the man is stealing, he isn't thinking about it, and that's next to impossible."

"I don't get it. Chavez is so sure."

Pablo shrugged. "Chavez gets what Chavez wants. Keep working on it. You'll waste a lot of time, just as I did, but maybe you'll get lucky."

"Any other advice? What about the Tau account?"

He frowned. "The less you have to do with that, the better. Just make sure that the money gets there. Nine percent of the Delta take gets transferred there on the twentieth of every month, rain or shine, no excuses accepted. If you're one day late, you'll hear from Samantha."

"Who's that?"

"Samantha Curbelo. She's in charge of the Tau account in Geneva."

"One of us?"

"No, she's a normal, but don't underestimate her. Don't mess with her, and don't ever cross her. She's a tiger, that one, and she's close to Chavez." He held up two fingers pressed together. "That close."

"Besides being a tiger, what's she like?"

"I've never met her, but from what I hear . . ." Pablo kissed his fingers. "But private property, you understand? Strictly for Chavez."

"I'll remember that."

"But you didn't," said Snake.

"Hey, who's telling this story?"

"Come on, cut to the chase, I can see what's coming. Your trouble is, you're trying to be too dramatic. It's obvious."

"What is?"

"What you're getting at. You tell me that Chavez was stealing, and you tell me that he was joined at the hip with this Samantha woman, so he had to be stealing from the Tau account, and she was in it with him. Right?"

Out of the darkness came a reluctant, "Yeah, that's about the way it was."

"How did you find out?"

"How else? I tapped her."

"I thought she was in Geneva."

"She was, but she had to come to Miami once, and I tapped her then."

With a hint of laughter in her voice, Snake asked, "Was she standing up at the time?"

"Not exactly."

"Were you?"

"Not exactly."

"I figured."

"Well, you know how it is."

"Sure I do. You and your passionate nature. So you tapped her in bed."

"Yes."

"And that's how you got into the thievery business."

"No. You're not as smart as you think you are. It wasn't like that at all."

I had been at Mendoza and Fitch for three months when Samantha flew into Miami to give me new instructions on the Tau account. I had been dealing with her in Geneva by telephone, telex, and fax, regularly diverting nine percent of the Delta take to Tau, but the new word was that Chavez wanted the split increased to eleven. This was the sort of instruction that had to be given face-to-face, and so she came to Miami to give it to me personally. She was supposed to stay for only a day, but one thing led to another, she stayed for three, and by the time she left I had the whole story straight from her head.

Chavez was using the Tau account as his personal retirement fund.

Figueroa was clean, a diversion to keep me occupied.

Why, then, risk putting a sensitive in at Mendoza and Fitch? Because Fidel had to have his Miami gossip, and only an ace could get it for him.

I got this all in one tap from Samantha, which tells you something about the way people think, or don't think, about sensitives. I mean, here is a serving officer of the DGI who should know what an ace can do, and yet she walks right into my range and lets me pick her brains. Go figure it out, maybe they don't have any brains to pick. It's as if they don't want to believe that we can do these things.

But we can, and I did, and once I knew what the score was, I had to decide what to do about it. My first instinct was to blow the whistle on Chavez by going straight to the top. You see, I was sure that Fidel knew nothing about what was going on, and that if he ever found out it would be Chavez up against the wall for sure. Yes, perhaps it's a sign of my political naiveté that I still thought of Fidel as the revolutionary purist, the idealist who would never tolerate corruption in any form, but that's the way I felt. And I'll tell you something else. I still feel that way. I'm out of it now, I don't care anymore, but I prefer to think that Fidel, over all these years, has never compromised his principles.

But how I felt then was unimportant, because I knew that there was no way that someone like me could ever get to the Maximum Leader. Chavez had too many friends in the highest of places, and I would have been blocked before I got started. No, if I blew the whistle the only thing I would accomplish was my own destruction. I was sure of it, and so, in the end, I did nothing. Not very valiant, I know. I had been passionately committed to nailing Figueroa when there was no risk to me involved, but I retreated from the thought of going up against Chavez. Retreated, hell, I caved in completely. The man scared me out of my wits. I wasn't very pleased with myself, but that's what I did. Nothing. On the twentieth of every month I continued to forward eleven percent of the Delta trading profit to the Tau account in Geneva, and I tried very hard not to think about it.

But life at Mendoza and Fitch went on, and since I no longer had to concentrate on tapping Figueroa, I was able to devote my time to my monthly gossip reports, and, more important, to the nuts and bolts of my daily work as a broker and financial consultant. I took pleasure in the work. It was, after all, what I had been trained for, and I enjoyed working with most of my clients: not the heavy hitters, but the average investors who were urgently trying to build for the future. Many of them were older people, and the future they were building was not for themselves, but for their children and grandchildren. There was a clique of them that hung around the office every day watching the Quotron, drinking strong, sweet Cuban coffee, and bragging about their adventures in the market the way younger men might have bragged about women. They were a good bunch of guys, about a dozen in all, and I got to know them well. In time I learned all about them, their work, their families, and where they had come from in Cuba. They were all so much older than I was, but they accepted me, not only as a broker, but as a friend. My cover story was that I had come over with the *marielitos* in 1980, and since most of them had been out of Cuba for twenty-five years, I was sort of a tie to the homeland for them. I'd like to think that after a while they looked upon me as something close to family. I certainly felt that way about them, which is why I tried to steer their investment programs into safe and conservative channels. But these were old men in a hurry to build, and, being Cuban, they were born gamblers. Their tastes in investments ran to the exotic, to the daring, and there were times when they came close to driving me crazy with the chances they took. Most of them were involved in a program of sophisticated, but risky, option plays that had done very nicely for them so far. They were making money, all right, but it wasn't the smartest strategy for people of that age. I tried to tell them that, but they wouldn't listen. The Dow was up over 2700, more than eight hundred points for the year, and they were on a roll. They were betting on the continued rise, and the way things were going they figured that they couldn't lose. I kept warning them to watch for a correction, but they didn't hear me. All they could hear was the jingle. They never had it so good.

"Stop," said Snake. "I've got it."

"I doubt it, but go ahead."

"You gave me the clue yourself. You said that you left Mendoza and Fitch in October of 1987. That was when the market crashed, wasn't it?"

"It was."

"So that was when you stole the money, right?"

"Right." It was a grudging admission.

"And it had something to do with those old men of yours?"

"Yes."

"Jesus." A thought struck her. "Their savings, all their money . . . you didn't . . . ?"

"I didn't. What do you know about the market?"

"Enough not to play it."

"The Dow Jones average?"

"It goes up, and it goes down."

"The American Stock Exchange's Major Market Index?"

"My eyes are glazing."

"I'll try to keep it simple. The Major Market Index, the MMI, is an index of twenty stocks offered for futures contracts by the Chicago Board of Trade. It works like this. Say, back in September of 1987, a customer of mine sold fifty put options of what they call the 'November 450' contracts. This means that on the third Friday of November, whoever bought those options is entitled to be paid one hundred times any shortfall of the MMI below the 450 level. But if the MMI doesn't go below 450 by that Friday, the buyer loses and my guy wins, he gets to keep what the buyer paid him. Say he sold fifty contracts at ten, then he gets to keep the 50,000. On the other hand, if the index *does* fall below 450, my guy takes a beating. How much of a beating depends on how low the index falls. Got it?"

"No. You said simple. That isn't simple."

Look, it's like off-track betting, but the payoff can be terrific. Back in October of eighty-seven, the guys in my Cuban coffeeklatsch were all into playing the MMI, and they were all betting that the market would keep on rising. Alberto Nuñez was a good example. Alberto was the patriarch of his family, he was in charge of investing not only his own money, but the savings of his sons and daughters, and a couple of cousins. He was doing good that year, betting on the rise, and he was the one who sold those fifty puts of "November 450." It's a simple bet. If the index stays over 450, he wins his 50K. If it drops a little below, he loses a little. But what happens if it drops a lot? What happens if it crashes? Alberto is in for one hundred times the shortfall, but Alberto doesn't think about crashes. Who wants to think about crashes?

But that's what happened. The market slipped on Friday, and crashed on Monday. Black Monday, and Alberto was in up to his neck. You wanted it simple, so I'll keep it simple. Alberto sold his puts at ten, and by noon on Monday the price of the option was thirty-five. This means that if Alberto wants to get out, if he wants to close out his position, it will cost him 175K to buy the fifty puts that will balance out his original trade. On the other hand, if he wants to tough it out, keep his position and bet that the market goes up again, he's facing a margin call of about 200K just to stay in the game. And that's payable on the spot, the next morning.

That's Alberto's position, very simple. What isn't simple is that Alberto doesn't have any 200K to ante up, and even the 175K wipes him out. Him, and the rest of his family. So Alberto is screwed, and so are all his pals in the coffeeklatsch. They've all been playing the same game, and that Monday in Miami they were all staring at disaster.

Not that they were alone. Maybe you don't know anything about the market, but you have to know what that day was like all over the country. You have to have read about it, or seen it on television. At the end of the day the Dow was down more than five hundred points; percentagewise that's twice the loss of the crash of twenty-nine. At the end of the day more than six hundred million shares had been traded, twice as much as the previous record. At the end of the day people were busted, dead, and dented. It was the kind of day that I won't try to describe except with one word: chaos. It was a kaleidoscope of chaos as we tried to trade our way out of a total collapse, and while our world was falling apart all around us, my little gang of Cuban senior citizens huddled in a corner near the coffee machine, fear frozen on their faces. Every once in a while, one of them would shuffle over to my desk to look at the Quotron, shake his head, and walk back to the corner to huddle again with the others. They were all in the same boat, and the boat was sinking. Not one of them had the capital to meet his margin call the next morning, and not one of them had enough to cancel his position. They were finished.

My mind was racing in different directions. I was working every phone on my desk, always with a heavy hitter on the line screaming instructions. I was in constant touch with our floor traders, or as constantly as the conditions allowed. I was juggling a dozen balls in the air as I tried to protect the Delta account, and at the same time I had to keep in mind that today was the nineteenth of the month, and that tomorrow, on the twentieth, I would have to make the transfer to the Tau account in Geneva. Rain or shine, no excuses accepted, that transfer had to be made.

Alberto Nuñez came over to my desk, looked at the Quotron, looked at me, and tried to smile. He didn't make it. He said, "Not so good, huh?"

"Not so good, Alberto. I'm sorry."

I tried to keep my feelings about these guys on a professional level. I told myself that they had had no business playing in such a risky market. I reminded myself of all the times I had tried to warn them off. I told myself that there are always losers as well as winners, but none of that helped. This wasn't just about money, this was also about pride and humiliation. These men were the patriarchs of their families, their families had trusted them, and now that trust was broken. These weren't the fat cats, these weren't the parasites that Fidel cursed in his speeches, the bloodsuckers who had looted Cuba, and then had fled to Miami. These were Cubans who could have been my uncles, and as each hour went by they began to look, collectively, more and more like my father at the end of a long day of cutting cane. Weary, hopeless, defeated.

And meanwhile there was the Tau account to prepare for tomorrow, eleven percent of the Delta take for the month, close to one million five to be deposited into the retirement fund of Patrício Chavez. Chavez, the man who couldn't be touched.

A million five. Just about enough to close out the positions of Alberto Nuñez, and the others.

I don't know when I decided to do it. I didn't make a conscious decision. One moment I was sitting there staring at those huddled sheep in the corner, and the next moment I was on the phone with my trader placing orders.

Alberto Nuñez, buy fifty MMI at thirty-five.

Juan Balat, buy thirty MMI at thirty-five.

Ignacio Brú, buy eighty MMI at thirty-six.

Teófilo Céspedes, buy . . .

I went down the list, all twelve of them, and in each case I bought what they had sold, enough to close out each position. And after each guy I executed an order to pay for the transaction. An order on the Delta account. The total was just under one million five. There was nothing left for the Tau account, but my uncles were out of it clean.

And I was out of it, too. I knew it in that moment. I knew that I was finished with the DGI, with Patrício Chavez, with Mendoza and Fitch, and with gathering gossip for Fidel. I was finished with all the high-class snooping. That's all that it was. I was finished with everything I had been trained to do, right up to that moment. I was out of it.

I gathered up my transaction slips, and went to the cashier's cage. There were half a dozen brokers in line, and they all looked shocked and shaky. They were drawing out cash, large chunks of it. There was no need for that, but they all wanted cash. That's the way it was that day. The one in front of me turned around and offered to sell me his BMW. He had had it for less than a month.

"I paid sixty for it," he said. "You can have it for forty. Cash, right now."

"I have a car," I told him.

"Not like this one. Thirty-five."

"Take it easy."

"Thirty."

I shook him off. When it was my turn at the window, the cashier asked me how much I wanted. She assumed that, like everyone else, I wanted cash. I had about two hundred dollars in my wallet. I was going out, and I wanted to go clean, but there was no sense in being stupid about it.

"Five thousand," I told her.

"That's all?" she seemed surprised.

I nodded, and she counted out the bills. I gave her my transaction slips, and said, "You see those old guys standing around the coffee machine? These slips belong to them. Pass them around after I leave."

"You going now?"

"There's nothing more for me to do around here."

I went to the garage and got my car. I didn't go back to my apartment. I was safe for at least twelve hours, but it was time to move quickly. I started driving north, but not too far north. Just far enough for a Cuban. Around here seemed just right.

"And you've been here ever since?" asked Snake.

"It's as good a place as any if you have to keep your head low."

"Are they looking for you?"

"I screwed Patrício Chavez. I have to assume they are. At least, here I blend in with the Cuban community. Here I'm Julio Ramirez."

"And what does Julio Ramirez do for a living?"

"A little bit of this, and a little bit of that. Mostly, I tell fortunes."

Snake laughed. "That old dodge."

"Sure, it's the easiest way for an ace to make a few bucks. I'm very big with the Cuban ladies here, especially the old ones. I tap their heads, and tell them what they want to hear."

"What a waste."

"It's reasonably honest work. That, and the frontons."

"Jai alai?"

"A jai alai game that isn't fixed is a very rare thing. I hang around the frontons, talk to the players, tap a few heads, make a few bets. Between that and the fortunetelling, I manage."

"It's still a waste. Have you ever thought of working for us?"

"I'm Cuban, Snake. If I worked for anybody, I'd work for Cuba, but I'm out of it."

"You won't stay out. No ace could. You'll get back in."

"I doubt it. Now it's your turn. What are you doing here?"

"I didn't make any deal with you. You wanted to tell me your story, and you did."

"The story was straight. You were in my head, and you know that."

"Yes."

"So I'm asking. What's a yankee ace doing in the middle of nowhere Florida?"

She did not hesitate. She had seen his head. He was really out of the game.

"It'a a weird one," she said, and she told him. Not all of it, just her part of it. The arson part.

"It's weird," he agreed, "but there has to be more to it. Do I get to hear more?"

"No, that's as far as I go. Sorry."

He accepted that. He thought for a while. "Watching this place by yourself, that's a lot for one person to handle. Do you want any help?"

"I was hoping you'd ask."

14

KILL *Calvin, kill Calvin. Oh God, how I'd love to kill Calvin.*

Just about everyone in the Cockatoo Lounge was thinking murderous thoughts about Calvin Weiss, and some of them were saying it out loud. As Weiss worked his way from table to table, greeting the first-timers on the cruise as well as the regulars, someone shouted from across the room, "You're dead, Weiss, your ass is mine," and someone else countered with, "I'll get you this time, Calvin, right between the eyes." There was laughter in the room, and Weiss paused long enough to flash the finger at each of the shouters before going back to his meeting and greeting.

The second purser, whose name was Fleckmann, saw the look on my face, and smiled. "It's a game," he explained. "We do it every trip. We call it *Killing Calvin*."

I didn't want to believe it. "You're kidding."

"Not at all. You see, it started a number of years ago on one of these trips. As soon as we cleared port, Calvin got up to his usual tricks, popping in and out of various beds and enjoying the favors of the ladies, and a time came when he didn't pop out quite quickly enough. Outraged husband, you know, caught a glimpse of him fleeing the scene, and wrung a confession out of his wife. That night the husband, a doctor from Pittsburgh as I recall, loudly and publicly announced that he was going to perform a rather exotic piece of elective surgery on our funnyman, and then he was going to kill him entirely. Well, Calvin got the word of the threat almost as soon as it was uttered, and, being a genuine coward and no fool to boot, he immediately went into hiding. It was our last night at sea, we were due back at Port St. James at eight in the morning, and all he had to do was lie low through the night."

"Did he?"

"Easily. There are dozens of hidey-holes on a ship this size, and, after all, there was only the one man looking for him. Calvin hid out, to this day he won't say where, and he didn't show his face until after the ship had docked and all of the passengers had gone ashore. He was pale and shaken, I can tell you. He said it was the most frightening experience of his life, and he swore that he'd never go through anything like that again, but of course he was wrong. The passengers saw to that."

"How so?"

"I don't know who actually started it, some of the regulars no doubt, but they turned it into a game. The idea of Calvin cowering under a bed was just too tempting to them, and so they announced that on the last night at sea, from eight in the evening until eight the next morning, Calvin was fair game. They made up a pool, each one kicked in a hundred dollars, and whoever killed Calvin won it all."

"You don't mean that they actually tried to kill him, do you?"

"No, no. In the beginning it was more like a game of hide-and-seek. Whoever uncovered Calvin, wherever he was hiding, would simply tap him on the shoulder, say, 'bang, bang, you're dead,' and go off to collect the cash. But it's grown into something far more sophisticated. There are rules, and time limits, and weapons. Not real weapons, of course. There are three allowable methods of killing Calvin: shooting, stabbing and strangulation. The ship supplies the weapons. We use those pistols that shoot pellets of paint, we use a Hollywood-type dagger where the blade slides back into the hilt, and for those who prefer strangulation we have a tasty little noose made out of black nylon. It's a little silly, I know, but the passengers love it. And for the winner, it can be highly profitable."

It may have started as a gag, but it was big business now. The ante was still a hundred apiece, but, according to Fleckmann, at least two hundred people signed up for the game every trip, which meant a jackpot that was never less than 20K. Registration took place in the Main Lounge on the last day at sea, the weapons of choice were distributed, and promptly at eight the hunt was on.

"Does he ever get killed?" I asked.

"Ever? He always gets killed. It has to be that way. I don't doubt that he could stay hidden all night, but that would never do. The passengers would never stand for it, and what would we do with all the money? No, Calvin knows how to play the game. Sometime during the night, usually on toward morning, he shows himself, and somebody pots him. It never fails."

"That leaves room for some chicanery, doesn't it?"

Fleckmann looked puzzled, then he got it. "You mean collusion between Calvin and a passenger?" He shook his head firmly. "The man may be a bastard when it comes to women, but he would never cheat that way. I can assure you that *Killing Calvin* is strictly on the level."

Which was what I was afraid of. I stood there trying to digest what I had heard, and what I came up with was mental indigestion. The assignment had been a bitch to start with, but there had always been a chance, a slim chance, that I would be able to pick the killer out of the crowd by tapping his head. Now that chance was gone. I didn't have a single person on board with murder on his or her mind, I had a couple hundred of them, and there was no way I could filter out fact from fantasy. My only edge was gone, and I felt like swimming back to Port St. James.

Fleckmann said brightly, "If you feel like risking a hundred, you might sign up for the game. You might get lucky."

I nodded absently. That's what Sammy would have said. My luck. Where was it now? There was a ship's brochure on the bar, and I fingered through it.

> Wait until you venture out shopping. Whether it's for straw baskets in Nassau, or for Spanish crafts in San Juan, for French haute couture in St. Maarten or just about anything in St. Thomas, you're sure to get a good price. So pack an empty fold-away bag for all the gifts, and don't forget your suntan oil.

Right. No straw baskets for Ben Slade, and no suntan oil, either. With my edge gone, my only chance was to latch onto Calvin and stay as close to him as I could. I was going to have to be his shadow. I was going to have to be his . . . friend. It was not a pleasant thought, but it had to be done. The only question was how to do it.

I watched as Calvin completed his circuit of the room, and left to repeat the performance in one of the other lounges. "Quite a guy," I said to Fleckmann. "Aside from chasing women, what does he do with his spare time?"

"He doesn't have all that much of it. You can say what you will about our Calvin, but he's a hard worker. He's on the go all day in the lounges and at poolside, and at night he emcees the two shows in the Steamboat Club."

"And after that? He has to do something to relax."

"You mentioned the ladies."

"All night?"

"No, not even Calvin. At about two every morning you'll find him in the casino, but the way he gambles, I'd hardly call it relaxation. He can be rather intense."

"What's his game?"

"He fancies himself as a poker player."

I managed not to smile. "Is he any good?"

"He thinks he is."

"But?"

Fleckmann shook his head. "A born loser, a hustler's delight. They stand up and salute when Calvin walks into the casino. There are men who have put their children through college on what they've won from Calvin. There are women who have supported a lover on what they take from him."

"And he keeps coming back for more?"

"I told you. He thinks he's good."

This time I didn't try to hide the smile. My luck had just kicked in again.

Seven hours later I sat across the poker table from Calvin Weiss and watched him squint at his hole cards. I had been sitting there for three hours, watching him get his head beat in. I figured he was down about three thousand, which wasn't a fortune by casino standards, but which was much too much if you made your living in a clown suit. Fleckmann was right, the man was a loser. Everything about him screamed loser, from the sweat on his face when he studied his cards to the way that he nervously riffled his chips. He played a fast, aggressive game. He rarely folded a hand, he rarely failed to call, and his raises were often silly. He played as if he wanted to lose, and he did a good job of it. I have seen this at tables all over the world, and it is always a sad sight to see, but never so sad that I don't take the money. In the past three hours I had taken my share, but I wasn't the only one. Everyone at the table was eating him up.

It was five in the morning, but the casino was running full blast. Once outside the U.S. territorial waters it was never closed, and it was never empty. It was filled with the people who weren't along for the straw hats in Nassau or the Spanish crafts in San Juan. They weren't along for the sun, or the pools, or the saunas, either. They were there for the action, and they kept the casino rolling around the clock.

The casino was a good-sized room on the Restaurant Deck, but like any other casino, very little space was set aside for poker tables. The people who run casinos want the gamblers going up against the slots and the blackjack, the craps tables and the roulette wheels. Those are the games that the house has to win. But poker players don't go up against the house, they bang heads with each other, and there isn't much in it for the management. Not that the house loses money on poker. For a few sticks of furniture and a couple of decks of cards, a table that charges ten dollars an hour for each seat should show an annual income of half a million dollars in any well-run casino. But that's small change by the standards of the times, and so they put the poker tables off in the low-rent section of the room where they won't interfere with the steady flow of money to the slots and the wheels.

Calvin squeezed his hole cards again, and took another peek at them. If he had asked me, I could have told him what was there. Two kings. I could have told him every card that had been dealt. The game was seven-card stud, and he and I were the only ones left; the other players had folded. There was about three grand on the table, enough to pull

Calvin even for the night, and he was sweating it out. This was the way our hands looked with the last card still to come.

Calvin: (Kh Kd) 10s 2c 9h 7d

Me: (Ah 6c) 6s 5d Jc 6d

Looking at the cards tells you the kind of game that he played. He was in love with those kings wired, and he was riding all the way with them. When I pulled the third six, he should have figured me for trips, and he should have dropped. In his spot, I would have. Of course, you could also ask what I was doing chasing along with a pitiful pair of sixes, but I wasn't trying to win. Just the opposite. Some people have to beat you in order to love you. Others have to be beaten. Calvin fell into the first category. Unless he could beat you, dominate and win, he didn't want to know you. If he could beat you, then you could get close to him, and that was what I had in mind.

I was high, and I bet five hundred, praying that he wouldn't fold. No fear. He was riding those kings all the way, and he called.

On the seventh card, I caught a useless seven of clubs. Before I tapped Calvin's head to see what he had drawn, I said another prayer that he had pulled his third king. I tapped, and he hadn't. It was the ten of hearts, and all he had was what he had started with, two kings. He waited for me to make my move. I checked. His eyes widened with surprise. He was expecting a heavy bet to force him out or make him pay, but I didn't want him out. I wanted him in, and I was the one who was going to pay.

"Those sixes not so strong," he muttered to himelf. "This guy Benny, he's been pulling my posey."

"The name is Ben," I said. I had said it before.

"Yeah, sure." He was still muttering to himself. "He's just rubbing my rhubarb with that shitty little pair. He raises and he raises, and now he checks. Horseshit poker, but maybe not. Maybe cute." He looked at me. "Which is it, Benny?"

"Ben."

"Yeah, sure."

He rubbed his chin. He scratched behind his ear. He was fighting greed. A pair of kings in seven-card is not a great hand, and he knew that he should check along and get a free ride, but if he did he might be costing himself money. If he bet instead of checking there was the chance that I'd call, and he wanted every dollar of my money he could get. On the other hand, if he bet, I might raise. He made up his mind, and pushed in a pile.

"One thousand," he said.

Something inside of me screamed *raise*, but that wasn't my job. This time I was supposed to lose. I could have simply folded, but I wanted him to win big. Besides, it was the company's money, not mine.

"Call," I said, and pushed chips.

He nodded. "What have you got?"

"I called you."

"Yeah." He flipped over his two hole cards. "You're looking at it."

"Kings wired." I tried to sound surprised. "That's all?"

"Look who's talking. It isn't much, Benny, but it's a hell of a lot stronger than your sixes."

It was a good deal stronger than two of my sixes, not three of them. I said, "You're a hard man to hustle, Calvin. A hard man." I folded my hand, and flipped the cards into the deadwood before anyone could see them.

Calvin grinned like a happy wolf, his relief written on his face. He pulled in the pot, and said, "Beautiful. Last hand of the night, and I finally hit."

One of the players asked, "What's this last hand business?"

"That's it, I'm out." There were a few unhappy voices around the table. Calvin said sharply, "Quiet, you vultures. You beat on me all night, and I finally get even. You can pick my bones tomorrow."

"Take it and run, I don't blame you," I said. "That's enough for me, too."

He gave me that wolfish grin again. "That last hand got to you, huh? Took some of the starch out of your shorts."

I shrugged.

"Come on, let's cash in, and I'll buy you a drink." He had beat me, and I was his.

We visited the cashier's cage, and then went to the bar. At five in the morning, we were the only customers. He ordered a scotch, I had the same, and he sank onto a bar stool. Some of the air went out of him then. “Sweet hand,” he said when his drink came. “Lousy pair of kings, but they held up. You gotta have faith.” He raised his glass to me. “That last hand saved my ass, Benny. I thank you, my wife thanks you, and my children thank you.”

“Look, I asked you before. Would you stop calling me Benny?”

“Yeah, sure. What do your friends call you?”

“Ben. Just Ben.”

“You're lucky. You know what my friends call me?”

“What?”

“Collect. They call me collect.” He looked at me expectantly, his eyebrows jerking. “Get it?”

“No.”

“Ben, it's funny. My friends call me collect. On the telephone.”

“Now I get it.”

“So how come you're not laughing?”

“Because it isn't funny.”

“It is, believe me it is. I know funny, and that's funny.”

“It isn't. Actually, it's very sad.”

He thought about that, staring into his glass. He looked up, scowling. “What's that supposed to mean? You trying to say that I don't have any friends?”

“Do you?”

“You gotta be kidding. You see the way they treat me around here?” He did a Durante. “I got a million of 'em, a million of 'em.”

“Name one.”

He laughed. It was a bitter, unpleasant sound. He was muttering to himself again. “My friends call me collect. I like it, I like it. You're wrong, it's funny.” He called for another drink, and when it came he gulped it. “What's all this about friends and friendship? You some kind of a philosopher?”

“No, just another poker player making conversation after a long, hard night.”

“A horseshit poker player. You should have raised on the last card. You would have knocked me out.”

“Not you. You were in love with those kings.”

“Yeah, maybe.” He looked at me directly. “Friends. You got any friends?”

"Four of them."

"I mean real friends."

"We're like a family."

"Lucky." He motioned to the bartender for a refill. He had been drinking steadily at the table, but he wasn't showing it yet. "Benjamin, the philosopher. You're right, don't let them call you Benny. Who ever heard of a philosopher called Benny? Well, you're right, Mister Philosopher, I don't have any friends. I got a million guys want to call me Calvin and shake my hand. I got a million broads want to hop into bed with me. And I don't have a friend in the world. I got zilch. Zero. Nada."

"You have a wife and children. That's a lot."

"Bullshit. What do you know about my wife and kids?"

"Not a thing."

"I've got a wife who hates my guts, and I've got kids I never see. That's what I've got." He put his face close to mine. "You see, Mister Philosopher, I'm not exactly stupid. Maybe I talk too loud, and I act like a *shmuck* sometimes, but that's part of my job. I'm not unintelligent, and I know exactly how empty and sterile my life is." He made a sweeping gesture with his hand. "This is your life, Calvin Weiss. The S.S. *Carnival Queen*."

"You're breaking my heart."

He looked surprised. "What's with the tough guy? You started this friendship *shtick*."

"I just hate to see a grown man feeling sorry for himself."

"Well, fuck you and your four friends. You think I never had a friend in my life?"

"Did you?"

"Like this." He held up two fingers pressed together. He looked at the fingers, and laughed. "The short one is me. You remember the old comic strip, Mutt and Jeff?"

"Sure, the short guy and the tall guy."

"Right, so let me lay a piece of trivia on you. You ask ten people today who was the short one and who was the tall one, and nine out of ten they'll say that Mutt was the short one. Mutt, short—right? Wrong. Mutt was the tall one. Don't ask me why, but he was. I know, because my friend was the tall one, and he was Mutt. Mutt and Jeff, that's what they called us. We went everywhere together, we did everything together, and nobody ever had a better friend. So it wasn't always this way, Mister Philosopher. I had a friend once, a damn good friend."

"When was this?"

"Oh, Christ, a long time ago, back in college. A little place you never heard of, Van Buren in upper New York state. Yeah, Mutt, Jeff, and the Pom-Pom Queen, we were a team. Later on there was the Poodle, but she really didn't count. It was just the three of us, two guys and a girl, the classic triangle. It would have made a great soap. The all-star jock, the campus comic, and the prettiest girl in seven states. Here, take a look."

He got out his wallet, and laid a snapshot on the bar. It was an old picture of June, and she had been stunningly beautiful. The woman I had seen in the motel room was a beauty, but the girl in the photo took your breath away. I murmured something appropriate, and Calvin nodded.

"We were both in love with her," he said quietly. "Mutt and Jeff, we both wanted to marry her. One of us did."

"You?"

"*Ta-da*." He raised a fist in a victory sign. "I got the girl, and I lost my best friend."

"Sore loser."

"Ah, come on, it had to be that way. We didn't think so, but it had to be. He wouldn't have been human otherwise."

"At least you got the girl. He got nothing."

"Lucky me."

"You don't sound happy about it."

"It was a mistake, Mister Philosopher. My mistake, and hers. She married the wrong guy, and she's been letting me know it ever since." He looked at his watch. "Jesus, I gotta get going."

"To bed, I hope."

He grinned. "Definitely to bed, but I didn't say what bed."

"At six in the morning?"

"Nothing like a sunrise *shtup* to start the day off right." He slid off his stool. He smiled shyly, and it changed his face. "Good talking to you. Almost like talking to a friend."

"Get some sleep."

"All in good time. Stop by the casino tomorrow. I can use the money."

I didn't want him to go just then. There was more that I wanted to know about him, but there was no way that I could hold him there. I decided on a quick tap, a grab bag to see what I could come up with. I went in as he was standing there, and I came out as he walked away.

It was a grab bag, all right, with all sorts of surprises in it. I stood there trying to absorb what I had gathered, and Fleckmann walked into the casino. He saw me at the bar, and came over. He looked neat, clean, and disgustingly well-rested.

"You look awful," he told me. "Up all night?"

I snarled at him.

"That bad? Been playing poker?"

I snarled again.

"Oh dear, someone needs his breakfast and a few laps in the pool."

"Sounds good, but not right now. How does one make a telephone call, you know, ship to shore?"

"Ship to shore, how quaint. What century are you living in? You go to your cabin, you pick up the telephone, and you make your call."

"That's all?"

"Electronic wonders."

I found some coffee on the way to my cabin, and took it with me. I called the Center, and asked for Sammy. The duty officer said that he was sleeping. I told him to roust the bum out. As I waited, I regretted, not for the first time, Sammy's carefree attitude about codes. He refused to use them. That was spy stuff, not for us.

Sammy came on, and said, "Where are you?"

"At sea."

"As usual."

"Cute. Something came up that's bothering me."

"Is this an open line?"

"Yes, and I'll be careful. If I say Pagliacci, do you know who I mean?"

"Yes."

"It seems that Pagliacci went to college at a small school in New York called Van Buren. That bothers me. Do you think that it should?"

There was a silence, then he said, "I don't like talking about this on an open line."

"Yeah, and you're the one who won't use codes. Loosen up, who do you think is listening?"

Another pause. "Van Buren is the school that's playing Polk in basketball. Vince's assignment."

"That's what I thought. Coincidence?"

"It damn well better be, because if it isn't . . ."

"I know, it makes it a whole new ballgame. If these things are connected . . ."

"They can't be. Ogden was out of his skull when he made those assignments."

"That's been our assumption, but what if he wasn't?"

"I don't want to think about it."

"I'm afraid that we have to. If these things are hooked up . . ."

"Hold it, you're jumping too fast. All you have is a coincidence so far, a tenuous connection between two of the assignments. What do you expect me to do about it?"

"I don't know, but I don't like it. I just tapped Pagliacci's head and came up with some names that should be checked out. Will you do that for me?"

"Let's have them."

"Back in Van Buren, he had a couple of close friends in his senior year. One of them was a girl named June Honeywell, aka the Pom-Pom Queen. She later became Mrs. Pagliacci."

"I'll check her out. What else?"

"A guy named Hassan Rashid, his best friend. He was an exchange student from Lebanon, a jock. Do you want to know what sport?"

"No."

"Basketball."

Sammy sighed. "I'll check it. Go ahead."

"One more. There was another girl that they called the Poodle. Her name was Julia Simms."

"Shit."

"What?"

"I don't have to check that one. Julia Simms has been dead for years. She was the mother of Lila Simms, the kid that Ogden set up for the rape."

15

THE time that The Prisoner spent in the squad room each day after the exercise period was a time of reflection for him, and, being a man with a disciplined mind, he tried to limit those reflections to a single topic at a time. Sometimes he thought about the value of his work, sometimes about the nearly useless existence that he now led, sometimes about the past; and when he thought about the past he often thought of the women he had known. These were not entirely erotic reminiscences for, as he would be the first to admit, he had not led a life of sexual adventure. In truth, discounting the casual connections of a soldier, he could number only four women who had given his life new dimension and meaning.

The first, of course, had been June, and with her there had been no coming together at all, but only the trembling of two magnetic bodies facing pole to pole, the space between them never closed. There had been kisses, yes, and touches, but nothing more than that, and it sometimes amused The Prisoner to think that this first great love of his life, the one against which the others were measured, had been so innocent, so chaste. And on further reflection, he wondered if, perhaps, that very innocence had preserved his love, like a fly in amber, over all the years that had passed. For the love still lived, if only in amber, and in these times of reflection he could still take it out, gaze at it, and marvel at its purity.

But if his time with June was a time to remember, his time with the Poodle was a time to forget, had he not been a man of such intellectual discipline, he would have long since forced all thoughts of her from his mind. But this was a luxury that he could not allow, for to forget about the Poodle would have been, by his standards, an act of cowardice. He had not conducted himself well with her. To use an unfashionable phrase, he had taken advantage of her love for him. He had used that love as an instrument of revenge. He had used that love as a bellows with which to reinflate his pride. In the end, he had allowed her to be crushed by her love for him, and for this he was deeply ashamed. A case could be made, he knew, for saying that in a sense he had taken her life. Exaggeration, yes, but it was a thought he had lived with for years. Over those years he had taken many lives, both by direction and by his own hand, and none had stayed with him that way. Only the Poodle, and, of course, the little girl on the plane.

Which led his thoughts to Zahra. In his dreams about that airplane operation he was never sure which of them had beaten the child when she started to scream, beaten her until her face was shattered and her eyes were sightless. In the tricks played by his memory, sometimes it was Amir who had done it, sometimes Murad, and sometimes, in a twisting of truth, himself. But it never was Zahra in those dreams, and he wondered why. Certainly not because she was a woman, for he had seen her kill savagely. Perhaps, because she was *his* woman? Did his connection with her convey an immunity in his dreams? Perhaps. He would have liked to have asked her what she thought of such a concept, for she was a woman of strong opinions, but he had not seen her in years, and now she lived in Paris, undercover. He missed her at times, but he knew that he missed her physical presence less than he missed her sharp and ranging mind. Of these four women that he often thought about, hers was the only mind to match and excel his own. They had lived and worked together for three years, most of that time in Paris, and he had come to depend on the way that she could cut to the core of a complex problem, grasp the essentials, and organize the answers. She was a true revolutionary, with the revolutionary's disdain for the unessential, and she had broadened his life with her intellect. It was for this that he loved her, and if the physical side of that love had been less a passionate coupling than a comfort shared by friends, it had seemed enough at the time.

At the time, but not now, upon reflection. Lying in the squad room on a flat pallet, stripped to his shorts and with his eyes closed, he could see the irony woven into these three loves. How ironic that there had never been a consummation to the first, great love of his life. How ironic that the finest of them all should wind up being crushed by the weight of her love for him. How ironic that the one whose intellect he had admired most, had failed to ignite any fire for him. How ironic that only with the fourth of these women, the one who should have meant the least to him, was he able to enjoy a time of rich sensuality.

It was a most improbable love affair. He was twenty-four when he met Maria-Teresa Bonfiglia, and she was thirty-five. He was Muslim and she was Roman Catholic. He was virtually penniless, and she was doubly wealthy, both from her marriage and from the fees that her voice earned. His was a star that was still obscured, and hers was a star that was firmly fixed in the world of grand opera. She made dreams come true on stage, while he had only extravagant dreams of the future of his people. She was a woman who knew exactly what she wanted to do with every day of the rest of her life, and he was a man who prayed every day for guidance into tomorrow. She was the mistress of the magnificent gesture, and he was the master of self-effacement. They could not have been more different, but when they made love they were very much the same: warm and wild, tender and savage, grasping and giving. When they made love, they were not improbable at all.

It lasted for almost a year, and the time went by so quickly that when it was over it seemed to The Prisoner that they had been together for only a matter of weeks. But it lasted from September to June, and it was a time of high excitement. That was the season that Maria-Teresa sang twenty-four Butterflys, twenty-two Toscas, eighteen Neddas yoked to eighteen Santuzzas, twelve of the Puccini Manon and eight of the Massenet, a record thirty-nine Susannas, and a raft of other rôles. She sang in Buenos Aires and in Rome, in Vienna and in Paris, at La Scala and at La Fenice, at Covent Garden and at the Met. She sang all over the western world—including an ill-advised Eva at Bayreuth—and The Prisoner was never far from her side. He sat through every performance that she gave, stood through every green room reception, faded away when photographers approached, and claimed his love only when her public had released her. It was a time of richness and contentment, and if he had any doubts about a would-be revolutionary playing lap-dog to a pampered darling of the Nazarene world, he kept those doubts to himself. He knew that it was too good to last, and he was determined to squeeze out every drop of it. It was almost as if he could see the austere life that waited for him, and knew that now was the time to store up memories.

He was right, it was too good to last. It started in September, and in June she told him it was over. Why? Because it was time to be over. There was a marriage that she had ignored for a year, there were children to reclaim, there was the wheel that turned her life and still was turning. He had ridden that wheel to almost full circle, and now it was time to step off. To his credit, he stepped off gracefully. He accepted what had been granted to him, and he walked away as filled with memories as a camel is with water when he comes from the well. His wheel was turning, too, it was time to go on to something new, time to find a purpose, and he found it soon enough when he met Zahra in Paris, and she introduced him to the cause that would occupy his days.

The cause, yes, always, but still there were times for memories. He switched on the phonograph, the battered old friend that helped to keep him sane, and searched through his stack of records. He found her Tosca, put it on, and lay down to listen. It was an old recording, over-used, but the pureness of her line cut through the hisses and scratches. As always, he was transported close to tears by her voice.

The tears of a killer, he thought. The tears of a warrior. The tears of a celibate monk. He turned the volume up for the *Vissi d'arte*. Such sadness. Yes, she gave her life for art, and mine . . . ? He knew very well what his life was for, and he knew very well how it would end some day, but until that day there were memories. Like these. He closed his eyes, and let the music roll over him.

16

IT took Sammy nine hours and an incredible amount of Langley muscle to spring Vince out of Atlantic City. He couldn't do it by himself, he didn't have the clout. He had to go to Delaney for it, something he hated to do, and Delaney had to go as high as the DDI before the local police would play ball. Even so, it took nine hours, and by the time Vince made the street there were only two days to go before the Polk-Van Buren game. When he called the Center, they told him to go to New York. Sammy and Delaney would meet him there.

The house on East Sixty-fourth Street that the Center used for a New York base was a four-story brownstone with a weathered façade. The top two floors were bedrooms, and the second floor was filled with a gleaming mass of electronic equipment. The interior walls of the ground floor had been knocked out to make one large room. In the days before Sammy took over it had been called the Operations Room, but now it was called the Saloon. Operations were still handled in the back of the room, but up front was an eighteen-foot mahogany bar complete with stools, rail, and a back mirror. There were "Wanted" posters of Old West pistoleros on the walls, a sepiatone of Lillie Langtry, and a Rubenesque nude in faded oils. Sammy had wanted to put in spittoons, but Langley had turned down the requisition.

Vince stood behind the bar, his preferred spot. Sammy and Delaney sat on stools. Vince dropped a single cube of ice into a glass, and poured a splash of Wild Turkey for himself. To no one in particular, he said, "I had some dynamite cognac down there."

Sammy asked, "Is it true that the Atlantic City slammer has slot machines in the cells?"

Vince nodded. "Every one a loser."

"As long as you're pouring," Delaney said pointedly. "Scotch."

Vince looked at Sammy, who nodded. He made the drinks, and pushed them across the bar. Delaney said, "Lay it out for me. How do you see it?"

Vince shrugged. "Nothing complicated. Domino gets close to Giardelli, and she uses his connections to set up the fix. As soon as I walk into the scene, she knows that I can blow her out of the water, so one of us has to go, Carmine or me."

"Why Carmine?"

"I've been thinking about that. I've had plenty of time to think."

"Don't be that way. We did it as fast as we could."

"Why Carmine, not me? Because the way that she sees it, I'm Company, which means that we're working for the same people."

"You're not. She's a freelance working for a dead man."

"I said the way *she* sees it. I think it was spur of the moment. She decided not to wax a company man when she didn't have to. All she had to do was keep me on ice until the time frame was over. So she does the job on Giardelli, and sets me up for it. She figured that by the time I worked my way out of it, *if* I worked my way out of it, she'd be home free."

"Where does Anthony fit?"

"I figure him for a recruit, nothing more. He and Domino, they put on an act about hating each other, but they're probably screwing like rabbits."

"You sure he's the one who slugged you?"

"No question. What have you got on him?"

"Middle-level muscle, name of Riordan. He and the woman have dropped out of sight. God knows where they are now."

"Have you been able to run down anything on Domino? Ogden got her out of Baghdad years ago. That should show in your banks."

"It doesn't," said Delaney. "He must have done it on his own. We still have nothing on her."

"Which leaves us where?" Vince turned to Sammy. "We've got the game coming up the day after tomorrow. What do we do now, coach?"

"Punt," said a gloomy Delaney.

"It's basketball," said Sammy. "I don't know, Vince, I really don't. You gave it a good shot, but it didn't work. The way I see it, we're out of options."

"We can't just sit back and let it happen."

"What else can we do?" Sammy spread his hands helplessly. "The Company gave us the job, we're bound by the rules that they established. The whole point here is to keep the Company clean, which means that we can't go public. We can't go to the cops, we can't go to the media, we can't go to the college. We can't do anything."

"I know what I'd like to do," said Delaney. "I'd like to get those two kids and beat their brains out."

Sammy sighed. "We can't do that either, even if we wanted to. You take those two . . . what's their names?"

"Holmes and Devereaux," said Vince.

"Polk doesn't have a chance without them. You take them out of the lineup, and Domino gets what she wants."

"Punt," Delaney said again.

Head-to-head, Vince said, *Sammy?*

Sammy kept a straight face. *What?*

There's a way.

Show it to me.

Vince showed him. Sammy started to shake his head, but caught himself. *No way. He'd never go for it.*

It's worth a try.

I'm not sure that I'd go for it, either.

What choice do we have?

It isn't a question of choice. It's a question of what's possible, and this isn't.

Ask him.

Why me?

Because that's what you get paid for.

Not nearly enough. Sammy cleared his throat, and Delaney looked up. "Vince has an idea."

Chicken.

"Vince?" Delaney looked confused. "Oh, you've been doing your number."

"It's just a thought, and I don't think much of it . . ."

"Thanks, buddy." Vince slammed his glass on the bar. "I'll tell it myself. Look, these kids sold out. They agreed to dump the game for twenty-five grand apiece, right?"

"Right."

"And we want them to play it straight, right?"

"Of course."

"So we buy them back."

Delaney frowned. "I don't follow."

"We outbid Domino," Vince said patiently. "We offer them a chunk of money to play to win. A big chunk."

Delaney's frown deepened. "Wait a minute. You mean we bribe them?"

"Call it fighting fire with fire. We double the offer. Fifty thousand each if they play it straight."

"Impossible." Delaney's voice was cold and stiff. "You're asking me to authorize the use of Company funds to bribe a couple of basketball players? Impossible."

"Why? I'm talking about a hundred grand. You spend ten times that much every time you knock off some South American politician."

"We don't do things like that anymore."

"The hell you don't."

"Look, it's out of the question. I mean, what if it ever got out? Our job is to keep the Company clean, not get it involved."

"It's already involved, up to the ass, and this is the only way out."

"Definitely not. Forget it."

I told you he wouldn't go for it, said Sammy.

How about giving me a hand?

I told you, I don't like it, either.

Maybe if you made a pitch he'd change his mind.

No way. He'll never do it.

Then lend me a hundred thou.

Be serious. I don't have that kind of money liquid.

I don't have that kind of money, period. But this is the only way to do it.

Getting a little emotional about this, aren't you?

Maybe.

Making it personal, aren't you?

"I guess I am," Vince said aloud. He came out from behind the bar, and headed for the door.

"Hold it," said Delaney. "Where are you going?"

"To work." He kept on walking.

Sammy looked into his head, and saw what he had in mind. He called after him, *She won't do it, you're wasting your time.* But Vince was out the door.

On the way over in the taxi, he realized that he should have called first, for there was no good reason why a woman as active as Ida Whitney would be at home at eleven in the morning. But she was. She showed no surprise when she saw him. She sat him down in her living room. She offered him coffee. She listened carefully while he spoke, nodding her head. He realized that he was speaking rapidly, almost wildly, and he tried to restrain himself, but the words came gushing out. Finally, he stopped himself in mid-sentence, and fell silent. He knew that he had made his case poorly. He waited. She looked at him with concern.

"What's wrong with you?" she asked. "You sound strange—not yourself."

"I'm not," he admitted, and his voice sounded strange in his ears, too high and thin. "Since the last time I saw you I damn near got myself killed, I got hit over the head, and I spent a night in jail. I am definitely not myself. I'm running on rocket fuel right now."

"Your eyes look terrible."

"Yours look lovely."

"Don't say things like that."

"Sorry, it's the rocket fuel. You haven't answered my question."

"What makes you think that I have access to that kind of money?"

He waved an arm in a gesture that took in the richly furnished room, the Traz original on one wall, the Catelot on another, and the bronze nymph by Giorgino. "Are you saying that you don't?"

"Lewis makes the money. I just spend it."

"That's not an answer."

She leveled her eyes at him, those eyes he remembered so well. They could be warm and liquid, or hard as bullets. They were hard. "I read the newspapers, Vincent. A name was mentioned here the other night. Giardelli. Now he's dead."

"Yes."

"Did you kill him?"

"No."

There was a silence between them. "Is that all you're going to say?"

"I'm sorry, but I can't answer any more questions."

"You're terrific, you really are. The other night you came barging in here and bullied Lewis into giving you a name. Now the name is dead, and you're here again, this time to ask me for a hundred thousand dollars."

"A loan."

"Whatever you call it, but you say that you can't answer. Just who the hell do you think you are?"

"An old friend."

"Well, old friend, this isn't going to work." Those eyes were flashing now. "Either you answer some questions, or this conversation is over."

He hesitated. "I'll answer the ones that I can."

She leaned forward. "Are you really a translator at the United Nations?"

"At times."

"Do you hold any other job?"

"Yes."

"Are you employed by any government agency, and if you are, is it federal, state, or local?"

She's good, he thought. Of course, she's been watching Lewis at work for years. "Federal."

"Can you tell me the name of your organization?"

"No."

"Would I know the name if you told me?"

"I doubt it."

"Is the work you do legal? I mean, is it within the law?"

"Sometimes."

"Is it in the national interest?"

"Always."

"Sitting here, right now, are you acting as a representative of your organization?"

"No. My organization has rejected this solution to the problem. They have refused to fund it. That's why I've come to you."

"I see. One last question. What the hell is so important about a God damn basketball game that an agency of the federal government has to get involved in it?"

Vince shook his head. "I can't answer that one, but I'll say this much. It's important to the government, it's important to my organization, and, of course, it's important to the young men involved."

"You'll have to explain that last part to me. The other night you made a strong case for trying to help two young black men who were about make the biggest mistake of their lives. Now you're suggesting that I supply the money that will compound the felony. So tell me this, old friend. How is throwing good money after bad going to help these young men straighten out their lives?"

Vince stood up, and walked around the room. He stopped in front of the Traz, and looked at it carefully. He stepped back, and looked again, staring into the geometrics of the composition. It told him nothing. He turned around.

"I don't have a good answer to that. You may be right, it may be throwing good money after bad, but it's the only move I can think of to make. Like I said, I'm running on rocket fuel, and I don't have much time. I can't let those kids throw that game. I can't."

He came close, and bent over her. Their faces were inches apart, and her scent was all around him. "That's it, the bottom line," he said. "Will you do it?"

She said faintly. "Is this part of your sales pitch?"

"Will you?"

"Why not ask Lewis?"

"I'm asking you. Now."

"Back off."

He straightened up, and stepped away. She stood to face him. Her eyes were warm again, but her face told him nothing. "A hundred thousand?"

"In cash."

"We'll go to the bank. I'll need ten minutes to change and call Lewis."

"Why Lewis?"

"He's my husband. I have to tell him where I'm going."

"You're going to the bank."

"I'm going to New Hampshire. With you." She smiled for the first time. "I go where the money goes."

At a certain point, it turned into a farce. Until then, Vince had been running on rocket fuel, the whine of engines competing with the throbbing in his head. There had been the rush to the bank to pick up the money, the transaction smoothly handled by an assistant manager who had thrown in a Vuitton carrying case as a lagniappe. There had been the rush to LaGuardia to catch the commuter flight to Manchester, the rush driving north in the rental car through driving snow, through Concord, and Franklin, and Bristol, and the rush to find a decent place to stay for the night. The place was called the Hunters' Lodge, and then there was the rush to their separate rooms, the rush to wash and change, and the rush to get a drink and something to eat.

Vince was holding an ice-filled towel to his head when Ida knocked at his door. She saw the towel, and asked, "What's the matter?"

"Where I got hit."

"You going to be all right?"

"No problem."

"Have you called them yet?"

"Just about to."

"Make it for the morning. It's too late to do it tonight." She had the bag with the money slung over her shoulder.

"Yeah, all I want tonight is a couple of drinks, a rare steak, and some sleep."

"The dining room is off the lobby. Make the call, and I'll meet you there."

She left, and he checked the team list from the Athletic Department. He dialed a number, and when someone answered, he asked, "Is this Willy Holmes?"

"Yes, that's right," said the voice.

"My name is Bonepart, from *Hoops* magazine. I interviewed you the other day, remember?"

"Oh sure, Mr. Bonepart, sure I do." There was a sudden enthusiasm in the voice. "What can I do for you?"

"I want to talk to you, Willy."

"Say, anything I can do to help the press, you name it."

"You won't be helping the press, you'll be helping yourself, kid. I want to see you first thing tomorrow morning."

"Tomorrow?"

"That's what I said, and I want to see Devereaux, too."

"Dion?"

"He's your roommate, isn't he? Is he there?"

"Well . . . uh, yeah."

"I want to see the two of you, together. I'm staying at the Hunters' Lodge out on the Parkland Extension. You know the place?"

"Yes sir, but . . ."

"No buts, Willy. I want to see you and Dion at eight in the morning, sharp. I'm in room number twelve. You got that?"

"Mr. Bonepart, you're going a little too fast for me here." Now there was a nervous edge to his voice. "Could you tell me what this is all about?"

"It's about your future, and it's about money. How does that sound?"

"Look, I'm not sure that I can . . ."

"You can. You don't have a choice. Either I talk to you and Dion, or I talk to your coach, and I think you know what I'll be talking about. Now, how do you want to play it?"

There was a long pause. "Just a minute." There was a longer pause, and Vince heard muffled voices. Willy came back. "You said eight o'clock?"

"That's right."

"We'll be there."

His head still throbbed, but the ice had helped. He went looking for

Ida, and found her in the dining room. It was a pleasant, quiet room with candles in sconces on oak-panelled walls, and a bluestone hearth that burned logs the size of an elephant's ankle. The linen was crisp, and the crystal on the tables twinkled. Ida had taken a table next to a window that looked out onto a moonlit snowfield. More snow fell, dancing down the window. Ida waved as he came into the room. In an angora sweater and a pleated skirt she looked younger than he could remember her being, younger than she could have been when he first had known her. As he took his seat, she asked the question with her eyes, and he answered, "Eight in the morning, both of them."

"How did they sound?"

"I only spoke to Holmes. He sounded edgy, but he'll show. They both will."

"I ordered you a drink. Wild Turkey, one rock, right?"

"Right." He smiled because she had remembered.

She read his smile accurately. "Don't flatter yourself. I remembered because Lewis takes it the same way."

"He got it from me. He never drank before he met me."

"I've ordered dinner."

"Steak?"

"Actually, I ordered venison for both of us."

"I said that I wanted a steak."

"I know, but the waiter talked me into the venison. He said he shot the deer himself. He was very persuasive. I just couldn't say no to him."

"That has to make him the luckiest waiter in the state of New Hampshire."

It wasn't very funny, but she laughed. Vince laughed, too, and it was at that moment, while both of them were laughing, that what they were doing turned into a comedy for him. Like a bad movie, he could no longer take the assignment seriously. It was a joke. He didn't give a damn who won some stupid ballgame. He didn't give a damn if Holmes and Devereaux were greedy little bastards who were screwing up their lives. He didn't give a damn that Giardelli got waxed; the world was better off without him. All he cared about was the moment, sitting in a romantic spot with a lovely woman he once had adored, and still admired. The rest of it was a farce, and he couldn't help laughing at it. He realized that Ida was looking at him strangely, and he heard the echo of his laughter in his ears. He had not stopped laughing. He was still laughing loud and hard. He stopped.

Watch it, he warned himself. Get a grip.

Ida asked, "Are you sure you're all right?"

"Just fine."

"How hard was that hit on the head?"

"I can still feel it, but I'm all right." The throbbing was worse. "What did Lewis say when you told him you were coming with me?"

"He said to take good care of the money."

"That's all?"

"If you mean what I think you mean, Lewis and I have the best of all possible marriages. We trust each other. I understand his needs, and he understands mine."

"An open marriage?"

"A free marriage."

"Permissive?"

"Understanding."

"No jealousy on either side?"

"Definitely not."

"Sounds ideal."

"It is."

He leaned across the table, and took her hand. "The other night you said that you used to be in love with me a little."

"A little, yes."

"I felt the same way, but I never said it."

"Just as well."

"There was Lewis."

"Yes."

"And now? How do you feel now?"

She shrugged, but she was smiling. "Some things don't change."

"Then what are we waiting for?"

"The venison, of course."

The venison came, and they agreed that it was delicious, but they did not eat much of it. They did not eat much of anything, and they barely touched the wine. They fiddled with their food with their eyes locked on each other, and finally, when they could rightfully say that dinner was over, they went up to Vince's room and made love.

It was a long time coming, years delayed, and everything about it seemed right. Their moves and their responses meshed. They rode the wave together, crested together, gasped and cried out together, and made the slow and lazy tumble home together, happily spent. It was their first time together, but they made love with a practiced ease. Everything about it seemed right, the machinery functioned, but in truth there was nothing special about it. There was an aspect of romance that might have made it special, the love that never made it years before now given a second chance, but it didn't work out that way. It was nothing more than a romp in the hay, and when it was done they both knew it. It was nothing special. It wasn't even sad.

They both fell at once into sleep, drained as much by the day as by their lovemaking, and hours later when Vince awoke it was to the sound of a scratching at the door. He woke with a bubble of laughter in this throat. He throttled it, and it never got past his lips, but it was a strange way to come up out of sleep. The room was dark, and the luminous dial of the clock said that it was just past four in the morning. He felt the warmth of Ida asleep beside him, tucked into the small of his back, and he heard her steady breathing. He felt the bubble in his throat again, the urge to laugh that, again, he had to control. It was all so funny, all of it now, not just the job. Now it was this business with Ida that seemed absurd, the candlelight dinner and the crackling fire, the passion rekindled after so many years, the rush to bed, the tumble and toss. And now the scratching at the door.

He heard it again. It was a tiny sound, like a cat in the night, but that was what had wakened him. It was the light and tentative sound that one made at four in the morning instead of a knock.

Another bad movie, he thought, and again restrained the urge to laugh. A French farce, that's what this is turning into. No, for a true French farce we'd have to have Lewis, the outraged husband, come crashing through the door.

The door swung open. The light went on. Lewis stood there staring. "You son of a bitch," he said. "I figured it was something like this."

Vince sat up in bed. "Lewis." Stuck for words, he said the first thing that came into his head. "I was just thinking about you."

Lewis snarled, "I'll bet you were."

The next thing that came into his head. "How did you get here?"

"How do you think? Drove all night through the snow while you were keeping warm with my wife."

"Lewis, don't jump to conclusions."

"You've been doing all the jumping around here." Lewis' hand went into his pocket, and came out with a small, flat pistol. "Let's see how you jump on top of this."

"Lewis." It was Ida, awake and bolt upright.

"You bitch, who did you think you were fooling with that story about the money?"

"It's true, the money is right over there in that bag."

"Just an excuse for a dirty weekend."

"It's only Thursday," Vince pointed out.

"You bitch. You whore."

"Don't you dare call me that."

"You said you had a permissive marriage," Vince complained. He was beginning to feel silly again. He turned to Lewis. "That's what she said."

"Be quiet," Ida hissed. She realized that she was naked, and she pulled the blankets up to her shoulders. "Lewis, put down that gun before you hurt somebody."

"You wanna see hurt, you're gonna see hurt."

"Close that door, people can hear."

Lewis kicked the door shut without looking at it. Vince tried to make himself small under the blankets. He muttered, "You said he didn't get jealous. You said that he understood your needs."

"Leave this to me, will you?"

"I heard that," Lewis said sharply. "What needs? What kind of needs do you have that I don't take care of?"

Vince leaned close to Ida. "You said you had an understanding."

"So I lied." Ida spat out the words. "I lied, all right? Now will you please shut up?"

"What needs, huh? You tell me that?"

"Honey, I know this looks bad, but I can explain."

Vince let her explain. He did not try to talk. He had enough to do to keep from laughing. He felt it in his chest and throat, and he had to work to keep it down.

Can't laugh now, he thought, spoil the big scene. Old Lewis, got a face on him like a tiger, snow on his hat and a pistol in his hand. Gentle Lewis, wouldn't swat a fly or step on a bug, but he's got this cute little pistol with a silencer on it, the kind that goes *phut*. Sweet little Ida clutching the bedclothes to her bosom, so modest, but why? Just Lewis and me, husband and lover, so why? Funny, that's why. The whole thing is incredibly funny, just the idea of my old friend Lewis Whitney shooting off a pistol . . .

Phut.

Lewis fired. The bullet went into the wall. Ida screamed, and dived under the covers. Vince threw his head back, and roared with laughter. He couldn't help himself, it came pouring out. Lewis stared at him in disbelief.

"What the hell are you laughing at?" he asked. "You think this gun is funny?"

Helpless with laughter, Vince couldn't answer. He nodded as he gasped for breath.

"Laugh this one off."

Phut.

Lewis fired again. This time the bullet went into the ceiling. Vince tried to catch his breath and began to hiccup.

From under the blankets, Ida screamed, "Stop laughing, you're only making it worse."

Phut. The wall again.

She's right, you have to stop, he told himself. It isn't funny. I mean it is, but it isn't. The man is out for blood, he's looking to kill, but I can't . . . can't stop. It's so ridiculous, a farce. I wanted a French farce, and I got it. Now all we need is for Domino and Anthony to walk in through that door.

The door crashed open. Domino and Anthony walked in. They both held pistols with silencers, the kind that go *phut*. Anthony was smiling; Domino looked grim.

Anthony said, "Drop it."

Lewis turned slowly to face them. He dropped his pistol on the floor. He said, "Who the hell are you?"

"Black hats," Vince explained. "The bad guys." His head was throbbing fiercely again, but his lips were stretched in a grin. It was still very funny.

Anthony said to Lewis, "Back up." He motioned with his pistol. "On the bed."

Lewis stepped back until he felt the bed behind him. He sat on the edge of the bed. He also sat on Ida's foot. Ida squeaked, and her head popped out from under the blankets. She took a look at Domino and Anthony, and dove back under.

"Close the door," said Domino. "We don't want to wake the dead."

Anthony kicked the door shut without looking at it. Domino came over to Vince's side of the bed. She stood over him. He grinned up at her, and said, "Tennis, anyone?"

One corner of her lips twitched. "Only if we play by my rules."

"I can live with that."

"I doubt it. You're not going to live with anything much longer. I let you off the hook once, but you couldn't leave it alone, could you?"

"Just doing my job."

"And I'm just doing mine."

"There's a difference."

"Not to me, there isn't. Who's the woman?"

"His wife."

"So how come you're the one without any clothes on?"

"Well, you know how it is."

"Yeah." Over her shoulder, she said to Anthony. "What do you think?"

"It could work," he said judiciously. "Husband discovers wife in love nest, kills them both, then plugs himself. Happens all the time."

"Make sure you use the same gun," Vince suggested.

Domino asked him, "Why are you smiling?"

"I don't know. I think it was the knock on the head that he gave me. Everything seems funny."

"Well, stop it. I don't like it."

Vince managed to pull his face into serious lines. "Better?"

"There's nothing funny about this."

"I know that. Deep down inside, I know that. Look, how about you let these two walk. They're civilians, they don't know anything about this."

"No way," said Anthony. "They all go."

Domino nodded. "Has to be. And it has to be now."

Lewis shifted on the bed so that he could see Domino. "Does this mean that you're going to kill us?"

"Yes."

"Is there anything that I can do or say that could get us out of this?"

"No."

"I control a great deal of money."

"No."

"And influence."

"No."

Lewis sighed. "Before you . . . I'd like to say something to my wife. May I?"

"We're burning time," said Anthony.

Domino hesitated, then she nodded. "Go ahead."

"Ida?"

Her face slowly appeared, the blankets under her chin. She looked up at her husband. Her eyes were filled with fear, but her lips and chin were steady. "Yes, Lewis."

"I don't have time to say much, but I want to say that I love you. I always have, I never stopped, and right now I love you more than ever. I'm sorry that it has to end this way, but I wanted you to know that, and I wanted you to know that . . . this business with Vince tonight, I forgive you—"

"You what?" She sat up. The blankets dropped, and she pulled them up. "*You* forgive *me*? What about that time with Martha Jackson? What about that hooker in Chicago? What about all those times you came home smelling like a perfume factory?"

"Hold it, there was never anything between Martha and me, she's just a colleague, that's all—"

"And what about the other one in your office, the fat one?"

"Ellen isn't fat."

"She's built like a bratwurst. It wouldn't be so bad if you had some taste."

"I married you, didn't I?"

"The one and only time. What about Mary Lou, and the other one, what's her name . . . ?"

She went on and on, and Vince began to laugh again.

"Stop it," Domino ordered. "Stop laughing."

But he couldn't. It was the ultimate insanity, husband and wife facing the end, and bickering right down to the wire. That was funny enough, but funnier still was the feeling that the best was yet to come. Because Lewis Whitney would never have driven through the night from New York to New Hampshire all by himself. Lewis did nothing by himself anymore. He didn't pick up a package, or open a door, or light a cigar by himself these days if he could help it, not with the small army that he had running around and doing things for him. He never would have come alone, he must have brought people with him, thought Vince, and if this is really a high-class farce a couple of heavyweights should come busting through that door right about . . . now.

A couple of heavyweights kicked in the door, and came into the room. They were tall, they were broad, and each carried a pistol with a silencer on it, the kind that goes *phut*. Domino and Anthony wheeled to face them, but they never got off a shot.

Phut. Phut.

Domino and Anthony went down. They lay without moving.

Ida squeaked, and went back under the blankets.

Vince laughed.

Lewis said to his men, "What the hell took you so long?" He said to Vince, "Stop that idiotic laughter."

Vince stopped, but not because he had been told to. Things just weren't funny any more.

"In all my years of practice, and at the fringes of government," said Lewis, "I have never seen an operation so misdirected and ineptly handled."

"It sort of got screwed up," Vince admitted.

"Sort of? I don't know what agency of the government you work for, and I don't want to know, but I'll tell you this. If this job is any indication of how your agency performs, I have serious doubts about the safety of the nation."

"I know what you mean. Sometimes I do, too."

"Under the circumstances, I think that you'd best leave the rest of this to me."

Vince threw up his hands. "Gladly. It's all yours."

"Did you really say that?" asked Sammy.

"Sure, why not?" said Vince. "It was his show by then, and I hadn't been doing so great, you know? Besides, my head still hurt."

"How is it now?"

"Better."

It was the next day, late at night, and they were alone in the Saloon. The place was dark, with only a single lamp burning over the bar. Sammy looked at his watch, and asked, "Time to call?"

"Give it another thirty minutes."

"So what happened next?"

"You wouldn't believe how efficient those heavyweights were. They got rid of the bodies like a pair of pros, which I guess is what they are. An hour later there were no bloodstains, the room was aired out, and everything was neat as a pin. By that time it was around six in the morning, and Holmes and Devereaux were due at eight. We settled down to wait."

"All three of you?"

"Just Lewis and me. Ida got dressed and went out to see if she could find a coffee shop open at that hour. It was awkward for her there."

Sammy grinned. "Putting it mildly."

"Don't make jokes. It seemed funny at the time, I was laughing my head off, but it really wasn't. We were three old friends, and it shouldn't have happened."

"But it did. What next?"

"Holmes and Devereaux showed up on time, and Lewis took over. I tell you, Sammy, those were two scared kids. They knew what was coming, and they didn't know how to handle it."

Lewis sat them down on the edge of the bed, and paced up and down in front of them like a courtroom lawyer examining a pair of hostile witnesses. "Let me introduce myself," he said. "My name is Lewis Whitney, I'm a lawyer, and I'm going to try to get you out of this mess you're in. Now, let's clear away some of the underbrush. We know for a fact that the two of you agreed to dump the game tomorrow night for twenty-five thousand apiece." Holmes started to say something, but a glare from Lewis shut him up. "Don't interrupt, I said it was a fact. The question now is what to do about it." He pointed a finger at Devereaux.

"You. How much did they pay you up front?"

The two kids looked at each other, then looked away. They were silent.

"Get it through your heads, it's over. You're cooked. Either you talk to me, or you talk to your coach, and then the police. Now, I'll ask you once more. How much did you get in advance?"

"A thousand dollars," Devereaux mumbled. Holmes nodded. "Thousand."

"When were you supposed to get the rest?"

"After the game."

"And I suppose that you took that thousand dollars and went out and bought yourselves some new clothes, a suit and some shoes, and maybe you took some ladies out for a big evening, right?"

Holmes looked Lewis straight in the eye, and said, "No, I didn't do anything like that."

"Just what did you do with it?"

"I put it in the bank. We both did. It's still there."

"The bank?" Lewis didn't try to conceal his surprise. "The bank?"

Devereaux drew himself up with a certain dignity. "I don't need any new clothes, and I already have a girlfriend. With respect, Mister Whitney, I think you've got the wrong idea about why we did this."

Lewis sneered. "Just a couple of misunderstood kids."

"No sir, I didn't mean that, but that stuff about clothes and women doesn't apply. Will is headed for med school next year, and that money was for his tuition. Me, my aim is to write poetry, and who ever heard of a rich poet? That money was for the future, Mister Whitney, not for having a good time."

"I'm touched." Lewis put a hand over his heart. "Thieves with hearts of gold."

"We're not thieves," Holmes protested.

"Thieves," Lewis repeated. "You throw a game and you're a thief, just like holding up a liquor store."

There was a pause, and Holmes said quietly, "That's something quite different, that involves violence. With something like this, nobody gets hurt."

"Nobody gets hurt, how many times have I heard that one? Look, spare me the morality of the nineties. You were ready to commit a felony, betray your team, your friends, and your family, and all for twenty-five thousand dollars. Think that over, and then tell me that nobody gets hurt."

"You tell 'em, Lewis," said Vince. "Tell 'em what it's like to justify the means with the ends. Tell 'em what it's like to turn your back on the ideals of your youth. You tell 'em, you should know."

Lewis scowled, but he didn't miss a beat. "As you can see, Mister Bonepart is a bit of a cynic. He doesn't think so, but he is. See that bag over there? There's a hundred thousand dollars in that bag, and he was going to give it to you to play the game on the level. He was going to outbribe you. And he talks to me about ideals."

A hundred thousand. Holmes and Devereaux looked at each other with widening eyes.

"Forget it," Lewis told them. "That was his approach, not mine. Mine is much simpler. I assume that you both have checking accounts?" They nodded. "Then you will each make out a check to me for one thousand dollars. That's Lewis Whitney, one thousand, and mark it legal fees." His voice cracked like a whip. "*Now.*"

They fumbled in their pockets, fumbled for pens, made out the checks, and handed them over.

"Thank you, you have now been relieved of your ill-gotten gains, and none too soon. You've been incredibly stupid in three different ways. You were stupid enough to risk your futures this way. You were stupid enough to take only a thousand dollars down, because I can assure you that you never would have seen the rest of it. And you were stupid enough to put the money into a bank account, thereby making the transaction a matter of record. I understand that you both are honor students, but you don't have the brains that God gives to clams."

Vince applauded. "There speaks your moralist, gentlemen. Next time get it all up front, and keep it in cash."

"There isn't going to be any next time for these two. Mr. Holmes and Mr. Devereaux are now honest citizens once again. They have left the life of crime behind them, and tomorrow night they are going to play their fucking hearts out for dear old Polk. Aren't you?"

The two young men glanced at each other quickly, glances sliding away. Willy mumbled, "Not that easy."

"Easier than you think," Lewis assured him. "I suppose that the people you dealt with made the usual threats?"

"Said they would kill us if we tried to back out."

"And they meant it," said Devereaux. "Those were two hard people. I never saw people so hard."

"A man and a woman?"

"Yeah."

"What would you do if I told you that those two people are out of your lives forever, that you'll never see them again, that they can't touch you?"

Holmes said slowly, "If that's the truth, I'd get down and kiss your feet."

"It's true, all right. And tomorrow night you two are going to play the best ball you ever played in your lives. And you know why?" He smiled at them sweetly. "Because if you don't, I've got people on my payroll who'll be coming around to see you. They won't kill you, they'll just make you wish they had."

"That won't be necessary," said Holmes. "We'll be in there."

They both stood up, and Devereaux said, "We'll do our best, but we can't guarantee anything. You understand that, don't you?"

Lewis gave them that sweet smile again. "Just win, that's the name of the game, because if you don't, you'll be having some visitors. That's *my* guarantee. Now get out of here, I've got some other business to take care of."

Forty hours later, standing in the bar of the Saloon, Sammy said, "I take it that you were the other business?"

Vince nodded. "I don't know what he had in mind, and I didn't wait to find out. I was out of there. I never did see Ida to say good-bye, I just headed for home."

"Cowardly."

"No question about it. I had enough of those guns that go *phut*."

Sammy looked at his watch. "Time to call."

Vince went to the telephone at the end of the bar, and dialed the number of *The New York Times*. He asked for the sports desk, then asked a question. He listened, and then he hung up. He shot a fist into the air.

"We win, Domino loses. Polk beat Van Buren, 78–62. Twenty-four points for Devereaux, and nine boards. Willy was in there, too."

"So that's it," Sammy said thoughtfully. "Polk goes on to the tournament, and Van Buren stays home."

"Mission accomplished."

"I guess so," said Sammy. "I hope so."

Vince caught his tone. "What do you mean?"

"I hate to do this to you now. You came out on top and you're on a high," said Sammy, but it had to be told, and so he sat Vince down and told him about Calvin Weiss, and June Honeywell, and Hassan Rashid, and the girl they called the Poodle, all those years ago at Van Buren College.

17

SEXTANT, whose name then had been Vlado Priol, was six years old when he saw his mother raped, and his parents killed. He witnessed those horrors while huddled under blankets in a dark corner of the cave on Mount Krn, and whatever he became in later life began on that night in the cave. But it would be a mistake to call that night the turning point of his life. That came ten years later when, with the help of David Ogden, he killed the man who had done the rape and murders.

This, he knew, made him a most unlikely candidate for his present assignment, and for the first time ever he was tempted to question the judgment of the man who had shaped his life. David Ogden had known him as no one else could have known him, then or since. It was Ogden who had found him stiff with fear beneath the blankets, Ogden who had buried the bodies of his parents, and Ogden who had taken him down off the mountain and into the home of the farmers who had cared for him for the next ten years. And it was Ogden who had returned as an agent of vengeance, had shown him how to kill his man, and then had taken him to America. Ogden had known both the boy and the man, had known what that night in the cave had done to him, and still he had given him this assignment. A job of rape. To the man who once had been Vlado Priol.

Why me?

He had asked himself the question over and over, and he could think of only two possible answers. First possibility. That those mushrooms in Ogden's brain had warped him entirely, and the assignment had been issued by a man without reason. Second possibility. That a sane and reasonable David Ogden had issued his orders with a total confidence in the man who once had been Vlado Priol. Confidence in the icy killer he had become, confidence in the faithful executioner of his wishes over the years. Perhaps even more than that, a confidence in the man who had seen first-hand the terror of rape, and would know exactly how to use that terror. Of the two possibilities, Sextant was obliged to believe in the second. He really had no choice.

But still, he asked, why me?

He asked the question as he sat with his feet extended in front of a hearth that produced a smoky, fitful fire. The house that he had rented was a cottage set off from the highway, and screened from the road by a stand of fir and pine. It was small, only a living room, a bedroom, and a bath, but it was enough for what had to be done. The girl and her friend were in the bedroom, bound and gagged, while Sextant sat in the living room with his animals. The animals were restless. Beer-gut, Richie, and Phil sat on the far side of the room, their heads together, muttering. The first case of beer had long been exhausted, and they had started on a second. They kept their voices low, shooting glances across the room at him, but they were straining at the bit.

It was Beer-gut who finally made the move. He heaved himself up out of his chair, and came across the room to ask, "Look, what's holding up the parade?"

Sextant did not bother to stretch his neck to look up. Staring straight ahead, he said, "I am."

"What the hell for? Let's get it going."

"When I say so."

Beer-gut shrugged. "You're the boss, but don't wait too long. Me, I'm feeling fine, but you get much more beer into Richie and Phil, and they'll start to lose their enthusiasm. You know what I mean?"

Sextant wondered, Do I know what he means? Academically, yes. If they drink too much beer they won't be able to produce an erection, and they won't be able to perform sexually. So, yes, I know what he means. But in another sense, since I've never had an erection in my life, I don't understand at all.

"I know what you mean," he said. "Just be patient."

"What about the boy?"

"What about him? You're being paid to do a job on the girl. That's all you have to worry about."

"I was just thinking that if you want me to start on the boy, just say so. No extra charge."

It took Sextant a moment to understand the meaning of the words. He smiled tightly. "As I recall, you were the one who once called me a faggot."

Beer-gut seemed surprised. "Shit, that don't mean nothing. Sticking it into a boy don't make a man a faggot. A hole is a hole, you know?"

If it were possible for me to feel disgust, thought Sextant, this would be one of the times to feel it. But it wasn't possible. That's something else I don't feel.

"Leave the boy alone," he said. "I want him to see it happen, but that's all. Keep your hands off him."

"You mean you want him to watch us do it?"

"That's right."

Beer-gut grinned. "Nice touch."

Is it? Yes, I suppose it is, a very nice tough. Sextant looked at his watch. Only just past eleven, not nearly late enough. That night on Mount Krn it had happened after midnight, and that seemed an appropriate time for it to happen now. It also seemed appropriate that the boy should see it happen. That other time a boy had watched, a much younger boy than this one, but still, that also seemed quite fitting.

He went into the bedroom, and closed the door behind him. There were two beds in the room. Lila lay on one of them, and Chicken on the other. Their ankles and wrists were bound, and their mouths were stopped with rags. They had been lying quietly, but when they saw him they began to struggle, straining at the ties.

"Don't do that," he said. "It won't do you any good."

They continued to struggle, and the sight disturbed him. He had seen it before, and it always disturbed him when people struggled to avoid their fate. He liked things neat and tidy, and all this thrashing was . . . undignified.

He knelt between the beds so that they both could hear him clearly. "Stop it. I can make you stop it, I can hurt you. Now stop."

The girl stopped struggling, but the boy continued to strain against his ties. Sextant sighed. "Very well, if you insist."

He put two fingers high on the back of the boy's neck, and pressed, feeling for the nerve. He found it, and pressed harder. The boy's body jerked violently, arching on the bed, and falling back. The breath went out of him, and his eyes rolled. It was as if he had been given an electric shock.

Surprised, Sextant removed his fingers. The reaction was extreme. He had used that touch many times, but he had never seen it work that way. He checked pulse and respiration, and watched as they came back to normal.

"Now will you lie still?"

The boy nodded weakly.

Sextant turned to the girl. "Are you going to behave yourself?" She nodded. On an impulse of curiosity, he put his hand on her breast. She flinched away from him. "I told you not to do that."

She lay still. He kneaded her breast gently, and after a moment he felt her nipple rise under his palm. As he continued to stroke her, he searched himself for a feeling. Any sort of feeling. Lust? Eagerness? Anything? No, nothing. Nothing at all. He could have been kneading dough to make bread.

Still kneeling on the floor, he turned to the other bed. He put his hand on Chicken's thigh, and the boy flinched just as the girl had. He slid his hand between the boy's thighs, and felt for his genitals. He cupped them, and began to stroke. Once again he searched himself for feeling, and once again he felt nothing at all. More flesh, more meat, that's all.

He shook his head, irritated with himself for having tried the experiment. It had been years since he had tried an intimate touching of a male or a female, and there had been no reason to suppose that anything had changed. He had always been that way, and he always would. He could play the charade. He could go through the motions either straight or gay, but that was all he could do. In the end he could do nothing, because he felt nothing.

What do they feel? he wondered.

He looked into the girl's eyes, and then into the boy's. Hers were filled with fear, but he noted with approval that the boy's eyes were narrowed into slits of concentrated hate. Good boy, he thought. If you're angry enough, you don't have time to be afraid. It was a lesson that he had learned early, and he had learned it so well that it had been many years since he had felt either anger or fear. He took no pride in the accomplishment. Anger and fear were simply two more of the emotions that he lacked. And yet, he did not think of himself as a robot, devoid of all feelings. Could a robot be thrilled by a Mozart quartet? Could a robot enjoy the patterned complexities of a Pirandello? Could a robot . . . He broke off the thought. He was what he was, and what he was most of all was the creature created by David Ogden. A man of ice.

He tried to remember what it had been like in that short period of his life before David Ogden came into it, but his memory stopped at his life in the caves. The people of Cankar's partisan band were mostly countrymen, small farmers and woodsmen who had taken to the mountains in July of 1941 when the call had gone out for resistance to the invaders. Few of them were Communists, but they all supported the right of the Communist Party to direct the resistance. All of them detested the king, the government-in-exile in London, and the rival Chetnik guerrillas operating under Mihajlović. Even the youngest of them felt that way, and the youngest had been Vlado Priol.

It was, in many ways, a wonderful time for him. To live in a cave, to eat by an open fire, to wear goatskins, wash rarely, and roam the mountainside was a dream come true for a six-year-old boy. And if the caves were often cold and damp, the fires sooty, the goatskins itchy, and the diet a monotonous routine of bread and beans, still he had a loving mother who held him close in the night, a father who was brave and strong, and as the older brother that every boy needs and rarely has, he had David Ogden.

And he had the safety of his mountain. There was a war going on all around him, brutal and savage, but he saw little of that. The men went down the mountain to raid, they returned, and sometimes a familiar face would be missing; but, in truth, the war had little impact on him. Mountain born, he knew as much from instinct as from being told that he was safe on the heights of Mount Knr, for the caves were unreachable to anyone not a son of that soil, and it was unthinkable that one of their own might betray them that way to the Germans. Unthinkable, until it happened.

And it happened, it definitely happened. He looked down at the girl, and at the fear in her eyes. "And it's going to happen to you, too."

Lila heard the words, but she didn't know what they meant. Chicken also heard them, but he knew all too well. He knew not only because he had been explicitly briefed on Sextant's intentions, but because for the past few minutes he had been inside Sextant's head. Inside, tapping, and receiving the man's thoughts loud and clear. As clear as it had been in the old days, his young days when he was twelve, and thirteen, and fourteen years old, when tapping had been a part of his nature, and never a chore. Back before the power had started to fade. As clear as that.

At first he couldn't believe his luck. At first he thought it was only luck. At first he thought it was just for the moment, and that it would fade. But it didn't fade, it stayed loud and clear, and after a while he began to understand that something strange had happened. It had happened when Sextant had touched his neck, had pressed those nerves and caused the pain. The pain had been bad, but there had been something more, an electric shock that had shot to the top of his head, and then had . . . changed something. He didn't know what, but the change was there.

And now, for the past few minutes he had been tapped into Sextant's head, listening loud and clear to the childhood memories of Vlado Priol, the memories of a horror that had come in the night. Through Vlado's six-year-old eyes, he saw most of the band leave the caves that afternoon, off to hunt and to raid with Cankar leading and Ogden as second-in-command, barreling down the mountain on their short and stubby skis and leaving behind only those men who had families. He saw the mountain day blend into mountain night, the familiar routine of fire and food, the mother stirring the pot and the father oiling the parts of an ancient Enfield. He felt the silence of the night, the embrace of trust and safety, and then the sleep.

And then he saw the rest of it.

Memories, thought Sextant, and again he wondered if these memories of his were made up of things that he actually had seen, and heard, and felt, or if they were only recollections of the stories that Ogden had told him later on. He tried to sort them out. He remembered the *pop, pop, pop,* of rifle fire in the night, the rush of his father to the mouth of the cave, and the harsh, quick words of his mother ordering him to lie quietly as she buried him in a mound of goatskins. He remembered the cries of alarm that went up around the camp, the orders shouted in German, and the *crack* of a grenade rolled into a nearby cave. He remembered peeking out from under the goatskin pile to see the three German soldiers rush into the cave and club down his father before he could fire a shot. He remembered watching the soldiers taking turns with his mother, and that when the first one did it to her she screamed and struck at him with her fists, that when the second one did it he hit her until she stopped screaming, and that when the third one did it she did not scream at all. He remembered when they shot his mother and his father. He remembered when the fire went out, and he lay there in the cold as the Germans left the mountain. He remembered when his own people came back the next day, and when David Ogden found him half frozen under the pile of skins. He remembered it all, but never clearly, only as a story that someone else had told him. He did not question that it had happened, he knew that all too well, but there were times when he found it hard to believe that he had actually been there, and had seen it with his own eyes.

This feeling of unreality stayed with him over the next ten years when he lived without David Ogden in his life. The raid on Mount Krn finished Cankar's band as an effective partisan unit; they could not operate without a haven in the mountains, and so in twos and threes the men drifted away to join other bands. The OSS recalled Ogden to Italy, but before he left he brought Vlado Priol to a trusted man named Debanjak who worked a farm on the outskirts of Kopor, and there the boy stayed until the war was over, and eight years after that, treated as a member of the family. He was sixteen years old when Ogden came back to help him to kill the man who had murdered his parents. Not the German soldier who had pulled the trigger—only God knew where he was—but the traitor who had led the German troops up the face of Mount Krn in the middle of winter. Only a local man could have done that, and it had taken Ogden ten years to track him down.

He came back in June of 1953, slipping over the border between Zone A of Trieste and Zone B, and then down to Kopor. He wore rough clothing, and he carried the papers of a tractor driver from Rijeka. He came to the farm in the middle of the night, and threw pebbles at a window until Debanjak came to the door. The farmer stared, and then opened the door wider.

"In the kitchen," he said. "Quietly. The house is asleep."

He lit a single candle, and they sat at the table. From his pockets, Ogden took a pistol, a paper sack, and a bottle of whisky. When Debanjak saw the bottle, he went for glasses, and poured. Ogden pushed the paper sack across the table to him, and said, "Tobacco, English, the kind that comes in a tin. I took it out of the tin to be safe."

Debanjak nodded his thanks. "What about the pistol? Is that for me, too?"

"For the boy."

Debanjak sighed, a wordless sound of understanding. "He isn't a boy anymore."

"I know. That's why I brought the pistol."

"You found the man?"

"I know who he is, and where he is."

"In the name of God, how did you do that after all these years?"

Ogden shook his head. The workings of the newly formed CIA were none of the farmer's concern.

"Who is he?"

Ogden shook his head again.

"The boy will kill him?"

"It's his right."

"It's his right," Debanjak admitted, "but what happens to him afterward? He goes with you?" Ogden nodded. "How?"

"The same way I came in. You're asking a lot of questions. That's not the way I remember you."

Debanjak looked down at his glass. It was empty. "Maybe it's the whisky. I'm not used to drinking it. Besides, I never thought I'd see you again. Now you come after ten long years and say that you're taking the boy away."

"I'm sorry, but it has to be that way."

"I understand that. If he kills the man, he can't stay here, but he's been with me for ten years, and that gives me the right to ask some questions."

Ogden poured whisky for them both. "Yes, you have the right," he admitted. "I'll answer what I can."

Debanjak leaned over the table. "Just one question. Why now, after all these years?"

"It was never really finished, we just didn't know his name. Now we do. He said something to someone, and that someone told someone else . . ." Ogden shrugged. "That's how these things happen. It got back to my people, and we decided to close the books."

"Your people have long ears."

"And long arms. Tell me about the boy. What is he like?"

"I told you before, he isn't a boy, he does a man's work on the farm. What's he like? He's strange, that's what he is."

"In what way?"

"Just strange." Debanjak searched for words. "He's a quiet one, doesn't talk much, does his work. He's . . . he's a cold one. Never laughs, never sings, never shows anything on his face. He has no friends, never jokes with the girls, never causes any trouble. Even when I had to beat him. You understand that while he was growing up I had to beat him once in a while?"

Ogden nodded. In Debanjak's world a young boy had to be beaten regularly in order to curb a natural rebelliousness, and to instill a respect for authority.

"Even then, he never showed pain, he never showed fear, and I never saw a single tear in his eye. Never."

"Is that so unusual?"

"Listen, in this country boys don't cry as a rule, but every boy cries at one time or another. But not this one."

"Not even when he was a child?"

"In ten years I have never seen him cry."

"Perhaps he doesn't have any tears left."

"Perhaps."

"Do you think he will be able to kill?"

"Who knows that about any man? You'll find out soon enough, won't you?"

"Yes. Go and wake him now. I want to start before dawn."

Debanjak's hand was on the whisky bottle. He started to pick it up, then put it down. "Listen, friend, you come here in the middle of the night and you tell me that you are taking him away. I understand the need for that, but there are ways of doing it, and giving me orders in my own home is not one of those ways."

Ogden said carefully, "It was not meant as an order. I'm sorry if it sounded that way."

"Ten years, you see? Like family."

"Yes. Would you wake him, please?"

"Of course."

"There is no need, I'm here," said a voice from the doorway. Vlado stepped into the pool of light that the candle threw. His feet were bare, and his nightshirt was stuffed into a pair of trousers. He was fresh from sleep, but his eyes were clear.

Ogden looked at him carefully. He saw a boy grown into a man, slight of build but clearly muscular. He looked for signs of the boy he had known, but could see none. It was a disappointment. He asked, "Do you know who I am?"

"Yes. I was listening, but I would have known you anyway."

"How much did you hear?"

"All of it. I heard the pebbles on the window."

"You move quietly."

"When I have to."

Debanjak cleared his throat noisily. "Did I teach you to listen at doors?"

Vlado did not look at him. His eyes were fixed on Ogden. "No, but you said that I'm strange. Strange people listen at doors."

"I meant no harm by it."

"I know that." To Ogden, he said, "Did you mean what you said about taking me with you?"

"Yes."

Vlado finally looked at Debanjak. "May I go?" Debanjak nodded. "Then I'm ready."

"You know what has to be done?"

"I'm ready for that, too. I've been ready for ten years. It's something I should have done then."

Ogden looked at him curiously. "Then? You mean that night?"

"Yes."

There was a long silence, and then Ogden said, "You were a child. There was nothing you could have done."

Vlado shook his head. "I should have done something."

"That's foolish talk. Did you have a pistol?"

"You know that I didn't."

"A knife?"

"No."

"They would have shot you down."

"I know, but I should have done it. I should have fought, and died. That's the way it was in the mountains. One fought, and one died. You know that. Even I knew that, and I was only a child. But I didn't do anything. I just lay there under that pile of skins and let them do that to my mother."

Ogden sighed. "Do you think about this often?"

"Every day."

"You'll feel better about it after you kill him."

"Maybe."

"You will. Now go and get dressed. Don't take much with you, just enough to fill your pockets. We'll leave when you're ready."

When Vlado had gone upstairs, Ogden said to Debanjak, "Did you notice that he didn't say hello to me? He never touched me, or reached for my hand. He never said a single soft word, and he used to be like a little brother to me."

Debanjak shrugged. "I told you he was a strange one."

Debanjak gave them a bottle of water and a small sack of plums, and they left with the sun just up as they headed southeast for Rijeka. It was a journey that could have been made in two hours by car, but walking took them the better part of the day under a sun that was soon hot and heavy. While they walked, Ogden talked and Vlado listened. The name of the traitor was Josip Koller, and he had done it for money. There had been no politics involved, none of the Royalist-Communist rivalry that had split the Yugoslav resistance movement during the war. Koller had led the Germans up the mountain for a price, the price had been paid, and the secret had been kept, until now. At the end of the war he had moved out from under the shadow of Mount Krn and had settled in the seaside city of Rijeka where he had established a small business selling paper and twine. Now, eight years later, he was a respected citizen and a prosperous merchant. He had never married, and he lived alone. He was an easy target.

"He goes to sleep every night about ten," said Ogden as they walked along kicking dust. "We'll go in around midnight. One shot and it's over."

"While he's asleep?" Vlado asked.

"Easiest way."

"I want him awake. I want him to know why he's dying."

"Negative. This is a job, and we don't have time for dramatics. In and out, understand?"

Vlado nodded. "All right, all I want to do is kill him."

"That's it. Any questions?"

"I thought I wasn't supposed to ask any."

"There was one I was sure you'd ask. I thought you'd want to know if we were sure that Koller is the man."

Vlado looked at him in surprise. "Is there any doubt?"

"Not in my mind, but nobody's perfect. In this business, mistakes get made all the time. What if we've targeted the wrong man?"

Vlado thought for a while as he trudged along. He shrugged, and said, "Then that's his bad luck, I guess."

Christ, he's an icicle, thought Ogden. That's what I was hoping he would say, but he sure as hell isn't the same kid I knew on that mountain.

It was six in the evening when they came to the outskirts of Rijeka, and they found a shady hollow on the side of a hill where they could rest and wait for darkness. They ate the plums, and Ogden went over the workings of the pistol and the silencer until he was sure that Vlado had it right. Then they slept, waking when the first breezes of the night found their faces.

Just after midnight, Ogden led the way down into the city, and to a small house on a side street near the port. The street was still, and there were no lights. They went around through a garden to the back door, and Ogden dealt with the lock. He edged the door open, and it creaked.

Ogden whispered, "Let's see how quietly you can move with your shoes on." He led the way down a corridor to a room with an open door. He motioned Vlado through the doorway. The room was filled with the odors of must and sweat, and the sound of heavy breathing. Faint light came through the shutters, enough to see a man asleep in a bed. Ogden pointed to the man, and then to his own temple. Vlado nodded. He walked to the bed, put the pistol against the man's head, and pulled the trigger. There was a flat *crack*, louder than expected, and Josip Koller was dead.

A fat woman in a long nightdress walked into the room. She opened her mouth to scream. Ogden had his pistol out, but Vlado turned and shot the woman square in the chest. She went down, and lay without moving. Ogden checked both bodies.

"Done," he said. "Out, and no talking."

Back on the street, they walked quickly and silently down to the port. There were lights in this part of town, but not many of them, and two waterfront cafés still open. Rickety piers jutted into the harbor, and Ogden made for one that lay in darkness beyond the second café. A rowboat was tied to the end of the pier, and Ogden motioned Vlado into it. He climbed in himself, and cast off.

"You row," he said, breaking the silence. "Straight out past the mole."

When they were under way, Vlado said, "Did you know about the woman?"

"No. I told you, mistakes get made all the time."

"Was I right to shoot her?"

"Yes, it had to be done. I would have done it if you hadn't."

"Good. I wasn't sure. Where are we going?"

"Italy. Keep rowing. There's a fishing boat waiting about a mile off shore."

"You told Debanjak that you were going out the same way you came in."

"Yes," Ogden agreed. "That's what I told Debanjak."

An hour later the fishing boat loomed out of the darkness, and they were taken aboard, the rowboat abandoned. The fishing smack was old and the crew was older, two ancient mariners who spoke to Ogden in a grunted Italian that Vlado did not understand. Ogden said, "There's food in the cabin if you want some."

"No," said Vlado. "I'm not hungry."

"How do you feel?"

Vlado thought about that. "Empty."

"Then you should eat."

"Not that kind of empty. I thought it would make me feel good to kill him, but it didn't. I didn't feel anything. It was like a game. I pulled the trigger, and he was dead. The same thing with the woman. I felt nothing."

Ogden nodded.

"That isn't right, is it? It shouldn't be that way."

It sure as hell shouldn't, thought Ogden, but he said, "Different people take it differently. Don't worry about it."

They sat on the deck with their eyes astern, watching the florescence of the wake spread out behind them. Ogden started to fill his pipe, but one of the Italians said something, and he put the pipe away.

"No lights," he explained. "We're still in Yugoslav waters. Another hour before we're out of the gulf."

"And then?"

"Four hours, maybe five to Rimini." He saw Vlado's blank look. "In Italy."

"Italy. What happens to me then?"

"A car to Rome, and then we fly to the States. America."

"America." Vlado said it softly. "And then what?"

"I have a home for you in a place called Maryland with a good family, people I know. A new name, new papers, a school. You have a new language to learn, a whole new life. I have it all arranged."

Vlado tried the word. "Maryland?"

"That's it."

"And you? Where will you be?"

"I'll be around. You'll see me once in a while."

"Once in a while." Vlado was silent, staring out into the night. "Ogden, I don't want to go to Maryland, and I don't want to go to a school. I want to stay with you."

"I know. I'm sorry."

"Couldn't we do it that way?"

"Not now. After a while, maybe. After you've done some growing up, but not now."

"I want it to be now."

"I know."

"Please."

Ogden shook his head. Carefully, almost delicately, he put an arm around the boy's shoulders, and held him. Those shoulders began to shake, and he held him closer. He did not look at him. The kid was crying for the first time in ten years, and he deserved a little privacy.

"Listen, what the fuck is going on?"

Sextant, still kneeling on the floor between the two beds, was jolted out of his reverie by the rasp of Beer-gut's voice behind him. He shook his head, leaving that other time reluctantly. He did not turn around.

"For Chrissake, let's get this show on the road. It's stupid sitting around like this."

"Get out."

"God damn it, you can't . . ."

"Get out," Sextant repeated. His voice was low and controlled, but it was deadly. Feet shuffled, and the door closed behind him. Sextant still had not turned. His eyes were on the two young people on the beds, shifting from Lila's terrified face to the hatred burning in Chicken's eyes.

So long ago, he thought, sitting on the deck with Ogden's arms around me, crying my heart out. And for what? Because I had killed a man and a woman? Certainly not. Because I had just found Ogden again, and was about to lose him again? Perhaps. Because I was finally able to cry for my mother, and what they had done to her? That, yes. Definitely yes, but after that no tears. No tears when Ogden left me with those people in Maryland, and no tears when he came back for me three years later. No tears when he sent me to kill the senator in Chile. Or the Jew in Cairo. Or the bomb in the garage in Santa Monica. Or the Canadian jet with all those people on board. No tears for any of those jobs, or for all the jobs in Nam and after Nam. Never a tear, and now, after all those knives in the night that I drew for David Ogden, the wheel comes round again. Rape, the short and ugly word like a stab in the dark. Why me, David? I'll do it, of course. I've always done whatever you've asked, but I have to tell you, David, that I do not want to do this one. There it is, flat out. I do not want to do this.

I do not want to do this.

Chicken heard the words that rang in Sextant's brain like the tolling of a hollow bell. He heard them clearly, just as he had heard all the rest of it. He had heard it in Slovenian, the mother-tongue that Sextant thought in, for, like any other sensitive, he could absorb a language from another man's mind. He stared up into Sextant's eyes, and was not surprised to see sorrow there. He stared into Sextant's mind, and was not surprised to see a sadness without limits. He tapped in further, and saw the warping of the boy who had become the man. And he saw that the man was a fraud. He thought of himself as a man of ice, without compassion, but he was wrong, the compassion was there. It was twisted out of recognition, and it was buried so deep that it could only be sensed by a sensitive. But it was there, and Chicken knew that he had to get it to the surface.

Take the gag out of my mouth, he thought. *Take it out.*

Nothing happened. Sextant continued to stare at him.

Take out the gag. He repeated the thought over and over. He knew he was wasting his time, but it was all that he could think of to do. He squirmed on the bed, and Sextant looked at him curiously.

"Full of hate, aren't you?" he said. "You'd love to cut my heart out, wouldn't you?"

Chicken shook his head. *Take out the gag.*

"You don't? Well you should. I would, if I were you."

Chicken shook his head again. *Take out the gag.*

"Don't even know what hit you, do you? One minute you're walking along with your girl, and the next minute . . . well, here you are. Don't know how, don't know why, and you don't even know what's coming next."

Chicken nodded. *Take out the gag.*

"Yes? Yes what? You do know what's coming? You smart enough to figure that out?"

Chicken nodded. *Take out the gag.*

"It's not going to be pretty, son. Believe me, I know. And there's nothing you can do about it."

Chicken nodded violently. *Take out the gag.*

"You think there is? You're wrong, boy, nothing at all. All you can do is keep on hating. Hating helps a lot."

WILL YOU TAKE OUT THE GOD DAMN GAG.

Sextant frowned. "You want to tell me something, don't you?"

Chicken nodded.

"Sure, why not, but keep your voice down. You start to yell and I'll hurt you bad." Sextant's fingers worked quickly, and the gag came off. "Well, what is it?"

Chicken grimaced as the gag came off. He worked the muscles in his face, and he wet his lips.

"Come on, you wanted to say something."

Speaking in Slovenian, Chicken said, "I have a great deal to say, Vlado Priol."

Sextant's eyes narrowed at the sound of the language. A knife appeared in his hand, and the point pricked the skin of Chicken's neck. In Slovenian, he said, "What do you know about Vlado Priol?"

Chicken swallowed hard, and tried for a steady voice. "How can I talk with a knife at my throat?"

Sextant lowered the knife. "Talk."

All the way, thought Chicken. Roll the dice. "I will continue to talk in Slovenian because I don't want the girl to understand. Your name is Vlado Priol. You have other names, one of which is Sextant. Your control is . . . was, David Ogden. Your assignment is the rape of that girl over there. Are you aware that your mission has been aborted?"

More to himself than to Chicken, Sextant muttered, "It can't be aborted. Gibraltar rules."

"Nevertheless, it is."

"How do you know these things?"

"I work for the same people that Ogden worked for. The same people that you have worked for from time to time."

Sextant came close to smiling. "You? How old are you?"

"Sixteen. The same age as you when you killed Josip Koller."

A silence, and then Sextant said quietly, "You're a dead man."

"I don't think so." Chicken was amazed at his own calm.

"You are. After that you have to be."

"Think, Sextant, you're supposed to be one of the bright ones. How many people ever knew about you and Josip Koller?"

"Only one, Ogden, and he's dead."

"Then how did I know? Would Ogden have talked, would he have told anyone your secret?"

"Never."

"Then how did I know?"

Sextant thought. "You're one of them. You're a sensitive."

"Top marks."

"Ogden told me about you people, but I never really thought . . ."

"Now you know."

"And soon you will be a dead sensitive."

"Are you sure? That means you'll have to kill the girl, too."

"Obviously."

"But your orders from Ogden clearly forbid that. As I recall, he said, *I do not want her life, in fact I forbid you to take it.* Isn't that so?"

Sextant frowned. He shook his head slightly, as if disturbed by a buzzing insect.

"Those were your orders. Tell me, in all your years with Ogden, did you ever disobey an order that he gave you?"

"Never."

"Did you ever put your personal safety above his wishes?"

"Never."

"But you're going to do that now, aren't you?"

Again, that insect buzzing. "Sometimes . . . sometimes it is necessary for the agent in the field to . . ."

"Disobey," Chicken said firmly. "The word is disobey."

Sextant's head went down. "Yes."

"Now listen to me, Vlado Priol." Chicken spoke rapidly, the words tumbling out. "If you can disobey one order, you can disobey another. There is no need for this thing to happen. I've been inside your mind, and I know that you don't want to do it. I know that the idea sickens you, and that you are doing it only out of loyalty to a dead man. But how much longer can you go on being loyal? All your life you've been doing things for David Ogden. Isn't it time that you did something for yourself? Isn't it time . . ."

Later, after it was all over, Chicken would look back and wonder how effective his plea might have been if he had been given a chance to finish it. But he never did. The door swung open, and Sextant's three animals spilled into the room. They were beer-drunk, they were weaving on their feet, and they were angry.

"Time's up," growled Beer-gut. "We want that little girl, and we want her now."

Richie, behind him, said, "Yeah, I wanna piece of that cute thing."

"We tossed up coins," said Phil. "I get to go first. Odd man in." He giggled.

In quiet Slovenian, Chicken said to Sextant, "Call it off. You can't let this happen."

Sextant said nothing. Still kneeling on the floor, his head was down and he was sunk in thought.

Go for it, thought Chicken. Go for it all the way. In English, he shouted, "Okay, boys, it's party time. Come and get her, she's all yours."

Sextant's head snapped up. "What are you doing?"

"It's what you want, isn't it?"

The three men rushed to the bed. Beer-gut ripped the ties from Lila's legs, and the other two tore at her clothing. Her hands were still bound, but she fought with her feet, kicking out as Richie tugged at her ski pants. She screamed, but with the gag in her mouth it sounded like a muffled moan. She twisted from side to side until Beer-gut pinned her shoulders.

"Get those God damn pants off," he grunted.

"Lie still, bitch."

Sextant, still on his knees, watched without moving. He seemed turned to stone.

"Well," Chicken whispered, "is this really what you want?"

No answer.

"Why don't you take the gag out of her mouth? That way you can hear her scream."

No movement.

"Just the way your mother screamed."

Still stone.

Richie had Lila's pants down around her knees. Phil had cut the ties on her hands, and was trying to get her sweater over her head. Beer-gut leaned over her, trying to kiss her.

"Still the good little soldier?" asked Chicken. "Still following orders?"

No answer.

"That's about what I expected. The last time you hid under a pile of goatskins."

Sextant finally looked at him. In the plaintive voice of a little boy, he said, "I was only six years old."

"Yes, and how old are you now?"

"Damn you," whispered Sextant. "Damn you."

Sextant came up off the floor in a single fluid motion. He plucked Richie off Lila and flung him against the wall. He caught the back of Phil's neck with the edge of his palm, and Phil crumpled to the floor. Beer-gut yelped, and backed away from the bed. Sextant hit him once, almost casually, in the belly, and he doubled over, retching.

Sextant turned back to Chicken. The knife was in his hand again. He cut the ties on Chicken's hands and feet.

"Get her dressed, and get her out of here," he said. His face was wet with tears. For the second time in forty years, Vlado Priol was crying.

18

OF the four agents that David Ogden chose to carry out his last requests, Gemstone was the one least motivated by a blind loyalty or by the money involved. True, she was loyal to Ogden and indebted to him, and true, she welcomed the sizable sum that had been deposited into her Zurich account, but Gemstone would have done the job for virtually anyone, and for nothing, if necessary. She would have burned down your barn for five bucks and the cost of the kerosene, and she would have burned down an orphanage just for the hell of it. Gemstone, whose name was Louise Abruzzi, was a firebug, a torch, a pyromaniac, and burning things down was more than just a job to her. It was her food, her drink, and her love life rolled into one.

She came into Glen Grove on the twenty-fifth of February, three days before the beginning of the time frame, and she spent those three days observing the Southern Manor from a room in a similar establishment directly across the street. By the end of the third day she knew exactly how she was going to do the job, and she spent the next day assembling the equipment she would need. With that accomplished, she left the rooming house and checked into a decent hotel on the other side of town. She was ready to roll on the job, but she was safe in the time frame and she could afford to give herself a day to let the anticipation and the excitement build inside of her. The anticipation was part of it for her, and she relished every minute of it.

Whenever time allowed, her routine for the day before a job was unvarying. She made it a time of complete relaxation as she drifted into a dreamlike state, thinking about the fire the next day, and of all the fires that had sparked her life over the years. This time was no exception. She started with a dip in the hotel pool, pleased that at her age she was still able to wear the most radical of bathing suits without embarrassing herself, then a light breakfast, and then she stretched out in the sun beside the pool to drift and dream. As usual, she let her thoughts wander back to when it all had begun. She no longer wondered why she was the way she was, but she still found it odd that she had been twenty-eight years old before she had become aware of the fires that were burning inside her head.

The year was 1970, and she was stationed at the Third Surgical Hospital at Binh Thuy, which was not a good place for an Army nurse to be that year. It wasn't the shelling so much. They were rarely shelled closely at Binh Thuy, the Air Force unit a few miles away drew most of the incoming, but they were operating around the clock and the strain was heavy. It wasn't just the wounded, either, not the legitimate wounded. There was a lot of dope going down at that time, medics coming to work stoned on horse, shooting up in the bathrooms, shooting up the patients who could pay for it. And the other kind of shooting, the gunfights. Guys coming into the hospital full of holes that the VC never put there. Gunfights among themselves almost every night, and always when the town was off-limits and the guys couldn't get in to see the girls. Stoned MPs and stoned GIs shooting it out in the compound; it was scary, and later, after she had set the fire, they tried to make a case that she had cracked under the strain. It's nothing to be ashamed of, it can happen to anybody, they told her, and she finally went along with it although she knew it wasn't so. She said, yeah, that must have been it, I must have flipped, because she wasn't going to tell them what really had happened, and she had to say something.

What she did was burn down the supply building at Binh Thuy. She did it in the middle of the night, and she did it by pouring gasoline around the base of the structure and setting it off with a homemade

Molotov cocktail. It was an amateurish way to do it, but she didn't know anything about setting fires then. The foundation was cement block and the roof was tin, but the rest of it was wood, and it cooked up quickly. By the time that the fire squad arrived the roof was glowing pink; there was nothing to be saved, and later the CID investigators told her that she had roasted a half-million dollars worth of government issue.

She didn't try to deny it. She told them exactly what she had done, but when they asked her why she had done it, she went silent. She wasn't going to tell them that at the moment it had seemed like the most satisfying, pleasurable thing in the world to do, and so she had done it. She wasn't going to tell them that she had done it the way she would have eaten an apple if she had been hungry, or taken a drink if she had been thirsty. She wasn't going to tell them how she had felt when the flames went up.

"What's going to happen to me?" she had asked. There were two of them, a major and a captain, and both had been civilian cops.

"All we do is file the report," said the major. "Saigon makes the charges."

"How bad could it get?"

"You could pull some time. Why did you do it?"

It was perhaps the tenth time they had asked the question. As she had all the other times, she shook her head silently. The major nodded to the captain, who got up and left the room. When he was gone, the major said, "I'm old enough to be your father."

"No, you're not."

"Maybe an older brother. You want to tell me, just me, why you did it?"

She shook her head.

He shrugged. "I'm going to put down in my report that you cracked under the strain. Otherwise, you're looking at some heavy time."

"What strain?"

"You joking? All the wounded, all the shit that goes down here? You cracked, that's all."

"I've been a nurse for seven years. I don't crack."

"Suit yourself."

"If I say that I cracked, that makes me a nut case. They put me in a psycho."

"Not necessarily. What do you say we stop horsing around. You want to tell me what it felt like?"

His eyes were laughing at her, and she realized that he knew. She managed to say, "I'm not a nut case."

"Oh, yes you are. I've been a cop long enough to know exactly what you are."

"How much time am I looking at?"

"Could be five to ten."

"That much?"

"Could be."

"I guess I cracked under the strain. I just flipped. It's been hell around here."

"Now you got it."

The report was filed in Saigon, and while the wheels of justice were turning she was confined to her quarters with an MP on guard outside the door. She welcomed the confinement. It took her away from the physical and emotional pounding of the war, and it gave her a chance to think about what she had done, and what her future might be. She figured that if she was lucky she would be booted out of the Army, which meant an end to her nursing career, and that at the worst she would wind up in jail. She was wrong on both counts. Seventeen days after the report was filed she was visited by a middle-aged civilian with a warm smile and an easy manner who introduced himself as David Ogden. The interview took place in her room. Ogden took the only chair, and she sat on the edge of the bed.

"First of all, let me assure you that I'm not with the CID," he said. "I represent a civilian organization that's interested in your case."

"Which organization is that?"

"We'll get to that in a while. First, I'd like to ask you a few questions."

The questions he asked were about her childhood, her education, her vocation for nursing, and her feelings about the war. She answered them easily, warming to the man. Like the CID major, he was almost old enough to be her father, but unlike the major, he gave off an air of trust and confidence. For the first time since the night of the fire she started to relax.

"These questions," she said. "All that stuff is in my file."

"I know," he agreed, "but asking questions is a way of getting to know someone. Now I'll ask you for something that isn't in your file. When was the first time you ever felt like setting a fire?"

She stiffened, and the feeling of trust evaporated. She did not answer.

Ogden nodded as if he had expected that reaction. "Without wishing to appear overly dramatic," he said, "you should understand that your fate, your future, rests entirely in my hands." He showed her two envelopes. "This one contains the orders for your court-martial on charges of second degree arson, wanton destruction of government property, and half a dozen other infractions. If you go to trial, I can personally guarantee you a guilty verdict and a heavy sentence."

"I cracked," she said softly. "The strain."

He brushed that aside, and tapped the second envelope. "This one contains your honorable discharge from the United States Army. Clean record, no charges brought, now or ever."

She stared at him.

"Before I leave here today, I am going to destroy one of these envelopes. Which one depends on you, and how honestly you answer my questions. Is that understood?"

She nodded.

"I'll repeat the question. When was the first time you ever felt like setting a fire?"

"The night it happened, here at Binh Thuy."

"Never before?"

"Never. Look, I know it sounds like a lie, but I never had that feeling before. You know, that I wanted to burn something."

"Wanted to, or had to?"

"It's the same thing, isn't it?"

"It could be. Never before?" She nodded. "All right, it happens that way sometimes. What do you remember about that night?"

"Everything."

"Clearly?"

"Clear as a bell. I know that I could make a better case for myself if I said that I had a blackout or maybe that things were fuzzy, but I'm trying to be straight with you. I remember everything."

Ogden said softly, "Tell me about it."

She told him about the cans of gas from the motor pool, swishing them around the base of the building until they were empty. She told him about the gas in the empty beer bottle, the rag for a wick, the match, the *whoosh* as it caught. She told him how she stood and watched as the flames crept up, burst through the roof, and stretched to the sky. She told him how she knew that she should run, but how she couldn't. How she had to stay and watch, no matter what.

"You knew that you'd be caught?" he asked.

"It didn't seem important at the time. I know that sounds crazy, but that's the way it was. I had to watch."

"Yes, I understand that. Now, I want you to tell me what happened while you watched. Will you tell me that?"

She did not answer.

"I'm asking you to trust me, and to tell me." He held up the two envelopes. "Remember, it's your choice."

In a small voice, she said, "I wet my pants."

"Yes, that often happens. And something else happened, didn't it?"

"Yes," in that same small voice.

"Tell me."

"Do I have to?" He nodded. She looked away from him. "I had an orgasm."

"Yes, that also happens."

"More than one." She laughed jerkily. "I don't know how many times . . . those flames, I never had anything like it." She put her hands over her face.

"Bingo," murmured Ogden. He moved to sit beside her on the bed. In a comforting tone, he said, "Relax, it's all over now. No more questions."

She still would not look at him. From behind her fingers, she said, "I'm so embarrassed."

"Don't be. It's happened to other people."

She lowered her hands. He gave her one of the envelopes. "You're out of the army, you're a civilian. Do you want to watch me tear up the other one?"

"No, I trust you." She meant it. "What happens to me now?"

"You can go wherever you wish, do whatever you please. I can have you stateside in a matter of days, if that's what you want. But you have to consider one thing. I dislike the word 'normal,' but what you did the other night could never be considered normal behavior, not by anyone. You know that, don't you?"

"I'm not crazy."

He shrugged. "You're a pyromaniac, you show the symptoms. Do you know what a pyromaniac is?"

"Someone who likes to set fires?"

"Someone who is obsessed with setting fires. Someone who gets pleasure out of it. Enormous pleasure."

"But I never did it before."

"Some people start late. Believe me, you're a torch, a natural."

"I promise, I won't do it again."

"Do you mind if I say that I don't believe you? Torches don't quit. It's not something you have any control over. Look, the way I see it, you have three courses of action open to you. Do you want to hear them?"

She nodded dumbly.

"You can do nothing about it, and try to lead a normal life. Frankly, I don't think that will work. Somewhere down the line you'll set another fire, and another, and one day you'll get caught. You won't walk away from that one. Is that what you want?"

"Obviously not."

"An alternative is to go into psychotherapy. The condition is treatable. Perhaps not curable, but treatable."

"I told you, I'm not a nut."

"And you don't want to lose what you just found, do you."

She smiled for the first time. "Hell no, it's too good."

"Then I suggest that you come to work for me. You'll make a good deal more than you did as an army nurse, and you'll report only to me."

"Doing what?"

"Setting fires. Only when I tell you to, and only under strictly controlled conditions, but that will be your job. To set huge, blazing fires."

"What if I get caught?"

"You won't, not if you're working for me."

"I really don't know much about setting fires."

"You'll be trained. If you want the job, you'll leave this evening for a place called Quon Trac. We have a training camp there that specializes in . . . in the sort of work I have in mind for you. After a month at Quon Trac, you'll be ready for your first assignment."

"Fires? Just fires?"

"Just fires." He saw the look on her face, and he smiled. "What is it?"

"Nothing, nothing at all."

"You were getting excited, weren't you?"

Again the jerky laugh. "Yeah, I guess I was."

"Well, how does it sound to you?"

"It sounds like heaven."

And it was, she thought as she lay beside the pool, her eyes closed against the Florida sun. Years and years of heavenly fires, and now he wants one more. One last fire tomorrow for the only man who ever truly understood me. All the others were for me, David, but this one is for you, and I'm going to make it a beaut.

"They had a chance and they blew it. It could have been a diplomatic coup," said Mike Teague. He pronounced it *coop*. The old man propped up in bed, a stained and wrinkled pajama top showing over the covers. He had a three-day growth of stubble on his face, and his wispy white hair stuck out in all directions. "It coulda solved the whole Cuban business in one stroke of the pen. You know how?"

"How?" Julio asked politely.

"Baseball, that's how. Cuban people are crazy about baseball, right?"

"Right," Julio agreed, conjuring up childhood memories.

"So here you got the National League, they add two more expansion teams, which is stupid in the first place because you got too many teams already, not enough major-league talent to go around, but that's something else. So they add two more teams, and who do they pick? Miami and Denver, that's who. Okay, nothing wrong with that, but can you imagine what happens if they pick Havana instead of Miami?"

"Havana?" Julio started to grin.

"Don't laugh. You put Havana into the National League and you got Cuba back on our side again. I mean, what's stronger, communism or baseball?"

"Baseball, of course."

"See what I mean? It brings the countries together."

"It's a thought," Julio admitted.

"A thought? It's a natural. You know, Castro was a ballplayer once, a good one."

Julio nodded. The story of the Maximum Leader's tryout with the old New York Giants was a part of Cuban folklore. Havana in the National League? It was a crazy idea, but like most of Teague's ideas there was a germ of sense in it. That was why he enjoyed spending time in the old man's room. He was a cranky old goat, but he had a never-ending fund of sports stories, and the walls of his room were covered with photographs. There were boxers with names like Tiger Arroyo, Battling Benny, the Williamsburg Kid, the Chocolate Kid, and Kid Kelly. There was a photo of the Brooklyn Dodgers, with Mike Teague the assistant trainer. There were team photos of the colleges at which he had worked: the Bowdoin lacrosse team, the Hamilton football team, the Van Buren basketball squad. There were photos of track men breasting tapes, a discus thrower at the moment of release, a vaulter caught in midfight. Every photo was signed; Mike wouldn't have any other kind. Julio was the old man's favorite audience. He had heard the stories so many times that he knew most of them by heart, but he always listened politely.

Julio, check in. The thought came winging from somewhere near.

Right here, Snake, he replied. *All quiet.*

Where's here?

Mike Teague's room. You?

In the parlor with Mrs. Costigan.

Right. Check again later.

They had divided the days into eight-hour watches so that each could get some sleep, and now at four in the afternoon they were both awake, circulating around the house and waiting for Gemstone to make a move. As he signed off with Snake, Julio felt a touch of excitement. As much as he hated to admit it, it felt good to be back in harness again, doing the work of a sensitive, even if the job was nothing more than standing guard over a ramshackle rooming house. And it was a pleasant change from the daily routine of hanging around the fronton, and telling the fortunes of elderly Cuban ladies. His only regret was that this renewed connection with Snake had not yet led to a renewal of intimacy. The eight-hour shifts made that impossible, but once the job was over . . .

He broke off the thought, and asked, "Did you ever see any baseball in Cuba?"

"Couple of times in the forties. The Havana Sugar Kings. You got some crazy fans down there."

"Was that when you were with the Dodgers?"

"Jesus, what's the use of me telling you things if you don't listen? I was with the Brooklyns in fifty-three, just that one year."

"Sorry." There was an electric razor on top of the bureau. Julio tossed it onto the bed. "Give yourself a shave, you look like a bum."

Teague let the razor lie. "The hell with it, I don't need it."

"Come on, Mike, the nurse will be here soon. Don't you want to look good for the nurse?"

"That old cow."

"Hey, she's a nice lady, Mrs. Coombs."

"Cow," Teague repeated, but he picked up the razor. "Maybe you were thinking about that Cuban runner I trained that time."

"Who was that?"

"Christ, don't you remember anything? That's him on the wall over there. To the left of the door, about halfway up."

Julio peered at the faded photo of a man in a warmup suit. It was inscribed, *a mi bien amigo, Miguel Teague.* It took him a moment to make out the signature. He said in surprise, "You worked with Alberto Juantorena?"

"Bet your ass. Fastest son of a bitch over a quarter mile that I ever saw in my life."

"You never told me, Mike, really you didn't. He was a hero in Cuba when I was a kid. When was this?"

"Seventy-six Olympics in Montreal," Teague said with a certain smugness. "Won the four hundred meters in 44.26. He was one *rapid* bastard."

"That's amazing. I thought you were still at Van Buren in seventy-six."

Teague shook his head sadly. "If I told you once, I told you a dozen times. I quit Van Buren after the seventy-five season. That was the year that we beat Polk in the big game, and then we won the tournament. That's the Van Buren team over there."

Julio followed Teague's pointing finger to another photograph on the wall. There were ten players standing or kneeling, with the coaches in the center, and Teague off to the side. There was no way that Julio could have known it, but one of the men in the picture was Hassan Rashid.

Julio, are you tapped in? Julio? Snake sounded hurried.

Go.

We're on. Mike's nurse just showed up and it isn't Mrs. Coombs. She says that Coombs has the flu and she's the substitute. She's on her way up.

Gemstone?

It figures, doesn't it?

Did you tap her?

No time. I'm coming up behind her.

There was a knock on the door, and a woman walked into the room. She wore a nurse's uniform, and she carried a black bag. She smiled at Teague, and started to say something. She never got the words out. Julio grabbed her wrist, twisted it, and pulled the bag away from her. He threw it across the room, and in the same motion he twisted her arm behind her back. He got his other arm around her neck in a lock. She screamed and struggled as he pulled her against him. She fell forward to the floor, and he lay on top of her, pinning her. She kicked, and a heel scraped his shin.

"Cut it out," he muttered. "I'll break your neck if I have to."

She stopped struggling, and went limp. She felt warm and soft under him. Snake came pounding into the room. She had half a sandwich in her hand.

"What the hell?" said Teague. "What the hell?"

Tap her, said Snake.

Going in now. Come on along.

They went in together and poked around. They went through her head from the attic to the basement. They checked the closets and blew dust out of the corners. They mowed her lawn and spaded her flower bed. They gave her a thorough housecleaning, and when they were finished they had nothing. She was nothing more or less than she was supposed to be.

Martha Rattigan, registered nurse, Snake said disgustedly. *On substitute duty for Ellen Coombs. She's clean.*

And she's twenty-six years old, added Julio. *You might have mentioned that she was young before I made a fool of myself. Gemstone was in Nam with Ogden. Does she look old enough to have been in Nam?*

I think she's angry.

Wouldn't you be? What's the sandwich?

I was hungry, Snake said defensively. *Who gets a chance to eat with these hours?*

Teague said, "That's a nice solid lock you got there, Julio. I used to train a wrestler once."

I think you'd better let her up, said Snake. *Unless you're enjoying yourself in that position.*

I'm tempted. It's the closest I've been to a woman in a while.

Poor darling. Now let the nice lady up and apologize like a good boy.

I've got a better idea. At the count of three I'm going to get to my feet and run like hell. You do the apologizing. One.

"She's pretty cute," Teague observed. "Maybe I shoulda shaved."

Wait, said Snake. *What do I tell her?*

Tell her I get this way when the moon is full. Two.

But the moon isn't full.

Tell her I'm an escaped mental patient. Tell her I was abused by a nurse when I was a child. Tell her I have a thing about uniforms. Tell her anything you please, but I'm out of here. Three.

He jumped to his feet, and ran from the room. He hurried down the stairs, and stopped at the first landing. He heard the nurse's strident voice complaining, and Snake's soothing tone as she tried to calm her. He grinned, took a deep breath, and danced down the rest of the stairs to the parlor. Mrs. Costigan was there, and she wasn't alone. With her was a middle-aged woman with grey hair and a distinguished bearing. Mrs. Costigan was holding something in her hands, and on the floor was a salesman's sample case.

Mrs. Costigan said, "Julio, come and look at this. Isn't it lovely?"

Julio came closer to see what she was holding. "A clock?"

"Not just an ordinary clock."

"Not at all," said the other woman with a practiced smile. "Hello, I'm Stella Amsell, and I represent the Jefferson Timepiece Company of Wilmington, Delaware. What Mrs. Costigan is holding is a faithful reproduction of a Seth Thomas grandmother clock, slightly reduced in size, but otherwise the exact same clock that was first produced in the Thomas factory in 1871. It's a beauty, isn't it?"

"It certainly is." It was about three feet long and a foot high, the body sculpted of gleaming walnut that curved gracefully around the clock itself.

"And it's free," said Mrs. Costigan.

"Actually, it's a promotional gift," said Mrs. Amsell. "Normally, this clock sells for one hundred and thirty-nine ninety-five, but we're giving away a limited number of them to a selected group of people in the community."

"People like me," said Mrs. Costigan, beaming.

"People like you," Mrs. Amsell agreed. "We're hoping that your friends and neighbors will see this handsome reproduction perched on your mantelpiece, and will admire it so much that they will want one for their very own."

Julio said, "That's a lucky break for you, Mrs. C."

"I was picked by the computer. It picked me out of all the other names."

"You and several others," said Mrs. Amsell. "I still have some other stops to make." There were four more clocks in the sample case at her feet.

Snake, Julio called, *get down here.*

I can't, she answered. *I've got my hands full of nurse. She wants to call the cops.*

Get your ass down here now. I think I've got Gemstone.

Julio went into the woman's head. He did a deep and careful tap, as comprehensive as the one he had done on the nurse upstairs, and when he was finished he knew as much as he wanted to know about Stella Amsell, aka Gemstone, aka Louise Abruzzi, onetime army nurse.

Snake came into the room, still with her half-eaten sandwich. Mrs. Costigan introduced her to Mrs. Amsell, and showed her the clock.

Snake made the appropriate sounds of admiration, as she said to Julio, *Have you tapped her yet?*

She's Gemstone, all right. Take a look for yourself.

Snake went in and out of the woman's head. *What a sweetheart. The device is in the clock. Did you catch how it works?*

It's a sophisticated job. The clock itself is the timer, and it ignites a tube of compressed thermite that throws a jet of flame under high pressure. Should be as hot as a welding torch, burn down anything from a barn to a battleship.

Only if it's undetected.

She has it set for one in the morning.

What next? You going to jump this one, too?

I think we can do better than that. He told her what he had in mind.

You running this job now?

Not at all. You asked me to help, and I'm trying to. What do you think?

I like it, but how do you know she'll react?

She used to be a nurse.

So was Mrs. Costigan. And speaking of nurses . . .

Not now.

I think you can get to that one upstairs. She was doing a lot of complaining, but I think she enjoyed that roll on the floor.

Not interested.

Really? As I recall, you were doing some complaining, yourself.

Listen, my onetime lover, once this job is over you and I are going to find ourselves a quiet place and we won't come up for air for days.

We'll see about that, but right now it's time to get to work.

Make it good.

The other two women were debating where in the parlor to put the clock. Mrs. Amsell was partial to the mantelpiece, while Mrs. Costigan thought that it would look better on the sideboard. She put it there, and both women stepped back to take a better look. As they did, Snake took a bite of her sandwich, and began to chew. Then she stopped chewing. She made a strangled sound deep in her throat, and a look of panic came over her face. She gasped for breath, but no breath came. She made another strangled sound, and the other women turned to stare at her. She put one hand to her throat, and her other hand stretched out in appeal.

Julio shouted, "She's choking."

"The sandwich," said Mrs. Costigan.

"Somebody do something."

"Help her."

"Heimlich maneuver."

"I'll do it, I'm a nurse," said Mrs. Costigan, but Mrs. Amsell was ahead of her. Moving quickly, she got behind Snake, and wrapped her arms under the rib cage. She went through the motions of the Heimlich maneuver once, again, and a third time. A gummy wad of food shot out of Snake's mouth, and fell to the floor. In the scene that followed, Snake sat slumped in a chair, breathing shallowly. Mrs. Amsell received congratulations modestly. Mrs. Costigan cleaned up the mess on the floor. Julio hovered around the edges.

Sipping a glass of water, Snake asked, *How was I?*

Too good. You had me scared.

Did you make the switch?

Nothing to it. All the eyes were on the star.

"Are you feeling all right?" asked Mrs. Amsell. She and Mrs. Costigan had finally settled on the mantelpiece for the clock.

"Thanks to you. I can't thank you enough."

"Not at all, I was happy to help."

"I could have done it," muttered Mrs. Costigan.

"I'm sure you could have," Mrs. Amsell assured her. "Now, will you look at the time? I'll have to run."

"This must be heavy." Julio picked up the sample case. "I'll give you a hand with it."

"That's kind of you. Good-bye, Mrs. Costigan, and I hope you enjoy your lovely clock."

Julio took the case out to the car, and when he came back, Mrs. Costigan was still in front of the mantelpiece, admiring. "You know, this is the first time in my life that I ever got something for nothing. Never won a lottery, not even a door prize."

"Your lucky day," said Julio. "You want a beer to celebrate?"

"Don't be silly. When did you ever see me drink beer?"

Julio went to the kitchen and came back with two beers. He gave one to Snake, and they raised their bottles in a silent salute. Snake asked, *Where did you put the case?*

In the trunk, with the hot one facing the gas tank.

What if she gives the others away?

Never happen. Those spares were just window dressing.

She might dump them.

She might, but I doubt it. She's a torch, and there's only one thing on her mind right now. She has to see it burn.

We'll see.

That we will.

They saw it in the middle of the night, sitting on the front porch. There was only the sliver of a moon, but there was enough light to see the street, and the street was empty. They sat side by side on the glider, waiting. They had been waiting for almost an hour.

"What time is it?" asked Snake.

"Almost one."

"What if she doesn't show?"

"She'll be here. She has to see it. That's the biggest part of it for a torch."

"That nurse . . ."

"Which one? There were three of them here today."

"Come on, the one you jumped. I really think you got to her. She asked me about you before she left."

"Like what?"

"All sorts of things. I could see that she was interested."

"What did you tell her?"

"Well, I said that you were Cuban, and a man of passion, and . . ." She stopped as a car turned the corner, and rolled to a stop down the street. "Do you think . . . ?"

Julio was silent for a moment, and then he nodded. "It's Gemstone. I just tapped."

Snake shivered. "Not me. I wouldn't want to be inside that head right now. What time is it?"

"Just one o'clock. It might take a while."

"How long?"

"Long enough for the flame to eat through the metal. Might be a few minutes."

As he spoke, the car exploded into flames. The explosion rocked the street and rattled windows. A figure was flung from the wreck. It looked like a flaming doll. It was also a screaming doll. The doll rolled over and over in the street, burning and screaming.

"Gemstone's last fire," said Julio. "I hope she got a kick out of it."

"It's the least we can wish her."

The screaming stopped. Julio tapped. "She's gone."

"Feel like calling the cops?"

"Let someone else do it." Lights had begun to show in windows. "Now that the job is over, would you like to tell me what it was all about? Why did she want to burn down this place?"

"Would you believe me if I said I didn't know?"

"No."

"I'm sorry, Julio, but I really can't say anything."

"I didn't think you would." He stood up. "Your room or mine?"

19

REMEMBER when you were a kid in school, and after the summer vacation your first assignment in class was to tell all the other kids what you did on your summer vacation? Well, here is what I did *not* do during my fun-filled eight-day cruise aboard the *S.S. Carnival Queen*. I did not lie beside the pool with a drink in my hand, and watch the girls go by. I did not play deck tennis or shuffleboard, I did not try my hand at skeetshooting, and I did not drive a bucket of golf balls into the Caribbean. I did not dance all night with the lovely ladies, nor did I see the inside of any of their cabins. I did not take a carriage ride through the winding streets of Nassau, I did not visit the tomb of Ponce de León in San Juan, I did not go snorkeling in St. Thomas, and I did not shop the sophisticated boutiques of St. Maarten. All I did, aside from eat too much, was keep a constant watch on Calvin Weiss, and play high-stakes poker with him every night. Even there, I didn't have the pleasure of winning, because I still was throwing him hands every time I could. I would not have minded any of this if, during all that time, I had pulled even a single lead on Madrigal, but after six days at sea and in ports I knew nothing more than when I had started. By then it was Friday and we were homeward bound, cruising off the coast of Hispaniola. We had one more day at sea, arriving back in Port St. James early Sunday morning.

"It's impossible," I reported to Sammy by telephone.

"Your favorite word."

"Look, you try it. I go around all day tapping heads, and all I get is *Let's kill Calvin, let's kill Calvin.* There are more than two hundred people into the game so far, and that's all they think about."

"And Madrigal has to be one of them."

"Maybe."

"Nothing maybe about it. If he—assuming it's a he—hasn't hit so far, then he's going to try it the night of that game, tomorrow night. It's his best shot."

I had to agree, but I didn't see what good it did me. "All I can do is continue to stay close to Calvin."

"What about Saturday night when he drops out of sight for the game?"

"I'll have to take my chances. Nobody knows where he goes."

"Not good enough. You'll have to be with him every minute that night."

"How am I supposed to do that?"

"Think about it. How much does the winner take out of that pool?"

"About twenty grand."

"And how much of the company money have you lost to Calvin so far?"

"A little under ten."

"Then don't you think it's about time that you started winning?"

"Oh."

"And don't tell me that you would have thought of it yourself."

"I would have."

He hung up.

That night, Calvin greeted me with an exuberant whoop as I sat down at the poker table. I was his buddy, but I was also his pigeon. "This is my boy," he explained to the table. "My boy Ben is better than MasterCard and he's better than American Express. He is my personal cash machine, I just push the right button and he throws money at me."

There were grins around the table. They had seen how often I had locked horns with Calvin, and had come out second best. I told them, "Not tonight. Tonight the worm turns, the empire strikes back, and the meek inherit the earth." I said to Calvin, "Let's make it easy on ourselves tonight. I'll cut cards with you now, one time and one time only, for fifty grand. Then we can have a couple of drinks, and relax."

His eyes narrowed. "You serious?"

"Sure. Look at all the time we'll save."

I wasn't serious at all. There is no way that I can control a cut, but I knew he wouldn't go for it, and I wanted to shake him right from the start.

"No," he said slowly, "let's do it the hard way."

"Suit yourself. Whose deal is it?"

That was about one-thirty in the morning. Four hours later a sweating, shaken Calvin Weiss asked me if I would take his personal check. He had been playing on markers for the past hour, and I had his IOU's for a total of forty-three thousand stacked in front of me. Three of the other players were also holding his paper, and he was in for over fifty large. He didn't have that kind of money in the bank, I knew that from tapping his head, but he wanted us to take the check. He was broken, and I was the one who had done the breaking, but I couldn't feel too sorry for him. Even with my particular advantage, I can't completely break a player, wipe him out and put him in debt, unless he insists on playing bad poker. There is no rule in the book that says that you have to play every hand and meet every raise. But that was his game, and it got worse when I started to turn the screws. After an hour of it he should have had the sense to cash it in and call it a night, but he went on chasing dreams until the sun was up and the coffee was cold. And now he wanted us to take his check.

The other people who were holding his paper weren't happy about it. They hadn't minded taking markers in the middle of the game, but they had figured on a settlement. Now they were being offered a piece of paper that was worthless in the middle of the ocean, and might be worthless on land as well. Trouble was, it was Calvin Weiss, a fixture in their lives, and none of them wanted to offend him. They looked at each other, unsure. I made it easy for them.

"I'll buy your paper," I told them, "and I'll take Calvin's check for the total."

They were so relieved they practically threw the paper across the table at me. I paid them with chips, and put their markers with mine. The total came to fifty-three thousand and change. I showed the figure to

Calvin, and he nodded. He whipped out his checkbook, and made out the check with all the aplomb in the world. He slid it across the table.

"Thanks, Ben. Appreciate the courtesy."

That finished the game, and the others drifted away, some still looking for action, some to bed, and some to the casino's hash-brown breakfast, which was the best food served on board.

"Have a drink with me," I said to Calvin.

He shook his head, grinning. "Gotta see a lady about a pussycat."

"Not this morning. We have something to talk about."

"Some other time."

"Now," I said firmly.

The grin was gone. He didn't like the tone of voice, but he went to the bar while I cashed in my chips. When I joined him, I didn't waste any time on it. I said, "Your check is no good. You know it, and I know it. What are we going to do about it?"

"Ben, baby, what are you talking about? You put the check in and it clears, no sweat."

"Bullshit."

"Bullshit, your ass. I'm telling you it's good."

"And I'm telling you it isn't." I went into his troubled mind, and plucked out a figure. "You've got maybe three thousand bucks in that account, give or take a little. Your house and your cars are hocked to the hilt, and all you've got is your salary."

"How do you know what I've got?"

"What difference does it make? It's true, isn't it?"

He stared at me, suddenly deflated.

"So let's get one thing straight. The check is n.g., right?"

He shrugged, and looked away.

"So I deposit the check when I get home, and it bounces."

He wouldn't look at me.

"Then I write a nice little letter to the Carnival Lines with a photocopy of your bum check enclosed, and you're out of a job."

"It never gets to that," he mumbled. "I figure to cover the check."

"With what? Calvin, please stop snowing me. You're talking now the same way you play poker. You're dreaming. There's no way in the world that you can cover that check."

"If you're so sure of that, why did you take it?"

"To save you the embarrassment. Why the hell did you write it if you knew you couldn't cover it?"

He sighed. "I figured . . . I'd figure something out."

"Like what?"

"I know some people who could maybe cover it."

"Fifty?"

He nodded.

"And you pay back sixty?"

He nodded.

"And a broken arm for every payment that you miss?"

He nodded.

"You're dreaming again. You'll never be able to make the payments. Not even the interest. You don't have enough arms and legs."

"Very funny. I make the jokes."

"I'm not trying to be funny, Calvin. I'm trying to help you out of a hole. There's a way."

He was instantly alert. "I'm listening."

I told him. A slow, sad smile worked its way across his face. "You know how much money I could have made doing that, I mean, all these trips. But I never did it, never once. I always played it straight."

"There's always a first time."

"Yeah, this time. Let's get it straight. You get to be the one who kills me, and I'm off the hook. You tear up the check, right."

"Right. No cash for you, but you owe me nothing."

"You'll still be losing. You'll only get about twenty."

"The other way I get nothing."

"All right, you got it."

"It's a deal?"

"I said you got it, didn't I?"

"There's one more thing."

"There always is."

"Wherever you hide out tomorrow night, I stay there with you. All night, until it's time to make the kill. Until the game is over."

"Trusting bastard, aren't you?"

"I can't afford to take a chance. You can see that, can't you?"

"Yeah, I can see it."

I grabbed a few hours sleep and got up at noon, in time to sign up for the Kill Calvin game in the Main Lounge. The officer in charge was Fleckmann, the second purser. I gave him my hundred dollars, and in return he gave me a receipt, an identification card, and one of those toy pistols that shoots pellets of paint. The paint came in three different colors: red, yellow, and blue. I chose yellow.

"Any particular significance?" asked Fleckmann.

"Cowardice. Real guns scare me."

He grinned. "Good hunting."

I took the pistol back to my cabin and examined it. It was roughly the same size and shape as the Walther in my suitcase. As far as I could tell without opening it, the paint was stored in the grip and was expelled in the form of pellets by a cartridge of compressed air. There was a Degas print on the cabin wall, the usual ballet dancer. I aimed, fired, and the pellet landed square in the tutu. I had no way of knowing how it would work at a greater range, but I didn't care. I had no intention of carrying the toy. I threw it into the suitcase, and tucked the Walther into my waistband under my shirt. Real guns really do scare me, but going up against Madrigal with a paint pistol scared me even more.

I spent the afternoon and the early evening trying to keep Calvin under observation, but it wasn't easy. He kept bouncing all over the ship, from lounge to lounge and group to group, whipping up interest in the game that night. It was a ridiculous sight, all those people flaunting their toy pistols, fake daggers, and lacy little nooses. I caught up with Calvin outside the Carousel Room, and pulled him aside. It was seven-thirty and the game began officially at eight.

"When do you disappear?" I asked.

"Very shortly. One minute you'll see me, and the next minute you won't."

"With all these people watching you?"

"I've been doing this for years. Don't follow me too close. Give me maybe half an hour, and make sure that nobody sees you."

I still don't know how he did it, but one minute he was in plain view, and then he was gone. A moment later, someone said loudly, "Hey, where the hell did Calvin go to?" But by then it was too late, as a bell rang to announce that the hunt was on.

I gave him his half-hour, and then joined him in his hidey-hole. It was a lifeboat, but not any old lifeboat. Both the port and the starboard sides of the Bridge Deck were lined with lifeboats hanging from davits, each about fifteen feet long and protected by tarpaulins, but the boat farthest aft on the starboard side was something special. Twenty-five feet long and painted a fire-engine red, it was a power launch that was built like a miniature tugboat with an enclosed cabin and a tiny wheel-house. Inside the cabin were two bunk beds, a folding table, a chemical toilet, and a sink. Not all of the comforts of home, but enough of them including the bottle of Scotch that Calvin had brought. The only inconvenience was that we could not show a light.

After I had settled onto one of the bunks, I asked, "Do you always use this place?"

"Always. It's amazing, I mean you'd think that somebody would check this out, but it's never happened, not in all the years I've been doing this. Sometimes I can hear them outside on the deck, but they never look here."

"How long do you stay?"

"Depends on how I feel. Sometimes I can catch some sleep in here, but if I can't then I get it over with early. Two, maybe three in the morning. I just show myself until somebody zaps me, and the game is over. You want a drink? It's gotta be from the bottle, I forgot to bring glasses."

He passed over the bottle. I took a slug, and gave it back. "That's all there is, so pace yourself," he said. "I could get it over with quick, you know, but I like to give them their money's worth. That okay with you?"

It was very much okay with me. I wanted to stay with him for as long as I could. "All night if you want to."

He grunted, and I took that for an agreement. We settled back into the bunks, shaking down for the night. It was dark in the cabin of the launch, and I could barely see his face. We passed the bottle back and forth, taking tiny sips.

"I shoulda brought some peanuts," he muttered.

"Peanuts are for sissies. Is it all right to talk like this?"

"Long as we keep it low."

"How do we pass the time? 'Sit upon the ground, and tell sad stories of the death of kings'?"

"*Richard Second*, Act Three." He laughed shortly. "You patronizing me, quoting Shakespeare to a comic?"

"I didn't mean to. I'm sorry if it sounded that way."

"Forget it. I got a thin skin about things like that, comes with the line of work I'm in. You see the way people look at you, and you know what they're thinking. A comic, he's got no feelings. He's got no sensitivity. All he knows is how to drop his pants and make people laugh. We're not supposed to be like other people."

" 'And yet, if you prick us, do we not bleed?' "

"You gonna do that all night? Besides, that's about Jews, not comics. I know, I'm both." He was silent for as long as it took for each of us to take one of those ladylike sips from the bottle. "You remember that friend I told you about?"

"Mutt and Jeff?"

"The funniest part was that he was an Arab. An exchange student from Lebanon. Mutt and Jeff, the Arab and the Jew."

"And the Pom-Pom Queen."

"You got a good memory. You're not married, are you?"

"No."

"I didn't think so, and I can usually tell. Listen, what I said the other night about my wife . . ."

"You don't have to tell me anything."

"Yeah, but I want to. Whatever I said about her, I didn't mean it to sound like I'm blaming her. I've got a screwed-up marriage, but it isn't her fault. She just married the wrong guy."

"You don't know how it would have worked out with the other guy."

There was just enough light for me to see him shake his head. "You wouldn't say that if you knew Hassan."

"Mutt?"

"Yeah. Hassan was the straightest, sweetest guy who ever lived. Sure, we both loved her, but the way he loved her was different. Let me put it this way. If she had married him, she'd be happy today. And so would he. The marriage would have lasted, and the love would have lasted, too. That's the way he loved her. Forever."

"Nothing is forever."

"Like I said, you never knew him. But it was different with me. I'm a fuck-up, and I've always been a fuck-up. All I knew was that I wanted her. So I woo'd her, and I won her, but it was still a fuck-up."

" 'Men are April when they woo, December when they wed.' "

"Enough. Pass the bottle." I heard it clink against his teeth. "You know the line from the act after that, the one about the clown?"

" 'It is meat and drink to me to see a clown'?"

"That's it. Meat and drink. Remember that."

"What happened to Hassan?"

"He took second best. Consolation prize."

"The Poodle?"

He did not answer, and he was silent for a long time after that. Once he mumbled about not bringing peanuts. Once he grunted as he took off his shoes and stretched out on the bunk. After that I heard his even breathing as he slept, and then I heard him turn over.

"Ben, you awake?"

"Yeah."

"What time is it?"

"About two."

"Listen, you got that check of mine with you?"

"Uh-huh."

"Could I have it back now? I mean, once we walk out of here and you zap me, it's over. So could I have it back?"

There was no reason not to. The check had served its purpose. I dug it out of my pocket, and handed it to him. I heard him rip it in half, and then in half again. He said, "Thanks. Is it enough to say thanks?"

"Don't get sloppy on me. Go back to sleep."

I heard him turn over again. My own eyes felt heavy, and I fought the temptation to close them. Only a few more hours and the hunt would be over, but I was beginning to get the feeling that I was guarding an empty castle. If two hundred players in the game couldn't find Calvin, then how was Madrigal going to do it? Only through a stroke of luck, and the professionals of David Ogden's world didn't operate on luck. So how? If I were Madrigal, how would I . . . ?

And there it was. So simple, really.

"Calvin."

"What?"

"How much did the other guy offer you?"

"What other guy?"

"You sold me out. You made a deal with someone else."

He was silent.

"Didn't you?"

"No, I swear I didn't."

I went into his head. He was lying. It was all there, screaming guilt. He had made the deal, all right, and someone was waiting out there on the deck. I said quietly, "How much did he promise you? Half of it? More?"

"Hey, do you really think I'd do something like that?"

"Which was why you had to have the check back. How much, Calvin?"

He sighed. "Half. Guy comes up to me yesterday afternoon, makes me the offer, and 'I did greedily devour the treacherous bait.' "

"No more Shakespeare. Talk."

"Look, do you know how often I get a proposition like that? At least once every trip, and I always say no. But I figure, I already sold out to you, so why not? Ten grand from him, and if I can get the check back from you I'm home free. Which is just the way it's working out."

"Cute."

"Remember, I told you I was a fuck-up."

"So you did. And, of course, you told him where you would be hiding."

He shrugged. "How else?"

"Which means he's waiting out there now."

"That's the deal. Hey, where are you going?"

I was off the bunk and moving aft to the cabin door. "Calvin, you're right, you're a world-class fuck-up, and if you want to do something right for just once in your life you'll stay here and keep quiet. You understand? Don't move, not for anything."

"What are you going to do?"

"I have an investment to protect."

I went out of the cabin on my belly, rolled over the side of the launch, grabbed the davit, and dropped to the deck. I took out the silenced Walther, and let it hang in my hand at my side. The Bridge Deck looked dark and deserted, and I did not try to hide myself. Madrigal would be looking for Calvin, not for me.

I started forward, leaving the launch behind me, and I felt his presence before I saw him. He was about a hundred feet up the deck, and I went into his head as soon as I got within range. It was a cool head, uncluttered. He had what he saw as a simple job to do, and he was ready to do it as soon as Calvin showed his face. With what as a weapon? I tapped deeper. One of those paint pistols? Not likely. I pushed harder on the tap. Yeah, a paint pistol, but then I saw what he had done to the toy they had given him in the Main Lounge. He had modified the paint mixture with a strong dose of—I had to stretch for it—Saxitoxin-D. Talk about biological assault with a vengeance. One drop of that on Calvin's skin, thirty seconds to kill him, and the beauty part is that it comes out looking like a heart attack. Very sophisticated high-level Agency equipment. The night was warm, and I was suddenly chilled.

I saw him then. He was standing with his back against the rail. It was too dark to see his face clearly, or to tell his age. He nodded as I came near.

"Hi, there," he said in a low, smooth voice. "You playing the Calvin game?"

"That's right. You, too?"

"I was, but I think I've had enough. Time to turn in. Good luck, and happy hunting."

"Thanks, but I'm not hunting anymore, Mister Madrigal. I found what I was looking for."

He stiffened, and then forced himself to relax. "Well now, what have we here?"

"I'm a messenger, and if I know your name, then you know who sent me."

He stood motionless. "That's impossible. He's dead."

"There are other people who know who you are."

"What's your message?"

"Your assignment has been aborted. At the highest level. It's over."

"That's also impossible."

"Don't give me that crap about Gilbraltar Rules. We're playing by new rules now." I showed him the pistol. There was light enough for that. "My rules."

"Is he up there in that launch?"

"Maybe you didn't hear me, I said that it's over. If you try to get him, I'll have to stop you."

"I'm unarmed."

"Except for that pistol in your pocket."

"That pistol is a toy, a paint gun for the game."

"And the paint is loaded with Saxitoxin-D."

"Christ, how the hell . . ." He thought about it. "You're a sensitive."

"And you're a murderer, but not this time. Reach into your pocket and take out that toy. Take it out by the barrel. If it comes out any other way, you're dead. Take it out, and toss it over the side."

"I don't give up my weapon, not to anyone."

His voice was hard. I was inside his head, and I could feel the anger there. He was working himself up to make a move.

"Take it out and toss it over."

"And if I don't?"

"This pistol is silenced. It wouldn't bother me one little bit to blow your head off, and dump you over the rail."

"You? I don't think so." He blew out air like a bull snorting. He was still working up to it. "Sensitives are gentlemen, they play by the rules. They don't do cold-blooded murder."

"Let's not find out. Come on, the toy."

He was ready, he had decided to do it. Inside his pocket, his fingers closed around the pistol, one finger on the trigger. I could see it all inside his head. He was no more than six feet away from me, and I knew what a drop of that paint could do.

He shook his head. "No, you'd never do it. Not a sensitive. Not a gentleman."

He started to pull the pistol from his pocket. I shot him twice, and the bullets hurled him back against the rail. The pistol never came out. He stared at me, his eyes wide with shock and surprise. They were starting to glaze.

"Gentlemen don't cheat at cards, either," I told him, but he did not hear me. He was gone. He sagged against the rail, and I caught him before he could fall. I grabbed an arm and a leg, and rolled him over the rail. It was a long way down, and I never heard the splash. I threw my pistol after him, and looked up and down the deck. It was empty.

I heard a scream, and I jumped. I heard another, and another. They were coming from the launch. I sprinted aft, scrambled up the davit, and swung on board. I went through the cabin door shoulder first, and stopped. Someone had turned on a light. Calvin lay flat on the bunk, and he was covered with red and blue spots of paint. Two young women stood over him, toy pistols in their hands. They were screaming at the top of their lungs.

"We killed Calvin, we killed Calvin."

One of them saw me, and said, "You're too late, we got him first."

Calvin looked up at me, grinning, and shrugged.

"You can have him," I told them.

I went back to my cabin and tried for a few more hours of sleep, but I awoke in the middle of a dream. Someone had accused me of cheating at cards, and I was trying to hide under the poker table. I hit my head on a table leg, and that was what woke me up. It didn't take a genius to figure out a dream like that. I tried to laugh it off, and I called Sammy.

"Ball game's over," I told him. "The good guys won."

I heard his breath go out. "What about the bad guy?"

"He tried to go swimming, but he wasn't very good at it."

"Any problems with the suits?"

"None that I can see. Fill me in on the others. How did Snake do?"

"A winner."

"Terrific. Vince?"

"Another winner."

"Martha?"

"She broke her leg."

"Christ. What about the girl?"

"She's safe." He told me what had happened. "Chicken really came through."

"Sounds a little dicey. What if she talks about what happened?"

"What's there to talk about? Nothing actually did happen, did it?

Chicken has her convinced that it was a party that got out of hand."

"She bought that?"

"She's not the brightest," Sammy admitted. "Chicken says she'll keep quiet, and I'm going with his judgment. He's changed a lot, Ben. He's grown up."

"As long as she doesn't tell her grandmother."

"I have a different sort of problem with the grandmother." I heard the change in his voice. "Jessup turned it up. It seems that Ogden had an intercept mounted on her mail for years."

"On Violet Simms? What the hell for?"

"He was reading every letter that she wrote, and every letter that she received. Not the agency, just Ogden."

"I don't get it. What does it mean?"

"I'll know more about that after I speak to the lady. I've asked our friends to pull her in for questioning."

20

IT was the day of the imam's weekly visit to the camp in the Libyan Fezzan, and, as always, he had brought with him the letter for The Prisoner that arrived each week at the embassy in Rome. Like all the others, the letter had travelled far, but swiftly, from a small town in New York state to a blind address in Paris, from there to the embassy, and then on to Tripoli in the diplomatic pouch. The Prisoner retreated to the privacy of the squad room, and held the letter in his hands for a while before opening it. It was his one link with the outside world, and his eyes noted all the familiar details. The cheap stationery, the American stamps, the Rockhill postmark, the return address in a spidery script: 29A Linden Avenue. The Prisoner pressed the envelope to his forehead, then to a spot over his heart, and only then did he slit the flap and open his weekly letter from Violet Simms.

Along with the letter, two newspaper clippings and a photograph fell from the envelope. He reached for the picture first, and stared long and hard at the daughter he had never seen in person. She was dressed for skiing, posing in front of a snow bank, and she was smiling at the camera, unaware that she was smiling for her father. He put the photograph aside to cherish later, and turned to the letter.

The weekly letters rarely varied in content, but he treated each one as if the others had never arrived. First there was news of Lila, and all seemed well. Good health, good grades, dances, parties, even a skiing trip won in some sort of a contest. All quite normal for the world in which she lived, and all quite different from the world of her father. No problems, at least for this week.

He read on. Mrs. Simms never failed to follow the form, always reporting on the required subjects. Nothing new to report about Mike Teague, living out his days in the Florida sunshine, frail and in constant need of medical attention, but still alive. Good old Mike, only a trainer on the team, but a surrogate father and any-time-of-the-night confidant to a Lebanese kid in a strange land with strange customs. Without Mike, it would have been hell. Without Mike, it would have been impossible. Hang in there, Mike, hang in there. He read further. No news about Calvin or June, but then there rarely was. What news could there be from the ruts of a marriage grown into a routine? Still, the marriage existed, and that was all he needed to know. Other news? Not much of anything. That world on the other side of the planet, the world in which he once had lived, seemed quite unruffled.

He picked up the newspaper clipping from the *Albany Times-Union*, and the headline jumped out at him. POLK DEFEATS VAN BUREN 78–62. Damn, a disappointment. For a while it had looked as if the Cavaliers might beat the Bulldogs and go on to the tournament. He allowed his memory to slip back to his own Van Buren days, the frenzy of the game nights, the stuffy gyms, the squeal of sneakers on hardwood, and once, only once, the indescribable thrill of trotting out onto the floor of Madison Square Garden, the blinding lights and the roar of thousands. He had made it, his team had made it, but it had not happened since to Van Buren, and now another chance was gone. He smiled at his emotions, knowing them to be a weakness, and put the clipping aside.

Fresh emotions washed over him as he read the second clipping. DIVA IN FAREWELL TOUR, read the headline in *The New York Times*, and the text of the story told of triumph after triumph as Maria-Teresa Bonfiglia bade adieu to her adoring public in cities across the country. San Francisco, Dallas, Cleveland, Chicago, and the final appearance only ten days away at Carnegie Hall in New York. He stared at the clipping, entranced, then put it aside and went to the phonograph. He selected a record, and stood with his hands clasped behind his back and his head sunk in thought as her incomparable voice filled the room singing the "Vissi d'arte." He remembered the first time that he heard her sing it, and he remembered the times when she had sung it just for him.

"And now that voice will be stilled," he murmured. "How sad. Memories, I will have only memories. How long can a man live on memories?"

No longer, he decided. It was time for him to go out into the world again, time for an end to his *hegira*, and he was amazed at how easily the decision was made.

Go, he told himself, go now. There is nothing to keep you here. Not the imam, not the committee in Beirut, not the men, not all the vows and promises made. I have given so much, and I have asked for so little in return. This I must have, and no one will dare to say no to me.

An hour later, dressed in western clothing and with money and papers in his pockets, he drew a vehicle from the motor pool and began the drive north to Tripoli. He was right. No one had dared to say no to him.

21

THIS is a voluntary statement by Mrs. Violet Simms of 29A Linden Avenue, Rockhill, N.Y., on this date. The statement was made to Mr. Samuel Warsaw of this department. This memorandum is restricted to internal use only.

SAMMY: We'd like you to tell us whatever you can about the letters that you have been sending over the years to the man you know as Hassan Rashid.

VIOLET: First of all, I haven't done anything illegal, and as far as I'm concerned I haven't done anything improper or immoral, either. I know what moral is. I'm a churchgoing woman, have been all my life, and I know the difference between right and wrong. I haven't done anything to be ashamed of. If you want to talk about shame, you ought to talk about the shame that my daughter put on me, having a baby without a husband that way. All I've done is try to raise Lila the best that I could, and I couldn't have done it without the money from Hassan. He's been generous to me, kind and generous.

SAMMY: Are you aware that the man you know as Hassan Rashid is the terrorist that the world knows of by the single name of Safeer?

VIOLET: So you say. Since I've been in this place that's all I've heard, that he's one of those people who blows up airplanes and does those terrible things, but as far as far as I'm concerned it's all a lot of talk. I haven't seen any proof that Hassan is this Safeer fellow, and until I do I just don't believe it. It's been a lot of years since I last saw Hassan, but it's been my experience that people don't change all that much over the years. You start out with a basically decent human being, and that's what you wind up with, more or less. And decent was what he was. What he is. Not that I felt that way about him right from the start. I had some funny feelings then about Arabs, and I didn't like it one little bit when Julia started to throw herself at him. Threw herself at him like a slut, that's what she did, and that's where the blame lies, not with me.

SAMMY: You don't blame Hassan for what he did to your daughter?

VIOLET: What did he do? She threw herself at him, didn't she? A man is a man, isn't he? He did what any other man would do, and she got exactly what she was looking for. Got herself pregnant without a husband, which doesn't mean much to some people these days, but it still does where I come from, and I begged her to tell him before he went home after college. He had to go back to his people, didn't he? Well, she should have told him then that she was pregnant, but she wouldn't. I tell you, I almost got down on my knees and begged her to, but that girl was so stubborn, so filled up with pride. Wanted to see if he'd send for her, wanted him to prove that he loved her before she would tell him. Love, my foot. She knew who that man was in love with, everybody knew, and he took up with my Julia only after June turned him down. Well, I guess she got her proof. He never did write to her, never did ask for her to come to him, which only goes to show how little he thought of her throwing herself at him that way. A man thinks you're cheap, and he treats you cheap, it's always been that way and it always will. Some people might find fault with the way that he treated her, but she had only herself to blame. He was a decent person, and he proved it later on when I needed him.

SAMMY: When was that?

VIOLET: When the baby came, and Julia died. God's judgment? I try not to think of it that way, but it's hard to escape the thought. In the end, it doesn't matter, does it? I lost my daughter, and suddenly I had a baby to care for. That's when Hassan—I'm sorry, but I can't call him Safeer—showed how decent he was. All it took was one letter from me explaining the situation, and the money started coming. Now, remember, as far as he knew it could have been anybody's baby, Not that it was, it was his, all right, but how was he to know that? And even if he knew, how many men would do the right thing that way? Well, Hassan did. The money started coming, and it never stopped, right to this day, deposited every month like clockwork in my bank.

SAMMY: What did he ask for in return?

VIOLET: Nothing much, nothing more than any father would ask. He wanted to hear about his child, wanted to know how she was growing up, wanted to see some photos once in a while, that's all. Little enough to ask for what he was doing, and I can be like clockwork, too. I've been writing once a week without fail, first to Beirut and later to that address in Paris, never missed once over all these years. I tell him about Lila, and all the other things that he wants to know. He always wants to hear about Mike Teague, who was like family to him once, and all about that singer, too.

SAMMY: What singer is that?

VIOLET: The opera star with that funny name. Maria-Teresa something.

SAMMY: Bonfiglia? Maria-Teresa Bonfiglia?

VIOLET: That's it. Any time her name is in the papers, I send him the clipping. And anything about the Van Buren basketball team. And anything I hear about Calvin and June, of course.

SAMMY: Why, of course?

VIOLET: Because they were all so close in college, the three of them. My Julia was never a part of it, she just tagged along. That's why they called her the Poodle, she was like a pet. But the other three were the best of friends, and if you want my opinion, Hassan never got over it when Calvin and June got married. If you want my opinion . . .

SAMMY: Yes?

VIOLET: I think that Hassan has always been waiting for the marriage to break up. There, I said it. Not very nice, but that's what I think, and that's why he wanted me to keep him posted about it. If anything ever happens between Calvin and June, you can bet that Hassan will be Johnny-on-the-spot.

SAMMY: You think he still wants her after all these years?

VIOLET: I'm sure of it.

SAMMY: Would he come back here to get her?

VIOLET: I'm sure of that, too.

SAMMY: What does Lila know about this?

VIOLET: Nothing, and I'd like to keep it that way. She thinks her father died in an accident just after she was born.

SAMMY: But she knows that her parents weren't married?

VIOLET: She knows that much, because of her name. She doesn't have to know the rest of it, does she?

SAMMY: She won't hear it from us.

VIOLET: Good. I don't want her hearing all that talk about terrorists. Her father is a fine, decent man, not this Safeer person you're talking about.

SAMMY: Would you say that he loves his daughter?

VIOLET: Of course he does, what a question. Everything that he's done over the years proves that he does.

SAMMY: Then why has he never tried to see her?

VIOLET: (No response.)

SAMMY: It's because he can't, isn't it? He hasn't been able to show his face for years.

VIOLET: (No response.)

SAMMY: It's because he's an acknowledged terrorist who is wanted by the police in virtually every country in the western world. That's why, isn't it?

VIOLET: All I did was write some letters. They were personal letters, family letters. There was nothing in them that would interest anyone else.

SAMMY: You're wrong there. They were of very great interest to someone else. A man named David Ogden read every one of them.

"So much for brain damage," said Sammy. "We read this job wrong from the beginning. There was nothing damaged about Ogden's brain. It was working fine right up to the end, trying to flush a master terrorist out of hiding. His goal was to get Hassan Rashid, the man we know as Safeer, onto American soil, nail him, and try him in an American court.

There were seven of us in the conference room at the Center, the five sensitives, Jessup, and Delaney. We had all just finished reading the Simms statement. Martha's copy dropped to the floor, and she muttered "damn" because she couldn't bend to pick it up. Her leg was still in a cast. Snake retrieved it for her.

"You're going too fast for me," said Delaney. "Are you saying that Ogden had an intercept going on Mrs. Simm's mail?"

"That's it."

"A *private* intercept. Not Agency?" He turned to Jessup. "Is that possible?"

"I'm afraid it is," Jessup said somberly. "You don't know how David worked. He ran Operations like a private kingdom. Look at those agents that he used, Madrigal, Sextant, and the others. People we never heard of. If he could do that, then he certainly could have mounted a private intercept on her mail."

"Ogden got to know Safeer from these letters," said Sammy. "He knew him inside out. He knew exactly what buttons that he had to push to move him out of his sanctuary."

"I still find it hard to believe," said Delaney. "How could he know how the man would react?"

Martha asked, "Do you have a daughter?" She knew that he did.

Uncomfortable, Delaney said, "Yes."

"How would you react if she was raped? Wouldn't you risk everything to be with her? Wouldn't you travel halfway across the world to crucify the bastards who did it?"

Delaney conceded the point with a shrug. "What about the other assignments?"

"Sound off," Sammy ordered. "Ben first."

"June was his first real love, maybe his only love," I said. "What would he do if he heard that she was suddenly a widow, available and vulnerable? I think he'd come running."

Snake leaned forward, and said intently, "Mike Teague was like family to Hassan. What would he do if the old man got burned out of his home? To tell you the truth, I don't know. But I'm sure he'd make some kind of a move, and he might have come here to make it."

"All right, I'll buy it so far," said Delaney. "But a basketball team?"

"They were the pride of his youth," Vince explained. "If you don't dig sports, then you won't understand it, but if Van Buren had made the tournament, I think there's a good chance that he would have tried to be here for it."

"Maybe a single button would have done it, maybe not," I said. "But Ogden wasn't taking any chances. He pushed them all at the same time."

"And it almost worked." Jessup shook his head sadly. "It was a masterpiece, a typical Ogden operation. Safeer hears that his daughter has been brutally attacked. He hears that the woman he loves is free to marry. He hears that his old friend Teague has been burned out of his home. He hears that his college team is going to the tournament. Damn, it's a psychological blitzkrieg, he can't resist it."

"He would have come over," said Delaney. "I'm sure of it."

"Damn it, if we had only known. We killed a beautiful operation."

"You mean, you would have let it happen?" asked Martha. "The rape, the murder, and all the rest of it?"

Jessup looked uncomfortable. "It's hard to say . . . I mean, if we could have gotten our hands on Safeer . . ." His voice trailed off."

"Talk about brain damage," Snake crowed. "Just look at him, he's ready to kick himself. He would have done it, all right."

Jessup said stiffly. "That's academic now. You stopped them. You stopped them cold."

"You sure did," said Delaney. "Four out of four."

Sammy said quietly, "Four out of five."

They stared at him, and there was silence in the room. So they had missed it. The five of us had caught it, but the two normals had missed it. It had nothing to do with being a sensitive. It was there, right in front of them, but they missed it.

"Five?" said Jessup. "You said five?"

"The singer," said Sammy. "Maria-Teresa Bonfiglia."

"What about her?" He still didn't see it.

"Mrs. Simms sends clippings about her to Hassan."

"So what?" said Delaney. "So the bastard likes opera." He didn't see it, either.

"You remember Ogden's lockbox?" Sammy said patiently. "The right-hand side contained envelopes, one for each of five women. They were Sarah Brine, the actress; Jenny Cookson, the anchorwoman; Carla MacAlester, the senator's wife; Vivian Livingstone, the socialite; and Maria-Teresa Bonfiglia, the soprano."

"My God," said Jessup. "Could it be a coincidence?"

"I don't think so. In the left-hand side of the box were the assignments to Ogden's four agents. I made the assumption, I guess we all made the assumption, that the right side was for personal use and the left side was for business, but we were wrong. The envelope for Bonfiglia was different from those of the other women. Students?"

"No erotic photos," said Vince.

"No love letters," said Martha.

"Correct, just the contract for the farewell tour. Ogden never had a romantic relationship with her. He arranged for the tour, he underwrote the expenses, but he wasn't paying off a sexual debt the way he did with the others. He knew that Safeer would hear about the tour. He was pushing one more button."

"How?" asked Jessup. "What has Bonfiglia got to do with Safeer?"

"I don't know," Sammy confessed. "But Ogden obviously did, and he used it to set one last piece of bait."

"The fifth button. Her final performance is next Thursday at Carnegie Hall. Are you saying that Safeer will be there?"

"David Ogden knew his man. If he knew him as well as I think he did, then yes, I think he'll be there. Sorry, folks, but that's the way I see it. It isn't over yet."

22

It should have been over for us, but it wasn't. We had done our jobs, and the rest of it should have been left to the proper agencies. If Hassan Rashid, aka Safeer, was really going to risk his neck by coming into the country to attend the farewell performance of an overage opera singer at Carnegie Hall, then the job now belonged to Immigration, the FBI, and the NYPD in that order. I say "if" he was coming because I wasn't anywhere near as confident as Sammy was that he would show. I agreed with Sammy that Ogden's operation had been brilliantly conceived. (That it also had been unblushingly evil was something else again.) But to me the brilliance had resided in the timing of the events, the sequential pushing of all the buttons, and not in any single one of them. Taken all together, they would have created what Sammy had called a psychological blitzkrieg, but I had my doubts that any one of them alone, save perhaps the attack on Lila, would have been enough to do the trick. So I wasn't at all comfortable about this night at the opera, and I would have been more than happy to bow out of the job at that point, but we were stuck with it for one simple reason. Nobody knew what Safeer looked like. Plastic surgery had changed his face and his fingerprints entirely, and careful schooling had done the same for his voice, his speech patterns, and his accent. We had to assume that with the manufactured papers available to him, he would have no trouble clearing Immigration into the country, and that he would be virtually unidentifiable once he was here. If his purpose had been simply to enter the country, there was no way in which we could have stopped him, but he had a theoretical goal, and that made it possible. I say theoretical because I still did not fully believe that he was coming, but the assumption was that he was headed for Carnegie Hall, and that's where we came in. Only a sensitive had the ability to spot him in a crowd and set him up for the suits, and so we still were on the job.

In addition to these doubts, I was unhappy about the situation for a number of reasons, the most important of which was that I had just killed a man. Madrigal had been right in what he had said just before I pulled the trigger. We may not be quite the ladies and gents of the intelligence world that he thought we were, but we do like to think of ourselves as being something different. No one knows better than a sensitive how filthy and corrupting the life in that world can be, and we try to insulate ourselves from the worst parts of it. The title defines the attitude. We are sensitives, with an inbred sensibility to the cares and the woes of humankind. What else could we be, being privy to the hopes and despairs of everyone around us? We work with our brains, not our backs, and we leave the mechanics of the game, the sweat, the grime, and the inevitable violence to others. But there comes a time, as it had come to me, and it had not come easily. I had taken a life, and that was no small thing to me. I had taken it to save myself, and to save Calvin, but that did not help my sleep at night.

Another intruder in the night was June. No, not romance. I carried a gleaming memory of her alabaster body wrapped in a cheap motel towel, but it was a memory to be filed under lost chances. When I thought of her in the night it was with sadness, not passion. Sadness for both of them, actually. Calvin and June, who should never have married, and who now were bound together only by two small sacks of marital cement. A not uncommon situation these days, but a personal one to me for I had intervened in it. I had pointed a finger, playing God, and had said that this one shall live and this one shall die. By killing Madrigal I had kept her pitiful marriage alive, and now I was being asked to point that finger again and help to destroy the man she thought she should have married. Mutt and Jeff, and the Pom-Pom Queen, and what would have happened to Hassan Rashid if he, not Calvin, had won the woman? Do we still speak of winning women? We certainly speak of losing them, and Hassan had lost. What would he have been with June at his side? Not Safeer, I was sure of that, but what? And what did it matter to me? Another intruder that clashed with my sleep.

The final source of my discontent was the way in which we were to be employed on the job. We were to be the eyes and the ears, spotted around both inside and outside of Carnegie Hall on the night of the concert performance. We would search, we would find, and we would point the finger. After that it would be up to the FBI and the NYPD, working together, which was fine with me. Lou Ritter was heading up the FBI team, and Captain Dennis Costello was the man in charge for the police. I had worked with Ritter before, and I could trust him as much as I could trust any normal. He and Costello would work from an unmarked command truck parked on Fifty-seventh Street opposite the hall, and Sammy would be there with them. So I had no complaints about procedure, and no complaints about command, but I had plenty to complain about when Sammy told me that I would be working with Chicken.

It was Sammy's decision that we would work the Hall in pairs, fifteen teams for a total of thirty sensitives. With Martha out of the game and Sammy needed in the truck, this meant pulling people off other assignments all over the country, and using some of the kids. I had no objection to working with the juniors, they were as good as any other sensitive for this kind of work, but I did object to working with a screwball like Chicken. I knew that he had gotten his touch back, and I knew that he had come up smelling like roses on the Sextant job, but that didn't mean much to me. The touch could go as quickly as it had returned, and the only reason he had wound up looking so good was because he had been so bad to start with. To me he was still a loudmouthed juvenille braggart without a shred of responsibility in his nature, and I wanted no part of him. I told that to Sammy, and I got the answer I should have expected.

"In the first place you're wrong, he's changed," Sammy said. "In the second place I don't care a fig about your personal preferences, I'm not changing the assignment sheet. And in the third place, if he really is so bad then he can only profit from working with a seasoned pro like the great Ben Slade."

So there I was, stuck with the kid who had broken Martha's leg, and who had come within a deuce of blowing the Sextant assignment. And to make matters worse, he was totally unrepentant, and all puffed up about what he had accomplished on that job. To hear him tell it, no one else had rescued a damsel in distress since the days of St. George and the dragon, and what he was proud of most was that he had done it all with his mouth. He had used no violence, fired no weapon, wrestled with no bad guys in the mud. He had talked his way out of a losing situation, and he wore the accomplishment like a rakish halo. This did not endear him to me. I, the seasoned pro, the great Ben Slade, had been forced to take a life.

I complained about the pairing to Martha, and she advised me to live with it. It was Saturday morning, the day of the Bonfiglia performance. "Ride it out," she said. "He's only a kid, what harm can he do?"

"I can't believe you said that. Look what he did to you."

"That was partly my fault, I should have kept an eye on him." She can be disgustingly fair-minded. "Besides, he's changed."

"So everybody tells me, but I don't see it. I'd rather be working with you."

"That's sweet, but I'll be in the truck with Sammy. What's really bothering you?" I shrugged. "Let Mama take a peek." I let her into my head, and she frowned. "The woman? June?"

"Do you ever get the feeling that you've played God once too often?"

She snorted. "About twice a week. Come on, sweetie, you feel guilty because you took out Madrigal? Keeping her husband alive was your job. What else were you going to do?"

"Nothing. That's half the problem."

"And the other half is Safeer. You want to nail him, don't you?"

"If he shows up."

"If? Can I come back in for another peek?"

"No."

"You don't want him to show, do you?"

"Please, spare me the profundities."

"Just trying to help."

"If you really want to help, do me a favor tonight and keep a tap on Chicken from the truck. Let me know if you think he's going to pull one of his crazy stunts."

She looked doubtful. "The range may be too much."

"Give it a try, please."

"He really bothers you."

"He makes me nervous," I admitted.

It rained that night, a light, steady shower that did nothing to cleanse the air or the streets. I welcomed the rain. I thought that it might cut down the crowd and make our job easier, but it didn't. The Hall was sold out, all two thousand two hundred forty-seven seats and sixty-three boxes, and no one was burning tickets that night. We were set up by late afternoon, and between the FBI and the plainclothes cops we had about seventy bodies in the area. Sammy gave our gang the final instructions in the truck. He had us broken down into three squads. The first would work the sidewalk outside the Hall, and the lobby area. The second would work the Parquet section, which is what Carnegie calls its orchestra. The third was assigned to the various balconies. Sammy had it set up like a radio net, one group reporting to the next, and the next, and then out to the truck.

"You tap individuals, not groups, as they approach the building," said Sammy, "and you tap everyone, including women. You report anything suspicious, but you do not, repeat not, approach the subject. You pass him along to the next squad until his seat is noted, and that's it. Once the performance has started, assuming that we haven't landed anything, you withdraw from the main hall. During the intermission you repeat the procedure on people passing in and out of the main hall and, again, if we don't have anything, you withdraw. We do the final screening when the audience leaves the hall after the concert. Now remember who you're dealing with here. This guy kills the way you blow your nose. Very casually. So let's not have any heroes here tonight. Your job is not to apprehend, only to report. No heroes, you understand?"

"You understand?" I asked Chicken as we crossed Fifty-seventh Street to the Hall. "Don't screw up tonight. You pull one of your stunts and I'll have you shoveling horse shit all summer."

"You don't have to worry about me," he said jauntily. "I'm on the team now. I'm a happy camper."

"You're a pain in the ass and an arrogant little prick, so don't blow me any smoke. Just do your job."

"I told you, Ben, I'll do it. I learned a lot on the Sextant job."

"You learned that you were lucky, that's what you learned. And who said that you could call me Ben?"

That got to him. First names were always used at the Center, regardless of age. His jauntiness crumbled at the edges. "What should I call you?"

Collect, I thought. Calvin's line. Call me collect.

"Collect?" he asked, puzzled.

Sloppy of me, he had picked up the thought. He had his touch back, all right. "Yeah, sure, call me Ben. Call me anything you damn well please."

There is nothing grand about the entrance to Carnegie Hall, just two steps up from the street and you're in the small lobby with the box office windows on the far left. It isn't until you walk into the main-stage auditorium that you begin to feel the grandeur of the place and, standing at the back of the Parquet, your eyes rise up to the four glittering horseshoe tiers that converge on the stage. Eighty feet above your head a double halo of chandeliers spreads a buttery light that suffuses the atmosphere and picks out the intricate wreaths and scrolls on the walls. Serried rows of seats slope down at a steep but pleasing angle. The Hall is just over one hundred years old, saved from the wrecker's ball and still going strong, singing songs of better days.

My squad covered the lobby and the Parquet, and I took up my position at the top of the center aisle as the first of the ticket holders began to trickle in. Chicken stood beside me. The setup made for easy tapping. As each person walked by I did a quick tap, in and out, and Chicken did the same, backing me up. It soon turned into a dull routine.

You getting anything? asked Chicken. *Anything at all?*

No, but keep alert. Don't let up.

Look, I've been thinking . . .

Don't. Whenever you think you have an accident.

When I was on the Sextant job . . .

If I hear anything more about that job, I'll puke. Get back to work, and stay on it.

All right, all right, I'm on it.

He was on it, I was on it, we all were on it, but by the time that the house lights dimmed we had turned up nothing. The message came from Sammy in the truck. *Everybody out of the Hall.* We gathered in the lobby, and Sammy came through again. *Don't bunch up in there. Some of you get out on the street and move around. Be back in time for the intermission.*

I went across the street and climbed into the truck. Ritter and Costello were there, hooked up to their people, and Sammy and Martha. I didn't see any smiling faces.

"Anything?" I asked.

"Zilch," said Sammy. "A couple of false alarms."

"Then we might as well pack it in and go home. He isn't coming."

"It's still early."

"The house is full. He'd be here by now."

"We could have missed him going in. We have two more cracks at him."

"Damn it, you're kidding yourself. He isn't here."

Ben. It was Martha. Costello and Ritter were looking at us curiously. *Let's keep the discussion inside the family.*

Sorry. It's just that I don't think this is going to work. I never did.

You don't want it to work. That's why you're so sure he won't show.

What's all this? asked Sammy. *You don't want it to work?*

He's afraid of what's going to happen if we nail this creep tonight.

Leave it alone, I told her. She had taken a really good look in my head.

It's nothing to be ashamed of. If Safeer goes down tonight, right here, everything about him comes out in the open. Lila finds out that her father is a cold-blooded killer, June gets robbed of her one decent memory, and Teague finds out what happened to the boy he treated like a son. So Ben would feel better if he didn't show up.

Fuck you, Madam Freud, I said. *Were you able to keep a tap on Chicken?*

As much as I could. You're hurting him, Ben.

He'll live. That kid is made of solid brass.

She flipped me a mental sigh. *When you get like this I can't talk to you.*

I went back to the Hall for the intermission screening, and once again we turned up nothing. Some of the audience went out onto Fifty-seventh Street to smoke, some gathered in the lobby, some stayed in their seats. We screened everyone who moved past our positions, and to cover the ones who had stayed in their seats we sent a few aces sauntering up and down the aisles, tapping as they went along. Nothing. Upstairs, downstairs, inside, outside. Nothing. When the second half of the program began, we withdrew again from the Hall. We gathered in the lobby and on the sidewalk, and Sammy made a speech to the troops from the truck speaking head-to-head, all hands tapped in.

Quiet down and listen up, he said. *The fact that we haven't spotted this bastard yet doesn't mean that he isn't here. In a crowd like this we could easily have missed him, but we still have one more crack at him, so don't let down. I want you on your toes when the concert ends and the people start coming out. Tap them once, tap them twice, tap them three times if you get the chance, and report anything you find. Send it straight in to me in the truck, and then get out of the way. The Feds and the cops will take it from there. Stay with it, gang.*

Tucked away somewhere I have a program of that concert at Carnegie Hall, and if I looked at it I could tell you what Bonfiglia sang that night, but I don't remember any of it. All I remember about the second half of that concert is pacing up and down Fifty-seventh Street in the rain with Chicken at my heels, waiting for it to be over. My mood was foul and angry, made worse by what Martha had said. Yes, I wanted Safeer caught, I even wanted him killed, but I wanted something better than that for the memory of Hassan Rashid.

"Ben," said Chicken.

"No," I said, and that was the end of that conversation.

We went back to the Hall, and took up our positions. Through the closed doors we heard the applause and the calls for encores. She sang one, and then another. They forced her to sing a third, and then it was over. The applause died down, the doors swung open, and the crowd came pouring out.

I tapped and I tapped, and I got what I expected. Nothing. The crowd thinned down to a trickle. Still nothing. I went into the Hall to take a final look around. Anyone who has worked as an usher either in Broadway theatres or in halls such as Carnegie, Avery Fisher, or the Met will tell you that people exit from an auditorium in three different ways. There are the taxi hunters who rush for the door as soon as the curtain begins to fall, there are those who exit in an orderly fashion, and there are the very few who sit stock still while the others leave, reluctant to remove themselves from the scene. Still captured by what they have seen and heard, they can sit that way, unmoving, until they are politely told that it is time to go.

Ushers call them the rocks, and from where I stood at the back of the parquet I could see five of them still seated. An usher moved from one to the other, saying a few soft words to break the spell of the evening and send them on their way. Each one, when spoken to, responded with a blank stare, and then a reluctant nod. They began to leave slowly. One of the women had tears on her cheeks, and one of the men did, too. The man with the tears came up the center aisle. He was tall, with sloping shoulders, and he moved with an ambling gait. I nodded, but he did not return the nod. I doubt that he even saw me. He was still in another world. I tapped him lightly.

Ben, said Chicken.

Yeah, I know. It's Safeer. And I missed him.

We both did.

Yeah. You missed him because you're sixteen years old. I missed him because I wanted to miss him. I raised the volume. *Sammy, I've got him. He's coming up the main aisle heading for the lobby.*

You sure?

No question. He's about six three, one eighty, dark and clean shaven. Dark blue suit, light blue shirt and tie. He's alone.

Got it. I heard him speaking vocally to Ritter and Costello, passing it on. *Okay, Ben, we take it from here. Stay out of it.*

Gladly.

Safeer was at the top of the aisle, going through the door. I sprinted up the aisle, Chicken close behind me. I swung the door open just enough to give me a crack for vision. I was out of it, but I was going to see it happen. It happened quickly.

The lobby was clear of civilians. There were five FBI agents in the area, one of them a woman, and they all were trying to look as if they belonged there. Two were near the front doors, staring out at the rain, two were looking at the list of coming concerts, and one was leaning against the wall near the box office window. Safeer started across the lobby to the front doors, and the five began to move.

The two at the door turned to face him. The two at the poster moved slowly to come up behind him. The one at the box office window started for the center of the lobby. Pistols appeared in their hands.

Safeer stopped. He glanced over his shoulder and saw the two behind him. He stood still. A woman carrying a canvas sack came out the box office door. She did not see the pistols, and she started across the lobby.

The agent nearest the door shouted, "Get back. No, damn it, no."

Safeer moved with the instincts of a man who had been hunted for years. He took two quick gliding steps and swept the woman in front of him, his arm around her neck. She shrieked. He put a small flat pistol against her cheek. His eyes swept the room. No one moved. Safeer sprang back, dragging the woman with him like a panther with its prey. He kicked open the box office door, and backed inside. He kicked the door shut. The agents stared at each other. Not a shot had been fired.

Just short of an hour later I sat in the truck with Sammy and Martha. Lou Ritter was at his bank of phones, and Captain Costello was at his. The truck was crowded with police brass, but they were letting Costello carry the ball. He had been there before. So had I. He was talking on the phone with the mayor.

"Yes sir, we're in telephone communication with him," he was saying. "He's holed up in the box office, and what we have here is your basic hostage situation. He has three women in there, and he says he's going to shoot one of them in ten minutes unless we meet his demands." He listened. "He wants what they all want, safe conduct to JFK and an aircraft out of here to Tripoli. No, no money. Yes sir, exactly. We have the streets around the Hall secured, we have a SWAT team standing by, and we're about to send in a negotiator. No, a specialist, a federal man. I've worked with him before." Costello, listening, looked at me and shrugged helplessly. He was lying to the mayor. We had never worked together, but he had worked with Martha and Vince on a hostage job, and he knew what we could do. "Yes sir, the chief is here, I'll put him on." He handed the phone to one of the brass, and turned to me.

"Mayor wanted to know why we aren't using one of our own people," he said. "It was a little difficult to explain."

I nodded. The mayor was new on the job. He had a limited amount of experience, and a limited federal clearance. He didn't know about folks like me. Costello knew. People like me made him nervous, but he knew that there was no one better than a sensitive in a hostage situation. All of us had done it at least once.

"You don't have to make this your pigeon," Sammy said for perhaps the fifth time. "I can send in Vince or Snake. You've gotten yourself involved."

"You've got it backwards," I told him. "I'm the best for the job *because* I'm involved."

Martha put her hand on my arm. "You're carrying a load of guilt about this. Don't let it get in the way."

"I let him get by me. I was trying to play God again."

"Just get those people out. Don't think about anything else."

"I let him get by."

"Ben, you're on," said Ritter. He was handling the phone to the box office. "We're feeding him the usual bullshit about the aircraft, getting it ready, mechanical delays, blah, blah, blah, but he's getting real antsy. Says to get over there now or he starts shooting."

"On my way. What's the drill?"

"We've cleared the lobby. You go in with your hands out in front of you, and you go straight to the box office window. It's like a teller's window, with bulletproof glass. You belly up as close as you can to the window, and put your hands in sight on the ledge. He'll talk to you through the window."

"How does he sound?"

"Cold. Almost casual."

I asked Sammy, "Any instructions?"

"You've been there before. Promise him anything, but give him *bupkis*."

I left the truck and started across the street. Fifty-seventh was empty of traffic, cordoned off, and bright with lights. Chicken caught up with me and matched my stride. I said, "What do you want now?"

"Thirty seconds."

"I don't have thirty seconds." I kept on walking.

He grabbed my arm and pulled. I was so surprised that I let him pull me around. "Damn it, you listen. Just for once, you listen to me."

"Thirty seconds."

"It may not mean much, but it worked for me on the Sextant job."

"Christ, that again?"

"Just one thing. Don't speak to him in English, use Arabic. You speak to him in his mother tongue, get it? It worked for me. I spoke to Sextant in Slovenian, and it rocked him, it really did. It took him right out of the rôle he was playing. And don't call him Safeer, call him Hassan. That worked for me, too."

He stopped, and looked at me expectantly. I tried not to grin. He wasn't being a wiseass, he was really trying to help, and I could not get myself to tell him that what he was suggesting was basic to the job. It was something we all had learned years before. He had learned it too, but at his age when you learn something like that you think that you've invented it.

"I'll try it that way," I told him. "Thanks. Anything else?"

"No, just that. Uh . . . take care, you know?"

"I will."

I went into the lobby of the Hall. It was brightly lit, and empty. I kept my hands in sight as I walked to the box office window. I got as close to the window as I could and put my hands on the ledge. His face appeared in the window. It was a cold face, with eyes that showed nothing.

"Peace be with you."

"And with you peace."

"I am the negotiator," I said in the Cairene dialect. "I am here to make sure that all goes smoothly."

"There is nothing to negotiate. You know my demands. Is the aircraft ready?"

"It will be ready shortly. There have been some delays."

"Ground transportation?"

"It is being prepared."

"Standard answers," he said disdainfully. "The standard tactic, delay and delay. That will not work with me. I want the transport now, or the killing begins."

"I cannot give you what I do not have. Be patient. It is a matter of minutes."

"While you surround the place with troops."

"The place is already surrounded. I must know if the hostages are safe."

"They are safe. They have not been harmed."

"I cannot see them."

"They are lying on the floor. Shall I shoot one in the leg so you can hear her scream?"

"There is no need for that. Just be patient. As soon as I get the signal, you will leave for the airport."

By this time I was into his head, combing through it quickly, searching for whatever I might be able to use. Considering the circumstances, his mind was under remarkable control. At the top of his thoughts was how we had found him, and he put it into words.

"Do you know who I am?" he asked.

"We know you."

"How did you know I was here? Was I betrayed?"

"Do you really expect me to answer that?"

"No, of course not. What is your name?"

"Benjamin."

"As you know, I am called Safeer. Have you done this work before?"

"Yes."

"Then we may speak as professionals. As you know, my position depends on your belief that I will kill, and since you know who I am, you know that I will." He spoke as if quoting from a textbook. "If my demands are not met, I will kill, and I will kill again. I am willing to kill even if it means losing my last hostage, which means that I too will die. I am not afraid of death, Benjamin. Death is my brother, and when the time comes for me to join him I will do so willingly. You know this about me, you know that I mean it, and so we must stop all this talk about delays." He looked at his watch. "Either my ground transportation is outside within ten minutes, or I will kill one of the women. Is that understood?"

So far the conversation had been going along the classic lines for a terrorist and a negotiator. It was time to change the script. I said, "No."

His eyes narrowed. "No? What does that mean?"

"It means that Safeer would certainly kill that way, but not Hassan Rashid."

He handled it well. His mind whirled, but his face did not change. He raised the pistol and pointed it at me.

"The glass is bulletproof," I reminded him.

He lowered the pistol. "What do you know about Hassan Rashid?"

I told him what I knew. I told him about the lonely exchange student who came to Van Buren and learned to play basketball. I told him about fatherly Mike Teague, and Mutt and Jeff, and the Pom-Pom Queen. I told him about the Poodle, about the baby, about the monthly payments to Violet Simms. I told him all about myself, and he listened carefully.

"Who else knows all this?" he asked.

"I am the only one," I lied.

"And who are you besides being Benjamin?"

"A man who knows many things. A man who knows how to keep secrets."

"There is no aircraft, is there?"

"No. There never was. There never will be."

"Then you have condemned these women to death."

"I don't think so."

He looked to his left, and down at the floor. He pointed the pistol in that direction, and fired. I heard no screams. He had taped their mouths.

Ben, what the hell is going on? It was Sammy. *Was that a shot?*

Keep the troops back. I'm inside his head. He fired a shot into the floor, no damage. He's trying to mess with me.

"What do you think now?" Safeer asked.

"I think that Hassan fired that shot. You killed no one."

He looked at me with wonder in his eyes. "How well you seem to know me."

"I know you as a brutal murderer."

"I have killed."

"And I know you as the man who dreams of the little girl on flight 307. The girl with the broken face."

The wonder remained. "You know that, too? What else do you know about me?"

"I know that you are going to die tonight."

He gestured with the pistol. "Then these on the floor will die with me."

I shrugged. "*Inshallah*."

He shook his head. "No, I do not believe that. Not you people."

"Listen to me, Hassan." I put my face as close to the glass as I could. "You are going to die because you would never surrender. I know that without question. But there is more than one way to die. If you make us take you by force, if you make us kill you, then I can promise you that the whole world will learn about Hassan Rashid. June will learn about the man she once loved. Lila will learn about her father. Even old Mike Teague will . . ."

"Stop that."

"Is that what you want?"

"You know I don't."

"Then you are left with the obvious alternative. And if that happens, only Safeer dies. Hassan Rashid lives on."

"What makes you think I would do something like that?"

"Because you are weary of living. Because you are weary of killing. Because you are weary of dreaming."

"The little girl with the broken face." He was close to it. I went into his head and saw how close he was.

"Yes, that one."

"Amir did that. Or Murad. Sometimes I cannot remember."

"No, you remember. That is why you dream."

"Did I really do it?" He asked it as a true question.

"You did."

"Yes, I suppose I did. But who killed the children of Gaza, the children of the camps, the children in the Bekaa? Those I did not kill." He shook his head. "Still, it would be good to rest that way."

"A form of peace." He was right on the edge. "What difference does it make, today or tomorrow?"

"I should never have come here, but to hear her one more time . . ." He looked at me directly, and I knew that he was going to do it. I didn't have to go into his head again. I knew. "You took a big chance with the hostages."

"Perhaps."

"When have I ever been merciful?"

"Never, but perhaps the time had come."

"Perhaps. I have your promise about what the world will know?"

"You have it."

He looked at the pistol as if it were the first pistol he had ever seen. "It is not an easy thing to do."

"Easier than some of the other things you have done."

"Oh yes, Benjamin, I can assure you of that. Much easier. In the words of Muhammad Taqi Partovi Sabzevari . . ." He paused.

"What words?"

" 'It is Allah who puts the gun in our hand, but we cannot expect him to pull the trigger as well, just because we are faint-hearted.' "

He put the gun in his mouth and pulled the trigger.

I turned on my heel, and walked out of the Hall. As I walked out, agents ran in. I leaned against the side of the building, then slid down to sit on the sidewalk with my head on my knees. I felt the rain on the back of my neck. Chicken stood over me. His cheeks were wet, but that could have been the rain. Then Snake and Vince were there, Sammy and Martha with her crutch.

Sammy knelt beside me, and said. "You were terrific. You did it."

I shook my head.

"You did. You've been trying for years, and you finally did it. You finally talked somebody to death."

Is that funny? I wondered. I must ask Calvin. Calvin knows funny. "The potential was always there," I said. "I just never tried hard enough."

Sammy gave me a hand to stand up. "Let's go home."

ABOUT THE AUTHOR

Herbert Burkholz is a native New Yorker who has lived much of his adult life in Spain, Mexico, Italy, and Greece. Formerly Writer-in-Residence at the College of William and Mary in Virginia, he is the author of eleven books, and his articles have appeared in *The New York Times Magazine*, *Playboy*, and other publications.